The Home of Urban Islamic Fiction

Tried & Tested

↩

Umm Juwayriyah

As Sabr Publications
155 River St
West Springfield, MA 01089

Cover art by Reyhana Ismail
Book and cover design by Leila Joiner
Editing by Dominique Scott

ISBN 978-0-9981791-1-7

Tried & Tested

And certainly, We shall test you with something of fear, hunger, loss of wealth, lives, and fruits, but give glad tidings to As-Sabirin (the patient ones).

Surah Al Baqarah: 155

Dedication

For Sabura Faatimah Muhammad, Atiyah Ibrahim, and Umm Saalih Khalilah

(May Allah grant them all paradise)

Acknowledgements

Ummi & Abi: Thank you for loving me and being there for me and my family whenever and however you can. I am so grateful that Allah gave you both to me. May He be pleased with you and reward you both in this life and the next. Juwayriyah: Mama loves you so much, girl! I appreciate all that you do: from reading my work, washing dishes, or helping out with your sister and brother begrudgingly. I see it and see you growing, and every day I pray for you! Bin and Hind, my littles, Mama loves you to the moon and back. My big brothers, thank you for your continued support of your little sis.

I also want thank Widad (Linda) Delgado for introducing my writing to the world and believing in my voice when I just 22. Leila Joiner, thank you for your continued support, business, and patience. Deborah McNichol, thank you for always being willing to help when I need it. To all the writers, artists, and friends inspiring me: LaYinka Sanni, Brooke Benoit, Reyhana Ismail. Latifa Ali, Layla Abdullah-Poulos, Najiyah Maxfield-Helwani & Daybreak Press, Papatia Feauxzar, SISTERS Magazine, Azizah Magazine, Dilshad Ali, Jamilah Alqarnain, Hend Hegazi, and Dominique Scott – thank you all.

Abo Binyaameen: Thank you for all of your help and patience! May Allah bless you.

To my readers: Thank you for supporting Islamic Fiction.

#MuslimGirlsRead

Chapter 1

It was all a dream. The humid, funky air and peeling wallpaper were bad enough. But the gangs of bold cockroaches that dashed from the cracks in the wall and grabbed each and every crumb that hit the floor or countertop made my skin itch like a bad case of eczema. Then there was the broken fridge door that leaked water all night and the flimsy, spotted curtains that smelled like an old man's ashtray. "What the heck am I doing here?" I hated thinking about what had put me here. I was the only one to blame, though. The weight of it was full of heartache. My bag lady chronicles were deeper than Erykah Badu's rifts and runs from the '90s. My truth was clear: this was where that one wrong decision to trust the wrong person on an ill-fated night had brought me.

Now I was finally alone staring at the orange-brown rust stains streaked over the kitchenette's concrete floor. It wouldn't have been so bad if my solace wasn't constantly being challenged by the voices and antics of noisy neighbors running through the hallways all times of the day and the night doing Lord knew what. Oh, and then there was the sound that came from the front window: the drip, drip, drip, splatter, splatter from the side pipe that ran down from the upstairs motel rooms carrying that brown sewer water. But the real deal was that late – very late – at night symphony of rat-a-tat-tats screaming all around and beneath the room every other hour that forced me to Rambo crawl on all fours into the dark closet and sleep with my eyes wide open. This place - this whole city was no longer familiar to me. I was home, but it didn't feel like home.

Still, I was grateful I had got away. That lock and key I'd been under was finally gone. The motel was crappy and cheap, but I got what I paid for. A thirty dollar a night sanctuary for the depressed, tired, drunk, drugged out, broke, and nowhere else to go travelers. Fortunately for me, I only fell in two of those categories. I could relate to all of them, at one time or another, though.

When I heard the hard thumps on the door, it didn't alarm me. She was right on time. I grabbed the soft cream Pashmina hijab from the dusty plastic night stand, wrapped it neatly around my hair, grabbed the small metal bat that I kept in front of the door with one hand, and opened the door with the other. Ready.

"Buenos dias," she sang duly. "It's check-out time." The long-legged, visibly pregnant Latina in front of me declared. Her long black hair extensions swung rhythmically back and forth to the silent tune of her bobbing head. The tips of the braids were dyed pink and red. The same color of her acrylic nails. "You gotta go pay up Fresh at the front desk or get'ta steppin' today. A'ight?"

"Sure. Thank-you," I said. The woman's eyes rolled at me as she sucked and then slurped on a cherry red blow pop like she was both infantile and X-rated. She finally looked me up and down and furrowed her eyebrows. She was obviously thrown off by my politeness or my appearance or my presence here all together. "So, okay…I'mma be down in a few." I continued in a more familiar vernacular.

"Yeah, whatever, honey. Just make sure you checkout with Fresh and none of them other fools down there, ya heard?" she said with an attitude and sauntered away to go bang on the next door. I lingered in the doorway for a little while longer wondering if maybe she would look back and recognize me from before. But she didn't. I closed the door and went back in the "hole" as I had been referring to the room for the last week.

My one bag was already packed. I was here. I'd been here. Only a cab ride and a short walk separated me now from my mother, the house I'd grown up in, and everything I'd left behind. I didn't know why I stayed in this motel for a week. Then again, I did. I'd left home over a decade ago without as much as a *"As salamu alykum".*

Twelve years of separation from family, friends, and everything I'd grown up with to live *the life.* A life full of all the stuff TV made look important, fun, and worth giving up everything and everyone to have. It was easy to find, but holding on to it almost cost me my life. Once upon a time, my life had looked so good from the outside. I had money, a handsome husband, cars, parties, and trips... but then came the drama and pain! Allah knew I never meant to take it that far. I really did try to get away several times. But he wouldn't let me leave. He said he needed me. He said he would change. And I believed him. Life had been so hard, I started to even hate the air I swallowed. Thing is, as much as I had hated the last twelve years that I lived in limbo with Mateo, I still didn't know if I could stomach this life again either. The lady was right though, *I gotta get'ta steppin'.*

At the front desk was a group of *thuggish-ruggish-bone* looking guys dressed in the latest hip hop apparel. I suspected they were a lot older, probably more likely in their mid to late 20's. I instinctively clutched my Lana Marks handbag a little tighter and walked straight forward to the front desk. I wasn't scared of them, I told myself, but I was a little. Mateo employed guys like them. He had always told me not to show them any fear.

I rung the bell, then turned to the group of guys and said, "Excuse me, but have any of you seen Fresh?" None of them responded. They continued talking and throwing dice like I wasn't even there. I rung the bell again and again and again. I still didn't see anyone approaching the front desk, but I had got several of the guys' attention. They looked annoyed. I didn't care, though.

"Ay, shorty – shorty!" One of the guys from the group called out finally. "C'mon now, half pint, chill with that bell. It's too early for all that, nah'mean?" he reasoned. He was a tall and thin, Dominican judging by his accent. It was strange how he reminded a little of a younger Mateo. I shook the thought from my mind. He was the last person on earth I'd wanted to see. Especially, not here. Not now. I'd gotten a taste of air, of freedom. Could he be spying on me with these guys? Nothing was too farfetched for Mateo. He was half crazy and always hated when I beat him at anything. I would never make the mistake of trusting him again, Insha'Allah.

"Look, it's almost noon. I need some service so I can check out," I shot back.

"You can leave them bills with me, *mi Morena*. I got you," he said, now smiling a crooked smile and proudly showing off his expensive teeth jewelry. "I'll make sure Fresh gets at it," he assured me. But I knew a scammer when I saw one. The woman from earlier had told me not to give the money to anybody but Fresh. The last thing I needed upon my return home was drama from some strange man hunting me down for a measly $210 dollars.

"Yeah, thank you, but no thanks. I'll wait on Fresh," I told him with a small smile. And thank goodness, I didn't have to wait long. No sooner had the words slipped from my mouth did the man I was looking for arrive.

"Someone looking for me?" Fresh chuckled. He came around the desk and politely said, "How may I help you, sistah?" I had assumed Fresh was also going to be some thugged-out over-grown kid too, but he wasn't hardly. Fresh was a little over six feet, with clear and smooth peanut buttery brown skin with chocolate eyes. He was a little on the pudgy side with a noticeably soft tummy that was clearly well fed, an evenly trimmed haircut, and a nicely manicured beard. He wore creased quality gray slacks, a pale aqua-blue short sleeved polo shirt, and a pair of leather hush puppies. Fresh had no visible tattoos, gold teeth, or jewelry hanging on or off of him. He looked like a normal guy, nice even.

"I need to check out," I said clearing my throat. I pulled the room key out of my handbag and placed three one-hundred dollar bills on the desk while the group of guys watched. Fresh grabbed the key and pulled an old-school log book from under the desk and began flipping through pages like we were back in caveman time. When he got to the right page, he slid his fore finger down the list of guests until he came to the right room and name.

"Imania Colon – room 090. That you?" he asked quizzically with an arched eyebrow, like he didn't believe the writing.

"Yes, it is." I assured him. I was ready to leave. I was really ready to go see my mother. I repeated that to myself again, *I was ready*. Finally, I wanted to go home. Fresh reached under the desk again and fumbled around with something before taking my money and putting it in a security box. He then counted one hundred and ten dollars out loud and then laid my money plainly on the table for all to see.

"You know," he said walking from behind the counter back towards the hall he came from. "…you look really – *really* familiar. I don't know no Colons… but, I knew someone long ago, a Muslimah from the Hill district. She…"

"I ain't from around here. I'm visiting some old college roommates and business associates. Thank you for the discount." I made up the story as fast as I could. It was a filthy habit, one that my parents had never tolerated from my siblings and me growing up, but Mateo had insisted on it. He didn't want any of his associates knowing where we came from and I played my part, a little too well, I guess. The guys began to laugh, at my expense no doubt.

"Yeah, yeah," Fresh said. "We have a lot of those types around here. They stop by the Birch Inn all the time." He chuckled sarcastically.

"I am sure they do," I replied with as much sarcasm as he had dished out. Then I walked towards the exit without looking back.

"Jibril," Fresh said.

"Huh? Are you talking to me?" I twirled around and asked, knowing already that he was.

"My name. It's Jibril. Jibril Ibrahim. And well, *Salamu alaikum*, Imania Colon. Welcome back to Pittsburgh."

I turned around and pushed through the doors as fast as I could. I had to get away from Fresh – Jibril – or whoever he wanted to be. I couldn't even respond to his salaam. I hadn't asked him for his name. What made him think I would even care? I kept speed walking. What in the world was I doing back in Pittsburgh? And staying around Hill district at that? I would hate Mateo for the rest of his life. That, I knew for sure. That man had known exactly who I was when he walked in the front office. I wasn't Imania Colon, even when I *was* Imania Colon. I had been lying to myself for so long. Now it was all gone, just like that. I was going to have to get used to being me again, the real me: Iman Shahidah Johnson.

I walked down about four blocks before I stopped, out of breath and tired, tears clouding my vision. I saw a bus stop across the street, but a cab was coming. I stood close to the curb, put my hand in the air, and waved. It was too hot to be on some musty and slow bus. I wanted to go home. I was ready. I was ready to start over.

Oh Allah, please help me be ready!

The cab stopped by the curb and I got in. A beautiful East Indian man with dark velvety amber skin and dark curly hair sat up in the driver's seat. The smell of spicy curry filled my nostrils. "Where to, miss?" he asked softly.

"Webster Ave, please."

They say you never forget where you come from, and I hadn't, but where I had come from had changed. Was this really Hill district? It couldn't be. The streets were in the right places and yet they looked completely different. The houses and the people had changed beyond words. I know when I had lived here it wasn't the best neighborhood in Pittsburgh by far. By my time, it had been several decades since Hill district had been a cultural hub and playground for such Harlem Renaissance greats as the poet Claude Mckay and the Pulitzer Prize winning playwright August Wilson. By my time, Hill district was a "*poor, but we got just enough*" type of neighborhood. I knew I grew up in the hood and yet I still remembered the grass being green, the trees being tall and alive, sidewalks that were clean, and happy people with somewhere to go.

Funny thing was, back then I didn't like it. I couldn't see the beauty in what I'd had. Nothing had been enough for me. I'd hated the Hill. I'd hated Pittsburgh. I'd been bored and sick of all the "Muslim girls can't dos" my parents and community had constantly dished out. I'd felt trapped like a royal letter written with a fountain pen and then stuck inside a cheap bottle with a corkscrew. I'd always planned to get out by any means necessary...

"Would you be needing help with your bag, ma'am?" the cab driver asked.

"No, that won't be necessary, sir. I only have this one bag," I said as I looked down at the wide mouth Tuscan Italian leather duffle bag I had with me. "But thank you anyway." I grabbed my bag, pulled the shoulder strap over my body, and opened the door.

As I rode in the back seat, I recited surah Al Fatihah, the opening chapter of the Qur'an, to myself over and over again. The cab driver kept looking up and checking me out in his mirror. I was sure he thought I was deranged or perhaps even pious. I was neither. Yet, I'd renewed my faith in my Lord and His words in the Qur'an right when it was decreed for me to do so.

It hadn't been easy or even something I had willingly sought after. It had been on dark nights after a drunk Mateo would fight with me like I was his enemy rather than his garment. When he got tired of me and my crying, he would leave to go hang out with his side chicks or his brothers or cousins. It was those moments when I was so low, I'd beg the earth to crack open and swallow me whole. It never did, though. Instead, Allah would beckon for me to remember Him. I'd lie on the floor reciting surah al Fatihah or al Ikhlas or An Nas. I would recite all night long until the throbbing stopped or I lost consciousness.

I'd wanted to run back home so many times but something had always stopped me. That something was... me. I got in my own way each and every time. What would my Abu say? Would my own father refuse to talk to me? Would he tell me he hated me? Would he call me a *kafir*? Would my Ummi slam the door in my face and disown me?

Each time I dreamt of those horrors, I'd wake up in cold sweats with an empty heart and black eyes, and reach for that bottle of something strong to drown out those horrors so I could black out again. Those days, living was worse than my dreams.

"How much do I owe you?" I asked and the cab driver turned away and looked at the monitor in front of him.

"$25.00," he said.

I reached in my purse without showing any facial expression, and pulled out one twenty-dollar bill and a ten-dollar bill.

"Keep the change," I said out of habit like I was still being kept by my husband.

After the cab pulled off, I stood in place breathing quick like an asthmatic. My chest felt tight and my head was spinning. I had purposely told the cab driver to stop a couple houses down from my mother's home. I knew I would need these last moments to reflect and muster up the last drops of courage I had to be brave enough to squeeze from my soul. Then I took one step. Then another. And then another. Soon I was walking up the old worn, rickety gray steps to 459 Webster Ave as my heart thumped with fear.

The porch looked the same but so much smaller now that I was a full-grown woman. There were two old lounge chairs right in front of the bay window. They were dusty and looked worn from nothing but time. A stack of old newspapers and grocery flyers were in the right corner and a couple of kids' bikes and a basketball were over there too. As I looked around the rest of the porch and the torn-down neighborhood that surrounded it, I wondered who the toys belonged to. A tear escaped from my eye as I pondered over the fact that my older brother or even one of one of my younger siblings could indeed have had children. My nieces and nephews.

"What you looking for? You lost or sum'thing?" A tall, lanky brown sugar skinned boy with mesmerizing hazel brown eyes was suddenly standing in the doorway and asking me. I hadn't even heard the screen door open. When I used to live here, it would always squeak. "We don't want to buy nothing you selling and we already know who Jesus really is, if you with them Jehovah's," he spat at me quickly. I pulled my hijab down further over my forehead and neatly wrapped the loose ends across my neck before walking over to the door. I didn't know who the boy was and he obviously had no idea of who I was either. More than likely, he was a relative I'd never met before.

"Is this still Muneerah Johnson's residence?" I asked.

"Why? Who want to know?" he replied with mean, furrowed eyebrows. And that's when I knew I wasn't going to get anywhere with him.

"Okay. Well, is your mom or dad in for me to speak with?" I said, trying my best to politely end our conversation. The boy looked me up and down and without any notice shut the door, screen and all, right in my face. I was completely unnerved. I knew my mother didn't allow disrespectful children around her. Good *adab* was required by everybody who walked through our doors, including our friends. Black sheep were swiftly handled and put in their rightful place. '*Reverence the womb that bore you or your hard head will make a soft behind*', Ummi had always recited to my brothers, sister, and me, remixing a verse of Qur'an with an old-school threat. Neither one of my parents had ever hit any of us. But then again, we knew better than to really test either of them.

I dropped my bag on the side of the porch, opened the screen door, and started banging on the door with my fist. I saw the boy peek out the window briefly, but he wouldn't come back to the door. I couldn't believe this. Some child had the nerve to shut me out of my own parents' home. I got so angry while banging on the door, I hadn't noticed the car pull up in front of the house. But I saw the woman rush out and run right up to the porch. We met on the bottom step.

"As salaamu alaikum," I greeted the young woman politely, trying my best to regain my composure and assuage her fears. It was too late for that, though. She had a look of pure terror written all over her face.

"Wa 'alaikum as salaam," she replied shakily with a petite, extended hand. "Um, is there a problem, sister? Who are you looking for here?" she asked me as she placed a bag of groceries onto the porch. She looked young, 25 or under for sure. She was dressed in conservative Muslim attire: a dark emerald-green outer jilbab and a black cottony, circular type hijab that came to her waist and swallowed most of her small body frame. She was also visibly pregnant.

"Yes, I'm looking for Muneerah Johnson. Is this still their residence?" I asked and the young woman smiled, now relaxing the tension that had been on her face.

"Of course it is. Are you a friend of Ummi's?" she asked me as she walked up the rest of the steps. We both reached down for her groceries at the same time.

"Yes," I responded and she let me take the bag. "I guess you can say that. I'm Iman, her eldest daughter." Before I could say anything else, the young woman gasped loudly and pulled me into a tight embrace.

Yasmeen, as I learned her name was, welcomed me back into my family's home and made me feel more at ease than I had ever felt when I had actually lived there. But then again, I was happier to be to here now than I'd ever been before. Inside the house, everything was almost the same besides the new paint on the walls and the new curtains in a couple of the rooms. Maneuvering around the house again came like second nature.

Yasmeen instructed me to settle my things in my old bedroom. She said Ummi was out at a doctor's appointment and that Masud, my youngest brother and her husband would be bringing her home later. Masud had been only 10 when I'd left with Mateo. He'd been a little kid in all aspects and a geeky, shy one at that. It was surprising that he had married so young. But the way Yasmeen swooned with joy every time she said his name, I couldn't help but think that the pesky little boy I'd once known well had matured into a sweet and dependable man and husband that I knew absolutely nothing about.

After praying the afternoon prayer with Yasmeen and devouring my Ummi's leftover breakfast like I was Goldilocks, I headed upstairs to my old room to finish unpacking. Thirty minutes later, I heard the floor outside my room creaking back and forth in the same position. I knew someone was out there, so I got up and cracked the door open.

"Would you like to come in?" I asked with a good idea that it might be my young but rude nephew, Hasan. The door opened further and as I suspected, Hasan, my oldest brother Shareef's son, stood before me. "You can come in, if you like," I suggested, but he didn't move.

"Are you really my Aunt Iman?" he asked me bluntly as he leaned against the door's frame.

"Yeah, that would be me, Aunt Iman, I guess," I replied while I continued to hang my clothes.

"How we know you not just some fake or probably some crack head pretending to be Aunt Iman? Auntie Ameera told me you were dead. There's no such thing as ghosts. So whatchu' doing here?" he questioned me. For ten, I had to give the boy credit, he was swift. He asked me a question that still left me puzzled. The life I had lived before returning here felt like a dream, a really horrible dream. The truth was it had been very real. Ironically, I actually did feel like a ghost, a fragile shell of my real self wandering through the night and day. How could I explain to a ten-year-old that I'd been tricked by a conniving, fast talking, handsome man into giving him total control of my life? How could I explain that I had turned my back on my whole family? How could I explain that I had walked away from my Creator? There were no easy, kid -friendly answers for Hasan. I guess Ameera had been right, I had been dead.

"I tell you what, why don't you ask me something – anything that only your real Aunt Iman would know? You can ask me five really tough questions. If I know them, then you'll know I'm not a fake or a crack head pretending to be your Aunt Iman," I said sitting down on the bed facing him in the doorway.

"And if you don't know – you leave," he said snidely and shifted his body to an upright position. "Question number one," he started without giving me any notice. "Hmm…where was my real Aunt Iman born and on what day?"

"Those are actually two questions, not one," I informed him.

"Ennnnnn." He made a sound like a game show buzzer. "Wrong answer. Strike one."

"Okay, okay, have it your way. I was born in this house, in the kitchen to be exact. January 11, 1971. In fact, your father and I have the same birth date. What's the next question?" I asked while I watched Hasan roll his beautiful almond shaped hazel brown eyes at me. He was clearly annoyed.

"Question number two: Does Aunt Iman's brothers or sister have middle names and if so, what are they?" he asked me and started humming the Jeopardy theme music.

"Okay, I got this. No. None of them have middle names, just me."

"Ennnnnnnnnn" he said again, much louder this time with a wide smile. "Wrong answer. Strike two."

"Huh? I am not wrong!" I protested bouncing up off the bed and stomping my feet on the weak wood panels beneath me.

"Yeah, you are," he teased.

"No, I am not little boy."

"Yeah, you are. You're a fake," Hasan yelled.

"No, I'm... wait. You little rascal. You tricked me," I said walking towards him.

"No, I didn't. You got it wrong fair and square," he said standing toe to toe with me, only a foot shorter with no signs of fear.

"You didn't say dead or alive," I yelled, completely frustrated now.

"The *real* Aunt Iman should know!" he yelled back at me powerfully in a tone that was stronger than his years, carrying a frustration and anger that frightened me. Did he not like me or did he have his own problems?

"Hasan – his middle name was Khaleel. He's dead. My older brother was hit by a car two weeks before I was born," I managed to say through a whisper. It had dawned on me that my oldest brother Shareef had named his son after his first sibling and friend. "What's your next question?" I asked returning to sit on the bed, much more composed.

Hasan continued to question me game style until he finally gave up around Maghrib time. He had gone way beyond the agreed upon five questions, but I didn't oppose him. For some reason, I think we both needed it. After he left, I made ablution, prayed, and then fell asleep.

I awoke to the sound of light tapping on my door. I had to blink my eyes several times to adjust them to the darkness. The room was pitch black now. It had to have been after Isha – about ten or eleven at night. Realizing that I had missed a prayer, I rose from the lumpy queen-sized bed slowly, stood, and walked to the door. Pausing, I quickly ran my hand through my shoulder-length straight hair and pushed my bangs away from my eyes as I opened the door.

"Allah! Laa illaahah illallah," my mother squealed and jumped up and down, lifting her full body up. "It is you! It is you! Iman! Allah! Ya Allah, my baby is home," she kept repeating and then finally reached out and grabbed me. We hugged, we rocked, we touched each other's skin, and we cried deeply for a long time. I wanted to tell her I was sorry and how much I hated the way I had treated her and my father all those years, but she kept shushing me silent. My Abu had returned to Allah three years ago. I had run out of time with him. I couldn't afford to let that happen with Ummi. Somehow and some way, I was going to have to find a way to make real amends.

Chapter 2

The honeymoon I was expecting to embark on with my long-lost family, didn't happen. The first couple of weeks home weren't as sweet as I thought they would be. In fact, it felt painfully awkward. I didn't feel like I belonged in their world. It was like I didn't know what to say or do or where to sit or even when to eat. Sometimes I didn't even know how to talk to any of them. Ummi was still that sweet giving woman she had always been, but something was missing. She'd changed too. I didn't feel like we were connecting. I'd hoped it would be the easiest to reconnect with her – she'd carried, born me, and nursed me, but I was struggling. Some days I would catch her staring at me like I wasn't even her child. When I would look at her, she'd smile coyly and turn away. I could tell she was probably wondering why I was back too. I had intended to tell her everything that first night in my room, but Ummi had refused to listen to my story. I continued to offer her my pleas for forgiveness hundreds of times since then, yet I knew it wasn't what she deserved. We needed to really talk. I needed to tell her my whole truth. It felt like my family didn't care to really know who I'd become. Maybe I was rushing them.

The good thing was I loved them all. My heart swooned for them. I felt so good being around them and hearing their voices again. Mas'ud was as handsome as they came. He'd grown into the spitting image of our Abu: tall, athletically lean, clear café au lait skin, broad shoulders, dark and fearless brown eyes, and super curly hair. He even had Abu's big ole' beard and he wore glasses. He was so well spoken and mannered, but he had few words for me. Whenever I was near, he'd make sure to go ghost. On the days when I caught him coming or going, I'd study every line on his face in sheer amazement. He was always playing around or joking sweetly with Yasmeen. From what I could tell so far, he was definitely a kind, doting husband and a hard worker.

My little brother was a mechanic at a car garage during the day and attending Allegheny Community College at night. He helped Ummi out with all her bills. In return, he and Yasmeen stayed in the attic's three rooms. I understood why Yasmeen was always smiling. Her husband treated her like his most treasured gift. I'd never had that in my marriage.

Mateo had said nice things to me when we first met, but as soon as I got on his turf, around his people, I was treated like nothing more than his handmaid. Don't get me wrong now, I was a well taken care of maid. Over the years, Mateo had given me some pretty nice yearly bonuses and perks: the Lexus SC300, lots of expensive jewelry, and summer vacations in the Dominican Republic. But what's wealth without faith, safety, trust, and love?

I spoke with Ameera, my younger sister, earlier in the week. She'd called and Ummi had broken the news to her. I think Hasan or Mas'ud had already told her because she didn't seem surprised or shocked or anything. In fact, she was as cold as ice. Ummi had told me prior to our brief talk on the phone that Ameera was married with three children and lived in North Philadelphia. Ameera basically repeated the same and hung up without asking me anything about myself or where I'd been all this time. It was another strange and disconnected encounter with a sibling.

I didn't know what I had expected from her. I guess she'd given me what I deserved. We had once been close, though. Three years apart, we slept in the same room, sometimes even in the same bed right up until I disappeared. We shared clothes, a closet, secrets, and friends. It was Ameera that I thought about and prayed for the most when I left. I had wanted Ameera to get out of the Hill and do well and be happy.

She was a beautiful girl and had always been smart. I hoped she was using her talents and not wasting her life away.

When I had asked Ummi about Shareef, she changed the subject and acted like she didn't know what I was talking about. It had been weeks and Hasan was still here but I hadn't seen his father once. I got the feeling she was hiding something from me. I didn't press her. I knew my mother well enough. Hiding other people's faults was what she did best. 'If it don't concern you, don't stick your nose it', she'd always told me growing up. But Shareef did concern me. He was my big brother and I wanted and needed to see him. So, I did the next best thing. I talked with Yasmeen, who was fast becoming my closest relative. While we were out washing clothes Sunday morning at the laundromat up the street, I knew it was the perfect opportunity to get her to talk to me.

"How long has Hasan been here with Ummi?" I asked while putting coins in a washing machine.

"Oh, hmm, let's see. He probably moved in with her right along the same time me and Mas'ud did. So, that's about a year and a bit of change," she said, putting a load of dirty clothes into a machine.

"That's a long time," I replied sitting down and watching my two machines spin my clothes.

"Yeah, I guess it is. You want an orange or lime pop from the vending machine?" she asked, walking towards the back of the small store.

"I'll take some water," I said taking some quarters from my bag to give to her as she came back towards me. She waved them away. "When's the last time anyone heard from Shareef?"

"At the hearing," Yasmeen said in between sips of her drink.

"A court hearing?" I shrieked. "What was he doing at a court hearing?"

"Being sentenced," she replied indifferently. I almost choked. My big brother was incarcerated? That didn't sound right at all. Shareef had been Abu's rock. It was Ameera and me who had tested the waters and made all the splashes. Shareef was our Yoda, always a step or two away, waiting to steer his two mischievous sisters back home unharmed.

"You okay? You need to stand up and get some air?" Yasmeen asked me while I suffered through a coughing fit.

"Fine. I'm fine," I finally managed to say. "Where is he – where is Shareef now?" I asked standing up to allow more air in my lungs.

"Oh, Allah. I am sorry, Astaghfirullah! I am so sorry, Iman. I didn't know you didn't know. I assumed Ummi or Mas'ud had told you by now. Shareef, he's at a facility up in Chester," she said, much more warmhearted. She swung her legs in a different direction. She was dressed conservatively, as usual, in a long, loose black overgarment, a long beige hijab, and dark leather sandals that she insisted on wearing with socks.

"No – it's okay. I guess I knew something was up. I just didn't have all the information. What's Shareef in for?" I asked, scared of the answer.

"Aggravated assault, parole violation, and a suspended license, I think. I'm not absolutely sure if he was charged with the license part. But I know it was suspended, alright," she said. I sat back down next to her and dropped my head into my hands covering my face as tears streamed down my cheeks. Allah, this couldn't be real! We were both silent for about five minutes until I managed to form words again.

"Where's Hasan's mother?" I asked hesitantly.

"You know what, that I don't know. I've never met her. She was around before my time. Hasan was living with Shareef over in East Liberty until he caught the case last year."

And there I had it. Not the whole story or even half of the story. I held enough pieces to see a small part of it. I had my issues that Allah knew I was busy struggling to try to work it out, but Hasan, at the age of ten already had his too. By the time Yasmeen and I finished washing, drying, and folding all the clothes and then driving home, I knew what my first task would have to be. I had to connect with Hasan. I owed it to his father.

They say absence makes the heart grow fonder and, in my case, that was mostly true. Being around my family again allowed me to see how much I'd really missed having them in my life. But for my family nothing spelled loving like cold hard cash. The money I had taken with me when I left Mateo was supposed to be more than enough to keep me comfortable for at least a year or so. But after discovering some of my family's financial problems, I did what any daughter would do: I handled it.

My Ummi was on Medicare and had been receiving social security payments since Abu had returned to Allah. She didn't have a job, so that was her only real income. With Shareef incarcerated, Hasan had no resources. He was totally dependent on Ummi and Ummi's backbone was Mas'ud. Mas'ud was the only one in the house working and that boy was working himself to death. He had a baby on the way to prepare for, too. Alhamduleelah, Abu and Ummi owned their house, so that was a big relief, but the house was falling apart. I knew coming back that I would need to get a job. I just didn't think it was going to have to be so soon.

I was fortunate, though. I had some education. Right after I returned to United States from the Dominican Republic, we had moved to Atlanta. When I saw how controlling Mateo was with me and his money, I enrolled in a nursing program at Georgia Perimeter College. Mateo played like he was so concerned with me going to school and stressing out over exams and stuff. But he was fronting. His real issue was me catching other men's eyes. He would drive me to school most days and pick me up. Even though he'd given me my own car, I wasn't allowed to drive it without another family member. I wasn't allowed to take morning classes. I wasn't allowed to stay late on campus to study in the library. I wasn't allowed to make friends with any students.

I wasn't allowed to take classes with male professors and he always wanted a tally on how many males were in my classes too. Mateo's list of can't-dos for me had been longer than my parents.

Thank goodness nursing was a field dominated by women because if it hadn't been, Mateo would've found a reason to force me to quit. That's when I knew something was really wrong with our relationship.

He fought with me for the whole two and a half years I was in the program, especially when I had clinicals. But I pushed through. I would hide my work, and study late at night when he was in the streets or out of town. I always kept my grades and achievements to myself to avoid setting him off or making him feel jealous. Evil Mateo wouldn't even let me walk at my graduation, but I didn't care. I had earned that paper with my legal name on it that said I'd graduated with honors. I passed the state licensure test and had that paper too. I knew there would be day I would get to use it. Now, was my chance.

The next morning, Yasmeen and I went to Ross Park Mall to go shopping. Well, more like go on a shopping spree. I bought new bedding for everyone, two new Harvey Ellis bed frames for Ummi and Mas'ud from Crate & Barrel, new curtains for the living room and kitchen from Pottery Barn, and three air conditioners because it was hotter than the open desert in the house. I purchased tennis shoes and some new dresses for Ummi from Sears (her favorite department store), a few new summer outfits for Hasan from Gap Kids, a pair of tennis shoes for Mas'ud and Hasan from Champs, and one of those Xbox game systems for Hasan from the game store.

Yasmeen and I could barely carry all the bags and boxes back to the parking lot. It was a blessing that the furniture stores had delivery services. There was no way in the world we could've fit any type of furniture in Yasmeen's old, beat-up Toyota Camry. After we finished shopping, Yasmeen and I stopped by the Cheesecake Factory and had a late lunch. I ordered the summer shrimp rolls and a salad and Yasmeen had the crab bites, chicken chili, and a salad as well.

As we chomped on our food, I reached into my pocket on my long-sleeved green chevron printed shirtdress that I had worn with a pair of black palazzo pants and a white pashmina scarf. I gave Yasmeen the rest of the money that I'd brought out that day, which totaled about $900. I told her to use it as she liked for her and my future niece. She looked down at the money and then back up at me several times in shock. I felt like I'd given her some type of contraband. So, I said to her,

"What? What's the problem?" Only I think it came out with a little bit more attitude than I intended.

"Well, I guess it's nothing for you, but," she said with a shrug of her shoulders while wiping a bit of chili sauce from the corner of her mouth, "people usually don't walk around spending thousands of dollars every day. At least not anyone I know."

"You know me, though," I said and continued eating my roll.

"Barely. Can you tell me, where did you get it all from?" she asked, putting down her half-eaten crab bite to look me square in my face. I could tell it was a question she really needed an answer to. I'd started going to the Masjid with Ummi on Saturday nights to attend the Islamic studies class. Every week, the sister who taught the class would go over in Arabic and English a new hadeeth with the small group of women who attended. Last week, I'd memorized that the prophet (sallallahu alyhi wa sallam) said suspicion was a sin in most cases. Yasmeen had been kind to me from the first day I had met her on the front porch a month and a half ago. I didn't want to give her any reasons to be suspicious of me. I was trying to build a good relationship with her. She was my strongest link to Mas'ud who still hadn't warmed up to me yet. I couldn't afford to mess things up with her.

"I don't mean to be nosy. I hope you understand, but your brother is not gonna let me keep this money if he doesn't know where it came from, ya know," Yasmeen informed me. I sighed, understanding completely.

She was right. Mas'ud would want to know. I'd seen firsthand how selective and cautious he was about all his affairs. And I certainly couldn't blame him. I was sure he'd had his fair share of shady situations growing up in the Hill and the fact was, family or not, you couldn't trust many people to put your best interests first.

"I get it, Yasmeen, and you're right. You both have every right to know where my money came from. So even though he hasn't asked me yet to my face, you can let him know for me that I've been saving this money for years. Some of it I earned and some of it my partner,

Mateo, gave me over the years. The rest of it came from pawning my jewelry and selling my car before I came back to Pittsburgh. You all didn't think I walked away empty handed, did you?" I said with a wink of my eye.

Yasmeen still looked serious. "To be honest, we don't really know what you did. I know you haven't said much about the last 12 years of your life with your partner, but from the little that I've gathered, he didn't seem like the type to give parting gifts. Did you even tell him you were leaving him?" she questioned me.

"No, he isn't the type to give parting gifts, that's why I started saving what I could. I wanted to leave him for such a long, long time, but I honestly was afraid. Then one day, Allah opened a door for me and I literally walked right out the front door with my bag. He went to London for a couple of days for business. He wanted me to come, but I told him I had the flu and was sick. As soon as I knew he boarded the plane, I packed and left.

"You walked away and didn't tell him anything?" Yasmeen asked again.

"Girl, I walked right out the front door, got in my car, and took it to a dealership and sold it. Took a cab to the pawn shop and dumped my whole jewelry box out on the counter," I recalled as tears filled the rims of eyes. "Got that money, took some Ibuprofen and took another cab to the train station, all in the same day." Hearing my getaway story out loud really felt powerful to my own ears. My life had been spared.

"That's some deep TLC movie stuff! What if that man is still looking for you, Iman? What if he comes here to Pittsburgh?" she asked, clearly concerned.

"I don't know, but I am praying he won't. I know Mateo is probably still angry at me and embarrassed even. But he always said he wasn't in the business of keeping a woman who didn't want to be kept. Out of sight, out of mind is what they say. Knowing him, he already has another woman wearing my clothes, eating the food I left in the freezer for him, and warming my sheets at night," I assured her.

"So, what happens when the money you have runs out? What are you going to do then?" she asked.

"Get a job," I said.

When Yasmeen and I got home later that night and brought in all of the new things it was like we were in Prince's video, partying like it was 1999. Ummi was speechless for the first time in about 62 years and it was because of a bit of happiness I gave her. She kissed my nose and called me her bunny. Allah knows it was probably one of the best feelings I'd had in a long time. I hadn't been called bunny in so long and it felt good. Hasan was so excited about the Xbox and, surprisingly, so was Mas'ud. He said a lot men played those games too. I didn't know one way or another, it hadn't been Mateo's thing. He was fond of street guys' games like Blackjack and dominoes. I was happy for my family, though. By the time I had showered, prayed, and made it into bed, I was exhausted. As soon as I laid my head on the pillow, my eyes closed. I whispered out loud to myself, Allahu Akbar, and then fell asleep feeling loved, warm, and safe for first time in 12 years.

Chapter 3

Mornings in the Johnson house were crazy. We all got up for Fajr prayer before the sun rose and scurried around to get in and out of the house's two bathrooms. Then Masud and Hasan would usually drive a couple of streets over to either Masjid Al Awwal or further on to the Islamic Center to pray with the other Muslim men in congregation. Yasmeen, Ummi, and I would pray together downstairs in the living room. After that, I'd drag myself back up to my room and fall back to sleep only to be reawakened by Hasan an hour or so later. It was so hectic and exhaustive, but day by day I was starting to really enjoy it. Hasan never went back to sleep after Fajr and now that I was his best friend (he actually told me that) he expected me to play the part. I didn't mind. In fact, I was glad to have Hasan's company. It was early summer time, so most mornings we'd cook breakfast for everyone, clean the kitchen, sort clothes, play Xbox of course, and roller-skate outside all before eleven in the morning. The boy made me smile from deep down in my core. He was bossy too, just like his father.

Eventually, I had to go job hunting, so I told Hasan that I wouldn't be able to play with him as long as usual. Of course, when I told him what I had to do, he insisted on tagging along with me. Ummi never let him go much of anywhere without her, so there wasn't much for him to do during the day besides sit on the porch, color, kick a ball, or ride his bike. I didn't actually have any job interviews lined up, I planned on dropping off my resume at some clinics and filling out as many applications as I could. Yasmeen had said I could borrow her car, so I gave in and told Hasan he could come. We left right after breakfast.

It was a sunny and warm day. I wore a pair of pale yellow wide-legged palazzo pants with a pale blue long-sleeved peter pan collared baby doll shirt, black leather wedge sandals, and my favorite white pashmina hijab. We drove through downtown, Strip district, Bluff, and Oakland. I needed to find a job as close to Hill district as possible. It would be at least a couple of months or so after I started working that I would be able to purchase a nice car of my own, which meant I couldn't work too far out since I would be relying mostly on public transportation.

My last stop was at the Hilltop Community Health Center. I didn't really want to work there because it was such a busy hood clinic, but as the saying goes, desperate times call for desperate actions. Hasan stayed in the car for all my stops since he didn't want to come with me. He'd been great so far.

I knew he was tired of waiting and I planned to reward him for his patience and good company with a trip to the mall for lunch and a quick stop at the arcade. I was so excited when I came out of the clinic to tell him the good news that I didn't notice until right when I got up on the car that the boy was gone. I didn't know if I simply screamed or laced it with a couple expletives. But my heartbeat dropped so fast, I thought I was going to faint. Then it started pounding, I started sweating, shaking, and felt nauseous all at the same time. If I had spotted a bottle of Vodka, I'd have downed it down in some alleyway. But I didn't have any. I had to deal with this sober. I had to find my nephew.

I ran frantically back into the clinic while I supplicated out loud. I thought that maybe he'd come in one of the other entrances looking for me since I'd taken a little longer than expected. I stopped by the front desk and asked the female attendant if she'd seen my nephew. I described him to her but it wasn't any use. She said she hadn't seen him. I started to cry right there in front of her. She offered to call the police but I declined her offer. Hasan had to be somewhere around there. He had to be, but the question was where?

I rushed back out of the clinic back towards where I had parked the car and every horrible thought that could come to me, did. I'd already caused my family enough heartache for a lifetime. I knew for sure they'd never forgive me if something happened to Hasan and I would never forgive myself either. I starting yelling his name and swung my body around in all directions but he was nowhere in sight. I saw a couple of different store fronts and a bodega a little bit up past the parking lot. I locked Yasmeen's car doors and began to speed walk up that way. For the most part, I knew I probably looked a little – well a lot – off walking the down the street talking to myself and crying, but I'd thrown my cool off. I was afraid.

The tears mixed with the brown mascara I had applied to my eyes that morning and was running down my cheeks leaving a muddied, messy residue. My hijab was crooked and loose and sweat was dripping off my forehead profusely. It was bad. When I finally reached the bodega, I cupped my hands and looked in the glass door but didn't see any children inside. Something told me to go inside anyway. I went in, looking around all the racks of snacks and vending machines, but as I expected, Hasan wasn't there. The store clerk, an old Latino man wearing a dirty New York Yankees baseball cap, watched me carefully as he sang along to an old salsa song by Tito Puente that was playing on a small radio behind his counter, but never said a word. Briefly our eyes connected. I felt like he understood without any words from me that I wasn't in there to cause him any trouble. He tipped his cap politely as I exited the store but I was too low-spirited to return the gesture.

Outside the store, I stood looking around again. I didn't see any children. I started sobbing loudly again as I walked. I didn't know where I was going, but I kept walking. I must have walked two blocks up before I came to an intersection. I didn't want to cross it because I was getting into unfamiliar parts. I looked back down the street and finally decided it was time to go back to the clinic and call my mother. No sooner did I turn around, I heard my name being called from across the street. Hasan and one other boy that looked around the same age as him was standing outside of a T-Mobile store.

I quickly crossed through the traffic on the busy street and ran over to him, praising Allah. Hasan greeted me as usual with a wide grin and clear, easy hazel eyes. I grabbed him by his shirt – one of the new shirts I'd bought him from Gap Kids, pulled him to me, and kissed his face.

"Are you OUT of your mind, boy?" I yelled through the tears. "I've been all over looking for you. You don't get out of the car I left you in without telling me. You must be out of your mind, Hasan!" Each word that left my mouth made my grip on his shirt tighten. I was seeing a pure, deep red.

"Yo," Hasan bellowed out trying to pull away from me. "Get off of me!" he demanded. His smile had dissipated and those beautiful hazel eyes turned hard like steel as he tried to match my macho. The little boy that he was with stood there watching us. Hasan looked more concerned about him, than about how I was doing and that angered me more.

"Get off of you? Little boy, do you know what can happen to you out in these streets? Children are getting kidnapped all the time. You better be glad I saw you! I was about to go call Ummi and that would have been your behind," I informed him. My energy had actually started to readjust to normal levels since I saw he was okay. But I couldn't believe he didn't understand the seriousness of his offense.

"Call Ummi over kidnappers? Aunt Iman, now you trippin'. We still in the Hill. Who gonna kidnap me here?" he asked. He folded both of his hands on his chest, cocked his head to the side, and smirked. "I'm a black boy and I'm almost as tall as you. Ain't no kidnappers kidnappin' me!"

"Okay, what about all the child molesters, dope fiends, and thugs? You're not that tough, Hasan, and whether you believe it or not you are a child and you'll be a child for the next eight years. Now, you listen to me and you listen good, boy. Don't you ever pull this kind of stunt with me again," I said and continued to give him the tongue lashing that he deserved.

A couple of people walking by turned their heads and gave me strange looks, but again I didn't care. I had to get Hasan told. It wasn't until some man came out of the T-Mobile store complaining about the noise that I momentarily took my attention away from Hasan. I turned around with every intention of giving the man a real live and uncut "around the way" Pittsburgh girl piece of my mind, with all trimmings – head bobbing, finger swaggin', and some choice words. That was until I looked up and saw his face.

"Well, well, well. As Salaamu alaikum, sister ...ah, Imania, was it?" he said laughing that same friendly laugh I had heard about a month ago, with the biggest Kool-Aid smile I'd ever seen as his pot belly heaved up and down. Hasan, with his grown-self, corrected him right away, giving all my business away.

"Imania? Who's that? That's not my aunt's name. Her name is Iman. Don't you remember her, uncle?" Hasan asked him.

"Yeah, Hasan, you're right. I do know your Aunt Iman, Iman Johnson. That's it," he said giving Hasan a wink while he held on tightly to the slick smile. "We go all the way back to the playground days," he replied putting way too much emphasis on choice words. "Hey, ah, how's those business associates doing, sister?"

"They're fine, they're all fine," I said, finally speaking up, but I was in no mood for games. My patience had been pushed beyond its limit once already and I was not about to be further humiliated in front of a group of children. "Let's go, Hasan," I ordered.

"Aww, Aunt Iman," Hasan whined sounding like the ten-year-old that he was. "Can't I stay a little longer here with Saud?"

"No, you can't. You know what you've done, so now it's time to go. C'mon." I started walking away but Hasan didn't budge. I stopped and walked back to him. "I said let's go."

"This is wack. I can't believe you're mad at me for nothing," he cried. I started to reprimand him, but I was cut off.

"Ay, *akh*, you gonna watch how you talk to adults. That's no way to speak to your own aunt, now is it? I think you ought to apologize," the brother, who still stood in the store's door said. Hasan looked at him and then at me before whispering a nonchalant apology. I accepted and restated my order.

"As salaamu alaikum, sister Iman and Hasan," the brother yelled out behind us in a tone that was far too hood for my tastes as we walked away. But he had offered the greeting.

"Wa alaikum as salaam, brother Jibril," I replied, this time loud enough for him to hear it.

Hasan looked out the window and was quiet the whole ride back home. I could tell by his slouched demeanor and twisted mouth that he was angry – at me of all people. I didn't care. Hasan had been wrong, dead wrong, and I had a right to be worried and afraid for his safety. I had absolutely no experience rearing children, but I'd been a big sister. I knew that sometimes children would have to be upset with adults. He'd have to get over it.

As I pulled into Ummi's driveway and turned off the car, Hasan looked at me with his big, light brown eyes and I was taken aback by the seriousness that he held within them. You could tell from his eyes alone, he already knew too much, had seen too much.

"Aunty Iman," he started and I nodded at his attention. "I know you were looking out for me, and I know I shouldn't have left the car like I did." He took a quick breath and blew it out hard. "It won't happen again. I promise."

"Insha'Allah, Hasan."

"Insha'Allah," he repeated. "You're not gonna tell my Jedda or Uncle Mas'ud are you?"

"No. Not this time, Hasan. But you are going to be punished. You made a bad decision, you scared the life out of me, and you behaved badly in front of your friend. So no playing the Xbox tonight."

"Aw, man! C'mon aunty, that's too much," Hasan whined.

"Sorry, Hasan, but I don't think it is. Lock your door when you get out and let's go inside the house so I can make you lunch."

Hasan got out the car and moped in the house as I walked behind him. I prayed I had handled the situation appropriately and that Hasan wouldn't take this as a deal breaker for our new friendship. We both needed this friendship and now wasn't the time to be thrown back to square one. Although, I also knew I couldn't afford to let him walk all over me. Either way, Hasan's situation was turning out to be much harder to build up than I had imagined.

Later that night, Yasmeen had invited me to go with her and Mas'ud to the Islamic Center of Pittsburgh to attend one of their friends' *aqeeqah* for their new baby. I was a little nervous about going to a welcoming ceremony for a baby because for sure there was going to be a lot of people there. Thus far, I hadn't even ventured out to Friday prayer services yet. Jumu'ah was always crowded with lifelong community members and that made it a no-go for me. The Tuesday nights' sisters study circle that I went to with Ummi was good enough. It was always a small group of sisters. Most of the attendants were new Muslims, so I didn't know them and, more importantly, they didn't know me. I was hoping because Mas'ud was younger than me and I didn't really know who his friends were when I was younger, they wouldn't recognize me now. And Yasmeen grew up in a different Muslim community so most likely her sister-friends here were new people too. Or at most, they hadn't heard of me.

I wasn't naïve. I knew very well I had been the focus of gossip in the community, at least for the first few years after I left. I also knew I couldn't blame them either. I had made the decision to do what I did and it came with lasting consequences. Everyone talked about someone at least once in a while. I did it a lot when I was younger: *"Hmph! You heard about how sister so-and-so asked for a divorce while she still pregnant or you know brother so-and-so's son be smoking after school with those non-Muslim guys?"* But the most common and scandalous gossip around the community growing up was, *"you know sister so-and-so done took her hijab off now? Is she still deenin'?"* Ghriba is what we called it in the Muslim community and it was considered more than a bad habit. It was a sin that many Imams talked about on Fridays during the khutbah to discourage Muslims from engaging in it. The real pious Muslims liked to front like they didn't do it, but they did. No one liked to admit that they did it. I guess because we often tricked ourselves into believing that talking about other people's weaknesses and sins would keep us safe from following into the same lizard's hole.

Like I said, I got it and I knew I still wasn't above it. I just didn't want to have to face the very people who dragged my name and my parents' names through the gutter. Really, my parents hadn't deserved it. They had done their best with me. They taught me Tawheed from the womb, the kept me around other Muslims, and they sacrificed and worked hard to take care of me. Ummi and Abu always reminded me to pray my five and to value my body by dressing modestly. For the most part, those were the teachings that carried me during the darkest nights. Still, it was me who had got caught up. It was me who had made the wrong choices, not my parents.

Anyway, after about an hour of procrastinating in my room, I finally shared my reservations with Yasmeen. She told me I should go, of course. Yasmeen was quick to remind me that the Islamic Center was the house of Allah. I had a right to go any time I wanted, not only on the days when it had few occupants. I knew that. But I couldn't help my feelings. I was scared.

"Keeping it 100, Iman, if they're gonna backbite you, they are gonna do it whether you come around or not. Just about everyone who knew you has probably already heard you're back anyways."

"Everyone knows I'm back?" I choked on Yasmeen's words as I sat on her new bed in disbelief. The thought of people knowing where I was and talking behind my back made my stomach knot up. It had been the reason I stayed at the Birch Inn instead staying at one of the five star hotels that I could have afforded to stay at downtown. I didn't want to see anyone. I was afraid of seeing anyone.

"Iman," Yasmeen started as she sat down on the bed next me. "I don't get it. I know I didn't know you back in the days, but you seem to be a really strong woman today. You left a horrible situation and you came back home and back to Islam. If you came back home for Allah like I think you did, then don't be ashamed," she said, trying to scoot her pregnant body off the bed again. "Here," she said tossing me a pale blue garment.

"It's a jilbab, practically brand new. It's way too snug for me in my belly and hips now. Why don't you try it on and see if it'll fit you? I think it suits you better anyway."

I glanced at the overgarment that she'd given me and looked out the door at the stairs. I could tell Yasmeen had no intentions of allowing me to stay home and act fearful. I got up and took the jilbab with me back downstairs to my room on the second floor. I quickly showered, combed my hair, and put on a full length, short sleeved sundress before trying on the jilbab that Yasmeen had given me. It was a lot cuter than the ones that I usually wore. It was made of very light crepe material. White decorative embroidery was on the bodice, sleeves, and the hem, and three small, white-silverish buttons went down the front. By golly, it was pretty and stylish. It *was* my style. I pulled it over my head quickly and went into the bathroom to catch a look of myself. A small smile emerged from the corners of my mouth. I looked like the old me.

By seven in the evening, Mas'ud was waiting on the front porch with Hasan for Yasmeen and me to come down. I put on my white hijab and paired it up with off-white leather strappy sandals, a long pearl necklace, and a couple of silver bracelets. When I finally came down stairs, Yasmeen was stepping out the door. Ummi was sitting in the living room so I walked over to her and offered salaams before I left.

"Oh, walaikum as salaam, honey. Keep an eye and ear out for Hasan for me, would you? He got a way of wondering off every now and again," she said, and I thought to myself, *now you tell me?*

"Don't worry, I will. You sure you don't want to come? You know there's enough room in Mas'ud's van for all of us."

"Nope, I'm too tired and getting too old to be hanging out late these days, Iman. My blood sugar was up today, too. 'Sides I'd much rather sit here in front of the air conditioner, sip on my iced sweet tea, and listen to the Qur'an on the computer. You go 'head and keep close to Yasmeen. You'll be alright, baby," she said sensing my misgivings. "Anybody try it, you make sure you tell Mas'ud who done it. All right?" Ummi instructed me and lifted the sweating cold glass of tea to her mouth for a drink.

"I'll be okay, Ummi. Insha'Allah, we'll see you later. Lock the doors behind me."

"You know I always lock those doors, girl. And one more thing, if your aunty Adilah is there with her sweet potato or pecan pie, make sure you bring a couple of slices home for me."

"Ummi!" I gasped. "You know you shouldn't be eating those sweets."

"Iman, a little sugar won't hurt me none if Allah doesn't allow it. Now go 'head and stop holding everybody up for you."

I shook my head, walked out the door, and closed it behind me. I knew I wouldn't be able to win any battles with my mother, at least not about the foods she ate, but soon enough I would have to have a talk with her about changing her diet and taking better care of her health. She was the only parent I had left. I still needed her in this life with me.

Mas'ud drove to the Islamic Center in a few short minutes. He took Hasan with him towards the brothers' side entrance. Yasmeen and I headed to the sisters' door through the front walkway. It was hard, but I forced a smile on my face as I entered. I extended my hand first and shook hands with several sisters. I even received some cold, stiff embraces from sisters I didn't know.

After Yasmeen introduced me to her friend Hasanah and her new baby boy, Khalid, I politely made my way over to a sitting area outside of the praying area that was equipped with a couple of old sofas, three folding tables, and about two dozen chairs. The sisters' prayer area was full of chatter. The women were laughing or talking animatedly as old friends did. The small children were running around or munching on snacks. But something inside of me was preventing me from breathing easily.

I kept glancing around to see if anyone was staring at me but they weren't. I had no idea why I felt so alone, so much like an outsider who was intruding on a private affair. I was ready to go back home where Ummi could keep me safe. But I didn't want to mess up the good time Yasmeen and Mas'ud were having. My heart started pounding and my head started throbbing. It felt like I was having a heart attack. I got up from the sofa, smiled politely at a group of sisters nearby fixing plates of food from the folding tables, and rushed over to the bathroom. After relieving myself, I stepped over to one of the four sinks and began to make ablution.

Catching my reflection in the mirror while I wiped over my head with the cold water, I jumped back from fright. It was him. I saw his reflection in the mirror. He smiled sweetly at first and then he began to snicker. He moved like a flash. Then he was suddenly standing right behind me. He tried to whisper in my ear, but I splashed water at the mirror and his reflection disappeared. Tears began to flush my eyes as my mind raced through all the horrible and loving nights I had shared with Mateo.

He'd been a monster and a knight. A friend and an enemy. A prayer and a curse. So many years together meant I left conflicted, hurt, shattered, yet weak for him. I hated that, deep down, pieces of me still felt connected to him. I hated that parts of me missed him and cared for him still despite everything he'd done. Mateo had robbed me of the best parts of my life: my youth. I hated that he had made me distrust myself. But most of all, I hated that the only way I knew to cope with those ugly, scary feelings was inside a bottle of something strong and haram for me. Whatever could snatch away and hide my feelings the quickest was the best. The hangover and heartache always left me for dead.

I stood at the sink, closed my eyes, and prayed for sobriety, but when I opened my eyes there he was again. This time he was in 3D in my vivid imagination. Tall as an evergreen tree, with smooth toasted almond skin, buff as the boxer he was, dark brown piercing eyes, freshly cut jet black, thick, wavy hair that was lined up perfectly, and smelling like his favorite Armani cologne. He looked more distinguished than he'd ever really been. He stood in front of me wearing one of his most expensive dark blue tailored suits with spit shined shoes, sneering at me. His look said it all; I was nothing and no one without him. I stuck my fingers in my ears and closed my eyes. I didn't want to hear him; I didn't want to believe him anymore. I had proven after all that I could "be". I didn't need the cars, the trips, the house, his crazy family, or him. He hadn't given me a life - Mateo had tried to throw me into my coffin.

I leaned my back into the door of the bathroom and slid down slowly, pressing my body up against the wooden door to secure it closed. I needed to be alone. I didn't want to go back to Mateo; I couldn't go back to Mateo. But did I fit in here with these women? I closed my eyes and let the rapid flow of tears stream down my face and soak my cheeks.

Every day since I'd been back at home, I smiled and tried to laugh with everyone. I tried my best to fall back right in step with my family, trying to be the ideal Muslima, the devoted daughter, the proper role model to my nephew – as if I had it together. Who was I fooling? I couldn't even fool the imaginary Mateo, how had I thought I could fool my family? Were they really laughing behind my back at my failure in life? Or had they really forgiven me?

The light tap on the door startled me. I quickly stood up away from the door and went back to the sink and washed my face. When the door opened, an older sister dragged her body slowly through with several pans in her hands. "Oh, my word!" the plump woman squealed. "Get out of town! Would you look at you?" she said with a hearty laugh and then grabbed me, dropping the pans to floor and squeezing all 206 bones in my small framed body tightly into her sweet-smelling softness. I laughed and wrapped my hijab back around my head before placing my hands around her. "You remember me, don't you?" she asked. "Of course, you remember me, baby girl. We go way back. I practically raised you. And I helped your Ummi deliver you, right there in the kitchen. I caught you with my own two hands while Musa was outside waiting on the ambulance," she said without taking a breath.

"I couldn't forget you if I wanted to," I said clearing my voice and willing another smile to appear. "It's so good to see you, sister Adilah. You were like a second mother to my siblings and me."

"Still am, still am," sister Adilah said and hugged me tightly again. "You come on out of this bathroom, Iman. I didn't even know you were here. If I'd known, girl, I would've had you helping with the food or sum'thing. You remember my daughter – your best friend Fariba? She loves to cook still to this day. She don't like to clean. She always too busy. She dropped them girls off on me talkin' bout she got to go back to work. And you know I got almost ten grand babies now? Don't ask me how, 'cause I'm not in the mood for those stories. But half them out there tearing the place down 'cause they parents won't watch 'em right. Goodness, c'mon, Iman, c'mon and help me out here," sister Adilah yelled, pulling me out from the bathroom.

I didn't feel up to going back out into the sisters' *musallah*, but the sister didn't give me a choice. Underneath the fake smile, I was relieved. In the nick of time, Allah had sent her to help me before I tore myself down again. Shaytan almost had me, but, Alhamduleelah, I held on and it made me feel better. As the night progressed, I met a few new sisters and even talked with some women I had known before I left. I got in the mix: fixing plates of food, cleaning the soiled dishes, and playing with the children. I had less time to think about me and more time to think about this moment of my life and that felt good. By the time we prayed Isha, it was dark outside and most people had gone home. The Imam gave a short talk right after the prayer on repentance being a mercy from Allah to His servants.

Before then, I'd never thought of it like that. I always equated repentance with shame and shame was for wrongdoers, not people Allah had mercy for. I'd used it to dodge all the guilt. But the brother used verses from the Qur'an and statements from the Prophet Muhammad, peace be upon him, to explain otherwise. He'd said that shame was actually a characteristic of faith for the believers since only those who had faith would Allah allow to return to Him to seek His aide and pardoning and this was a mercy. As those who didn't believe in Allah were not concerned with shame, they were allowed to disregard their ills until the day of reckoning. It made sense and was just the right type of advice for me. I was proud of myself. It was another step closer to the healing that I wanted and needed.

When Mas'ud finally knocked on the sister's entrance to let Yasmeen and I know that he and Hasan were waiting in the car, it was well past ten in the evening. While Yasmeen prepared to leave, several sisters embraced me and invited me out to different events. Sister Adilah had given me a plate of food for Ummi, complete with three slices of her famous pecan pie. She told me to call her tomorrow so she could stop by and visit with me. Sister Adilah was a hoot. She reminded me of all the elder sisters I had loved in our community growing up. I had every intention to call her and sit with her from time to time. I figured she could help me to remember me.

As soon as I got in the van and sat in the back with Hasan, Mas'ud started asking me questions. "How you feel? You okay, Iman?" "Did you get enough to eat?" "Did you get to hold the new baby?" "Did you see aunty Adilah?" "What did you think about the lecture?" "How many new sisters did you meet?" he rattled off, one by one. I answered all his questions with pleasure. It dawned on me that this was the most talking Mas'ud and I have done in almost 12 years.

I realized that my baby brother was concerned for me and he was checking to make sure that his big sister was good. Even though he didn't talk to me much at the house, he was showing that he cared for me. It even felt like he had some love for me, too. We all talked the whole way home; laughing and sharing stories. When Mas'ud revealed to me that a few brothers had asked him about me, I was disappointed. Muslim men asking about me? I laughed out loud at the irony. If they only knew how messed up I was, they'd forget my name.

When we got home, Hasan rushed out of the van and started to run up the steps saying he was next on the Xbox. I shut that down real quick. How quickly children forget. I walked up before him, turned on the porch light, and reached into my purse to pull out my key, but the door flew open.

Chapter 4

"Oh, Allah! Wow, it is you! Subhan' Allah! It is you," sweetly sang a short, bronzed skinned, slightly plump woman with beautiful oval shaped hazel eyes. Her eyes were young but pained, with deep dimples in both of her cheeks, and a button nose. She stood in the doorway wearing a shiny black overhead *abaya* with a fresh blackened bruise underneath her left eye. She quickly embraced me and began to cry. "I never stopped praying for you," she whispered in my ear.

My hands instinctively reached up and found their way around her chubby, soft body and I slowly pulled her as close to me as I could. She smelled familiar and I knew I knew her. I loved her. And I'd never stopped praying for her either.

"Ameera?"

I asked as I stepped into the house followed by Hasan, Mas'ud, and Yasmeen. My eyes zoomed in on my mother. She cried softly as she held a pretty, chubby little girl with thick, black curly hair, buttery skin, and big dark brown eyes. She looked about one or two.

"Yeah, Iman! You know it's me, sis!" Ameera said so excitedly. "I ain't know what to expect, but I had to get here to see you. I couldn't stop dreaming and thinking about how you would look now," she looked me up and down and smiled before hugging me again with tears in her eyes. "Black don't crack, baby! You still look exactly the same --- better. Allahu Akbar! My sister is alive!"

Ameera held my hand tightly as we walked into the living room. Mas'ud and Hasan were already playing with Ameera's older two boys. I locked eyes on the one that favored me for a few seconds. From his dimpled chin to his nose to his eyelashes to his mouth, it was like looking into the face of a child I was supposed to bear.

"His name is Imran," she said laughing. "That's my oldest. He's seven. Ya'll could be twins, right? And the other one is Munir," she said turning her full body over to the other side of the room. "He just turned six. He look like Ummi, don't he?" she asked me, still laughing. "And my baby girl, Saba, is all her father so far!"

I sat down on the old couch and those old springs squeaked underneath my weight. I made a mental note to order a new sofa. But I shifted my focus quickly back onto Ameera. Ameera, my baby sister that had the black eye. It was either surreal or too real for me take in. I nodded my head at her. Ameera thought I was agreeing with her, but I was demonstrating my confusion. It was like everyone was looking at her, seeing her, but not really seeing what I saw. My little sister had been beat up. Didn't they care? My veins were getting hot and itchy; I had to let it go.

"Who did it?" I asked in a low, shaky voice as I took the straight pins out of my *hijab* and removed it from my head. I was trying so hard not be disrespectful to Ummi or her house, but Ameera's behavior had me on fire.

"Did what?" she shot at me like she still knew me and wanted to go head to head.

"Who the hell punched you in your damn eye, Ameera?" I yelled at her as I stood up and walked over to her and pointed to her face.

Ameera's mood instantly deflated. She slumped her shoulders, rolled her eyes, slowly inhaled her breath, and swallowed it up in my face. "Really, thanks a lot, Iman. I'm here...for you. This," she said, pointing to her face, "Was all because of you." She spat at me like I had actually told her to take punch for me. She pulled the bottom of her abaya up into her hand and quickly walked over to Ummi and snatched her baby, Saba, from her then stormed into the kitchen without any more words for me.

Ummi then shot me a look that said she was disappointed in me. I threw my hands up. "Hasan, go on and take the boys upstairs to your room and put their stuff away. Help them get ready for bed," Ummi ordered him as she guided the boys to the stairs.

"Okay, Jeddah. When I finish can I play Xbox?"

"No!" Ummi and I yelled in unison.

"Tomorrow, Insha'Allah, Hasan. I got you, bro!" Mas'ud told him. "Ya'll go head to sleep. See ya'll at Fajr, Insha'Allah,"

"As salamu alykum," the boys sang out sadly and moped up the stairs.

"Wa alykum as salam," we all responded.

Mas'ud turned to me and said, "Iman, I know where your heart is, but she's mad stubborn. She's not gonna talk to you about it like this. I've tried for years with her and Umar. Her husband got his issues, but, you need to understand, so does Ameera."

"So what then? Ya'll sit around and let Ameera get beat up whenever he feels like knocking her around?"

"Did I say that?" Mas'ud questioned me sharply.

"What are you saying, Mas'ud? My little sister walks in here with a black eye and you sitting playing with the damn kids? This isn't right. Ummi this isn't right!" I said, turning to address my mother.

"Iman, listen to me girl, you're mad and I understand that. But everybody got to find their own way. Your Abu and I tried our best to raise our kids the best we knew how. But ya'll done grown up and went your own ways. Ameera done got out here, like you, doing what she want. She married who she wanted and they do what they do. That's how she done chose to live. She got to find her way. Just like you did. Insha'Allah, she will too. Leave Ameera be, please."

Ameera came back into the living room balancing her big baby on her hip and holding a Styrofoam container of food in the other hand. She plopped down on the old sofa next to Ummi and the springs hissed slowly like a tire losing air. Then she propped her daughter next to her on the sofa as she began to eat her food. She looked up at everyone and smiled so kindly, it scared me. She'd really had lost her mind. "It feels so good in here now. That cool air is refreshing. I know ya'll happy ya'll got those air conditioners. Ummi, you out of grape pop, too!"

"I'mma get up and get to the market tomorrow morning, Insha'Allah. Make sure you write it down on my list so I don't miss it. Alright, y'all, I'm going to bed," Ummi said pulling herself up off the old sofa slowly. "Y'all be good to each other. This is the only family you got. See ya'll at Fajr, Insha'Allah."

"Good night, Ummi," I said.

"As salamu alykum and good night," Ummi said to us. Yasmeen and Mas'ud got up too and followed behind Ummi.

"As salamu alykum wa rahmatullah," Yasmeen offered to us meekly as she followed behind her husband.

As soon as everyone had vacated the room, I turned my attention back to Ameera. She was still sitting on the sofa shoveling food into her daughter's mouth like she was feeding a baby bear. My anger was bubbling up again. I had heard Ummi's advice and I knew she was right. I also knew I wasn't in the best position to judge Ameera's marriage, but I had to. I never fought back because I didn't have anyone there to protect me. No one ever reached out to me and said, "You're dying. Get out of there or let me help you!" No one came for me. I was here for Ameera right now.

"You know that that food can't save you, right," I said walking over to her and sitting down on the couch beside her and baby Saba. "Or change how it feels,"

"Don't do that, Iman. Please, Allah! Don't come out your mouth talking sideways 'bout stuff you don't know squat about. You don't know nothin 'bout me, my family, or my man," she said putting her fork and Styrofoam down. She snatched her diaper bag off the oak floor and pulled out a package of baby wipes and rubbed the grease off her hands and Saba's face.

"I am not judging you, Ameera," I assured her.

"Oh, really now? What do you call this then? 'Cause it sure feels like you are to me. And it's the same thing Umar did to you. He don't know you and gonna talk about you. I got him together good! I stood up for you! I always have. I might not win every fight, but I don't lie down and get whopped up on either, believe that."

"Okay, so he hits you and you hit him back and ya'll fighting and roughing each other up. How is that a marriage for you to be in? How is he putting marks on your face and you still calling him your man?" I questioned her.

"Iman, do you see the word stupid on my forehead? We don't fight every day or even every freaking month. But some couples fight, *Mizz Iyanla* - even when they love each other. You of all people should understand that. According to Moody, you were the one getting your behind beat every other day. That ain't my life. Me and Umar got our issues, plenty, but like I done told everybody in this house, we *are* working on it. So, respect that and respect my choice. If I need help, I know how to get it," Ameera barked at me.

"Fair enough," I replied putting my arm around her shoulders. "I honestly don't like your choice, Ameera, but I will always respect you and the decision you make to work it out with your husband. But I want you to know this: while I," I told her pointing to myself, "was getting my behind beat, I knew exactly who my enemy was! I love you. And I want us to have time together so that I can get to know you and your kids, Insha'Allah. "

"I love you too, Imani! And that's why I am here," she told me and gave me a kiss on my cheek. Ameera had always been sweet and easy to like, like our Ummi. She had a temper and didn't like being pushed into a corner, but she was just as easy to forgive. Ameera was exactly who I needed to see, hug, and love. Allah was the Best of Planners.

By the time Ameera and me fell asleep it was almost time to get back up for salat. The house was full and the bathroom situation was now dead serious. I had to wait ten minutes in a line of women to relieve myself and make ablution. The boys took over the downstairs bathroom and the rest of us were all upstairs. Yasmeen and Ummi were the problems. They moved slow and had the weakest bladders, so Ameera and I had to go last. Mas'ud took all the boys with him to the masjid to offer Fajr. Yasmeen, Ummi, Ameera, baby Saba, and me stayed behind and prayed in the living room.

After the prayer, Ameera read the Qur'an to us in Arabic. Yasmeen read the English translation. Ummi sat rocking herself in her chair smiling as she listened. She finally started snoring right before the boys got back. I covered her with a throw blanket and went into the kitchen to cook breakfast. Ameera and the baby tagged behind me.

"You gon' have to fill me in on how you manage to stay so trim and slim," Ameera commented. "These babies done put a hurting on my waistline," she said as she munched on some grapes.

"You sure it was all the babies or some of your eating habits too?" I asked her.

"Wow, you got jokes, really?" Ameera teased.

With a light giggle and a generous smile, I shook my head from side to side to indicate my jest. "Seriously, I'm telling you the truth 'cause I love you. Food wasn't my addiction, but I have some. I know it's tough, I know," I explained.

"Yeah, well, I joined Weight Watchers online. You seen all that weight Jennifer Hudson done lost with them?" she asked me as she gobbled up another handful of the fruit.

"You can't believe all that was with Weight Watchers. She probably has trainers, chefs, and therapists working with her too. But she does look fab. I met her once at the Essence Festival in New Orleans." I shared with my sister as I reminisced back to the pictures Mateo and I and some of his family members took with her. He'd choked me right before we left the hotel to go to her concert. He'd been smoking and I was downright tipsy. I rode in the back seat with my sister-in-law Evelyn. Mateo sat upfront with his older brother Manny. They were having fun. I was living in fear. I burned that picture and all the other pictures in the albums that we'd taken together the day I left.

"Really? So, you was rolling like that to Essence festivals and what not? How come that man ain't never brought you back home to visit then?" Ameera asked me as she whipped some eggs and cheese together in a bowl and then poured it into the sizzling hot frying pan.

I heard her question but I didn't really feel like answering it, so I ignored her. The ugly truth was that I couldn't blame Mateo for my disappearing act completely. Mateo had actually offered several times to bring me home to visit. He even bought us plane tickets to go visit Abu when he heard he was sick in the hospital. But I couldn't get on that plane. I didn't want them to see me before I was ready: clean, sober, and free from my monster.

"I had ah...filled out some job applications the other day. Please make dua for me that Allah blesses me with something and soon! I need to help out Ummi and Mas'ud! He got that little baby girl coming real soon, Insha'Allah," I explained while I chopped the potatoes and onions for home fries.

"From the looks of it around here, you've helped out a lot already. I need you to come to Philly and sprinkle some of that makeover money on my house - heck, in my whole life," Ameera said, laughing like a jackal again. She laughed on and off the whole morning. When we cooked, cleaned, served the food - Ameera was either talking or laughing or talking and laughing.

Ameera had been the little sister that would crawl in bed with me and tickle me when I was sick and draw smiley faces in my school books. She had been one of my closest friends when we were little girls. The thing was, neither of us were little girls anymore. Now she was a grown-up woman with children and a husband that possibly had a really bad problem. I was a grown-up woman with a lot of issues who had ran away from a fighting husband. I couldn't understand why she was still laughing. Wasn't nothing funny anymore.

Ummi, Yasmeen, and Ameera left out after we prayed salatul Thuhr and went to the market for food. I stayed behind with Mas'ud to watch the rest of the kids. Hasan loved being the big cousin. Imran, Munir, and Saba followed behind him like little ducks.

"Flip - your- wrist, Imran! You gotta, like, flex the controller like you really hitting a baseball! Here," he said getting up off the couch, "let me show you *again* how to do it." He was being bossy, but I thought it was cute. I gave him the controller and told him to keep playing with the other kids. I walked to the front door to go outside with Mas'ud. He was sitting on the porch watching Saba ride on one of the push toys.

"Hey, Moody!" I said as I pulled the end of my hijab back to middle of my chest and straightened the creases in the fabric on my head. "I am sorry for talking to you like that last night. It wasn't right."

Mas'ud looked up at me and smirked. "We're good, Iman. Ya'll Johnson girls are real tough stuff. I don't want none of it. I do what I can, though," he assured me.

"It must have been tough dealing with Ameera all this time now with Shareef and Abu gone and all," I noted.

Mas'ud shrugged his shoulders then exhaled. "Ameera is ... she's fiery and it's hard for her to control herself. It's even harder for other people to deal with it, you know," he explained before extending his hand and pushing Saba back and forth some more. "She visits us a lot more now. I think she knows that she needs to do better. Truth is, I used to fight with Umar and then turn around and fight with Meera too. It didn't help. They got this toxic relationship and if you try to attack either of them, they join together and attack you.

"So, I had to stop. I send them both reminders about Allah and her responsibilities to her children, them standing in front Allah and having to bear witness against what she exposed them to – and I pray for her and wait. Good thing is, with you being here now and coming out from what you did, that's gonna force her to confront some of her issues, Insha'Allah," he told me hopefully.

"Why do you think that?" I questioned him.

"Ya'll was close. She lost the most, I think, when you know, you left us. She looked up to you and was following behind you and then she didn't really have that support any more. She just did dumb stuff for no real reason. She got in a lot trouble. Her and Abu fought a lot. It was hard on her, so I think she took the first brother that she ran into. She didn't let us really check him out either," Mas'ud explained. "Shareef likes Umar, though. I mean overall."

"Why?" I asked.

"As men, we can tell when brothers are knuckleheads and when they're rough around the edges. Umar is real rough around the edges, but he ain't no hoodlum. Abu could've really been a good mentor for him. He would've trained him, ya know," Mas'ud said through a short laugh. "I know Umar tries hard with Ameera and he loves her. Problem is, sisters like Meera don't make it easy for brothers who are already rough around the edges to do right. Two hot heads together isn't the best recipe. She got what she got. She wanted to get out of Pittsburgh."

"So, what about you, Mas'ud? How come Shareef's issues didn't become your issues like my issues shadowed Ameera?" I asked him.

"Who said they didn't?" he said matter-of-factly before picking up Saba off the push toy and handing her to me. "She needs to be changed." He walked into the house and went into the living room with the boys and I heard them all moan when he turned off the television and told them to go get ready for the masjid. I stood there on the porch and watched them for a little before I went into the house to look for Saba's diaper bag.

After I changed Saba's diaper, I took her upstairs to my room, the room I was now sharing with Ameera and her, and laid her down for a nap. I took out a sheet of paper, a pen, and grabbed a book to write on before sitting back on the bed softly so as not to wake Saba. I sat for a couple of minutes and then the words flushed my mind:

Dear Shareef:

Assalamu alaykum! In case you didn't recognize the name, yeah, it's me, your sister, Iman. I pray you've been well and safe in there. I miss you more than you know. I know you probably heard already, but I wanted to let you know that I am back in the Hill with Ummi. I'm trying really hard to fill in your shoes and help where I can. It's not easy being here, but Insha'Allah, I'm not going anywhere. Ameera and her babies are here too. She needs all our help to make the right decisions. Hasan is such a great little boy. I love him a lot and I am so thankful to have him in my life. I know we have a lot to talk about. So, I am going to come and see you soon. I want you to know I love you and that whatever is going on with you in there, it isn't your place. You belong with us. So, keep your head up and stay focused. We need you here. I need you here.

Your Sister,

Iman S. Johnson

After I finished writing my letter to Shareef, I fell asleep next to Saba. She smelled so sweet, like pure love, baby love. Holding her next to me was like holding onto a piece of cloud or a soft marshmallow. It didn't matter, though. She was my blood, which almost made her mine. I hated that she'd had to see so much violence in her short time on earth. I hated that Ameera didn't understand that Saba deserved better.

I had known soon after our moving into together that Mateo wouldn't be a good father. He was mean, angry, broken, and often prone to physical violence. The first time I had a miscarriage, I finally understood what people meant when they said Allah was the Just during calamities. I never thought sadness and happiness could co-exist. But they could and I was living proof. My heart had ached so bad I thought it would fall out when the doctor told me that they could no longer hear my baby's heart. But in that moment, I exhaled so deeply and it felt so good. I made the decision right there in that hospital bed that I wasn't going to have a baby with Mateo. I had an IUD implanted into my uterus to make sure that I didn't have any more slip-ups. It didn't work good enough, though. Every once in a while, I would get pregnant. Each time Allah found a way to bring about justice for me. Three miscarriages and one stillborn in twelve years were hard, life changing events each and every time. But it would have pulled me into a depression I might not have had the strength to crawl out of if I had brought four children into this world with a monster for a father and a fool for a mother. All children deserve the best. Allah gave it to mine by choosing to keep them with Him.

I woke to the sound of more laughter and an empty bed. I rolled my eyes at the sound of Ameera's voice, but I needed to get up and pray. I figured Ameera had probably come in and took Saba downstairs, so I made wudu and offered salat by myself.

By the time I finished praying, the thick aroma of frying fish and sweet cornbread baking had wafted into the room and was taunting me to come find it. I salamed out of the prayer and rushed down the stairs only to be met by sister Adilah's big smile.

"Now there she is," she said. "We've been waiting on you to wake up for an hour now, sleeping beauty!"

"I didn't know you were coming by, sister Adilah. I would have delayed my nap to catch up on your company," I said as we shook hands and embraced. "As salamu alykum."

"Wa alykum as salam, Imani! You know I didn't come alone. I brought some of my grandkids. And you remember, my son?" she asked.

"Which one?" I replied but when I looked out onto the porch, I saw him. He was standing next to Mas'ud chatting as he held baby Saba in his arms comfortably. Saba was a friendly baby, but the way she rested her head on his shoulder and wrapped her little fingers around the crevice of his neck said that she knew him well. He turned and looked right at me with that same stupid smile and laughed at whatever Mas'ud was telling him. I stepped back away from the door and pulled on the ends of my hijab making sure I was fully covered. Ameera stomped heavy footed into the room wearing her black abaya, her face covered in her veil, carrying a tray of glasses. She shot me a silly look and said,

"Don't play dumb, girl. You ain't been gone long enough to forget Jibril Ibrahim!"

Why was this man always around me?

"Yeah," Sister Adilah chimed in, "You know Jibril was a bit sweet on you, Iman, when ya'll was younger," she finished.

I glanced at him outside the door once more but I couldn't find those memories. I walked away from the conversation as politely as I could. It didn't make any sense for sister Adilah to think I was ready to talk to her or anyone else about marriage. Muslims were so quick to rush into marriage, like it was the world's best solution for every ill. Maybe if I was 16 again, I'd blush, make sajdah, and scribble his name in my secret diary. But I wasn't 16. I was 30. I'd seen too much. I knew way much too. Marriage wasn't any fix.

"So, what brought you around to our block?" I asked her as I sat down and picked up one of her pretty granddaughters, sat her in my lap, and kissed her cheeks.

"Well now," she huffed and grimaced as she closed our front door, shuffled her feet into the living room, and plopped down next to me. I had a feeling it wasn't going to be good. "Your Ummi called me over 'cause she worried 'bout you and Ameera," she divulged. No sooner did the name slip out of her mouth than Ameera popped her head in from the kitchen with a confused look that said what she had already told me and everybody,

"Yeah, chile, I said Ameera too. You might as well come on in here and sit down," sister Adilah ordered.

Ameera whipped her whole head around and looked back in the kitchen at Ummi and this time I was the one cackling! I knew Ummi probably wouldn't offer Ameera any eye contact. She was in there cooking and humming and playing with some of the kids like she didn't know what was going on.

"I don't know what this is about, Aunty. Did I do something to you that I don't know about?" Ameera asked as she took a seat in the old La-Z-Boy by the door.

"You ain't did nothing to me, Ameera. It's worse. You doing something to your own self," she informed her.

"Like what?" Ameera asked her boldly with a bit more attitude than I was comfortable with her dishing out to our elder.

"First off, lift your niqab when you speak to me, girl! I ain't no stranger," she instructed.

"I...I...I got stuff, the flour and stuff all over me. I need to-"

"You need to cut out all those stories, Ameera. How many times you think you got to roll up here looking like you done been hanging out with the *Taliban*? Your Ummi tired of your mess. Your brothers are tired of the crap. We all done had enough. It ain't fair! How do you think your mother feels with you walking around her house banged up?"

"I...what ya'll want from me? You acting like I can't come to my mother's house now? Is that what you're saying? Where am I supposed to go, if I can't come home when I need to?" Ameera said softly through tears.

"Ameera, you know good and well that ain't what I'm saying. This house, this community you were raised in, we about this deen and Allah. Forbidding the good and enjoining the good, that's part of praising Allah. That's part of the sunnah. Is it not?"

"Yeah!"

"Then you gonna have to make up your mind what you gonna do about what's going on in your life, Meera. Fix it or let it go - for the sake of Allah. But you are gonna decide one way or another, even if we got to make it for you. 'Cause at the rate things are going, something is gonna give. You know, I had a mind to send the boys back up to Philly. But your mother wouldn't let me. She's a better Muslim than me this time. But I'm warning you sis, that husband of yours ain't got no more chances. If he don't know how to handle you and you don't know how to handle him after all these years - we gonna have to handle the both ya'll. Jibril, Hamad, Ya'coob, and Mas'ud been ready to go see him again 'cause some folks got to get sense knocked into them."

"So now you telling me that Ummi wants me to leave my husband? That ain't cool, Aunty. I got children—"

"Your children been watching you two rock and roll. You knocking on him and he's knocking on you. Fighting fools, the both of you. So how are you being just with them? That's right, you got them

babies watching all that foolishness and what they really need is for
their mother and father to protect them. They need they family and
community to protect them too. They got rights over all of us. Let
me ask you this: you ever see your father fighting on your Umm?" sis
Adilah asked Ameera.

"No, but..."

"Well then, how you thinking your children deserve less than you?"

"They don't. I don't want any of that for them. But ---"

"You need help with that attitude of yours! And ain't nothing
wrong with admitting that, Meera. I been you, little sis! Been that sister
fussing and fighting with my children's father at night and rolling
through the streets like the Muslima of the year during the day. Playing
like I had it together, praying Allah didn't snatch the cover off my life
and reveal the truth to everyone around. You got to make a step for
you, to Allah. He's there, ain't He, Iman?" she turned around and asked
me. I couldn't even speak. The tears were caught so far down in my
throat, I was afraid to let in any new air. I nodded at her.

"You know, I think it's about time for ya'll to hear my story. I don't
share this with everyone, but once upon a time 'cause that's how all
crazy stories begin, I called myself falling in love with a young king.
He had the most handsome face and smoothest, deep baritone voice.
He sounded like a young Barry White. And I used love me some Barry
White when I was younger. But he dressed different and he had a funny
name. All he talked about was Allah. He told me Allah was the Lord of
all the worlds. I was raised Baptist, so all I knew was Jesus. Until then,
I thought I was saved from the world. Come to find out, I didn't know
much about my creator, the Most High. I couldn't get the stuff he was
telling me out of my head. He had such an amazing life, I thought,
because in the late '60's it was all about Black folk knowing who they
were and being proud and being intelligent and dignified.

"We were reclaiming our true selves, we thought. I didn't mean to
hurt my family or the guy I had been courting. George Gregory was a
real nice guy and all, but man, I couldn't shake off whatever Aqil had

put on me. I went on and married him and took my shahadah the same night. Aqil Ibrahim and Adilah Ibrahim became us. Some of the best years of my life were with Aqil. We studied and read Qur'an together every night. We helped start the Islamic Center and the foodbank! Aqil worked like a horse and never complained. He cooked and even cleaned up the house too. He pushed me to go to school to better myself. I'd go to school and take classes in the morning while he watched the kids. He wanted me teach in the community. I am telling ya'll, that man was so good to me. He was so good to me, I thought I wasn't good enough for him. But we had Allah and we had each other and that's all I thought I needed. Those were some golden days. It wasn't until after I had Fariba, my last baby, that the strong young king started dibbing and dabbing with them drugs. I don't even know how or why or when it started. He be out all night. He came in at fajr, call the adhan, and he be so high, he'd fall asleep before he could finish.

"We lost our first home that he had worked so hard to get for us. He never whopped up on me physically. But I became enraged. I was losing my world. We argued and tussled all the time towards the end. He be gone for days at a time. The kids loved him so much; they would cry and I would cry with them. When Aqil would show up, I'd knock him upside his head hoping to knock some sense into him. But it didn't work. By the time when he started stealing my baby's pampers' money, I knew I had lost the war. I knew there wasn't nothing I could do for him. Eventually, I had to go crawling back to my parents for help. I was angry and embarrassed. Allah had brought me right back to where I had run away from. But I wasn't the same. I'd learned a whole lot about life and its purpose and who Allah was. I'd been given something beautiful and special called Islam. Your Umm was there, too. She wouldn't let me have no pity party for myself. She told me to get up and take care of myself and my kids.

"I got up and prayed tahujjud one night that I was feeling so low and I asked Allah to make a way for me and my children. It came. It came, you hear me?"

"The religion is advice." We said: To whom? The Prophet (saaws) said: "To Allah and His book, and His Messenger, and to the leaders of the Muslims and their common folk." (Muslim)

After sister Adilah left that night, Ameera and me cleaned up the dishes and the kitchen. Then we prayed Salatul Isha, the final prayer of the night. We played with the kids and then put them all to bed. Funny thing was, Ummi didn't say a word to Ameera or me. The whole night I could feel her angst. I actually saw her, I think, for the first time since I'd been back as more than my mother. She'd been through so much her whole life and her face, with skin looser than it's ever been, much duller than it had ever been, hid bones much weaker than they ever been. Old age and heartbreak and weariness were painted on her body and I knew some of those colors came from my own brush of selfishness and despair. Ummi...

"Ummi?" I called out to her from the kitchen where I sat alone drinking a cup of lemon ginger tea. I had a feeling she was getting ready to go to bed.

"Yeah, Iman? You all right?" she asked peeping her head into the kitchen.

"Yeah, I'm all right. Are you?"

"Yeah. Why you asking me questions this late at night? I've got to go to bed."

"I just...I just want to know that you can talk to me too. I won't break, Insha'Allah."

"I know that, Iman. I carried you for nine months in my womb and then birthed you. Stop thinking all the daggone time. 'Salamu alykum."

"Wa alykum as salam."

Stop thinking? I wasn't sure how to do that yet. Most nights when I closed my eyes, I saw things that I couldn't or wouldn't repeat. His name still made me nervous. The sound of his voice still felt authoritative. It was like being caught in prison. I was in Mateo's mental prison. But, maybe it was time to break free once and for all.

Chapter 5

The next morning, I stayed up as usual with Hasan, Imran, and Munir after the Morning prayer. We made French toast, eggs, and beef sausages for the family. I made oatmeal and egg whites for myself. Then, at eight in the morning, I took the boys out to the park to run around. As I sat on a bench watching them toss their football back and forth, my cellphone rang.

"Hello?"

"Hi. May I speak to Miss Johnson?" a female voice requested.

"This is Miss Johnson. How may I help you?

"Miss Johnson, this is Sandy Parks from Hilltop Community Health Clinics' HR department. I've reviewed your application for the registered nurse position and I would like to schedule an interview with you. Are you available tomorrow around ten a.m.?"

"Sure, that would be good."

"Great. So, you have our address already?"

"Yes, I do."

"Perfect. I am located on the second floor in suite D. Let the receptionist know you are here to see me. Please bring your license, resume, and at least three business references. Okay?"

"Oh, um, sure. Thanks."

"Thank you. I look forward to seeing tomorrow, Miss Johnson."

I clicked the end button on my new smartphone and threw it in my Coach clutch bag feeling troubled. Business references? Who was I going to get to act as references for me in Pittsburgh? Everyone one I knew here were my relatives. It always had to be something or another with me. I no longer felt like being outside, smiling, or having a time.

"C'mon ya'll. Let's get on back home," I called out to the boys as I stood from the bench. The littlest one ran over to me first and jumped into my arms. I couldn't help but smile at him. "Did you have a good time playing, Munir?" I asked.

"Yeah, Aunty. It is so fun here. I wish my Ummi would let us stay here forever."

"You don't want to go back to Philly? I thought you guys told me that Philly had so many great places and things to do?"

"It does," Munir said, then dropped his head away from my sight. "But ...it's not good. Ummi and Abu are not nice there."

"Hmm, I am sorry about that, Muni! It's going to be okay baby. Insha'Allah, we are gonna make sure your Ummi and your Abu are nice wherever you guys are. Hasan, get over here, now!" I yelled back over to the field. Hasan and Imran ran over to me while tossing the football back and forth. They were panting, sweating, and musty by the time that they reached me and it made me laugh out loud like Ameera would have. "P-U! It is definitely time to get home. You little guys need a shower."

"You saying we funky, Aunt Imani?" Hasan questioned me.

"Yes, I am," I told him laughing. I felt better. My nephews were such a blessing even in the fog of my mind, they shined through. Love shined through. "How about we stop by the store and get you guys some cold juice before we walk back home?"

"Juice and Doritos, too?" Little Munir asked as we started walking out of the park.

"Now, I didn't say anything about Doritos. We have fruit at the house. That's better for your body than chips. Too much salt."

"Aunty," Imran started. "Are you one of those vita-tarians or something?"

"Vita-tarian? Do you mean vegetarian?" I asked him laughing.

"Yeah, that too. It's like them weirdos that only eat grass, ants, and water!"

"No. I am not a vegetarian, Imran. But vegetarians don't eat ants and it's not nice to call people names like weirdos. If someone likes something that you don't, doesn't make them weird. It just makes them different, okay?"

"I think they are weird. My Abu said that Muslims are supposed to eat meat 'cause that was what Prophet Muhammad sallallahu alyhi wa sallam did. So, if you don't eat meat and stuff that makes you weird, right?"

"No, it doesn't make you weird, Imran. People have different habits, needs, and views. Some people don't like to eat meat because we have lots of fresh veggies and fruits that can help make our bodies healthy and strong and some people choose not to eat it because it kills off too many animals unnecessarily when there are lots of other healthier choices to nourish our bodies with. And eating meat isn't mandatory for Muslims, Imran. And did you know that Prophet Muhammad (sallallahu alyhi wa sallam) actually didn't eat meat very often?"

"My Abu said he ate it a lot and that Muslim men are supposed kill animals on Eid. My Abu knows more about Islam than you," Imran said matter-of-factly. I didn't really know how to respond to him. His father probably did know more about Islam than me in a *black and white, there is only one way to understand everything*' type of way. Plus, I didn't want to disrespect his father, especially not in front of little Munir who already had some conflicting views of his dad. But before I could find a quick retort, Hasan jumped in the water to save me.

"Aye, Imran, you need to watch how you talking to Aunty. She's family, right?"

"Yeah, but," Imran responded.

"Yeah, nothing! You ain't even listen to what she said. You trying to back talk her. She said not to call people weirdos. If you know like I know, you betta quit it before Jedda or Uncle Mas'ud pop your fresh butt when we get back. Just chill out, cuz! We ain't getting no Doritos. Dag!" Hasan said, reprimanding him and handling the situation better than I ever could have.

When we got to the convenience store on the corner of our street, the boys rushed inside. I reminded them again only to pick out 100% juice. I stood at the counter waiting on them and watching the door. For some reason, I still always felt like I had to watch my back. Yasmeen's words still rang loudly in mind, I really had no idea what Mateo was feeling or doing. He could retaliate against me at any time. Then what was I going to do?

"Imania Colon? Is that you?" a low, deep, male voice called out. Before I could look up, that same annoying cackle that made his pop belly heave up and down like he needed to vomit, let me know exactly who he was. He came out of the aisle wearing a black and white LRG raglan tee, black cargo jeans, black leather Air Jordan flip flops, and a white kufi, holding the hand of Munir in his right hand and a large grab bag of ranch Doritos in his left hand. The two other boys were right behind them.

"As salamu alaykum, sis. You didn't hear me calling you back there?"

"Wa alykum as salaam," I replied to Jibril and then turned away from him and addressed my nephews. "Now, ya'll already heard me tell you not to get any chips. Hasan, go take back the chips, please."

"Oh, nah, I told them I would spot them the contraband. If that's cool with you, Iman?"

"No, it's not cool with me, brother Jibril. They will not be getting any chips today and that is really final," I told him. He turned around to face the boys and screwed up his face and made them laugh.

"No problem. Little brothers, I got ya'll next time, Insha'Allah. Take the chips back, Hasan." Jibril grabbed the juices from the boys and started walking up to the counter as Hasan ran back to return the chips. I saw Imran suck his teeth out of the corner of my eye, but I let it go. What was more pressing was that I really hated that Jibril assumed I needed help with them. I rushed up behind Jibril and grabbed Munir's hand from him and pulled him to the other side of the counter.

"Look, brother, I got the juices. I don't need you to pay for them. All right?

"Chill, sis. I'm good," he said as he handed the female cashier a ten-dollar bill, bagged the bottles, and then handed him his change. Jibril then picked up Munir and walked out of the store. Imran and Hasan followed him out of the store and they left me standing there looking stupid. I was so hot. I came out of the store and they were halfway down the street. I didn't run after them. I took my time walking, thinking about what words I could use ever so delicately to slice his whole face off his head.

He stood at the foot of my mother's porch alone, leaning on the step with one foot drinking a bottle of Sprite at eleven in the morning like that was normal.

"Where's the boys?" I asked him.

"Oh, they went inside the house. Hasan said you told them they needed to go get washed up."

"Yeah, I did," I said, walking up the steps without the courage I had lost a half block up the street to tell him off.

"Aye uh, what's your deal?" he asked me right before I open the screen door.

"Excuse you?"

"Nah, that ain't what I'm talking about. Your attitude is the issue. You're mean and I wanna know what the deal with it is."

"Are you serious?" I said, turning around walking back over to the banister sitting down. "You came in the store and totally disregarded my instructions to the boys, then proceeded to act like you had more authority than me in front of them. And I have the attitude?"

"Iman, I'm not sure you know this - but I am not their enemy or yours. I'm a lifelong friend of the family. I've known them their whole lives, I am their brother in this deen and I love them. Heck, I am their uncle. I am invested in the well-being of the people in that house," he said pointing at the door. "You act like you forgot that we grew up here on this street together. And furthermore, I ain't even capable of disregarding you. Not in this lifetime."

Then there was silence. Silence so full and pregnant it felt like a burden. I sat there trying to process what he'd said to me for what felt like an eternity. Shame, confusion, old memories that finally came flushing back inside of me: the barbecues, sleep overs at the Islamic Center, Aunty Adilah's Friday dinners, the jokes, Shareef and Jibril hanging out in the back yard playing football, his sister Fariba jumping rope with me, all of us selling icees together, Ramadhan, the Eid outfits, the spit he put on my scraped knee when I fell off the monkey bars when I was eight. Allah, mercy, protection, and trust all swirled around in my mind like pieces of a puzzle I needed to put together. But something was still missing. I didn't have the faith in myself that I needed to put it all together. I was still broken.

"I don't know what to say," I told him.

"You ain't got to say nothing. Just hear what I am telling you. Anyway, my Ummi and some other sisters we grew up with are getting together tonight to start planning some of the activities for Ramadhan. You should go get in there and—"

"Probably not, Jibril. I don't really think that would be the best for me right now."

"Why not? I don't even see you at Jumu'ah. How you going to make new connections and build a base if you keep hiding from the people?"

"I am not hiding. I get out and do what I need to do. Plus, everyone in the community knows I am back already. So, what I need to show my face to every single Muslim for?"

"It ain't for them, Iman. You need to do it for you. Get over yourself, kid. You ain't the only one going through something or who has been through something or is still struggling with something. And I didn't have no place to runaway to! My screw-ups played out right on Front Street for everyone to see. We all got beat up, rolled over, played, schemed, and dropped kicked a couple of times. I chose to pick myself up and crawl back to Allah to save me. We all the same...."

"I guess. Hey, you know, I've been meaning to ask you about my brother. Have you been over to Chester to see Shareef?"

"Yeah, I've seen him and I see you changing the topic too."

"No, really, I am serious. How is my brother?" I asked him.

"Alhamduleelah, Shareef is good. He's in good health, doing his time, looking forward to the future, seeing his family and you, now that you're back. He's ready to get free to raise his son, Insha'Allah."

"Why is he there?"

"Complicated stuff from the past, mostly."

"I really want to go see him. Me and Ameera both, actually. I want to rent a car, but I don't have any credit or debit cards yet."

"I think you two should chill and wait for Shareef to get out. He probably got a good two to four months left. That's what I think. But let me run it past him and see if he's open to you two coming down there to see him."

"Why wouldn't he want Ameera and me to come see him? Especially me? I haven't seen him in almost forever."

"Think about why you haven't come out to Jumu'ah. What's holding you back?"

"Judgement, I think."

"Yeah, you got it right. I'll talk to him."

"Jibril, brother Jibril?

"Yeah, Sister Iman?" he said laughing as he shook his head.

"I need help with references. I have a job interview tomorrow morning at the Hilltop Health Clinic, but I don't have any business references available to use around here or... from before."

"Okay. That should be an easy fix. I can come back by after Maghrib and give them to Mas'ud. Anything else you need me to do for you, Imania Colon?" Jibril asked and then started cackling again. "I kid you, I really do! Lighten up!"

"You're not funny." I told him as I hopped off the porch banister and grabbed my bag off the floor.

No sooner than I did, a black, shiny Lincoln town car pulled up in front of my house and stopped. I could see a white man sitting in the front seat looking through a bag. I froze with fear.

"Ya'll expecting someone or something today?" Jibril asked.

"Oh, Allah, no!"

"Go 'head in the house," he commanded me. I turned quickly and yanked open the screen door, ran in the house, and slammed the front door behind me. Tears began to stream down my face and the pounding of my heart was back. Once again it was so hard and loud it felt like my heart was going to burst through my chest. Yasmeen and Ameera rushed over to me and the boys ran down the stairs probably because the door slamming had scared them too.

"What's wrong, Iman? Is everything okay?" Yasmeen, my sister-in-law, asked me as Ameera wiped the tears off my face.

I couldn't get all the words to form right in my throat. I didn't know anything for sure, but I knew inside of me that the driver of the car was here for me. And if that driver in the car was here for me, it was because Mateo Colon sent him. I slid down the door and sat on the floor crying. I had been stupid to come back home and put my family, the people who loved me in danger.

"Outside!" I told them. Ameera ran to the living room and looked out the window and then came back.

"Jibril is talking to some white guy. He looks like he is law enforcement, Iman. Not some crazy thug." Hasan ran into the living room and started giving us a play by play of what he was seeing.

"Uncle Jibril is pointing at his car. He looks like he telling him to take his behind back where he came from. Now the man is throwing his hands up like he bought to go in on Uncle Jibril. Oh, shoot. The guy walking back to his car now. Uncle Jibril is following him. You think he going to get his gun?"

"No!" Ameera and Yasmeen shouted in unison. "Get 'ya tail out of that window, right now, Hasan!" Yasmeen yelled.

"Uncle Jibril is coming to the door," Hasan told us before he shut the curtain and came running back into the hallway. "Uncle Jibril is at the door!"

Ameera looked at me and then looked at Yasmeen, before she grabbed her face veil and slowly tied it onto her head and secured the pin in her hijab while Jibril knocked on the door. "It'll be okay, Iman. All right?" she told me before she pulled open the door.

"Salamu alykum," Ameera greeted Jibril.

"Wa alykum as salam. Ameera, where's Iman?"

"For what?" I heard my little sister ask him.

"That man over there is an officer with legal papers for her."

"How do you know he is an officer, Jibril?"

"Cause, I saw his badge, Ameera. What type of question is that? Tell Iman to come out. I'm standing right here. He's not going to leave until she comes out and gets whatever he has for her."

Ameera closed the door and flipped up her niqab. "Iman, I think the guy looks legit," she said kneeling down to the floor next to me and Yasmeen. "I'll go out there with you. Let's get this over for the kids' sake. C'mon," she said pulling me up with all of her strength.

Imran handed me a wet wipe from the baby's diaper bag and gave me a hug. I could tell he was shaken up from seeing me cry. I smiled at him and hugged him back. "You're going to come out with me, Ameera?"

"Yeah," she said flipping her niqab down again, "let's go."

She opened the door and I took a really deep breath as I grabbed her hand and we walked out the door together. The tall, slender white man was balding and had a gray moustache. He wore a dark navy stripped polo with dark black dress slacks and a pair of black dress shoes. He smiled and began walking up to the porch as soon as he saw Ameera and me. He climbed the steps and smiled again. Jibril waved his hands at the man as if to explain he was close enough and he nodded his head.

"Mrs. Iman Johnson-Colon?"

I stepped up a little and nodded my head in shame. I was still married to the monster. "That's me," I said, raising my hand.

"You've been served," he said and handed me a legal envelope. "My apologies if I frightened you, ma'am! The instructions are included in the envelope. Have a good day." The process server turned around, walked down the steps, and got in his car. He was gone before I had even opened the envelope. Jibril and Ameera stood next to me as I read the summons.

I couldn't believe my eyes. I gasped before the smile pulled my mouth wide and I let out a cackle so sharp, I startled myself.

"Who is it from, Iman?" Ameera asked.

"Mateo!" I said singing his name happily for the first time in years. "He filed for a divorce!

Ameera threw her arms around my neck and pulled me into an embrace. "Alhamduleelah, you're free at last! You are free!" she said before kissing me on the cheek. Jibril stood there watching us for a minute with a screwed-up face. It was clear that he now had a bad attitude.

"So, I guess we know he knows where you're living at now, right?" he said. I hadn't really given it much thought, but Jibril was right. I'd been served and that would be reported back to Mateo's lawyers. Of course, he knew I would go back to Ummi's house. I didn't have anywhere else to go.

"Yeah, I guess it does," I said shuddering at the thought of the Mateo that lived in my mind laughing at me. I looked at Ameera and she looked as worried as Jibril did.

"Ya'll should go 'head back in the house. Tell Mas'ud to give me a call when he gets off work."

Ameera grabbed my hand and I clutched the letter to my chest and we walked back up the steps together and went inside the house and sat down in the living room. Yasmeen and the kids all came sat around me and Ameera, but I couldn't say anything. There really wasn't anything to say. My happy dance would have to be put back on reserve. My freedom song had been sung too soon. My hope had been deflated. Mateo had made his move and I would have to get back on the run again before he put my family in danger too.

"Imani, you betta not let that creep spook you out," Ameera lamented, breaking up the silence. "He ain't nothing but a Joe running game. Trust me, girl, he ain't 'bout that life. And if he is, Umar know some akhs who carry them burners."

"Ameera, what? Are you crazy, girl? Hush up talking like that around these kids. I am not going to let my stupid mistakes ruin any of you. I will do what I must to keep you all safe."

"Not alone you won't, Iman!" said Ameera.

"You can't do it alone, Iman!" added Yasmeen.

"Listen," Ameera continued. "You got Allah, you got your family, and you got you! That's an us situation. So we gonna work together, put our trust in Allah, and do what we got to do to keep us all safe. So, don't you dare go running off again in the middle of the night 'cause this time, I'mma come get your frail tail and bring you right on back home."

"Meera, I am not running, okay? I am tired of running and fighting. If he's coming for me, he's gonna have to take me dead."

"What? What type of mess ya'll in here talking 'bout 'round my grandbabies," Ummi asked, coming in the door to the living room with Mas'ud behind her. "Hasan, Munir, and Imran go head take these bags into the kitchen for Jeddah and put those groceries away," she instructed the boys as she sat down on the couch next to Yasmeen who was holding baby Saba.

"Ya'll good?" Mas'ud asked still standing in the door looking concerned. Jibril had probably texted him on his cell and made him leave his job.

"We're okay. I had an unexpected visitor pop up. It threw me off a bit." I tried my best to honest with him.

"I bet. I think now might be a good time for me to take you to the police station and file a restraining order," Mas'ud suggested. "We can go now while I am on my break."

"Yeah, that's probably the best idea yet. Let me go freshen up and I'll meet you in the car," I told him as I got up and walked up the stairs to my room.

The air in the house had started to feel stale. My stomach was doing somersaults and my knees were buckling with each baby step I took. I knew the restraining order was a useless piece of paper to stop a monster. Nothing would stop him from seeking his revenge on me now that he had me on a bullseye. Not my family and definitely not a stupid piece of paper. I had stolen from him as far as he was concerned. He didn't want me back, that I was sure. He had other women. Mateo didn't want me to be happy. But he had filed for divorce and whether he knew it or not, he was releasing me.

Mas'ud took me to the police station down on Centre Ave but they sent us over to the Family and Juvenile Court facility on Ross Street to file the protection from abuse paper work. Everything was real standard. I had to write a statement, submit a copy of my out of state license, and then speak with a legal advocate to go over the order before I could go meet with a judge to file the order. Mas'ud and I were sitting together in the waiting area when a short, white middle-aged female clerk with short brown hair wearing black slacks and a white sheer blouse and black leather heels came over and got us for the review.

She seemed really agitated from the beginning. She spoke real fast and loud, as if we were hard of hearing or second language learners while she reviewed the steps with me. I shot Mas'ud a look of disdain to acknowledge her shady behavior. She must have caught wind of it because she rolled her eyes upward, huffed, and then had the audacity to tell me: "This *is* how the process works in our country. You Muslim ladies come down here all the time when there is trouble with these type of guys, but never wanna follow the rules. It's a waste of time if you don't follow the rules of the law in this country." I opened my mouth to go in at her, but Mas'ud held up his hand and proceeded to do it with much more class than I would have given her,

"Ma'am, what in the world are you talking about? My sister and I are not foreigners. We're Black Americans, born Muslims. This is as much our country as it yours! Now, it's not our business how many other Muslim women have come down here for help, but I know one thing: they all deserve respect and some professional help. If it's asking you too much to do your job, go on and go get someone else to service us!"

The clerk gasped and then shook her head before jumping up, grabbing our paperwork, and walking out of the cubicle.

"Way to go, bro! That's that Johnson temper when you need it," I said teasing my little brother.

"She's an idiot. Thinking she know so much. Your husband on paper ain't even a Muslim. She need to claim his butt!" he quipped and we both laughed.

All in all, it took about three hours for me to get everything right and to see the judge to plead my case for the temporary protection order. I would have to go back to see the same judge and bring my evidence for a longer order to be issued. But for now, I had the paper. I felt bad that I had taken up so much of Mas'ud's time. He insisted on staying with me until everything was finished, which meant he had to call out from his job. I tried to pay for his time and give him some gas money but he wouldn't have it.

"You done enough already for me. I never did get a chance to say thank you for that money you hit off Yaz with. Shukran, Iman!"

"Whatever I have is yours – the both of yours. I am really proud of you, Moody. I know we didn't get much of a chance to get to know each other before…before my departure. But I feel really blessed to have this chance to know you now," I told him and then leaned over in the car kissed his head.

"Man, have you always been this sappy? I don't how you made it out there in the real world!" he teased me as he started his van up and pulled out of the court's parking lot.

"What? I am not sappy, Mas'ud. I am hardcore, Pittsburgh Steelers black and gold hard, okay? Right now, I am just being reflective," I offered in my defense.

"Whatever. But seriously, we need to reflect on this situation with your… ah ex-husband. I was talking with Jibril and he told me he had a contact with this brother who's a pretty decent family lawyer. You need to get representation for your official divorce and we need to make sure the dude is not trying run game on you or pull a fast one on us. You're not going to get anything out of the divorce, are you?"

"No! I already took the possessions I needed. Nothing else he has I want, except for my freedom. I want my freedom!" I declared, hoping that by saying it out loud it would strengthen my resolve to truly get away from Mateo mentally and to finally stop being afraid of him.

"All right, well, I am gonna drop you off, go pray salatul Asr at the Islamic Center, and then link up with Jibril and Ya'coob."

"Can you remind brother Jibril that I need the references?"

"Will do. As salamu alykum wa rahmatullah,"

I hopped out of the car and ran up the steps to the porch and went inside. Ummi was asleep on the couch in the living room but I didn't see or hear the kids. I tiptoed up the stairs and went in my room, but I still didn't see anyone. I knew that only meant that Yasmeen, Ameera, and all the kids were up in the attic hanging out in Mas'ud's spot. I opened the wooden door that led up to the attic, climbed the stairs two at a time, and was immediately met with silly baby talk from Saba.

"As salamu alykum!" I greeted when I entered Yasmeen's sitting room. There were toys, books, and crayons all over the floor. Baby Saba was standing at the edge of the child gate leaning over with her hands extended waiting for me to pick her. Ameera, Yasmeen, and all the boys were praying in neat rolls together. Hasan was standing up front of everyone leading them in the afternoon prayer. He was reciting silently to himself but I could see that he had his eyes extended checking to make sure my face matched my voice. He called out, "Allahu Akbar" and they all bowed down into ruku, bending forward to touch their knees, and then Hasan called out again, "Allahu Akbar" and they all prostrated to the ground.

I grabbed Saba up, crossed over the gate, and sat down on the black leather futon and waited for the prayer to finish so I could talk with my sisters. When Hasan gave the last salam and finished the prayer, he turned around quickly and scrunched his nose up before he told me,

"Aunty, you scared me!"

"I am so sorry, sweets. I didn't mean to disrupt your concentration. I thought I was being quiet."

"Well, you were being quiet. That's what scared me," Hasan revealed.

"Boy, you ain't got nothing to be afraid of up in here," Ameera reminded him. "We are all here together and safe, you hear? You better not fear anyone but Allah, anyway! Remember that. What's happening up at the police station?" my sister questioned me. Ameera grabbed up Saba as Yasmeen picked up the prayer rugs off the floor, but left behind all the toys for the kids to continue to play with.

"Meera, it was a sheer waste of time. We had to go over to the family court house; I filed the papers, met with the judge, and got some temporary protection," I explained.

"Sounds like your mission was accomplished to me," Yasmeen said, smiling before walking into the cute teal and white kitchenette that was equipped with a small fridge, sink, hot plate, and microwave. None of that had been there when I was little. Shareef and Mas'ud had added it to the attic a couple of months before my Abu had passed away, Ummi said. She'd told me that Abu had actually planned to list the house on the market and was making plans to move to Morocco for their retirement. He had started and completed several upgrades on the house with Shareef and Mas'ud's help. It pained me to know he hadn't able to see the remodeling project to the end and then get on that plane to Morocco with Ummi. But I felt content knowing that my father had lived a good, upright life as a Muslim man with integrity. He gave his all to his Lord and to his family. I trusted that Allah had the best resting place for him where he would finally be at ease, peace, and in complete submission to the Most High.

"Well, yeah, we finished the first part of the process. I gotta go back next week, and show the judge evidence of abuse in order for him to extend the order," I said sucking my teeth.

"What type of mess is that? What evidence they want to see? A broken rib? A black-eye? A soft heart?" Yasmeen quipped.

"Heck if I know. I probably won't go back anyway. Some of the folks were straight up rude. Mas'ud had to check the first clerk who came in to help me."

"He did not!" Yasmeen gasped. "Allah, I hope he didn't curse her out, did he? He didn't!"

"Yaz, stop playing. I ain't never ever heard my brother raise his voice, let alone curse. I don't think he got it in him."

"He does, ya'll. Not often, Alhamduleelah. He tries so hard to manage his temper – ever since Shareef got…" Yasmeen turned her head and looked over at the kids playing to make sure Hasan wasn't listening to us talk and then whispered, "you know what I'm saying. Mas'ud's been really bothered. I think he sometimes feels like he is carrying us all alone with Abu rahimahullah gone and Shareef away. It gets to him 'cause he's the youngest and he always had someone there to help him before. Alhamduleelah for the Ibrahims and Aunty Adilah for always being there for us," Yasmeen brought out a jug of ice tea and a bottle of water, probably for me. She slowly lowered her body down onto the low futon. I held her hand as she positioned herself.

"Guess, I ain't making it easy for him either," Ameera reflected.

"You are not making it easy for any of us," I told her. "I just got back here and I know I ain't gonna get a wink of sleep if you leave and go back to Philly."

"He is always worried about you, Meera. You know that. I wish there was more I could do for everybody," Yasmeen expressed solemnly. "I didn't grow up with my Abu. My parents divorced when I was a baby and then my Umm got on that marriage train, off and on, a bunch of times before she met my current step-father. But it took her plenty of years to find someone to treat her right. We went through a lot with all those different brothers coming in and out of our lives. I pray Allah makes it easier for me and Mas'ud and our baby. I want my baby to have a stable home like ya'll grew up in. I need my husband to be calm, cool, and collected. I don't want him stressing out all the time."

"That's totally understandable, Yaz. I apologize if my presence has added any discomfort or hardships in your marriage. Mas'ud is totally in love with you and is committed to you and that baby. I am just learning to stand up on my own two feet and my balance isn't the best yet. But I have no plans on sitting back and letting Mas'ud struggle to keep this family together alone. I am his oldest sister for a reason…and I am here to stay," I admitted to my sister-in-law.

"Alhamduleelah, we need you! And actually, I think Mas'ud has been doing a lot better now that you are here, Iman. And you too,

Meera. You know he loves this family and I think he wants ya'll all back together again. Shareef is the last piece he needs to really calm himself and relax, Insha'Allah."

"Yeah, I really miss Shareef, too. Ever since I got here, I've been feeling like Allah is trying to show me that maybe I should move back home for good. Ummi's health ain't the best and if you get a job, Imani, and Yaz has the baby, Ummi gonna need help with Hasan and stuff," Ameera reasoned.

"Is Umar gonna go for you and the kids leaving? How is a long-distance relationship gonna work out? Philly isn't around the corner. That's almost a 6-hour drive," I asked her before I grabbed the bottle of water and poured it into the glass. Ameera was quiet for a minute as she rocked Saba in her arms.

"I ain't figured all the logistics out, Imani. I know that I am almost 28 years old with these three kids, three Black Muslim kids at that! And they are growing up in world that ain't setup to appreciate their faith or respect their race. I gotta do better. I mean, you may not know this, but Umar has always been a good provider. He loves his deen and he loves us. But we getting too old to be fussin' and fightin' And I ain't gonna lie, I've started too many fights for no reason at all," Ameera shared.

"You gotta take it back to Allah, Meera, and make the best decision for you to draw closer to your Lord so that your kids don't start absorbing all that negativity," Yasmeen told her. "Especially for the boys. I remember when my Ummi was in bad marriages, I hated it. Shoot, I felt like running away all the time. But her situations were so bad, I was afraid to leave her there by herself. I thought I had to stay to protect her. But now my little brother Abdullah is sitting in jail for attempted murder at 19 because all that anger he held in all those years watching my Ummi get kicked and jumped on. He let it all out at the wrong time with the wrong person. Alhamduleelah, he is alive and back deening, but he might die behind bars. My Ummi gotta live with that…"

"It's crazy how difficult this life is," I offered.

"It's a test. This whole life is made to test and try us so that we can seek Allah's aid and guidance and make it out of here back to Allah and gain entrance into the gardens of paradise, Insha'Allah," Ameera reminded. "We got to hold on to the rope..."

"And not be divided," Yasmeen said finishing the verse from the Qur'an.

After talking to my sisters, we all went our separate ways. Ameera took the kids downstairs to the first floor to start on dinner. Yasmeen stayed up in the attic to finish cleaning up and take a nap and I went to my room to offer prayer. After I finished praying, I went through the clothes in the closet. I picked out my outfit, ironed it, and finally fell asleep.

When Imran came to wake me up for the evening prayer, I got up and saw a white envelope sitting atop the cherry wood vanity in the corner of the room. I grabbed it and opened it. Inside were five sheets of neatly typed reference letters on good paper. On the back of the envelope was a number written in black ink and underneath the number was the name of Attorney Hussayn Ahmed Al Ajmi written in cursive.

He hadn't forgotten. In fact, he was one step ahead of me. Now I needed to find my old phonebook to see if I could find someone in Atlanta who could tell me what Mateo was up to and if he had really moved on. It was risky to reach out to someone in his inner circle of friends, but it had to be done. I wasn't going to let him ambush me or my family. It was time to be the one to start the fight, like Ameera had done, and finish it for good.

I took out the references, put them in a business folder and put it in my purse, and then put the envelope on the shelf in the closet for safekeeping. I went downstairs to go pray with my family.

Chapter 6

The next day, I got up early for the Morning prayer. I didn't lollygag like I normally did with my sisters and nephews. I went right back to bed and gave my body its rights. And it was a good thing I did, too. I woke up again about a half hour later with cramps on my big day. By the time my alarm went off at eight thirty, I could hear that the whole house was up. I showered, washed my hair, combed it then slicked it back into a small puff at the nape of my neck. After I dressed and fixed my face and put my hijab on, it was nine thirty and I needed to get ready to go.

Ummi, Ameera, Yasmeen, and all the kids gave me salams when I came down the stairs. Ummi tried to get me to eat some of the leftover grits and eggs, but I didn't want to put anything heavy in my stomach or smell like soul food walking into the clinic, either. I grabbed a cup of yoghurt and two bananas and sat down and ate them quickly. Yasmeen gave me her car keys and everybody started making dua for me to be successful as I walked out of the door. I was smiling, trying my hardest not to cry. As I sat in the car and adjusted the mirror, it dawned on me that it had been over a decade since I'd had someone pray for my success and really mean it. It had been over a decade that someone had trusted me to go out of the house and do what I said I was going to do and return on time. It had been over a decade that I believed in me and that I was able, with the help of Allah, to make a way for me to do better. I smiled at myself in the rear-view mirror, started the car, and said *Bismillah* before driving off to my interview.

The interview was short and sweet. All the fears I had swirling around in my head as I waited to be called in to meet Ms. Parks dissipated when we shook hands. Ms. Parks was a warm, well-spoken Black American woman in her early 40's with short natural hair. She was dressed very Afrocentric in a colorful, cotton Ankara pattern shirt, a flowy white broomstick skirt, and natural colored espadrilles. She did all the talking and then asked for my references, which she glanced at briefly before offering me the job. She explained that the clinic would even pay for me to take a course to prepare for the examination that would switch my license over to Pennsylvania's. The clinic needed RNs desperately. The best part was after the first six months, I would be eligible for a raise and full benefits.

"Yes!" I blurted out before she could finish going over the contract. "Yes, I accept. Where do I sign?" I told her. Ms. Parks laughed.

"Awesome! We are always glad to get local Hill district residents from the community to join us here at the clinic. We serve the community and believe that our community members are the best people to help their neighbors heal, learn, and gain health. Welcome aboard, Ms. Johnson!"

It was an unreal experience, but it had happened. I signed the contract and received my first schedule to shadow with the nurse supervisor. I was given a name tag, a badge, and a parking pass, even though I didn't have a car yet. I headed home to share the good news with my family.

At home, I was greeted by a triple layer red velvet cake complete with cream cheese frosting that Ummi had made from scratch just for me. Win, lose, or draw she said I had already accomplished enough for her to celebrate. The sweet cake had been me and my Abu's favorite when I was younger. But it was a treat she only really baked up on special occasions. We could count on her every Ramadhan to make a couple through the month of fasting right along with sweet potato pies, and bean pies too. At our Islamic Center, soul food was also Muslim food. I remembered how Aunty Adilah would throw in the Caribbean flavors too. Besides her pecan pie, she also made the best peas and rice, ox tails, and jerk chicken.

Ameera wasn't as a good as Ummi or Aunty Adilah, but she had her days of perfection. Today was one of them. Her buttermilk fried chicken wings were spiced just right and were fried masterfully to a golden crisp. She even made skillet cornbread and her version of Abu's dirty rice that actually challenged his original recipe.

We all sat around eating and talking until it was time to pray the afternoon prayer. I'd had the perfect day and I knew how I needed to end it.

"Meera, you going to Jumu'ah tomorrow?"

"Yeah, of course. Why? You ready to come out?"

"Insha'Allah, I think I am. You going to the Islamic Center or heading over to Masjid Al Awwal?"

"Masjid Al Awwal, probably. Umar said he gonna come through, so if you riding with me you gonna have to play nice," my sister warned me.

"I ain't the one you need to be telling this to. And you know Aunty Adilah said Mas'ud and brother Jibril and the rest the Ibrahims gonna have to talk with him, right?" I reminded her.

"Okay and…? That's between him and our brothers. I am gonna sit in on it, though. I know the conversation that I have to have with my husband and I'm not afraid to have it. Imma say my peace and hear what he got to say and we will try to meet somewhere in the middle." Ameera suddenly sounded more mature than she had when she first arrived.

"You really are trying to hang on to your marriage at all costs?" I asked her.

"You not gonna understand, Imani – so why try? I know you been through your mess, but I am telling you, no, I am swearing by Allah, that Umar ain't all bad. He gotta a lot good qualities and he ain't the reason our marriage is a mess. I know we ain't no perfect fit. I can be honest and say that. But if he is willing to let me move back home and take the kids, what we need to get divorced for? Maybe being apart is better for us right now," she reasoned.

"Whatever you say, Meera. But remember I am on your side. Ride or die, Insha'Allah!"

"You so Joe, Imani!" Ameera said laughing. "Be ready to leave by twelve fifteen. I don't like to be late."

Once I got back into my room with my full belly, I had to resist the urge to fall asleep. I willed my eyes to stay open long enough to find that old phone book. I knew I had brought it with me when I ran away from Atlanta over two months ago. But did I burn it up with some of the other memorabilia? I couldn't have. I looked through all my things, but I had only come with one bag and a of couple smaller boxes that I'd carried in my hand.

I looked inside the closet and pulled out all the shoes I had lined up on a small shoe rack. And that was when I spotted a small, black book in the corner. I smiled and thanked Allah silently before reaching in and pulling it out. I sat on the floor with my legs crossed and flipped through the pages slowly as I dragged my pointer finger across the names of women and a few men that were approved friends or relatives of Mateo that he trusted enough to speak to me. But I knew exactly who I needed to call.

I needed to call someone who I had enough dirt on that whether they wanted to help me or not, they had to. I needed to call someone who shared my pain and that was only one person in that phonebook. I flipped the pages one at time until my finger finally spotted her name:

Evelyn Melendez-Colon: 567-224-0978

My estranged sister-in-law had been married to Mateo's older brother, Manuel. They'd had a tumultuous relationship as well. But Evelyn had been a streetwise girl with loads of goons in her own family living in Pittsburgh, around Atlanta, and behind bars. Unlike me, Evelyn came in the family knowing exactly what she was getting herself into. She even got into the Colon's hustles to make her own money and her own connections. When she finally had enough of the beatings, all the cheating, and hustling the Colon men were notorious for, she set Manny up.

She made it look like his drug bust by the Feds had been unexpected and completely due to his screw ups, but I was the only one who knew and had proof that it had been Evelyn all along. She had been working with the Feds, taping his conversations, and even planting drugs on him that she'd purchased in anticipation of his imminent arrest for a whole year.

When it all finally went down, Manny was sentenced to 15 years in prison and Evelyn didn't even have to testify against him. Mateo and his little brother, Diego, were heartbroken and inconsolable for months. Mateo always suspected foul play because the Colon brothers weren't in the dope game. They smoked every now and again, but Manuel never touched hard drugs. As for their business, he had even forbid the family from moving weight around. Mateo said it was because the drug game was saturated and too risky for Dominicans. But truth was, back in the early eighties, when his parents had moved stateside and ended up in the South Bronx, their dad couldn't find a job to save his life because he didn't speak good English.

Desperate to provide for his struggling family he had got caught up in the streets working with some two-bit hustlers who had got him hooked on crack. A couple of years into his full-blown addiction, he was shot in the head after robbing some kid dealers in Bed-Stuy before he could clean himself up and raise his boys.

Mateo's mom got out of dodge. They all ended up in Pittsburgh trying to start over. It would be years later, in the nineties, that I would run into Mateo while working at the library. He was an older high school drop-out, a hard-core hustler and gang member at 21. But I was so young and naïve back then from being sheltered in a Muslim home, I couldn't tell. He had a pretty smile, a dimple in his right cheek, and he was always dressed really nice and clean. I never even smelled cigarette smoke on him, let alone drugs or alcohol on his breath.

Mateo would come to the library at the same time every day and I thought he was nerdy. He liked books like me. I never expected that the Hill library was a prime spot for illegal activity and he was either making deals or picking up money, but he was. When he was done *"working"* he would come into the library and talk to me about different books. I was so impressed by his knowledge of so many writings and authors.

Many of the books I hadn't even read yet. I liked talking to him. It was innocent, I told myself. I was flattered that he even noticed a Muslim girl with a hijab on. Then he brought me a rose one day and told me he liked that I was covered and that his Abuelita back in the D.R. was the most beautiful and pious woman he'd ever known and she dressed like me, too. I let him give me a ride home and the rest ….it all happened too fast.

I remember there was a robbery that his brother Diego and another cousin were involved in that went bad. Somebody got shot. Their whole family had to leave Pittsburgh. Mateo said he couldn't stand to live without me. He needed me to come with him and his family to the Dominican Republic. It was only supposed to be for a couple of weeks. By the time we got to Atlanta two years later, I had seen too much. I had done too much. Mateo was controlling my life. I didn't want anyone to see me like that.

I looked down at Evelyn's number and grabbed the small cellular phone out of my bag and started to dial the digits. As the number began to ring, I took a deep breath and silently made dua for His help. There was a click and then I heard a familiar female voice that was airy and sprinkled with a sassy Latina and southern accent asking who it was. I froze for a moment knowing good and well Evelyn wouldn't be welcoming to my intrusion into her newfound safe life. But I had every right to the security she had found.

"Aye, uh, hey, Evie. It's me. It's Imania," I finally managed to drag from my mouth.

"Imania? Imania?" she questioned defensively as she annunciated each syllable in my name. "What happened? Who's dead? You bet not be pregnant again. I swear to God, yo!"

"Well, hello to you too. Hope you've been well."

" Nia, don't play!"

"Evie, can you just listen? I left. I am out! Haven't seen Mateo or anybody in months! So please. Help me!"

"What? Oh my God! For real? Oh my God, you really left? You're not there anymore! Mija, wow, I am so freaking happy for you. I pray to God, you bet not ever go back. You hear me? Don't ever trust him. Get back to your people and move on with your life. It ain't never happen, okay?" Evelyn warned me.

"I am trying, Evie. I am really trying to do that. But Mateo sent word up here to me that he wants a divorce. I don't know but I think he is gaming me so he can pinpoint me. Have you heard any news from them lately? Or anybody? I really need help from someone on the inside to help me out here," I explained.

"Nah! I haven't done that in years. I ain't trying to stick none of mines back into their business. I wish I could help you. I can't risk mixing up with mad dog Mateo or demented Diego. You understand?"

"What about Corazon? Isn't Mateo still sending you money for her?"

"What about her? That's money my daughter is due from Manny! We don't conversate at all. I get the check in the mail and cash it. That's it. Listen, I don't know where you going with this? But get to it!"

"Okay, can you have Cora speak to Mateo? He's not gonna suspect her either way! I need this Evelyn, please!"

"Wait a minute! I know you ain't just ask me what I think you did? Nia, you think using my baby as some decoy in front of your mad dog husband is a good idea? How crazy is that? Cora is too young for that crap. Besides, she don't need none of their trouble in her life."

"I am not asking you to put *her* in danger. You know I would never do that. Cora has always been safer than the both of us. Corazon Colon is Manuel's daughter and you know Mateo and Diego love her to pieces. They care about her and would give their lives to protect her. But, sweetie, you're a different issue. If word got back to Mateo or Diego about your involvement with the Feds - you could be in some real danger right along with me. I know too much, but what you did is on a whole other level."

"What'chu saying doe?"

"I am saying we both need to be safe. We both need to have real freedom and that can't happen if we don't support each other. You know how this works better than most. This is a small favor. You managed to get divorced from Manny and I need help to get mines from Mateo. I can't go back to Mateo and I can't have Mateo messing with my family either," I said, pleading my case with her.

"*Tato*, but this is crazy, Imania," she responded with a long sigh. "Look, give me a few days, all right. I'll see what I can put together. I got some family up your way still. They might be able to help you. I'll send you word when I got something. Be safe, you got me, girl!" she said and ended the call.

I hated having to pull Evelyn back into the Colon craziness. Allah knew that I didn't wish her or her daughter any harm. I had prayed many nights for their safety because that's what I had wanted for myself. The day Evelyn left, I had been so happy for her. She'd come to me with Corazon in her arms and told me what I had already known. She said she risked her life for Corazon and she wanted me to swear I would never mention to anyone what I knew. I gave her my word. We hugged and she told me to find a way to leave Mateo and she would be there to help.

That night, Mateo came to me in our room as I laid crying into my pillows. He thought I was just sad about Evelyn moving out of the house and taking the baby away from the family. He was immune to my painful existence with him. He didn't understand that my tears were for me and my longing to go back to my real family. As he laid next to me holding me like a loving husband, he shared with me that Diego didn't trust Evelyn and he was concerned about her too. I listened quietly without giving him any indication that I knew Evelyn was involved. I tried my best to assuage his worries. I reminded him that Evelyn and Corazon were his family and that he was responsible for them in his brother's absence. He nodded his agreement with me, kissed my forehead, and then left out as he did every night.

If Evelyn wouldn't use Corazon to get Mateo to talk, that only left her one other option, and that was Manny. Although it had been about seven years since he was sent away, I knew he was still involved in many decisions that Mateo made from behind bars. If anyone could get Mateo to stay at bay and move on, Manny could. But really, Manny had been the biggest monster of them all. If Allah had not changed his heart, I could be forcing Evelyn and her family right back into the lion's den.

That night, I tossed and turned and couldn't get any sleep. Ameera and baby Saba were both snoring on the other side of the bed. It normally didn't bother me, but now it was like I had to get away from it. I got up and went to the bathroom to relieve myself and make ablution. I gathered my prayer clothing and tiptoed downstairs to the living room. With so many people in the house sleeping, I didn't want to accidentally wake anyone up, especially not the boys.

I glanced at the clock; it was two in the morning. I pulled my prayer garments over my body and tied the khimar on my head to cover my hair then grabbed a prayer rug off my father's bookshelf to pray on. I had almost forgotten about the night prayers my father would make during Ramadhan with us until I caught Ummi one night praying alone. She was standing in the exact spot that Abu always stood in and reciting his favorite surah from the Qur'an in Arabic. As she recited and I listened, something inside of me was awoken. I remembered Abu, it was like he was there or I was back there in the days of my childhood standing right next to Ummi and Ameera. We were standing behind Shareef and Mas'ud and Abu was leading the prayer. The words were pulled out the back of my mind down into my throat and pushed out onto my tongue. In that moment, I recited a chapter from the Qur'an that I hadn't in years.

The Arabic words tasted so sweet, I wanted to hold them in my mouth longer and swirl them around and hit every point of articulation at the right time to match Ummi's voice and to match my Abu's memory. The 30 verses ended too soon. Ummi had completed her night prayer. But she didn't turn around and glance at me. She didn't question me. Her body stayed prostrated on the floor. She was making supplications for Abu. She was supplicating for me, Shareef, Mas'ud, Ameera, Yasmeen, and all her grandchildren. She was taking it all to

Allah, as she always told us to do. Allah was our ultimate protector and I knew that if I was ever going to feel safe again, I had to train myself to rely on Him with sincerity.

I laid the prayer rug on the ground facing the east and raised both of my hands up to my ears and then said, "Allahu Akbar" to begin my night prayers. An hour later, I finished praying and finally felt sleepy, content, and understood. I laid down on the old sofa with a throw blanket and fell asleep.

Later that Friday morning after breakfast, the house turned into a fast-moving assembly line. Ummi was ironing clothing for all the children and some hijabs for the women. Yasmeen was cleaning the house, and I was with Ameera bathing the kids who needed help. Friday was a day of prayer in Islam and every Friday, whether there was rain, sleet, or snow, all of my family found a way to gather together to go pray in the house of Allah. Mas'ud had gone to work early that morning, but he always took his lunch break during the prayer so he could catch the sermon and pray in congregation.

The Jumu'ah prayer on Fridays was actually a minor holiday for Muslims. In America, it was also a day for Muslims to gather in one place, remember Allah, pray, and hang out with other Muslims you might not see during the week. Unlike in Muslim countries where I heard a lot Muslim women didn't even come out to the masajid to pray because they had lots of female Muslim relatives to pray with in their homes, in America, Muslim women filled the prayer rooms. Back in the day, if you were looking for a Muslim, all you had to do was go to a Masjid or Islamic Center on Friday to find them.

Today, many Islamic Centers and masajid in America had evolved to fit the needs of the Muslims that they served. Some of them had community centers that included youth rooms, conference rooms, and dining halls as well for community events. My parents had always been members at the Islamic Center. They were some of the founding members along sister Adila and her first husband, brother Aqil, and a couple of other families. Yet, when I was growing up, Abu always tried to pray at all the masajid that opened up in Pittsburgh. It was a big city and new Muslims were always coming into the community or Muslims from other cities would come in and out as well. Abu always thought it was important for the Muslims to know one another and to build with them. I remember him always reminding me that the believers were one body and that we shouldn't separate.

So even though Ameera had grown up attending the Islamic Center of Pittsburgh, I didn't really think much of it that she liked to pray over at Masjid Al Awwal on Wiley Ave. It was one of the earliest prayer places in all of America. It was a smaller community but the members were known to be warm, tight, and active in dawah outreach. I was actually glad that my first time back at Jumu'ah, I could go and focus on the sermon. I didn't want to get caught up thinking too much about myself or others.

After I finished helping with the kids, I gathered my clothing and went downstairs to the bathroom to wash up. The boys were all washed, dressed, and smelling good like the Nag Champa lotion Ameera had them swimming in. They were sitting in the living room in a trance as they played the X-box and waited for the adults. Ummi was upstairs showering and Ameera was upstairs dressing. I quickly washed up, knowing Yasmeen still needed to get into the bathroom and she would likely take the longest time moving her eight-month pregnant body around.

The house was so full, I had to get dressed in Hasan's room. It's was still early summer but it was sticky hot outside. Funny thing was, I never really heard my mother, sister, or Yasmeen complaining about the heat or the effects it had on them as Muslim women. Inside, we all took our clothing and head coverings off as soon as we stepped across the threshold. Throughout the day, we yelled at the kids to turn up the air conditioners or to open the windows in the basement to draw in more cool air. But when it was time to go outside and wrestle with the sun's beams, we all covered and battled our way through the day without any hesitation.

I remembered when I was in high school, kids would always come at me with the most annoying question to ask a Muslim woman: "Are you hot in that?" It was as if they assumed that the hijab diminished our humanity. Or if the questioner themselves assumed they were immune to the effects of the heat because they had taken off most of their clothes. And since neither were true, the question seemed stupid to Muslim women and a waste of time. Most Muslim women knew the question was intended to make them feel bad. I would pop my head and roll my eyes at them before shooting back my own petty response, "Aren't you still hot when you're butt naked?"

Today I was hot for sure, but I wasn't going to sweat it. The art of dressing as a Muslimah during the summer months was all in picking out the right materials. Lightweight pieces that breathed and were roomy and flowy were necessary to allow perspiration to be wicked away from your skin to maximize your dryness. Cotton and cotton blends like Georgette, Rayon, Koshibo, Peach Skins, Jersey Knits and of course my favorite go-to summer fabric, linen, were the best friends of Muslim girls who dressed modestly.

Another tip was to reduce clothing, especially if you were going to fully cover your body like my sister Ameera did. She always wore outer garments that started at her head and then went down to the ground coupled with a face veil. What people who saw her didn't know was that Ameera wore only a long silk slip dress under her georgette abaya during the summer. It helped her to stay cool because her clothing was all lightweight, breathable, and it provided her with maximum breeze, despite her fully covered appearance.

I chose a simple full-length purple spaghetti strapped rayon maxi dress to wear and a black one piece jilbab that was embellished with rhinestones on the bodice, scrunch sleeves, and zipper down the side of the neckline. The jilbab had been a gift from my Aunty Adila. She'd told me one night that she had purchased it on her pilgrimage trip to Makkah, Saudi Arabia last year that her son Jibril had taken her on. It was beautiful, traditional, and most importantly a light crepe material that flowed perfectly for the hot weather. The last item I needed to be ready was my hijab. All the pashminas were still hanging in the basement drying, so I borrowed a hijab from Ameera. She liked the oblong scarves that were mostly imported from the Gulf. In the Gulf countries, black was the "it" color to wear. I grabbed a jazzy, sparkly one off the nightstand and a couple of her pins. I wrapped the hijab delicately around my head, shoulders, and chest and pushed the straight pins into the light fabric. I was ready.

Downstairs, Ameera was hopping around like a rabbit as she put the finishing touches on baby Saba who was dressed up in a pretty pink and yellow sleeveless sun dress and a pink Al Ameera hijab with lace. Imran and Munir were out on the porch with Hasan, and my mother was sitting in her La-Z-Boy.

"You look beautiful today, Ummi," I told her as I leaned down and placed a kiss on her cheek.

"You don't say? I've had this jilbab for years. Your Abu bought it from brother Riyadh who had the halal meat store. You still remember him, Iman?" she asked.

"Oh, yeah! Brother Riyadh who used to drive around selling meat out of his old pick-up truck?"

"Yeah, he sure did. He did that for years before he got that shop. Alhamduleelah, that brother was a hard worker."

"Mashallah, he was. Didn't he used to be married to sister Khadijah Rahman who had all those sets of twins?"

"That was him. They had three sets of twins. Them kids all grown up now. Khadijah moved back to Virginia after her and brother Riyadh divorced. She still there now, living with one of her boys," my mother informed me.

"Well what happened to brother Riyadh? I haven't seen him round the halal market yet," I asked.

"Imani, that brother been dead. *Rahimahullah*. He must have been at least ten years older than your Abu. He was probably in his late 70s when he passed away. I think his oldest daughter, Saarah, from his first wife is running that store now with her husband."

"*Innal lilahi wal innal ilayhi rajioon* – From Allah we come and to Allah is our return. I had no idea. So much has changed in the community."

"That's life. People come and go," Ummi reasoned. "You better go 'head now before Ameera start fussing with you. Hasan and me riding with Yasmeen over to the Islamic Center. I'll see ya'll later, Insha'Allah."

"All right, Insha'Allah." I said. I gave my mother another kiss, grabbed my handbag off the floor and headed outside. To my surprise, Ameera was already outside at her car strapping her kids into their car seats. I opened the door on the passenger side to her dark gray late model four door Audi wagon and got in.

Ameera threw her black Coach bag into the car and then plopped down into her seat, tugged on her seatbelt, dragged it into position, and snapped it shut before slamming her door.

"Imran, say the dua for travelling please. Munir you make sure you say it with him too, baby cakes," she instructed her little boys in the back of the car. And like the well-trained boys that they were, they began to recite the supplication in Arabic. Ameera started the car and immediately turned the air conditioner on full blast before she pulled out of my mother's driveway and sped down the street to the light.

Even with all the mess she had going on, I still admired Ameera. My little sister was a fighter for sure. She had a whole lot of get up and go embedded in her spirit that kept her focused on living her life as a Muslim woman and mother. She had definitely retained many of the lessons and advices Ummi and Abu had taught us growing up. Now she was passing them down to the next generation of Johnson Muslims. Her personality was confusing sometimes. Some days she had a lot of energy and was happy. Then other days she would bark at everyone, cry, yell, or sleep all day. I figured her marital issues were draining. Yet, I knew that today would be a good day for her. She had every intention of speaking up to her husband and getting her way, one way or another. Ameera was back in Pittsburgh for good. I had my sister back.

Ameera pulled into Masjid Al Awwal's parking lot and it was almost empty. We were one of the first families there. After we unpacked the kids and went inside, Ameera left baby Saba with me while she went to sign up for a meeting with the Imam. She said Umar had texted her and let her know he was in Pittsburgh on his way to the masjid. Unfortunately, I wasn't excited to meet my brother-in-law. I knew my nephews and niece deserved to see their father after so much time away from him. I was sure he missed his family as well.

People were weird like that. We had the ability to possess really nasty qualities and behave downright evil with someone, but at the same time be gentle and loving with a different and select group of people. Mateo was the same way. His mother and his brothers were the loves of his life. I never saw him lose his cool with them ever. In fact, he was extremely kind and patient with his mother and brothers. Diego, his younger brother, was reckless, wild, and immature. He always found some trouble to get into. Diego got on Mateo's nerves, but he held his cool with him mostly. It was different story with me.

While we were in the Dominican Republic living with his grandmother, Mateo changed a lot or maybe he was always who he was. I know it sounds cliché, but it felt like he became a different man overnight. Then he began to hang out with his cousins and drink a lot. Mateo wasn't one of those jolly, happy drunks. He was an evil drunk. He would curse at me using some of the filthiest words he could come up with. He would push me or slap me, but I always thought it was the alcohol, not Mateo. I was hoping things would get better.

The first time he all-out beat me was about a couple of months after we had moved to Atlanta. He'd been sober. We were out at the mall and had stopped at a fast food spot to get a bite to eat. A young Mexican busboy came over to clean our table and complimented my smile. He jokingly told Mateo in Spanish that he was lucky to have me. I smiled playfully at Mateo, but he wasn't smiling back at me. He then refused to let me eat my food and made another waiter pack it up for takeaway. The whole way home he didn't say a word to me. I didn't know what had set him off. I tried to be tender and talk about a book he had been reading to get him to calm down. He wouldn't budge. When we pulled up to the house he dragged me out of the car into the condo, up the stairs, and into our bedroom. Through my tears, I could hear his mother, Paola, at the door sobbing and pleading for him to tell her what was going on. Mateo ignored her respectfully and locked her out of our room right before he backhanded me with his open hand knocking me to the floor. Then he began kicking me all over my body with his brand-new Air Force Ones. He whupped me for about five minutes. Later that night, he put the sneakers in the trash. He'd scuffed the tops of them while he was beating me up. He no longer wanted them. He never said a word to me about what I did that angered him. I figured it out on my own. I never smiled out in public with him again.

Saba was wobbling around with some of the other toddlers and babies as I watched her like a hawk. The sisters' side had now swelled up to about 30 Muslim women and more than 20 young children that either were playing or sitting quietly on the floor next to their mothers. Imran and Munir were on the brothers' side with the men, waiting on their Abu. As soon as I noticed Saba getting too far away from me, I got up to go bring her back. I spotted Ameera out in the hallway talking to another sister who was covered in all black with a flipped-up face veil. Ameera waved at me and then put up her pointer finger to let me know that she wanted me to wait for her.

I stood holding Saba in my arms as the muezzin started to call the adhan for Jumu'ah. I glanced back at where Ameera was but she had disappeared, so I decided to take Saba back to my spot on the floor before a sister came in with another group of children and took our seats.

After praising Allah and the prophet Muhammad, peace and blessings upon him, the young Imam started right in imploring his listeners to seek purification of ourselves.

"...so my dear brothers and sisters, the process of soul purification is something that is continuous. It is an on-going process, a fight to keep our hearts clean, healthy, and in submission to Allah subhannahu wa ta'ala. As long you as you are alive on this earth, there will be something *or someone trying to divert you from the remembrance of Allah. Shaytan is an open enemy to all of us and no one is free from his whisperings. Maybe a brother is having difficulty praying on time, so he becomes ashamed and stops coming out to the masjid all together. Or a sister is having some difficulty after a divorce and so she begins to feel depressed and stops coming around her sisters in Islam because she is consumed by her situation. These are the exact times that we have to flee, not walk, but flee to Allah. Whatever trial you may be struggling with: drinking, drugging, and illicit relationships – we advise you, as we advise ourselves brothers and sisters, to return to Allah. Purify yourself.*

Tazkiyyah – soul purification – is one of the most important tasks that Muslims engage in after the worship of Allah! Why? Because Allah tells us in Surat Ath Thariyyat, 'I did not create the Jinn and the humans but to ya'budoon – submit to ME. We know we can't fix anything in our lives, let alone in this world, without first submitting to Allah and seeking His aid. Go back to Allah, brothers and sisters; go back to Allah brothers and sisters. GO BACK to Allah, my dear brothers and sisters always for that purification. But finding your way back for that purification will be difficult without the proper knowledge. Acquiring useful knowledge is the first step to purifying your soul because ilm – knowledge - is the foundation of deeds and it is also a guide. Na'am? In sura Muhammad Allah Azza wal jal instructs us by telling the nabi, "(O Muhammad) Have knowledge that there is no god except Allah and seek forgiveness for your sin and for the believers, males and females." Knowledge goes hand and hand with purification. You want purification, study the book of Allah. Study the Sunnah - the ways of the Prophet Muhammad and His companions, may Allah be pleased with them all. Study and practice what you know and seek Allah's help. You – We can't do it alone."

Some sisters were nodding their heads in agreement with the Imam quietly, others were wiping tears from their eyes, and still some were just entering the prayer area and offering the customary two units of prayer for when you enter the masjid. I was rocking Saba in my arms and she was finally drifting off to sleep so it was easy for me to take the words in. I was reflecting on the fact that I was not alone in my troubles. Of course, there were other Muslims all over the world struggling to find or to hang on to Allah because some type of addiction had them hostage. The blessing of being able to return to Allah for purification was tremendous. I hadn't even realized that I was almost six months clean now. While the desire was always hanging around in the creases of my mind and heart, I knew today it had been none but Allah to wash it away and keep it at bay.

Ameera had come and sat behind me and was leaning up against the wall listening to the sermon as well. I noticed that she had her face veil pulled up, revealing her face. The bruise under her eye had healed well. She had helped smooth over it with a bit of foundation. Either way, she looked distressed. I tapped her foot and shot her a smile to see if she would accept it. She turned her body the other way.

Once the prayer was over, several sisters greeted me with salams, handshakes, and embraces. Umm Saalih, an elder sister in the Pittsburgh Muslim community and a friend of my mother embraced me so hard my bones rattled. She talked and talked to me for about ten minutes before handing me a plate of food to take home to Ummi. Ameera had disappeared again, though. That girl was starting to get on my nerves. She was so worked up over Umar and nothing else. I started gathering up Saba's things and packing her diaper bag.

"Aunty," Imran said tapping on my shoulder. He was wearing an off-white thoub and a beige knitted kufi. "My Ummi wants you to come downstairs to the Imam's office."

"Now?"

"Yeah, she said for you to come now. I'mma watch Saba. Me and Munir," he informed me.

"Oh no, Imran. I don't know about that. Where is your father? Can you take Saba to him?" I asked him.

"Abu's down there with Ummi. He told us to watch Saba, too."

"Lord, what is this?" I said with a loud sigh. I would have felt more comfortable if Hasan was there to help, but he was with Ummi and

Yasmeen at the Islamic Center. "Okay, but you make sure you really watch her. Just 'cause she is sleep doesn't mean you can go running away. Ya'll sit right here with her and don't get up until me or your mother comes back. You got it?"

"Got it," Imran agreed.

I grabbed my handbag and reluctantly walked away from them. I didn't even know where the Imam's office was. The whole situation didn't feel right. Ameera had been acting funny since we got here and I knew it didn't take a lot to get that girl started. I hoped she would hold her peace long enough for Mas'ud and brother Jibril to get over here. I wasn't a fighter in any way, shape, or form.

As I stumbled closer to the Imam's office, Ameera's voice guided me right to the door. I knocked hesitantly a couple of times. When no one opened it for me, I pushed the door open, walked in and offered the salams. Sure enough, Ameera was in there showing out. She was yelling at a man that I assumed was Umar. The Imam was behind his desk standing up and trying to get her to calm down. Umar wasn't very tall at all. In fact, compared to my brothers, he was short and on the stocky side. Saba favored her father for sure. They had the same bright buttery cream faces and big, round dark eyes. Umar also had a big bushy beard that almost fell to the top of his chest. He wore a light blue Indian-styled khamees top that came down to his knees over light blue jeans that were creased and rolled up to his shins that he paired with white and blue Keds. His face was scrunched up and I could tell he had an attitude. He didn't look too happy to see me standing next to Ameera, either.

"See, akh, this is what I'm talking about here. She always running her mouth, cutting up, and doing stuff she ain't got no business doing. She's not well sometimes and I've had patience, but the putting hands on me?" Umar explained dramatically as he talked with his hands. "Then I'm the bad guy when I flip and defend myself. *Wallah*, she didn't have my permission to leave Philly and take my kids nowhere. I don't care if she at her mother's house or not," Umar noted unapologetically. "You know 'cause Ameera ain't always well. Driving that far by herself ain't even right. Something happen to them, then what? Who they blaming then? I told Ameera she leave, I told her she was divorced."

"Really Umar? Now, I'm sick all the time? Really, you taking it there? Whatever," Ameera huffed. "You don't have no business trying to prevent me from visiting my mother! You stay trying to make up your own deen. News flash: Umar's deen ain't Allah's deen! Mas'ud spoke to you and told you he'd come get us. What was the problem? You the problem, Umar! You want to make things difficult for me all the time. Even when nothing happening, even when I'm trying, you gotta start something up! You knew it was important for me to come see my sister but did you try to make that happen? No, you didn't."

"C'mon now, you really trying to play me like I'm brand new? You know everything, all the time, Ameera, right? But you didn't have my permission to drive from Philly to Pittsburgh, did you? That's the issue, that's what I'm telling you right now. I ain't got no issues with Ummi or Mas'ud," Umar told her as he pointed at me for emphasis. "I got an issue with you not listening to me, you running your mouth, getting in my face, and putting your hands on me whenever you don't get your way. You hit me. And then you left before Mas'ud even came. See, if you would've waited for your brother, we could've worked something out. You left and took my kids. What's that? I could've reported them missing, you know? That's child endangerment, you feel me? Imam, what's that? She divorced. That's what it is?"

As the Imam put his hand up to silence the bickering between Ameera and Umar, there was another knock on the door. I was relieved when my little brother walked in with brother Jibril and his two younger brothers, Hamad and Ya'coob. Ameera's family had shown up. I put my arm around her shoulder and hugged her close to me. Her face veil was wet. She still wanted to hang on to the last few threads of this marriage.

"As salamu alykum," Mas'ud and the other brothers greeted everyone. They all looked frustrated and annoyed. Tension was thickening. I sensed it was time for Ameera and me to leave. Mas'ud, towering over most of us, immediately stepped forward to let it be known he was there to represent his sister.

"My sisters don't need to be here. 'Cause what we need to tell this brother, Imam, is strictly on some man to man level. Time for discussing who did what and why is over. I don't have time for it and I'm sure you don't want to hear it either. All this brother needs to do is come to a resolution that's fair and just according to the Qur'an and Sunnah. Iman and Ameera, ya'll go home," Mas'ud ordered.

I nodded my head and brother Jibril opened the door for us to exit. Ameera started up again trying to explain she had a right to stay. I had to forcibly pull her out of the room. She was really acting up and showing out. It wasn't no use. Umar had divorced her. Mas'ud had no intentions of helping her reverse it.

As we walked away from the door, all the males' voices got louder. Ameera tried to make a dash away from me again to go back for Umar. I bore all 120 pounds of my weight down and held onto her arm before using all my energy to push her out of the hallway.

"Ameera Johnson!" I yelled at her once we got away from everyone. "We are in the house of Allah, girl! You betta act like it," I cautioned her sounding exactly like my mother would have. "You so worried about that man, you done forgot who loaned him to you and why."

"Imani, I still love him. I really do," Ameera revealed through sobs as I held onto her. A couple of sisters walked into the walkway we were hiding in. I shot them a disapproving eye. They quickly excused themselves and went back out.

"I love you, Ameera. Ummi loves you, Abu loved you. Shareef, Mas'ud, and the kids love you too. You're okay, you're going to be okay, Insha'Allah. Let's go home now," I heard myself consoling my sister. I wasn't sure about anything. I said what I thought she needed to hear. I told her what I had needed to hear during my own despair and I had hope. If Allah could pull me out from underneath the monster that had controlled me, surely His Love and Might was strong enough to heal Ameera.

By the time we got home, my little sister was exhausted. She didn't speak to any of us. She took her kids upstairs for a nap with her. I stayed up talking with my mother to fill her and Yasmeen in on what had gone down after Jumu'ah. We all tried to act normal for the kids' sake but the peace didn't last long. Later that night after we had prayed the night prayer and were getting ready for bed, the full storm hit. Mas'ud and the Ibrahim brothers broke the news to Umar that Ameera and the kids were staying in Pittsburgh for good. Umar lost it with them and accused them of breaking up his family. Mas'ud reminded him that he had pronounced the divorce in front of the Imam. If he wanted to reverse it he needed to go back to the Imam and seek his approval. Even still, Mas'ud didn't want Ameera in Philly anymore because it was too far away from our family. Mas'ud told Umar that he and Ameera had both proven they didn't know how to handle their issues without resorting to violence. Ameera needed to heal.

Umar wouldn't buy it. In fact, he was offended and reiterated his innocence before he called Ameera the attacker and Mas'ud a pushover for always listening to Ameera's crazy stories. Umar told Mas'ud he had a right to cancel the divorce if it was made in anger and that he was going to take his family back to Philly tonight. Mas'ud told him it wasn't happening. We all knew it was going to get bad when we heard Mas'ud start cussing into the phone, "You can come! I wanna see you come do it, Umar! You even look my sister's way and wallahi, I'm going upside your head, *ahk*! That's right, you so tough!" And just like that, the Johnson temper Mas'ud tried so hard to suppress had been let loose.

Sure enough, Umar ended up coming over to Ummi's house in the middle of the night, banging on the door and yelling at the top of his lungs for Ameera and his kids to come out. My mother had been the first to go out to the porch to talk to him and try to calm him down while Yasmeen held onto Mas'ud. I tried to keep Ameera up in our bedroom as best as I could. She was besting me this time. She was fighting me off with all her strength.

My heart broke when Imran started crying for his Abu as he watched me and his mother tussling. It seemed unreal that we were fighting and carrying on like that in my Abu's house. I felt like we had desecrated his very memory. The Johnson family, the Muslims on the block in Hill district, fighting each other. I had no words to explain why this was happening to my family. By the time brother Jibril pulled up in his car, Mas'ud had broken free from Yasmeen and had ran outside and was up on Umar. They were out on the sidewalk gripping each other's necks when Jibril fought his way between them and pulled my brother o ff Umar.

"Allah!" my mother wailed with tears streaming down her eyes as she fell down onto the porch. I prayed He heard her cries as we all stopped what we were doing immediately and ran towards Ummi. When the ambulance came and took her away, Ameera's problems were the least of our worries.

Chapter 7

The next couple of days, while Ummi was at UMPC Mercy Hospital, were terrifying and restless. Mas'ud, Yasmeen, Ameera, Aunty Adilah, and I all took turns staying with Ummi in the hospital. We also had to take turns taking care of the kids back at the house throughout the remainder of the weekend. Monday morning, Mas'ud and I both had to go to work. I was excited to finally start my new job, meet new people, and earn my own income. I didn't want my mother in the hospital sick. Every day after work, I drove Yasmeen's car back up to the hospital to go sit with her.

The news from the doctors was troubling. Ummi had suffered a minor heart attack and had chronic elevated blood sugars. While I had been aware of my mother's diabetes, none of us knew that Ummi was on high blood pressure medicine as well. She had been keeping it from all of us and that angered me. Her heart was working overtime trying to cleanse the sugar out of her body and regulate her blood pressure. With all the mess her children had going on, she was suffering mentally and physically. Ummi was doing too much at her age and health level. She needed to make some serious changes in her diet, get more exercise, and lower her stress levels. As a RN, I was sure I knew how to help her with the first two issues, but I had no idea what I or anyone else in the family could to do to remove the stress from our lives.

After the fiasco the night Ummi was hospitalized, Ameera finally had an opportunity to say her peace to her husband the next day. She humbly asked his permission to stay in Pittsburgh with her family. With Ummi in the hospital, Umar had no choice but to agree. Before he left, the Ibrahim brothers had gathered all of the brothers over at

Aunty Adilah's house. Aunty Adilah and brother Jibril mediated. Umar agreed to come to Pittsburgh every other weekend to attend Islamic counseling and anger management classes with Ameera. Umar also agreed that he would start looking for employment in Pittsburgh so he could be reunited with his family and build a better relationship with our families. None of us were sure if that was the best thing to do for Ameera and Umar or if it would even work. They were sure that they both wanted to keep working on their marriage. With our support and vigilance, I really prayed it would get better for them.

Two weeks later, we brought Ummi home to a house full of friends from the community and almost all her family. She was bit weak but all smiles when she saw some of her closest sister-friends and companions at our house welcoming her. Ameera, Yasmeen, and I had stayed up all night to make a healthy menu of lightly seasoned stuffed cabbage and peppers, chicken salad, baked sweet potato casserole, rice pilaf, and fruit salad. Yasmeen made several jugs of fresh fruit infused sparkling waters. Mas'ud, brother Jibril, and all the kids had worked together to fix up Ummi's room. They had painted her room an aqua color with white accents, installed track lighting, changed her curtains and bedspread, and removed an old bookshelf so she had space for the treadmill I bought her off Amazon.

At the end of the night, Umar arrived from Philly. He'd brought Ummi a bouquet of roses and a box of sugar free chocolates. She stood up and gave him a hug and thanked him for coming back to Pittsburgh to see about Ameera and his children. It was a beautiful night. I felt thankful that Allah had given us an opportunity to rebound. I had to be at work early in the morning so I went upstairs to prepare for bed. Right as I stepped in the door, I heard my cell phone ringing inside my handbag. I rushed to the closet to grab it before I missed the call, thinking it was my supervisor, Michel'le, from work.

"Hello?"

"Dimelo, Mami?" the male voice that came through the phone was deep, rich, and hauntingly familiar. On the sparingly good days when he was soft with me, he would greet me that way. It had been my sign he was in a good mood. Those were the rare times I could breathe, relax, and receive a little extra space to move around without his anger stirring up.

This time, it aroused fear in me. I couldn't respond. I heard him laugh and try to coax me to talk to him. I wanted to hang up. Everything in me wanted to retreat and escape the confrontation. I was so very afraid of him but the control had to end. I was pissed. He had probably gotten my number from Evie, no doubt. He knew I was back at home in Pittsburgh. I was not hiding. I was in plain sight, breathing without him. He needed to know that.

"A... *Aqui, Como tu ta?*" I heard my voice shakily come through the phone. *Be steady, Iman.*

"*Tato, mi amor, tato.* I heard you were looking for me and I thought it was funny since I've been looking for you too," he began. "You really, really surprised me, Nia. I would not have imagined in a hundred years that you would leave like that. Mama was so worried about you. I was worried," his speaking voice suddenly rolled into a yell. "*Di que!* I thought that somebody was crazy enough to hurt you. I thought you was dead. I was ready to start a war for you! Then bam! Diego finds out you right back laying up in your old hood." He laughed snidely. "I think the saying goes something like you can take the girl out of the hood, but you can't take the hood out of the girl. It's strange, you know. I worked really hard to give you a lot, Nia. I know now you never really appreciated any of it!"

"Mateo, don't do that. Don't, please," I heard myself begging him. "My family needs me."

"Really? Since when have you been concerned with *those* people? And for the record, did I ever stop you from going to see them? I don't seem to remember it going down like that, Imania. I remember you telling me that you couldn't deal with them. It was you who didn't want to see them. Now you their savior? What can you do for them? You don't even know them anymore," he said as the agitation in his voice began to rise again. I had to stand up for myself.

"I want the divorce, Mateo. I am not going to contest anything. I don't want anything. I am not going to say anything to anyone about nothing. This is where I belong and where I am staying for good. I've moved on. You have your family and I have mine. Let's end our marriage peacefully," I suggested.

"Peacefully, huh? You want peace now? Is that what this is all about? Is that why you put Evie up to talk to Manny and have him come at me? Seems to me you trying pit my brother against me?"

"No! I would never do that to you, Mateo!"

"You did it, Nia! You know, I was trying for us, Imania. I had hopes and dreams for us. I thought you had my back. I thought you were going to support me. I kept my word to you even when you betrayed me because I loved you. But check it out, for Manny, for Corazon, I'll let you have this one. I've moved on too since you wanna throw shots. I got a baby on the way that I need to focus on. I got to take care Mama 'cause they saying she got that dementia. Diego done caught another case that I'mma have to figure out how to make go away. Right when I need you to help me after I been helping you all these years, you walk out. Very classy, very mature, Nia." Mateo sighed. "I'll come get the papers from you next weekend. We'll talk, eat, drink, and end our marriage properly. If that's what you really want. I don't think it is, though,"

"Mateo, I do want the divorce! But I don't think we need to meet up. It's not necessary. I can't be alone with you. I am Muslim. And if Mama is not well, you shouldn't leave her. I've signed the papers. I can send them back to you next day FedEx," I pleaded.

"Imania, don't even try to come at me with that Muslim crap. You think I ain't read up about you Sunnis? I know you're my wife until those papers get filed and approved! And we are going to do this my way or it's not happening at all. You ought to be thanking me that I did not send Diego to come get you weeks ago and drag your behind back here. I left you be. All those years I was doing for you, breaking my neck to keep you looking good, taking you all around the world, and giving you everything I could get. I gave you my life. Now you gonna jump ship without looking me in my eyes? What Allah and your prophet say about a wife disrespecting and being ungrateful to her man? Huh? You had Mama crying her heart out over you, thinking something I did got you hurt, and you think there's no reason for us to meet?"

"You abused me!" I finally blurted out through sobs so deep it rocked my chest. "You hurt me, Mateo! All those years – all those years you beat me down in every way so I could be weak, so I could feel worthless. Love shouldn't hurt," I screamed.

"*Ta tu pasao?* I never broke your bones or sent you to the hospital, ever. You needed discipline. I never wanted to hurt you. I tried to help you be a better wife. A better woman. I tried. And you know, I was trying to get help, too! Look, I said you got the out. Be smart, Imania, before I change my mind. *Di que!* I am still your husband and I want to see my wife. I need to see my wife. Have the papers ready for me," Mateo warned me before ending the call.

The monster was coming for me.

I felt my body slide off the bed I had been sitting on and down to the floor. I threw the cell phone at the wall and held myself as I gave into a furious cry. Every ounce of goodness and joy that I had fought so hard to find back in Pittsburgh came pouring out of me, leaving behind a bitter and poisonous concoction of guilt, shame, and anger. I was stuck and overwhelmed in my sorrow from all the wrong choices I had made. Mateo had won yet again. He always had a way to beat me even when I was determined to be strong and win. And he said he had a baby on the way! A real baby! He'd made a real baby with another woman that quick. How was that fair? I didn't know whether to feel jealous or sorry for him. My stomach began turning and tightened and grinded my insides until I felt as if the food I had eaten would come back up.

The house I was sitting in suddenly became too small. My family and friends downstairs felt like strangers yet again. They didn't know how deep the issues that Imania Colon had ran from or how truly fragile she was. Ummi had yet to even let me tell her why I had left home all those years ago. She didn't want to know my story. She didn't care about my past. All everyone was focused on was whether I was moving on or not. "Alhamduleelah, you've moved on!" and "You're back, Mashallah! Keep moving on, sis." How in the world was I supposed to do that when my past still had a hold on me, physically and mentally? I couldn't breathe any more.

Panting for air, I got up off the floor and grabbed my cell phone, my handbag, and left the room. I went into the bathroom and washed my face before going down the stairs. As I walked past the living room, I saw my family from the corner of my eyes. They were happy. I wasn't. I opened the door and walked out quietly. At first I didn't know where I was going. I was walking under the bluish gray evening sky, feeling the warm summer breeze tiptoeing across my face, and crying from the depth of my soul. I felt like I was being pulled in a direction that I knew well, but was too weak to fight it. When I stopped walking, I was in front of Ace's Package store. I froze as a deep yearning rolled through me and settled in my dry mouth to taunt me. I peered into the display window and my eyes immediately spotted the Cayman Blue Vodka on one of the shelves and at that moment, I knew I was going to drink again. I'd lost.

"Aye, you know, I hear they have a two for one deal going on. You copping?" shot a soft, but annoying male voice interrupting me as I was about to take a step in the direction of the package store's door. I knew exactly who it was. Slowly turning around, I was greeted with a warm smile that showed no visible signs of judgment. It was the same one he'd shared with me at the Birch Inn months ago.

"You're following sisters now, brother? That's pretty lame, don't you think?" I questioned him. He laughed as he shifted his weight from one leg to another before he stepped closer to me. As usual, he was dressed clean in a pair of French blue Dockers, a white Polo, and tan Clark loafers with no socks. His hair and beard were freshly trimmed and lined up.

"Don't flatter yourself, kid. I have my orders. Escorting sisters in the community is something our fathers started 40 years ago. You know what this community is about. Chivalry is embedded in the deen for those who take heed."

"So, you are following me?"

"Escorting is the word."

"I am fine, really. You can tell whoever sent you, thanks. I'll go my own way from here on," I told him as I started walking away from the Package Store.

"Iman, would you come back here?!" Jibril yelled. I kept walking for a couple of steps but then I decided to stop. I turned around and walked back towards the package store and stood squarely in front of him. He pulled out his smartphone and started swiping the screen.

"Do you have a sponsor?" he asked me with a serious look that I had only seen once before.

"For what?"

"For help and support, Iman. You know someone you can talk to about stuff you need help with! So that you're not out here in these streets looking for help in the wrong things. There are people in our community who can help you. You just gotta reach out."

"Wow, you think I'm some junky now? Listen, you don't know nothing about me, *Fresh*, okay? I don't need your sponsors or help. I got this. I can take care of myself."

"But I bet you need that drink right about now, huh? Look, I done already told you I know what it is. You can pretend like you're towing the line, everything is okay; you're Muslimah number one, sister of the year, righteous and pious, praying and slaying *Shaytan* at every corner. Haven't you realized by now that it's not going to change whatever happened to you all those years you were out there? You look hurt. You act like you've been hurt. You act like you've made bad choices. I am sorry whatever happened to you happened. I am sorry that I couldn't have been there to help you and protect you. Allah put me here right now. I am offering you help right now. Take it. Don't let Shaytan win. Take the help," he barked at me.

Once again, the man had silenced the very core of my being and made me think about things that I had not thought about in years.

He reminded me so much of my father and Shareef. His very anger seemed firmly rooted in a sweetness, patience, and guidance I hadn't known from a man outside of my family before.

"You have a phone?"

"Yes," I coolly responded in a low, muzzled voice as I wiped tears from my eyes with the edges of my hijab. I reached in my hand bag and pulled out my small cell phone and clicked it on.

"The number is 412-349-1070 and the other number is 412-349-5050. The sister's name is Labibah Bey. She works over at Clover Recovery Center in East Liberty. She is going to be expecting your call, so try to contact her as soon as you can. Did you contact that lawyer I gave you the number for?" he asked. I shook my head no. Jibril huffed his breath before rolling his eyes at me. "Why not? What are you waiting for? We need to know what that man is up to sooner rather later," he reasoned.

"It's not going to do any good, Jibril! My husband is going to do what he wants with me either way because I messed up. I called someone I thought I could trust. Like a dummy, she gave him my number and now he said if I want the divorce, I have to give him the papers face to face. He's coming out here next weekend to get me," I told him as I fought back tears. "He's never gonna to let me be! It's never going to be over. I have ruined my entire life."

"What the... and you're only saying something now, Iman?" Jibril started pacing back and forth as he spoke. "You know you're hard headed, right? First of all, he's not your husband Islamically. Stop giving that man rights he don't have or deserve. Second, you're not meeting with him. Third, he *is* going to divorce you, Insha'Allah. We already been working to make sure it happens. And it's a good thing he's coming here, save us from taking a trip," he said matter-of-factly. "Call the sister when you get home. Let's go back, I gotta go make some calls and please, keep this to yourself. I'll talk to Mas'ud ."

"Who's we?" I asked after we had walked home in silence and had reached the steps to the porch.

"What?" he replied as he was getting into his late model Infiniti SUV.

"You said, 'we had already been working to make sure it happens'. Who else is helping you?"

"Shareef! Salamu alykum."

"Wa alykum as salam."

The next day after I prayed the Morning prayer with my family, Ameera, Ummi, and I drove over to the Allegheny Riverfront Park to go for a walk. It had been Ameera's idea. Ummi insisted she was strong enough to stroll for a few minutes. She promised us that if she needed to stop she would sit down on a bench. After Fajr was always the perfect time during the summer months to go outside. The air was crisp and at its coolest, there weren't a lot people out at that time, and it felt good to smell the fresh air, listen to the birds, and gaze at the water while you walked. After my break down last night, I was glad Ameera had invited Ummi and me out.

Ameera and I held Ummi's hand on opposite sides as we slowly strolled along the paved walkway together. Ummi wore a dark green overgarment made of a light Koshibo fabric with a black georgette hijab that she always pinned under her chin with a pair of black and white New Balance sneakers. Ameera had on her normal attire: a black overhead abaya and black niqab that she wore over a lyrca skirt and cotton tank top with a pair of red and black Nike running sneakers. I kept it simple in a gray jersey knit full length baby doll dress, a pale pink georgette hijab that I had borrowed from Yasmeen, and some white Keds. At first Ummi was quiet, but as soon as we took our first break on the bench, she opened up.

"I don't know how much longer Allah is going to allow me to stay on this earth, but I want you Iman and you Ameera to know that I love you both. Nothing that either of you have done has ever stopped me from loving you and wanting good for you. I have been praying for the both of you and your brothers before you all were even born. Some of those prayers, Allah is just now fulfilling before my eyes. And I bear witness each and every day that there is no power or might, except for Allah because without Him, it wouldn't have been possible. Your

Abu and I wanted to live in this life as Muslims and raise our children in a way that would make you good people. It wasn't easy, though. We weren't born and raised Muslim. We didn't know how difficult it would be for you all. We made a lot of mistakes," Ummi shared with u as her eyes began to drip tears.

"Ummi," Ameera said rubbing her hand. "You don't have to explain anything to us. You and Abu did your best with what you knew and with what you had. That's all that matters," Ameera consoled her.

"No, I don't think that's all that matters. I want you both to know that I am sorry. I really am. Whatever I did that hurt ya'll or made ya'll feel less than other kids, or decisions that we made for ya'll that wasn't well thought out or too harsh - I didn't do it on purpose. It wasn't easy. We tried, by Allah, your Abu and I tried our best."

"We know, Ummi," I reassured her. "But we need you to stick around a little longer. I need you here and healthy, Insha'Allah. We don't need to waste time thinking about how much time you got left. I want you and all of us to do the best with however long it is!"

Ameera and I helped Ummi up and we all continued walking for another ten minutes. On the way home, Ameera stopped at the Halal Meat Market and we bought some fresh chicken breast without the skin, stew beef, and lean ground turkey. While we were there, Ameera bought Ummi and me a fresh green juice smoothie made with spinach, a piece of ginger, kale, mango, and berries. Ummi kept acting like she was going to puke before she even tried it. When she saw picky eater Ameera gulping hers down, she gave it a try. It was a small step in the right direction towards better health for all of us.

Back at the house, Mas'ud and Yasmeen had the kids out in the backyard playing tag. Mas'ud was chasing the boys as he held Saba in his arms. She was giggling with delight. Yasmeen was pulling weeds out of the small box garden she'd started. It was a beautiful Sunday morning for sure. I was glad we were all home to enjoy it. After we gave salams to everyone, Ummi headed straight upstairs to take a much-needed nap. Ameera and I brought the groceries into the kitchen to put them away.

"You did really good out there, Meera! You think you can handle three days a week?" I asked her as I took the groceries out of the bags and handed them to her to put into the fridge.

"I think I can. I like walking. I wish I could run, though."

"Why can't you run? You used to run all up and down the block when you were little," I reminded her with a laugh as I remembered how quick she was.

"Oh yeah! Ummi used to send you and Shareef to come get me and bring me home. That used to be so fun."

"Yep, it was. You used to try to dodge us like a little footballer. Shareef would send me to one end of the street and he would chase you right on down to me so I could grab you and drag you home."

"Those were the days. I got too much of these babies' weight up on me now. Too much junk in the trunk to be out there trying to run with stuff jiggling, popping, and locking. I might hurt myself or somebody else," she told me and we both laughed.

"You got a point there. But Meera, it's not impossible to lose pregnancy weight gain. If you can commit to some changes in your diet and you stay consistent with the walking, you can be down ten pounds in a month' time."

"It's not that easy for me. I've also been on some meds that cause weight gain."

"What type of meds are you taking?"

"Aren't you noisy? Geez!"

"Just worried about you, Meera."

"I know. Anyway, so what's good with you? How's work?" she asked, changing the subject.

"Good, I like it a lot. I am learning and getting to know everyone on the team. It's actually really fun. Wonderful clients at the clinic and my supervisor, Ms. Michel'le, is cool peoples. I can see myself staying there for a while!"

"Michel'le? Wasn't that the name of that R&B singer back in the day?" Ameera asked me.

"Yeah, I guess it was. But she doesn't have a high-pitched voice."

"Okay, guess they ain't related."

"Nah, I don't think so."

"What you think about Jibril?" Ameera questioned me, quickly changing the subject once again as she started to wash the dishes. I shot her a look that told her to stop it. "I am serious, Iman. I think and I could be wrong, but I think you should give him chance."

"A chance for what, Ameera?"

"Marriage, silly. You're in your 30's, Iman. Grown Muslim women get married. It's the Sunnah and he's a good dude all around. That I will vouch for. He needs a wife."

"I'm sure he is and does, but I don't think I am ready for marriage right now."

"Really? Are you sure you're not telling yourself that because you're afraid?"

"Um, yes, I am afraid. I am also still legally married to Mateo. I also know that I need time to heal and grow on my own before I start dealing with someone else's baggage. What's wrong with that?"

"Nothing. I am not trying to force you to get married today, Iman. But I think you would benefit from love. Real love, you know, *I'm searching for a real love!*" she sang playfully. "Mary J style or not, you know, love can be healing. It can help you grow, too."

"What makes you think that man is even interested in me? And doesn't he have a wife or two and some kids all around Pittsburgh?"

"You funny. He's interested. We all can tell he is. He was interested back in the day and he still is now. And no, he doesn't have any wives. He's been divorced from his one wife for a long time now. He had married a revert from Mount Washington. They have a son. He's about Imran's age. She was a really nice sister."

"What happened to her? How come I haven't seen her out and about at the Islamic Center?"

"She's dead, may Allah have mercy on her. She died in a car accident a couple of years ago, out in South Side. Word around town was she had a drug problem. She might've been high or drunk or both during the accident. You have seen their son, though, you just didn't know it was him. Saud has been over here with Jibril several times. He's Hasan's buddy.

As I reflected on all the times that I had bumped into Jibril, I did recall a young boy around. The first time I'd seen the bright eyed little boy with chocolate skin was at the T-Mobile store when Hasan had wandered off from the car while I was at my interview. The next time was when Aunty Adilah had come by to address Ameera and me about our issues. The third time was at Ummi's dinner. It made me wonder why the brother had never formally introduced his son to me.

I finished cleaning and went up to my room to get ready to offer the afternoon prayer. My cellphone was lying on the dresser drawer. It reminded me of the conversation I'd had with Jibril the other night about finding a sponsor. I sat on the bed with my cellphone, clicked the phone on and searched for the contact he'd given me. Labibah Bey's name flashed on the screen and I hit the send button to call the sister. The line began to ring.

"As salamu alykum,"

"Wa alykum as salam. Is this this Miss Labibah Bey?" I asked.

"Yes, it is. May I ask who's calling?"

"Um, uh, this is Iman Johnson. Brother Jibril Ibrahim gave me your number."

"Oh, wonderful, Alhamduleelah, very good. I've been waiting for your call, Iman. How are you?"

"Good, Alhamduleelah…," I pulled the phone away from my ear and let out a harsh breath before I palmed my forehead. Now was not the time to lie and pretend everything was okay with me. I had to be real. I brought the phone back to my ear and inhaled before I spoke again, "um, well, uh, to be honest, Miss Labibah, some days are more difficult than others," I finally confessed.

"I am sure they are," Miss Labibah replied in a slow, silvery voice. "Recovery is an ongoing process. It never ends. But you have taken two courageous first steps toward long term sobriety: it sounds like you are sober right now which is the hardest step and then you decided to pick up your phone and give me a call. Allah has told us that when we take one step towards Him, He will take ten steps towards us. And when we walk towards Him, He will run towards us! Be sure, beloved, that you are on the right path. Some days are gonna suck and hurt you too, but believe me, after every single difficulty, there will be ease," Miss Labibah explained.

I don't know what it was about her, but I felt free to open up to her. She listened to me without interrupting or passing judgment. Whenever I doubted myself, she politely restated the sentence in a more positive way. We ended up talking for over a half an hour and I made an appointment to meet her the next day for my intake. Miss Labibah informed me that I would have to complete two weeks of one-on-on-one counseling with her and some of the other addiction counselors at Cloverleaf. Once I completed my intake and profile, I would move on to group sessions and sponsor assignment.

Brother Jibril had been right. I had been worrying about everyone else's issues and neglecting to take care of myself which was putting my sobriety in jeopardy. There were no short cuts to this problem that I had. I had taken what I thought was a short cut when I met Mateo and it had disastrous repercussions. I never foresaw how dangerous and selfish it was to cut my family out of my life. I didn't know enough about life, marriage, or even men to make a good decision about Mateo. When it came down to it, I had acted irresponsibly.

I had wanted a boyfriend because everyone else had one. I had wanted to go out to the movies with a guy, buy popcorn, a slushy, and then show him off to my friends. I wanted to be able to write love letters, get surprise chocolates on my birthday, and a jean jacket with our names airbrushed on it with hearts and rhinestones like other teenage girls got. I let a temporary feeling take me away from the very people who loved me, protected me, and who really wanted the best for me because I couldn't talk to my parents and tell them what I had been feeling.

I had been so concerned about what my Abu or other Muslims would think of me if I told them the truth that I lied myself right into the hands of a monster. The sad part was I wasn't a lone wolf. I saw other Muslim teens doing it and thought they knew something. I thought I could get away with it. We were fooled by wolves.

Muslim teens caught between two worlds were an epidemic in every Muslim community across America. I kept telling myself when I was working at the library all those years ago, that I wasn't doing anything wrong. I didn't go after Mateo. He pursued me. I never knew where that lie would lead me, but it took over a decade to dig my way out from it. I would never get that time back. I would never be able to un-live the experiences of my life. It all mattered.

I didn't know if Allah would ever bless me with a child in this life, but if He did ever choose to do so, I would teach my baby to talk to me openly. Pretending hurts and will eventually discolor your perception of honesty. At rock bottom, I didn't even know what honesty tasted like anymore. I was lying to Mateo, his family, and to myself. I needed therapy because I was weak. I needed therapy because I had developed behaviors that were unhealthy and routine. I needed therapy to learn how to be honest with myself. I needed therapy to learn how to speak up for myself and not feel guilty. I needed therapy to learn how to live a life that I wasn't ashamed of. I needed therapy because I wanted to love myself and others from the most honest part of my heart. Sister Labibah was my sign that Allah was running towards me. I needed to keep walking, one step at a time.

I put my phone away and grabbed my prayer rug off the vanity. I laid it out towards the east, adjusted my hijab, and raised my hands up towards my head before saying in a clear guttural tone, "Allahu Akbar."

The remainder of the week went by too quickly. I worked at the clinic from seven thirty in the morning until six in the evening every day. As a pediatric nurse, most days I was busy from the time I logged in with prepping and sanitizing rooms, taking vital signs, obtaining medical histories, and documenting them in the electronic medical records. With mid-summer upon us this week, my co-workers and I were buried with clients coming in for physical examinations and vaccinations.

Ms. Michel'le, my supervisor and nurse team leader, had dubbed me "nurse magic hands" after I spent the day drawing blood from over 40 toddlers and children without any one of them wailing, kicking me, or grabbing the needle out of my hand. Patience, clarity, and kindness were my superpowers. I took pride in the work I did and felt privileged to be able to have parents come in the clinic and trust me with their kids.

Wednesday morning, Ms. Michel'le left me a note that my training had been cut. She was informed that I wouldn't need to retake the National Council Licensure Examination for Registered Nurses because my tests scores were retrieved. That automatically made me eligible for licensure in Pennsylvania. During my lunch break she mentioned that the clinic had already paid the fees for my temporary permit to be switched and that I would also start my benefits and pay increase.

"Seriously, Ms. Michel'le, I don't know who to thank. I am glad everything has worked out so quickly and smoothly. I really wasn't sure how I was going to jungle those training classes, work, home, and everything else in between with a sane mind," I noted in between bites of my salad.

"Thank God! We are lucky to have you, Iman. You're a big help to our team. It's clear you have the skills, attentiveness, great bedside manners, and, most importantly, the heart to be here. You wouldn't believe how hard that is to come by in this field, but it is. Too many nurses rush out of school and come over here because they know we need the help, but they're not really here for the long haul or to help our community. They don't know how to reach out and relate to the people that we serve. They come to work to get a paycheck and some experience. This is home for me, so when a parent walks in the door with their sick or hurt child, it's personal."

"Yes, ma'am. It is very personal. How long have you been living in the Hill?"

"My whole life. Born and raised and will probably die here. I love this whole city. No, I don't live in the best neighborhood. But my husband and I own our house; we know everybody on the block, at our church, and this is where our family is. We are blessed to be here and to be able to give back to a community that raised us, nourished us, and helped us to become the people we are today. I can't walk away. Nope. I am needed here and that means the world to me," Ms. Michel'le explained with a wide smile that filled her cocoa brown skin and exposed one silver lined tooth. She picked up her cup of tea and sipped it slowly and then placed it back on the table before continuing. "It's cool that you speak Spanish," she added.

"Thanks. I didn't know I would have to use it so much. The neighborhood has changed so much."

"Yeah, it has. Not only in Pittsburgh, but all over America. Spanish is the unofficial language of this country. If I could go back to school, I would study it. Did you take it in college?"

"Nope," I mumbled, not really wanting to discuss it. But I knew Ms. Michel'le had heard me and would continue to press the issue.

"Well how did you learn to speak Spanish? I swear you sound like you one of them when you talk. All I can understand is Si and Hola," she told me through a light giggle. I got up from the table and picked up my tray and put the empty salad container and my water bottle on it and turned to walk away.

"I lived in the Caribbean for a couple of years…" I revealed allowing my mind the right to pull those horrible memories out and back into my conscious.

"Amazing! That must have been a great time. From Pittsburgh to the Caribbean with warm weather, sandy beaches, and coconuts, too! Shoot, what brought you back to this city?"

"My ex-husband," I began by stripping Mateo of any rights over me as brother Jibril had reminded me of the importance of doing. "He was a mean and abusive man. But he taught me the importance of valuing my family and community. Like you said, this neighborhood is home. I was raised and loved here!"

"Glory be to God, Ms. Iman," Ms. Michel'le said as she nodded her head and gave me that same wide smile with that silver lined front tooth again. "Yes, indeedy, we are lucky to have you back in the community and working here with us here at the clinic. You have a powerful testimony. If you ever want to share it with others, the clinic has a support group for women that would be grateful to receive your voice."

I smiled at Ms. Michel'le and thanked her for the offer before walking away with my tray. I wasn't ready to start leading others yet. Maybe one day Allah would bless me with the strength to go forward and help other women, but that time was not now. So far, I'd had only one meeting with sister Labibah. I shared my full story with her from start to finish while she sat and listened to me. Later she asked me questions to help me pull apart and decipher my own pain. It was painful and it broke me down to a place I had not ever allowed myself permission to go. Getting it all out was relieving. It was sorta like when you are sick to your stomach and feeling queasy all day and then right before the sun sets, you throw up. It's the best feeling in the world especially if you can go to sleep because you feel so much better. My first therapy session with sister Labibah felt like that. I learned that I had a lot of healing ahead and that I had to unpack it if I was ever going to feel better about me. Speaking about my past and being honest about the abuse that I endured was important to the process of healing and dealing with my truth.

Chapter 8

I finished working at around six thirty that evening and headed out to the parking lot to wait on my sister when I received a text message from her saying that Mas'ud had taken Yasmeen over to Magee birth center because she was having heavy contractions. I immediately dialed home as I sat down on a bench outside the clinic to wait on Ameera. After a couple rings, my mother's voice came through the phone.

"Wa alykum as salam, Ummi. It's Imani. Any word from Mas'ud and Yasmeen?" I asked her.

"No, not yet. They left maybe a couple of hours ago. Ameera on her way to get you now. Ya'll going to go head over up there to Magee?" Ummi asked.

"I would hope so. Yasmeen had asked me a few weeks ago about assisting her and Mas'ud during the delivery. You think you can watch all the kids and Saba without any of us there, Ummi?

"Ah, yes! I sure can. I am the oldest mother in the house and I know a thing or two about raising kids. Plus, Hasan will keep an eye on the boys. I'm really gonna be watching Sabby. Insha'Allah, we'll make salat, eat some dinner, I'll let the boys play a game or two, and then it'll be time for them all to wash up and get their butts in the beds while I read some Qur'an. Hopefully, by time ya'll get back they'll all be asleep."

"Sounds like a plan. Ameera is pulling up now. We'll call you once we get to there and figure out what's going on. Salamu alykum."

"Wa alykum as salam," Ummi responded.

I clicked end on my cellphone, tossed it into my handbag, and walked over to Ameera's car and opened the passenger door to get in

the car. My sister greeted me with salams as I tossed my bags into the
back onto one of her kid's car seats.

"You riding up to Magee, right?" I asked her. "I spoke to Ummi and
she said you can stay too, if you want."

"I might stay for a little. I don't do good with pain, blood, or sick
people so I'll probably cut out early,"

"Are you serious, Meera? You got three kids. How are you afraid of
childbirth?" I snapped at her.

"I like getting pregnant and carrying my babies. Having them is
a different story," she joked as she sped down the road. "Seriously, I
couldn't give birth without pain medication. That epidural is the
bizness."

"Yaz's birthing plan excludes all forms of medical intervention
unless it is medically called for. She wants to do it naturally."

"I know. I know. That's why I can't stay up in there. First time she
starts hollering, I'mma start crying. I be done called the anesthesiologist
for her myself. I don't see why women want to go through all that pain
anyway. That epidural is a blessing,"

"I don't know for sure, but from what I have read, many mothers
are concerned about drug interactions because it might cross their
bloodstream and go into their baby's. There's also some strong medical
research that suggests that epidural usage prolongs the second stage
of labor by a significant amount of time. It's a pretty difficult decision
to make. I don't think there is a right or wrong answer, just whatever
the mother-to-be and father are comfortable with. Mas'ud seems
supportive of Yaz's decision, which is good."

"Whatever," Ameera hissed with a giggle. She always surprised
me. I had assumed she was on the natural and crunchy mama band
wagon by many of her parenting decisions. I also knew being pro-pain
medication during labor didn't necessarily exclude her from being a
natural mama. However, she certainly wasn't a traditionalist in the
area. Ameera was always doing her own thing anyway. I couldn't figure
her out.

We arrived at the birthing center a little bit after six in the evening. Per the center's regulations, Ameera and I both had to register and receive badges before being admitted to the labor and delivery floor. I stopped at the gift shop and purchased some snacks and water bottles for my brother. I knew Yaz had brought her hospital bag with her and she had probably thought to put things in there for Mas'ud, but Mas'ud most likely hadn't brought his own stash.

Ameera had also brought an iPod that had Qur'an stored on it, a box of red raspberry tea, peppermint oil, a heating pad, and a pack of socks and slippers for the both of them. We heard Yaz moaning as soon we got to the door. Ameera shot me a look that let me know that she wasn't going to stay around for too long.

"As salamu alykum," Ameera and I greeted them in unison. I walked over to my sister-in-law and gave her a kiss on her forehead before sitting down in one of the chairs in the room. Yasmeen was standing over the hospital bed wearing her own full length short sleeve cotton bed gown and a short circular Al Amira hijab, rocking back and forth. Mas'ud was standing behind her rubbing her back.

"Wa alykum as salam," Mas'ud replied. "Just in time. Yasmeen's water broke and our midwife checked her. She's six centimeters already," he gushed with excitement.

Yasmeen moaned out loud in a deep, husky tone before she started rocking and shaking the rail of the bed.

"Oh Allah. Mas'ud, why don't you help her get in the bed and lay down? She might feel better to get off her feet?" Ameera suggested as she got up and handed Mas'ud the iPod.

"No, no, no. I am okay," Yasmeen assured us. "I have to stay up and moving to get thisssssss......aahhhhhh out," Yasmeen bellowed out in pain before she could finish what she was saying. Mas'ud turned on the iPod and selected surah Ar Rahman. The soft and melodic voice of Mishary Rashid Al-Afasy filled the room. The Kuwaiti Qur'an reciter was a favorite of Yasmeen and Mas'ud. They often played his recitations at night when they slept. "She's coming, bae. She's coming," Mas'ud promised her as he continued to rub her back. "Ya'll staying, right?" he asked shooting us a look of worry.

"Of course, Insha'Allah. We'll hang around for a while. But you got this Mas'ud. You're doing great supporting her. Ya'll can do this," I told him. I got up and went in the bathroom to make wudu. I had missed the evening prayer.

"That's right. Ya'll got it. So we ain't gonna stay too-too long," Ameera repeated as she sat in the chair with the television's remote in her hand and flipped through the channels.

"Can I pray?" I asked Ameera when I came out of the bathroom. "Where's your prayer rug, Mas'ud?"

"Go ahead. Nobody stopping you, girl." Ameera noted before clicking the television off as she rolled her eyes at me. Mas'ud paused the Qur'an as well.

As I was praying, the midwife, Abiola Ife, entered the room. She respectfully lowered her voice as she spoke to Yasmeen and gently helped her sit on the hospital bed as she checked her vitals again.Once I salaamed out of the evening prayer, I folded the prayer rug up and went over to see how Yasmeen was doing.

"Any changes?" I asked the midwife as she checked for the positioning of the baby's head with abdominal palpitations. Yasmeen bellowed out again and Mas'ud moved to the other side of the bed and sat behind her and began to massage her.

"Yasmeen is doing great! Fully effaced, about eight to nine centimeters dilated. This little girl is at zero station and is on the move," Abiola shared with us. "I got a feeling things are going to move really quickly now because our baby girl is about ready to make her entrance into the world. I am going to have the nurses start preparing the room. Is that okay with everyone?"

"We're ready," Mas'ud replied right as Yasmeen's contractions kicked up and she started wailing.

Mas'ud and I got Yasmeen up and into her bathrobe so that we could walk her in the halls while the midwife and the other nurses prepared the room for the delivery. Ameera stayed in the room. She said she wanted to call home to check on Ummi and the kids and call her husband. I smiled at her as she closed the door behind us. I knew the real reason why she didn't want to accompany us. It was fine any way; I was better suited to assist my sister-in-law and brother.

I held onto Yasmeen's bicep firmly on her right side and Mas'ud held onto her forearm. We walked her slowly stopping every four or five steps for her to yell, bellow, and wail through her contractions. Her legs started to become unsteady as the pain increased and she began to give into the pain. Right as we got back to the room Yasmeen started crying again.

"I... I... can't! I need to...ahhhh lay down. I can feel her moving!"

Abiola and Mas'ud helped Yasmeen back onto the bed. Abiola did a quick examination and announced to us that it is was time for Yasmeen to push. "This is going to go really quickly, Yaz! You can do this. You can trust your body, listen to it for when it's ready for you to push, okay, sweetheart. Keep breathing," Abiola instructed her. Mas'ud and I helped Yasmeen scoot her body down to the edge of the hospital bed and put on her feet into the stirrups. Ameera turned back on the iPod and once again Qari Mishary Rashid Al-Afasy was reciting Ar-Rahman to us while we helped Yasmeen push, scream, and fight her body to do what it needed to do. About an hour or so later, we all heard the first cries of Yasmeen and Mas'ud's daughter.

She was beautiful with wide dark eyes, long eyelashes, a full head of curly black hair, and pink puckered lips weighing in at a healthy seven pounds and five ounces. Ameera and I waited patiently for midwife Abiola to complete all the standard checkups, Mas'ud to get his kisses in, and Yasmeen to cuddle and nurse her before our turns came up to hold our new family member. Yasmeen sat up and handed her daughter to me. I fell in love. It had been such a long time since I had held a newborn baby in my arms. I rested my nose on her head and rocked my niece in my arms.

"All right, what name have you all decided on?" Ameera asked as she sat next to Mas'ud taking pictures of her with her cellphone. He was on the phone with Ummi reporting the details of his wife's delivery. He held up his pointer finger to let us know to hold on.

"I got a name for her. Now we're waiting on your brother to decide on his name for her," Yasmeen explained. "Are you ready yet, Mas'ud?" Mas'ud shook his head no while he continued to talk to our mother before he finally said, "At the aqeeqah."

"Nah, bro! That ain't gonna work," Ameera protested. "We are not going to be calling that girl baby. You can save the surprise for the community and strangers. I want this baby's name before Iman and I leave. You owe us that, partner!"

"I second that," Yasmeen added and we all laughed. "Give Ummi my salams, please."

Ameera and I hung out in the room laughing and chatting with the new parents for another hour. We even got to watch Mas'ud call the adhan in his daughter's ear softly as he rocked her to sleep. Ameera recorded it with her phone, of course. We headed home around nine at night with pictures, videos, memories, and the name of our brand-new niece. We'd been sworn to secrecy until Mas'ud had a chance to announce her name first at his daughter's Islamic welcoming and naming ceremony. I was pretty sure that Ummi and Aunty Adilah would get it out of him much more sooner. Once I got home, Ameera and I prayed the night prayer together and then headed off to bed. I fell into a deep sleep that was fulfilling, happy, and peaceful.

Thursday was a crazy blur. I had been so tired from the long night at Yaz's delivery; I had to drag myself out of bed. I was itching the whole time I showered, brushed my teeth, and dressed to call my job and call out. But I didn't. It was too early in my employment to not show up and jeopardize my work ethic or my money. The bills had been piling up since Ummi's hospitalization. We had the gas, water and light bills, renovations on the house that I had started spending money on, and Ameera's wagon needed new breaks. I had promised her I would contribute some money to fix them since she had agreed to help me with transportation to and from work. Plus, Mas'ud would be bringing the baby girl home in a couple days. We had all been chipping in to buy things for her arrival for months, but all those items were for up in Mas'ud and Yasmeen's living quarters. I still had to buy her some baby gear that would stay downstairs so we could all share in her care. Somehow, some way we would have to pull together to keep the family afloat.

As I went through the day taking care of different patients, I kept catching myself reminiscing. A year ago, I was in Atlanta trapped in Mateo's world. That world came with a four-bedroom condo, a two-car garage, a community pool, a community tennis court, and a walk-in closet complete with a couple of pairs of Christian Louboutins, trips to the Dominican Republic, Mexico, Jamaica and even London. I didn't have to do much but look after the house, watch Mama Paola, speak when he spoke to me, watch my eyes, watch my mouth, watch the company I kept, watch my heart, cook his food the way he liked, keep my body the way he wanted it, and protect my smile. Mateo said he was fond of my smile. I hated smiling for him, though. I hated waking up in that life with him. He was right; I had been so very ungrateful. I had been so very lonely and depressed. Nothing he did brought me any type of satisfaction. All of that was over now. My family was crazy and loving and they gave me real smiles. Even with everything that was going on with all of us, even with being tired from working, and worried some days, I loved it. I loved them.

I didn't take a lunch break that day. Instead I took a nap break in the cafeteria. I handled that shift like a soldier and clocked out at exactly six thirty. As I was waiting outside of the clinic with sweat dripping down my neck from under my hijab, I saw Ameera pull up in a car I wasn't familiar with. When she got closer, I saw her husband inside. Ameera was always playing games at the wrong times.

"Salamu alykum, hun," Ameera greeted me from the passenger's side of her husband's black late model Nissan Altima. I got in the backseat, closed the door, gave her a stern eye, and put my bags on the seat beside me before returning her salams. We rode to the house in silence. Now it wasn't that I hated my brother-in-law, it wasn't that. I didn't care for him or like him much. Right as we pulled into Ummi's driveway behind Ameera's wagon, Umar turned around and started talking to me.

"A'ight, so I know I didn't get much of a chance to talk to you and welcome you home during Ummi's dinner, Iman. And I know that the first time we met left a lot to be desired," he confessed. "You probably don't have a very good opinion of me. I can't blame you for that. In fact, it's my fault and I take, you know, full responsibility for that. I want to you to hear from me that I love my wife and I love my family. I wasn't born Muslim, wasn't even raised by my parents. I grew up in foster care in D.C. before I aged out and made my own way, found Islam and ....," Umar paused and looked across at Ameera who was sitting quietly listening to her husband speak to me. It was a first as far as I was concerned. "Dis ain't me shooting you no jive excuses. I don't need no sympathy from nobody. I just want you to understand where I am coming from. I ain't no perfect Muslim. I got some issues and Meera got some issues too. We are both aware of our issues. What matters is that we trying to get better every day, you understand?" Umar told me.

"Ameera knows and I am sure she has already filled you in as well of my past. I am not in any position to judge either one of you. I am living day by day searching for my Lord's mercy and protection. But the bottom line, Umar, is that Ameera is my little sister. Everyone in that house over there," I said pointing to Ummi's house, "is going to do whatever we have to do to keep her and those babies safe! It is personal and you're right, I don't want to hear your excuses. Keep your damn hands off my sister or it's going be what it is," I explained as I grabbed my bags to get out of the car.

"I hear you. I respect that. But you gotta hear me when I say, by Allah, I ain't never jumped up on Ameera. Your sister is the one throwing punches, pots, pans, and anything she can get her hands on when she get in her moods. I defend myself when I have to, but never intentionally try to hurt her."

"You defend yourself by punching your wife in the eye? Really, c'mon. Let's not..." I started as I sat up closer, feeling myself getting hot. Ameera had herself a real abuser. I couldn't believe that this brother was going to sit up in my face and try to blame the victim.

"Hold up! I didn't punch my wife. She caught an elbow or something after she jumped up on me in that jawn. Ameera jumped up on my back and pulled me down when I was trying to walk out the door. Ameera, you ain't tell her yet about your condition?"

"She don't have to tell me nothing. I know enough about domestic violence to know that Meera couldn't have hurt you. Do you understand that there is no justifiable reason for you to...?"

"Iman, I threw a plate at him," Ameera huffed out as she interrupted me and turned around to face me. "I did. I threw the plate at him and I pushed him out of the chair he was sitting in. We were arguing about me coming out here. He said we were gonna talk about it and then he got mad and said I couldn't come here for a visit blah, blah, blah. I got so angry. I threw my plate of food, it hit him. I got up and hit him upside his head and stuff, he grabbed me and tried to hold me down and it got crazy from there. It's embarrassing to admit, but I have fought this man so many times – but we are trying this counseling thing.

"When you left, Iman, I was so angry, man! I did a lot of things, a lot of bad things with bad people! I hurt a lot of people, too. I hurt me. So now I am trying to learn how to deal with all the anger and it's hard. I have started fights with Umar, I have hit him, cursed him out, thrown things, and I know that it's abusive and that with his past and struggles, I don't make it easy for either of us. We clash a lot. The meds the doctor gave me helps some."

"Meera, are you telling me that *you* are abusing your *husband*?" I questioned her with disbelief.

"If you wanna put it like that. I am abusive towards him," she admitted as a couple of tears dropped from the corner of her eyes. "Sometimes the anger is blinding. I don't even remember what I did. Highs are high, but the lows are scary." I watched as Umar softly wiped away her tears with his hand. I didn't know what to make of them. Was Ameera covering for her husband or had he really been covering for her? Did my little sister just admit to me that she was suffering from a mental condition?

"Like I said," Umar said, interrupting my thoughts, "Meera and I got our issues, but we are trying to work on them together and separately. I ain't never wanted to put Ameera out there and blame her for our troubles 'cause truth is, with her condition I know I don't handle her right always. I got a temper too. That's why you know, this separation thing might be best for us right now. I want the family to know, though, that I ain't giving up. I ain't 'bout to leave my family. Meera and my children are all I got besides Allah. We in this," he added as he nodded at Ameera and she smiled at him. He leaned over and kissed her forehead.

I got out their car after Ameera asked me to watch her kids until she returned. Even though I was tired, I knew my sister needed time with her husband. I didn't mind watching my niece and nephews at all. I hoped in between making up they would also carve out some time while he was here to actually talk to a real counselor. I didn't know what things Ameera had been through or the full extent of her condition. I did know that she needed to get real help and not try, like I had, to handle it on her own.

As soon as I got in the house, Hasan and Munir came running towards me.

"Aunty Iman, guess where we went today?" Hasan gushed as he hugged me. I knew Masud had picked them up with Ummi to go see Yaz and the new baby in the birthing center. I didn't let on, though. I took my shoes off and put them away before I walked into the living room and sat down.

"Oh, hmmm, I don't know? Where?" I finally responded to him playfully.

"Jaddah, me, Imran, Munir, Saba, and Aunty Meera went with Uncle Mas'ud to see Aunty Yasmeen and the new baby! She is so small."

"Yeah, she is. That's how Allah sends all newborn babies into this world. Small and in need of help. You guys are going have to help her out when Uncle Mas'ud and Aunty Yasmeen and the baby come home. You ready?"

"Aunt Iman, you know I am. I was born ready. Insha'Allah, she'll be another little one under my orders," he explained as he puffed his chest out and popped the collar on his Polo. We both started laughing.

Ummi appeared on the stairs holding big ole' Saba in her arms. She was taking her time balancing Saba on her right hip, gripping onto the railing with her right hand, and stepping down each step one at a time. Normally, I would have jumped up and grabbed Saba from her, but my body had turned off. I couldn't get back up. I was one breath away from sleep.

"Hasan, go on and get Saba," I ordered him as I laid back into the couch.

"I got her! Shoot, we almost done," Ummi protested as she stepped down off the last step. "Here, this came for you today," Ummi said as she came into the living room and handed me a letter. I willed my body into an upright position to inspect the letter and scope out its sender. Joy emerged from the corners of my mouth and spread across my whole face. The sight of my brother's name immediately energized me. I tore opened the letter with my fingers, unfolded the neatly tucked letter, a picture fell out and onto the ground. I grabbed it in my hands and placed it over my chest and dived into his words:

As salamu alykum wa rahmatullahi wa barakatuh,

Alhamduleelah! Allahu Akbar! Iman, it was mad good to hear from you, baby girl. I can't tell you how much happiness it brought me to see your name. I know Ummi, Ameera, Mas'ud, and the rest of the fam have loved you up and gotten their fill of their hugs and kisses, but you still have some coming from me. Believe that! Things are different at home in every way imaginable. I've heard you've been doing your thing, though. May Allah bless you and reward you for all of the good you have brought back with you. But take your time, baby girl. Make sure you are making time for you. Reflect, pray, and focus on healing. You don't have anything to prove to anyone. You have always belonged to us. We're family and whatever you need to get through, you'll have to learn that we are here to help you do it. We are all in your corner praying for your success!

Alhamduleelah, I've been good. Staying out the police way, working out in the yard, reading, working, and praying. I am looking forward to the day when I can sit with you, my boy, Ummi, and the rest of the family. Insha'Allah, my time is coming up soon. I've had a lot of time to think about my own mistakes, errors, and now I am focused on my goals for Hasan and me.

I don't want to make this too long. So, I'll leave you with the same reminder I remind myself with every single day: Whatever you need, ask Allah. He will respond. Don't lose patience. Tell Ameera, I said she needs to chill out and that I love her. Tell all the kids I love them. Hug and kiss my son for me. And promise me this: If you have any trouble, call Jibril. His number is 412-724-2967. I love you, Imani.

Asssalamu alykum,
Shareef Johnson

I glanced at the letter again and quickly reread it to myself before I turned the Kodak backed photo over. I studied it from corner to corner. My oldest brother stood in front of a colorful wall wearing a dingy khaki button down shirt tucked into khaki pants with black boots. Despite knowing his whereabouts, his presence shined through. Shareef stood straight up showcasing his full six foot plus broad but sturdy frame holding his large hands together in front of him. He looked intently into the camera. He neither smiled nor frowned. His golden brown freckled face was complemented by shiny black natural hair that hung down in hundreds of tiny locks. His face was adorned by a neat, short beard and moustache. His light brown eyes were clear and shone through simple black square framed glasses that made him look older than his 37 years, but it suited him well. I missed him. I really missed my big brother.

"What he say? He tell you when his release date is?" Ummi asked me as sat rocking Saba and turning the channels on the television with the remote control.

"No. He didn't say. He said he will be home soon, Insha'Allah."

"He's been saying that for almost two years now," Ummi mentioned in a low voice so that Hasan and the other kids in the front room playing didn't hear her.

"Well, what is the problem? How long was he was sentenced for?" I questioned my mother.

"That's done and over with now. There ain't no use rehashing all that all old news. And it's Shareef's problem, not yours, Iman. Insha'Allah, he'll get out and be reunited with this boy soon come," Ummi snapped at me.

"I think I have a right to know, Ummi. Shareef is all of our business. What ever happened with him, I wanna know."

"Hush up talking all loud in here, Iman. You wanna do something, pray for him. Ask Allah to set aright his affairs so he can come home, find a job and take care of Hasan without anybody messing with them."

I had bothered my mother. She was funny like that. Growing up, Ummi never talked about my siblings or me to the others. She considered it backbiting and that was a no-no. For sure, whatever happened to Shareef, I wouldn't be able to get it out her. I had already tried with Ameera, Mas'ud, and Yasmeen. None of them had given more than the other. I knew there was an assault charge, parole violation, and possibly a suspended license. But I had no idea where his troubles began. Who had Shareef assaulted and why? Why was his license suspended? And why was he even on probation in the first place? Nothing added up. It wasn't like Shareef had been dealing or doing drugs. He hadn't been in the streets at all from what others had told me. He had a job working as a barber and a security guard and his own apartment over in East Liberty. It was time for me to get answers. I had to go see Sister Adilah.

"Ummi, I am going to take Saba up for a nap with me. You can send the boys up too, if you get tired of them. I need to pray and get a little rest in before I go see Aunty Adilah later,"

"Yeah, okay. What time Meera say she coming back?"

"Later," I suggested not wanting my mother to worry about it.

I got up and folded the letter from Shareef, placed the picture of him back inside of the envelope, and stuffed them into my bag. Chunky Saba had fallen asleep in Ummi's arms and was drooling away. I picked her up, grabbed my bags, dragged us all the stairs, stumbled to my room, and crashed on the bed. After I laid Saba out and offered the evening prayer, I lied back down on the bed. I kept rolling from side to side and moving around my pillows. Memories of my family all together in yesteryears floated through my mind and heart. The tears rolled down my cheeks slowly as a wet spot began to spread out beneath my cheek. What if I had been the cause of Shareef's problems too and Ummi didn't want to burden me with it? Ameera had already admitted that her anger had developed when I left. Maybe I had hurt Shareef too. And Abu too. I had hurt him the most. It really was all my fault, I thought before crying myself into a deep sleep.

About two hours later I was awakened by a knock on my door. I thought it was Ameera, but when I reached over for Saba she wasn't there.

"Come in!" I yelled as I pulled myself up and wiped the sleep out of my eyes.

"You dressed?" I heard my little brother Mas'ud reply.

"Yeah, yeah, I am," I replied as I adjusted my shirt, combed my hands over the top of my shoulder length hair inside the pony tail holder before sitting up on the bed.

"Hey, salamu 'alaikum, sis! What's up?" Mas'ud greeted me as he came in the room wearing his work clothes. He sat down at the vanity in the front of the room.

"I'm good, Alhamduleelah. I had a long day and I was sleepy as usual. What's good with you, Yazz, and baby M.A.J?" I asked him playfully as I got up off the bed and stretched my body out. Mas'ud laughed at me when I recited his daughter's initials as him and Yasmeen had insisted that it be labelled on her hospital cot so that none of Yasmeen's friends from the community would be able to see her full name.

"You play too much, Imani. We good, though. Yasmeen and baby girl are due for check out tomorrow at noon so she sent me over here to get a different outfit for her than the one she brought. She keeps changing her mind about what she wants for baby girl to wear home. I don't know what the big deal is over a fifteen or twenty minute ride home," he admitted.

"I imagine it's a pretty big deal for a new mother. It's a first-time moment. Make sure you take a picture of them both before you guys get home. I want to see what face baby girl makes when the sun's rays hit her face for the first time," I told him and he laughed.

"She's going to be asleep. That's all she is doing. Eating, sleeping, and going to the bathroom."

"I don't care. Take a picture of my niece," I demanded.

"I will, Insha'Allah. Aye, Ummi said you was going over to Aunty Adilah's for that Ramadhan planning meeting. I can drop you off now if you want or were you going to drive Meera's wagon?" he asked.

"We'll since you asked and all, sure you can take me. I was going to take her car – but on second thought, I don't know if she'll need it. Are Ameera and Umar down there now?" I asked him.

"Nah, just Ummi. She said they came back through and scooped up all the kids and went out to eat," Mas'ud told me.

"Well why didn't they take Ummi with them too?" I wondered as I walked over to the closet, scanned through the hangers, and zoomed in on a pink and brown paisley baby doll jilbab made out Koshibo I had purchased online from sister a named Jenneh in New York.

"They didn't take Ummi because she ain't want to go out with Umar!" he explained. "You know she got a good poker face. She'll salam, shake hands, kiss cheeks, and still keep Umar at a distance until he shows her something to change her mind 'bout him."

"True! I can't say I blame her. I liked to bust a lung when Ameera pulled up with him to pick me up from work. I can't call it. I don't know what to think any more. What you think, Mas'ud? Ya'll made amends, right?"

"Not hardly, Iman. I am right back where I was when she got here: minding my biz until something jump off that requires my presence. Insha'Allah, they'll be cool with Ameera here and him out in Philly."

"Insha'Allah," I said as I pulled the jilbab over my head. I walked over to the vanity and pushed Mas'ud out of the way as I sat down and started wrapping and pinning a brown georgette hijab on my head.

"Alright, well, I'll be waiting for you out in the van," he told me before he left out the door, closing it behind him.

As I sat staring in the mirror with one eye and the other eye following my hands as I pushed pins in every direction to smooth out and perfect the fit of the fabric around my face, it dawned on me that I hadn't even prayed the night prayer yet. I stopped right before completion and yanked the hijab off my head and pins flew to the floor. Aggravated by my absentmindedness, I got up and threw my hijab on the bed and ran to the bathroom to make ablution. Knowing that Mas'ud was waiting on me in the car and that Yasmeen was waiting on him to get back to her and baby M. A. J in the hospital made me rush even more. I didn't like the way it made me feel, but I didn't stop, I splashed the water on my face once, pulled the sleeves of my jilbab all the way up and washed my arms and elbows, rubbed my wet hands over my head and then wiped my ears, before lifting my feet up into the sink to wash them up to my ankles. I dried off and then sprinted back to my room and grabbed one of Ameera's prayer garments off the coat rack she used to store her overhead abayas and long garments and pulled it over me and then laid it out in front of me in order to pray.

Chapter 9

I was still rushing when I recited surah Al Fatiha. Then I slid into surah An Nasr before I praised Allah, my Lord, and bowed down before I prostrated to the floor. It was at that moment that Shareef's face flashed before my eyes as I exalted Allah and I felt the tears again. I couldn't rush anymore, I felt a power greater than me slow me down and focus on what I was saying and who I was saying it to. I started to supplicate for my brother and my Abu and everyone I knew. Once I got to the last prostration, I exalted Allah and then mumbled supplications slowly for myself. I asked Allah to pardon each one of my sins, to protect me from myself, from the Shaytan, from Mateo, and any harm. I asked Allah to strengthen my faith and to bring all the good that would bring me closer to Him into my life and remove all bad energy, people, and thoughts that would take Him out of my life. After I salaamed out of the prayer, I sat for a few minutes on the prayer rug. I knew I needed to text sister Labibah, but I didn't have time.

Leaving my thoughts on the floor where I had prostrated, I got up and ran to the bathroom and splashed water on my face before running back, snatching my hijab off the bed and wrapping it loosely around my head. I pulled out a pair of brown leather ballet shoes from under my bed and slipped my feet into them, grabbed my bag, and quickly ran out the room.

I hollered salams out to my mother as I zoomed out the door and locked it behind me. I saw Mas'ud's van parked on the street with his lights on. He was sitting in the driver's seat reading. I walked up to the passenger door and tapped on the window.

"Salamu alaykum. Sorry for keeping you waiting so long. I had to make Ishaa," I explained.

"Not a problem," Mas'ud noted. "You won't be late with that group anyway."

Sister Adilah's house was around the corner on the next block. Cars were lined up and down her street. There weren't any spots left in front of her house. Mas'ud let me out in the street.

"I'll probably give Ameera a call when I'm done and see if she can pick me up, Insha'Allah," I told him.

"Give me a ring if you need too," he suggested.

I dodged between the cars passing by then walked up to the porch. The light on the porch made it easy for me to find the doorbell. I could hear female voices as I rang the doorbell. It was only a second or two before the door opened and I was greeted with salams, a handshake, and kisses on each cheek by someone very familiar.

"O-M-G, it's good to see you! My Umm didn't tell me you was going to come through," Fariba began. "I thought I was gonna miss out seeing you again!" She embraced me again.

"I was trying to get here. Didn't know I would run into you, but it is so good to see you, Reeba!"

Fariba, Sister Adilah's only daughter, had been a close friend of mine growing up in Pittsburgh. We were the same age, went to the same high school, and worked at the library together sometimes. Almost anything I did, Fariba did it with me. She was the only one who actually knew of and met Mateo when we first got to know one another. She knew about everything, except for the night that I actually left the city with Mateo and his family.

"You look real good, Reeba," I told her as I walked with her into the dining room that was full of sisters from the Islamic Center of Pittsburgh community. Fariba stood out in the room of mostly older women. She looked like a younger version of her mother. She was about five-five, with a curvy yet athletic build, and her skin was a rich umber brown that was offset by dark almond shaped eyes and thick black eyebrows. Fariba wore a colorful aqua blue and yellow intricately styled head wrap, a long sleeved hi-low flowy yellow top, several silver and copper necklaces of varying lengths, fringed suede earrings that looked homemade and a matching yellow maxi skirt.

As customary, I walked around the room offering salams to my elders and shaking their hands. When I got to Sister Adilah who was sitting on the floor on top of several large pillows, I kneeled down and gave her a hug and kiss.

"And where is your mother?" she asked me with a raised eye.

"Home. She was tired from watching the kids all day and her outing to the hospital to visit with Yasmeen and the baby. She sends her salams and love to everyone," I explained.

"That's right, that's right. Yeah, she told me this morning she had to go see Yaz and the baby. Should I go on out there tomorrow to visit them or what?" she asked me.

"No, Insha'Allah, they should be coming home tomorrow. Why don't you stop by tomorrow night? That'll give Yaz a minute to settle back in,"

"Okay, that sounds like a plan. Well, Imani, we done ate already. Fariba can bring you a plate. Sister Danah was going over the budget we had from last year. 'Cause we only a couple days away from the new moon, if that. Reeba, bring Imani a plate, please. Go 'head Danah with the rest of what you was saying," Sister Adilah ordered.

Sister Danah, an older short plumb sister in her 60's, dressed in a dark blue jilbab and a beige hijab, adjusted her reading glasses and started back into her presentation. I sat down on the floor next to Sister Adilah and listened.

There had been three thousand dollars raised since last Ramadhan from Friday dinner sales alone, another five hundred dollars raised through pledges during lectures, and three hundred dollars from the monthly sisters' events.

"We got enough for the Eid activities for the youth and the main Eid dinner. But, we gonna stretch ourselves thin during Ramadhan 'cause you know the Center is going to need to borrow some money for the iftars," Sister Danah warned us.

"That's about how it always goes," Sister Tahirah chimed in. "I think this year we need to suggest families join together and sponsor nights for iftar. They collect the money and we can buy the food and supplies at the halal meat market and cook the meals ourselves."

"Wait a minute," Fariba said objecting. "Who is the 'we' that is going to be cooking the meals for iftar every night for 30 days? I hope you don't mean us in this room?"

Sister Tahirah, a thin, middle-aged woman with Tortilla brown skin and long legs was dressed in all black. She rolled her eyes upward and turned her body around to face Fariba. "If you don't want to cook, Fariba, you don't got to cook. For those who can and want to secure some of the blessings for feeding the fasting people during Ramadhan, we can!"

"We tried it before doing it like that, right Ummi? And it didn't work. And just because the sisters' committee cooks the Friday meals doesn't mean we should saddle our members with cooking during Ramadhan. I got three kids, a job, and no husband. It's hard enough trying to get to the masjid and pray and read Qur'an every day without worrying about frying chicken and baking macaroni and cheese for 300 plus people. If families can get together and collect the money to sponsor an iftar, then they can get together and find somebody to cook it up too. That's all I'm saying, Tahirah," Fariba argued.

"The sisters' committee has an obligation to encourage the people to spend in the cause of Allah and make it easy for them," Tahirah advised. "Some families can donate the money, but they can't cook the food. I think the sisters' committee should handle it."

Sister Adilah raised her hand as if she was in school and waited patiently for sister Danah to call on her before she spoke.

"Let's take a vote. If you think the sisters' committee should take responsibility for cooking for the weekly – not daily – weekly iftars, raise your hand," she instructed. Sister Tahirah and her teenage daughter

Khalilah, and two other sisters raised their hands. "Okay, now, if you don't think the sisters' committee should take responsibility for cooking the weekly iftars raise your hand," she stated again. I put my hand in the air along with Fariba, sister Danah, sister Adilah, and four other sisters. It was a no-go. "So, what we can do now is assign Fariba and Tahirah to find a couple of halal caterers in the city that will be willing to give the sponsoring families a discount for bringing them business during Ramadhan. Then we can set the price and have it announced by the time the moon is sighted. Is that all right with you Tahirah?"

"Whatever. I am going do what I can to get those blessings for me and my family, Insha'Allah."

"If you want to cook, Tahirah, cook! I got other thangs to do during Ramadhan than cook."

"That's because you choose to have it like that. So, don't start no mess with me tonight, Fariba Ibrahim! I gave my ideas and you gave yours. A wah duh yuh!"

"Right back at you, Tahirah! You think you slick, though," Fariba griped before storming out the dining room as she waved her hand into the air.

Sister Adilah shook her head at me and sighed before she got up. "All right, ya'll two stop all that nonsense. Alhamduleelah, at least we have an idea of what we are going to be doing for the Eid. And we have some goals for the iftars. I say we meet next week. Same time but we might be in Ramadhan by next week, so Insha'Allah, if we are then let's meet up at the Center right after Maghrib so that we talk quickly and stand for the *qiyam*," she advised us and then walked over and hugged sister Tahirah. "and get those blessings for standing up and praying to our Lord. Shukran, sisters, for coming out and eating with us."

As the women gathered their things and started to clear out of the room, I got up and started picking up the leftover plates and cups. I carried them to the kitchen where I found Fariba putting up the food.

"Shukran, Iman. I was about to come out there and get that stuff," she told me as she handed me a plate of food. "I forgot to bring you your plate. Go on and get started eating before Umm come back here and start fussing at me about that too," Fariba insisted, causing me to laugh.

On the plate of food Fariba gave me were baked barbeque turkey wings, honey glazed carrots, pineapples and peas, white rice, and fried cabbage. Everything looked tasty, but too high in fat. I sloshed the food around the plate a bit and then settled on eating the carrots and rice.

"Don't tell me you're a vegetarian," Fariba sulked as if being a vegetarian was problematic. I laughed anyway because it was the second time since I'd gotten back to Pittsburgh that I'd been accused of being one.

"No, I am not a vegetarian. Just conscious of my health and the food I use to nourish myself," I explained.

"Oh, okay, consciousness, that's commendable. I try," she noted. "Every day is a battle. Watching my heart and protecting my faith is a full-time job, my health too often takes a backseat," Fariba confessed and then handed me a glass of ice water with lemon slices.

"Ain't it the life of this world, they say at least," I replied in between nibbling my food. "Hoping for the best though, fearing the worst."

"You know it. But the funny thing is, well at least to me," Fariba started at she washed the dishes, "is that all the stuff we go through being Muslim women here in America ain't too different than the stuff that Muslim women go through in third world countries."

"How so?" I questioned her.

"Poverty? Check! Lack of education or miseducation? Check-check! Good men shortages? Check! Lack of good health care? Check, again! Widespread abuse of women? Check! Listen, I've been married twice, I have three daughters to provide for. I have responsibilities that make it difficult and challenging for me to come out and pray at the masjid on Fridays and attend classes during the week because I have food to pay for, laundry to wash, and homework to check. I've chosen to wrap my hijab and wear skirts to soften the discrimination that comes with working in corporate America so that I can pay my electric bills on time. But what happens? I gotta deal with side eyes and snarky comments from folks that only stepped on a prayer rug about a week ago, and think they have the right to throw bones. The players are different, but we gotta fight through the same tribal games the prophet Muhammad, peace and blessings upon him, fought against. It's either you conform and drink the Kool-Aid so a sister's mouth stays shut or stick a toe out and wear a scarlet letter. We can't win for losing," Fariba complained.

"But you seem to speak up and you push back! You've always been strong, Reeba. Not all of us have what you have inside of you. Allah gave you strength," I reminded her.

"Chile, cheese! I don't want to fight *every single day* of my life. I am fighting the ignorance from non-Muslims at work, fighting in the streets because I am living in a low-income neighborhood despite having fought to get educated and then I come home or to the masjid and still gotta fight? When do we as Muslim women get to throw the armor off and be demure, unguarded, and be loved for being who we are?"

"Jannah, Insha'Allah," I insisted with a fake smile. "No really, isn't that the right answer? You know, I am not the best person to give you answers. I feel like I am right back where I was when I left over a decade ago. I am trying to learn and figure things out as things come my way," I admitted. "But I do know – or better yet, I have learned that nothing you desire or chase after in this world is going to really matter if you don't put Allah first. Love, success, men, and nice things are fleeting. Even when you give it your all, sometimes it's not going to be enough. People disappoint you and things break or go out of style," I reasoned with her.

"Ain't that the truth!" she said laughing. "Speaking of disappointment, just so you know Tahirah is married to my ex-husband. The first one. She's been married to him for a while," she told me as she took a seat at her mother's kitchen table next to me. She'd brought over a tray of chopped carrot sticks, salted cucumbers, celery, a bowl of hummus and a pitcher of lemon- water. "I married him my first year of college, had a set of twin girls a year later, and asked him for a divorce after three years in. He's a nice brother, but dispassionate, you know? We didn't really gel well. I didn't see it at the beginning because what did I know about men at 19? I'd never had one. So, he left bitter. I left hopeful that it was a misstep and better days and love from someone who could match my hustle would come, Insha'Allah. I didn't mess with him and always tried to make things easy for Mahir, my ex that is. He paid his child support and we split custody. Then Tahirah jumps in the picture and claims she wants to build. Okay, but actions speak louder. Everything is a problem for her. Mainly me. What I do, how I talk, who my friends are, what I wear, what I do with daughters, how far away we live, how I do their hair. Anything she can fuss about, she does! So, it started to carry over and she got her husband wired up thinking he shaykh of the year. Next thing I know they were both all in my business riding me hard.

"I got so sick of fussing with them, Iman, I left Pittsburgh, left my Umm, and took my girls, Habibah and Hadiyya, to Cleveland. Thought I found a square brother at the masjid out there to work with. Latif wasn't much to write home about, but I was willing to work with him and submit. So, check it, right after I got pregnant, he lost his job at Amtrak, okay? Mashallah, right? So, I go get a second job to keep things up and the loose ends tied. I fought to keep my mouth shut, tried to be supportive and encouraging and patient while I was pregnant, working, and still dealing with Mahir and Tahirah. So, one day, I was feeling sick at work so I leave my office and go get my girls from school and we head home. I walk up into the house and this man up in *my* living room with two other Muslim brothers that we knew from the masjid cutting and bagging coke! *Coke!* In my apartment," Fariba emphasized as she hit her hand on the table.

"Street pharmacists, huh? So, what did you do?" I asked her while munching on some fresh carrots and hummus.

"Honey, I lost it completely, okay? I was yelling like I had mad cow disease. Told them all to get out and threatened to call the police. I left out of there with my girls before they did and jumped in my car and drove to a motel. Next thing you know, I am on the phone with my Umm crying. I told her what I saw and you know Umm! She said, I'm sending the boys! Alhamduleelah, Shareef and Mas'ud came out there too."

"Really, when was this? Hasn't Shareef been gone for about two years?" I asked her.

"It's actually been twenty-three months. So, that mess happened a month or so before he got locked up," she revealed as sadness clouded her features. It immediately dawned on me that Fariba had to have inside information about my brother. I knew exactly which direction I needed to steer the conversation in.

"How did you end up resolving the matter?" I questioned.

"That was it! Like I was all the way done – done with Latif that day. You know how our brothers are, okay? They got him up out that apartment the next day. He cried and begged and pleaded with them. He even had the nerve to lie to them and say I didn't know what I saw. Told them he was trying to take care of his family. He claimed he wanted to save the marriage. I wasn't having none of it. I gave my jobs a one week notice then I got up and left Cleveland before the month was up. Shareef helped me to move to Morgantown."

"Morgantown?"

"Yep. Morgantown, West Virginia. I got settled in, found a little temp job to carry me over til I had my Hafsa and then bam - Shareef got locked up. Craziness. And so, Imani, I am sharing this with you because I've heard they said you went through some mess, but gurl, know that we *all* did. We all have gone through it and most of us are *still* in it."

"I hear you, Reeba. Thank you for caring enough to share. Sometimes people act like they don't know what to say to me," I explained to her.

"Who cares?" she smirked. "Really, let 'em kick rocks, Imani! You know my Umm always says we about this deen. I got Allah and I got my family and I am breathing. Anything else He blesses us with, it really is a gift, not a requirement for me to believe in His power in my life."

"Nothin' but the truth. Hmm, talk about perspective! So, riddle me this one: what in the world happened to my brother? Why is Shareef in prison?"

"You don't know?" Fariba eyes widened and she sucked your teeth. "Let me guess, they told you it wasn't your business, right?"

"Of course," I affirmed.

"Aunty Muneerah has not changed a bit. It's not really all that complicated. Shareef's ex-wife Renay, Hasan's mother, isn't Muslim."

"Really?"

"Girl, please. A whole bunch of the brothers we grew up with didn't check for us at all. My brothers included. But you know Allah is quick to call people into account. So, I guess Shareef figured out some time after Hasan was born that it's kinda difficult to be a practicing Muslim and raise a Muslim child *without* a Muslim woman," Fariba reasoned in between gulps of her ice water. "He tried to end it amicably, but you know how some women can get when we feel scorned. Honestly, though, I liked Renay in the beginning and I think Aunty Muneerah and Uncle Musa liked her too. She wasn't one of those club hoppers or always in the streets in some fitna type of woman. She was a decent lady and nice enough."

"So what was the problem? How come Shareef didn't stick in there and try to make it work out for Hasan's sake?"

"I think it was combination of things that built up. Islam is all we know so when we step out there with people who don't believe like us, don't live like us, and don't even want to, over time it kinda gets to you."

"Yes, the very things that you thought were cool, interesting, or exciting at 18 starts to wear you down and then hurt you at 25. Been there, done it," I said remembering my first encounters with Mateo and how intrigued I was.

"Exactly, so he got out of there. She put him on child support, as she should have. But he fell behind. That's pretty much where his legal troubles started. Renay would call the police on him when he would come to pick Hasan up or she would she skip out when it was his day.

They would fight and argue and it became this constant battle for him. Finally, Renay met a guy and moved on."

"What do you mean?" I asked.

"She dropped Hasan off to Shareef and bounced. We didn't see Renay for like six months. She would come and go and I think Shareef suspected that something was off. The guy she was with was shady. I know Aunty Muneerah got worried every time Renay showed up.

"Fast forward three years or so and Meera called me one night and said she seen some marks on Hasan's back when she was washing him up, I told her to tell Shareef. I thought that he would confront Renay and find out what happened and set some rules or whatever. It didn't go like that all. It blew into this really big debacle. Shareef ended up getting into a fight with Renay's guy and she called the police out. Shareef got arrested. She pressed charges and he got the parole."

"Okay, I get all that. What put him in jail now?"

"So, like I said it was right after all my mess ended, his license got suspended due to the child support being in arrears. He was driving dirty and got stopped on the highway by the police. The police found the unlicensed gun in the car."

"Oh, Shareef," I gulped then lowered my head into my hands. "A gun charge and suspended license will get you put in jail for sure."

"Plus the assault and battery charge he was on parole for. It's messy and I think he knows now that he made some very poor choices in his life that lead up to that night. But Alhamduleelah," Fariba fluttered her eyelashes and gave me a half smile, "after difficulty come ease," she mused.

"You're waiting on Shareef to get out?" I questioned her figuring she had dropped enough hints of their courtship for Stevie Wonder to see she had feelings for him.

"Honey, I am too old and done learned enough lessons to be waiting on any man in this world. This time, Imani, I am trying to wait on Allah to bring me what's best for me."

There was a light tap on the kitchen door. Fariba yelled out for her brother to enter.

"Salamu alykum," Jibril greeted us as he entered the kitchen dressed in a navy blue and white striped button down Polo, a pair of khaki pants, and brown loafers. He began rummaging through the empty pots and containers that Fariba had washed out. "Reeba, where my plate?"

"Would you stop acting like some wild animal? You could actually miss a meal or two, Jibril," Fariba teased her brother as she got up from the table and walked over to the counter where there was a stainless-steel microwave. She opened the door and pulled out a paper plate stacked high with all the food items that had been served.

"All right, now! That's what I'm talking 'bout. May Allah bless you, bless you real good, beloved," Jibril rejoiced right before grabbing a folk out of the dish rack. "Bismillah," he uttered as he dug his folk into the food and shoveled food into his mouth. "Are you working tomorrow?" Jibril asked.

Fariba turned around and looked at me, but I shrugged my shoulders. I didn't know who he was talking to. "You talking to me?" she asked him.

"Nah, Imani! She know I'm talking to her, Fariba," Jibril insisted. Fariba laughed.

"No, I didn't know you were talking to me. But to answer your question, yes. I have to go to work tomorrow," I told him.

"Okay."

"Okay, what?"

"Okay, we'll be around there," Jibril retorted.

"We who?" I pressed him further with a little giggle. Jibril sucked his teeth as he walked over to the table and sat down with us. He raked his hands through his beard and took out his phone.

Jibril pointed at me and said, "I don't know why you wanna play games now, but this situation is not really funny to me at all. We – the men in your family, will be up at your job tomorrow. Mas'ud will take you to work in the morning and Fariba and I will pick you up. You get any calls or requests; send them to Mas'ud and me. For real – for real, I think now is the time when we all need to make some serious du'aah to seek Allah's aid, His guidance, His justice, and His protection for all of us. This is a serious situation," Jibril reminded me before getting up and walking out the kitchen with his plate.

Fariba shook her head while munching on the rest of the food. Nothing else needed to be said. I had been avoiding thinking about this weekend the whole week. But Jibril was right. It was here and the fact that I didn't know what that monster was planning, was serious.

"Aunty Meera is outside," a young boy came running in the kitchen shouting. He jumped in Fariba's lap, grabbed a carrot off the plate and put it in his mouth. Fariba kissed him on his forehead. I looked closely in his face and recognized him this time.

"Are you Saud?" I asked with a smile.

"That's me," the little boy admitted in between bites of the veggies.

"It's so very nice to finally meet you," I told him. "My name is Iman. I'm Ameera and Mas'ud's big sister."

"And Uncle Shareef, too!" Saud corrected me.

"Yes, Uncle Shareef, too. He's my big brother, though."

"I know that," Saud said matter-of-factly. Fariba and I started laughing.

"Kids these days. They know all the business," Fariba noted.

"Indeed. All right, Reeba." I got up from the table. "We really need to link up. It's been too long. I missed you," I told her as she stood up, lightly gave both cheeks kisses and hugged me tightly.

"That sounds like a plan. Insha'Allah, things will blow over in the right directions for us both. Oh, I'll see you tomorrow."

I briskly walked back to the dining room and grabbed my bags. I wanted to offer my salams to Sister Adilah, but she was nowhere to be found. Fariba and Sa'ud walked me out to the porch.

"All right, Imani, As salamu alykum. Ya'll be safe, Insha'Allah," Fariba added. I had got all the way down the steps before turning around and walking back onto the porch.

"Fariba!" I yelled into the house through the screen. The sound of her slippers slapping the old wood flooring as she rushed back to the front door could be heard outside. "I had one more question about Hasan's mother. Where is she?" Fariba shook her head and her mouth widened into a turned down position.

"Jail. She was arrested right after Shareef got locked up. I think her guy and her were running some credit card fraud scheme that went awry." Shocked, but feeling relieved, I didn't ask her for clarification or more details. Once again, nothing else needed to be said. Ummi had Hasan by default. Both of his parents were locked up. As I walked back to Umar's car and got in, I silently thanked Allah. I hoped that whatever Hasan's mother did, that Allah would help her make a change in her life so that she could help raise her son. It was clear to me that my brother went to jail for trying to protect his son and I had a feeling he'd do it again if he'd had to. Still, I had to smile at the irony. The very woman who orchestrated his ruin, Allah saw fit to ruin her as well.

"What Aunty Adilah cook for ya'll?" Ameera asked me after giving me the salams. I let a quick smile ease onto my face and inhaled deeply before releasing it all. I laid my head back into the seat, crossed my arms, then squeezed my eyes closed. I dozed deeply with heavy breaths for all two or three minutes it took for Umar to drive down the block and around the corner to Ummi's house. I don't even remember getting out the car, if I said anything to Ameera, the kids, or Ummi. I remember falling into the bed, kicking off my sandals, and cozying up next to my warm Saba. For some strange reason, I couldn't remember exactly what I dreamt about either. Whatever it was, though, I know I felt comfortable, easy, free to move about, and walk in my essence inside that dream. That was the part that I needed to feel the most. That was the part that I dreamed about all the time – safety.

I had noticed in the last year or two, every single time something monumental was about to happen in my life, I would be lulled into deep sleeps. Some call it intuition, but I've come to think of it as recognition. I recognize now that Allah was preparing my body for tasks that He had waiting on me. Often it was the miscarriages or the fights with Mateo, but right before I got out of dodge, I knew Allah was preparing me to return home. My body started cleansing itself and I would be pulled into sleeps so deep, I couldn't wake myself up. Then, even without my permission, I experienced and entered my sobriety.

I had been praying for it five times a day for years, I dreamt of it every night, but I never knew I had the strength during my waking hours to stop. Living was worse, I thought. I didn't have it in me to fight it, I always told myself. But I kept praying and one day it was all over. The mere smell of alcohol started to nauseate me. My head would pound with furry if I even sipped a taste. I would vomit until my insides ground against themselves and brought me to my knees. I sobbed for hours because I knew I couldn't do it anymore. I was more afraid to be without it. But Allah finally prevented my body from accepting it. My body actually submitted to Allah before my mind was ready to admit we had a problem. All I could do was sleep, long and hard, deep breathes and vivid dreams. When I emerged from that unexpected detox, clear headed, I knew it was time to leave Mateo.

Now I'd come full circle. It was time to face him and my past, once and for all.

The sound of the adhan that I had set on my laptop resounded throughout my room. I rolled out of the bed, fell to the floor, and landed on my back. I jumped up to my feet and hit the stop button as the caller's voice instructed me to *"Hayya 'alal falah"* or to come to success. I recited to myself, *"as salatu khayroon minan-nawm"* that prayer was better than sleep as I wiped the sleep out of my eyes and tip toed over to the closet and grabbed my prayer garment and pulled over my body. With Meera's husband staying in the house this weekend, I knew to cover before going out of the room. He usually only used the bathroom downstairs but I wanted to be safe.

Slipping into my house shoes, I opened the door and staggered to the bathroom. Without Yaz and Mas'ud in the house, the bathroom lines had been greatly reduced. It had been nice for the short time it lasted. Today would be their homecoming. They would actually beat me home. Yaz was scheduled for discharge by noon, Insha'Allah. Hopefully, I would be coming home to Yaz and the baby girl and nothing more.

After relieving myself and making ablution. I headed to my mother's room to wake her up for prayer. As I got closer to the room, I could faintly hear her soft voice floating through the air sending words from the Qur'an. She was already up praying. I twisted the door knob, tip toed into her space, and sat down on her new bed to wait for her to finish her prayer. Moments later, she was sitting folded leg on the top of her pale pink and beige prayer rug. She turned her head to the right and then the left as she offered peace to the angels. As soon as Ummi spotted me, her face lit up like a full moon.

"Salamu alykum, Iman! How long you been sitting there?" Ummi said when she finally noticed me sitting behind her.

"Wa alykum as salam. Not long, just your last raka'ah. I came to wake you up, but I see you got me beat."

"I guess so," she responded with a giggle. I extended my hand and helped her pull herself from off the ground. "Woke up out my sleep needing to bow my head. Praying for everybody, here and everywhere. You gonna try and make it to jumu'ah today?" Ummi questioned me as plopped on the bed next to me and reclined on a stack of pillows.

"I don't know. I might try to cut out early. All depends on my patient load today," I explained.

"You ain't been to jumu'ah since you got that new job. And you ain't been coming much to the halaqah on Tuesdays either. You all right? 'Cause you know if you got something on your heart, Allah is best Helper," Ummi cautioned me.

"Of course, I know that, Ummi. Been a lot going on at work and I am new so I gotta keep up. Plus, I thought I told you I have therapy on week nights. It's the only time I can go," I reminded my mother, trying my best not to feel some kind of way by her tone. Sometimes, I felt like Ummi was still treating me like I was 16. It didn't feel good and most times it bothered me. I was a grown woman.

"What's this therapy thing you doing? And for what? You know those head doctors don't know enough about our way of life to be giving us advice. That's dangerous, Iman," Ummi argued.

"Ummi, she's Muslim and she came highly recommended. Going to see her is a good thing for me," I assured her.

"Oh! Well what you getting this therapy for in the first place?" Ummi questioned me. After inhaling deeply at her persistence, our eyes locked for moment. I didn't want to be rude. I knew she was trying to show me she cared. But she had to know that her delivery left a lot to be desired. Without dropping her eyes from my gaze, she shook her head before spitting out, "Never mind! Take care of yourself, Imani!"

I nodded my head again and forced a smile. I wanted to soften the mood. "I am going to try and see if Meera or may be Fariba can come and get me for jumu'ah today. So, Insha'Allah, I'll probably see you a little earlier," I offered her. Her face lit up again and she grabbed my hand and pat it.

"Insha'Allah, I hope you do that. This is going to be busy weekend with Yaz and the new baby coming home. Then we got to start preparing this house for the aqeeqah and Ramadhan, too. Alhamduleelah, this is such a blessing. Your Abu he'd be so proud. He would be pleased to have you and Yaz and the new baby here in this house. Alhamduleelah."

"May Allah bless Abu and widen his grave, ameen!" I supplicated for my father.

"Ameen. Ameen. Ameen!" Ummi agreed.

Spotting some light outside her windows from behind her curtains, I slid off her bed and stood up to leave. I walked over to my mother and leaned down to kiss her on her forehead. Lowering my body even lower I grabbed her in an embrace and hugged her tightly.

"What's all this for?" Ummi questioned.

"I love you, Ummi," I revealed and reminded myself. "I want you to know that." It seemed like basic etiquette and common sense, but I'd let over a decade go by where I didn't have the decency to speak to my parents or siblings or tell them that I loved them. With all the drama in my world, it felt right to tell her, especially since she was being difficult with me.

"I know that, Imani. And I love you too. Go'head and turn off the lights on your way out. Make sure those boys pray and that Ameera ain't left them unattended," Ummi instructed me.

"Got it. See you later, Insha'Allah."
"Salamu alykum."
"Wa alykum as salam."

Chapter 10

Just like that, my day had started. I offered the Morning prayer back in the quiet of my room. Then I headed downstairs still in my prayer clothes. Ameera, Umar, their kids, and Hasan were gathered in the living room laughing and eating like it was late in the afternoon. But it wasn't. The sun's rays had started to break-up the darkness of the night, though it was still quite early. Saba was wide awake, though, and waddling around in her pink Hello Kitty pajamas and pink slippers with her brothers and Hasan as they tossed her toy ball back and forth. I didn't have time to chat with Ameera now. I offered everyone my salams and headed back to bed. I had to be up and out in less than three hours. With Ameera and Saba sleeping downstairs with Umar in the small guest room that was also used as my mother's computer room, I had my bedroom all to myself. The good sleep was beckoning me to come back for another taste. I couldn't resist it.

Mas'ud came to pick me up right on time. He yawned long and hard and stretched his long, lean arms up into the air as I got in his van. His work shirt was half buttoned. His hair and beard were beady and straggly. I smiled and rubbed his head. It was clear that his little baby girl was making her presence known.

"I'm good. So, today make sure, you ah, keep your eyes open and ah, try to stay in contact with us," Mas'ud instructed me as he kept yawning through his words. "Hamad will be posted outside the clinic in the morning and Ya'coob will Insha'Allah get up here around noon. If you even receive a text from him saying 'hey' you let me know and you leave with Hamad or Ya'coob. If all goes well, Fariba and Jibril will be here 'round five thirty to pick you up. Umar and Jibril will be at the house til I get home,"

"And if he calls me and says he wants me to meet him somewhere, what then? I don't show up?"

"You definitely don't show up, Imani," Mas'ud told me as he turned his body to face me and pointed his finger. He was fully awake and alert now. "You call me immediately with the address. Then Jibril, Umar, Hamad, and me will go meet him. You don't go see him under any circumstances. Use your mind. Don't let him or Shaytan get up in your feelings. He ain't got no power over you – none. He can't hurt you any more, Iman, unless you give him the opportunity. Think smart and be safe."

"I know, Mas'ud, I know. I just don't want Mateo to get angry and try something stupid with any of you guys. I know him, and he…"

"Don't worry about us. Let us worry about ourselves. You take care of you. Listen and follow the rules we've put in place to keep you and everybody safe. Insha'Allah, everything will be fine."

"I hope so. And hey, do you think it'll be okay for me to go to jumu'ah today during my lunch break? Ummi wanted me to meet her over at the Islamic Center,"

"I'll let Ya'coob know," Mas'ud said as he pulled up in front of the Hilltop Clinic. "All right, Insha'Allah, I'll talk to you later, sis."

"Insha'Allah. As salamu alykum!" I offered the greeting as I opened the door to his van, grabbed my bags and got out. After I closed the doors and threw my bags on my shoulder, I adjusted my hijab then walked into the clinic.

Standing at the door for the office, I swiped my badge, whispered a supplication for strength, and walked into the suite. This was going to be a nerve wrecking day but I was committed to pushing through. I had my counselor Labibah Bey on speed dial, I had Ameera, Mas'ud, and I even had Fariba and Jibril. I had Allah. Mateo would not win this time.

The patients kept me busy all morning. Mas'ud texted me every hour. He arranged my pick-up time with Ya'coob after I spoke with

Michel'le. I wanted to give her a heads up that I was going off the premises during my lunch break for Friday prayers.

"You know that's fine, Iman! Any time you need to go, go! I wish more folks would go pray. Shoot, people walking around this here earth angry and upset 'bout stuff that they Momma or Daddy did to them in grade school. It's ridiculous. Pray on it and let it go. We need more prayers in this world!"

"I hear you. And thanks, Michel'le! I should be back right on time, if traffic cooperates."

"Iman, I am serious, don't you worry about it! Go and enjoy your service!"

Michel'le shooed me away with a smile as I thanked her again. Turning around, I headed down the hall toward the last examination room before I left for Jumu'ah. I turned the door handle and there sat a middle aged, olive-complexioned Latino woman. She was an attractive woman with peanut butter brown skin, chin length, curly dyed blonde hair, dark brown eyes, and impeccable make-up. She was wearing a pair of black skinny jeans that were ripped at the knees, a blush pink hi-lo tank that she finished off with a colorful pair of Jimmy Choo's strappy platform sandals. I knew they were Jimmy Choo's because I had had a similar pair with the matching handbag myself. They'd been gifted to me by the devil himself. I'd worn them out with love every chance I had got for months. I'd left them in my closet back in Atlanta purposely. She was overdressed for the appointment for sure. I glanced around the room looking for the seven-year-old child, Danny Reyes that was listed on my chart.

"He's in the bathroom," she offered. "We've been waiting like forever," she complained as she turned around and picked up the matching handbag from the table behind us.

"My apologies, Mom. We try our best to keep our appointment timings as accurate as possible. Fridays are super busy. While we wait for Danny can you tell me what brings you in today?"

"Yeah, Danny been having trouble at home seeing stuff like forever. But then the nurse at his day camp said he failed the um, seeing test or exam or whatever. So, he can't see, right? I wanna get a referral now for the eye doctor before school starts back up and get him some glasses."

"Okay, that's an easy fix," I told her as I walked over to the computer desk. I logged into the system and pulled up his chart and began to add notes for the doctor. Danny, a thin boy with the same peanut butter brown skin as his mom and dark, thick curly black hair and a huge smile busted into the room.

"Mami, is this the doctor? She's so pretty," he said.

"No, Danito. We still waiting. This the nurse."

"Hi, Danny! I'm nurse Iman. Thanks for being so patient and kind. I'll take your vitals and then doctor Brown will be right in. Is that cool?" I asked as I gave him a full lookover.

"What the heck is that?" he asked me boldly as he walked right up to me and tugged down on my stethoscope. She popped the little boy in the back of his head before grabbing and shushing him at the same time.

"That's a really good question, Danny. The vital signs are a bunch of measurements of how your body is working. I have to check four things: your temperature, your pulse, your breathing, and your blood pressure – but the last one is not really a vital sign. My bosses make me do it anyway," I told him as I picked up the thermometer, grabbed a new protector seal and put it onto the device. I stuck the thermometer into Danny's mouth. Holding his arm, I placed my first and second fingers on his wrist and pushed down. When the thermometer beeped Danny raised his other hand up and pointed at it and mumbled, "It's ready."

"Thanks for all of your help, Danny. You'd make a great nurse or doctor one day," I advised him as I finished recording all of his data into his file on the computer. As I was getting ready to submit the update, I saw that Danny had been diagnosed recently with Fetal Alcohol Spectrum Disorder. He had already been enrolled in our collaborative care program for children with complex or chronic health issues. But his Mom hadn't brought Danny into the clinic since he'd been diagnosed.

"Mom, before I go, I want you to know that Danny is already enrolled in our collaborative care program. He doesn't have to wait for referrals," I reminded her as I got up. "All you have to do is call our family care coordinator, Vanessa Bruins, and let her know what's going on with Danny. From there, nurse Vanessa will take care of the rest. Danny can be seen by his doctor, me, the nutritionist, the psychiatrist, the psychologist, and our developmental specialist all on the same day and that way we can discuss his care plan and make all the referrals you need and save you some trips."

"Really?" she asked, raising her eyebrows and smiling.

"Yep. Just give Nurse Vanessa a call and she'll take care of you. All righty, Danny, you're all ready for Doctor Brown. It was nice meeting you,"

"Nice meeting you, too!" he said as he gave me a high five.

"Thanks, nurse Iman. If I have any type of questions about Danny, can I call the office for you?"

"You bet. I am here from seven thirty in the morning until closing. Take care now," I told her as I walked out, waving good-bye to them. Back in the staff room, I washed my hands and took off the pink and white flower printed scrub top that I wore over a long sleeve white t-shirt and white cotton maxi skirt. I reached into my bag and pulled the navy ruffled koshibo jilbab that I had packed and pulled it over my head. I went to the bathroom and inspected the garment for wrinkles but surprisingly couldn't detect any. After rewrapping my hijab, I grabbed my bags and headed out of the clinic.

As soon as I stepped through the sliding doors, the sun's heat engulfed me. The chill that had clung to my skin all morning long from the clinic's central air instantly melted away. It was doggone hot. Squinting my eyes to see as I approached the curb to get a better look, I heard a horn beep twice. I waved my hand out as I watched the car approach. I could see Fariba sitting on the passenger side of her brother's black late model Toyota Highlander.

"As salamu alykum," Fariba and Ya'coob greeted me once I got in the car.

"Wa alykum as salam. Thanks for the ride, Ya'coob."

"Don't even worry 'bout it, sis," he told me as he pulled out of the clinic's parking lot. "Everything going okay on the inside?" he asked me as he chewed on a Miswak stick and steered the car.

"Yeah, so far so good. Alhamduleelah. Hey Reeba, you playing hooky from work, too?" I questioned my friend and she laughed. Fariba was dressed coolly in a rayon burnt orange and navy blue tie dye baby doll dress embellished by bell shaped sleeves and small black rhinestones on the bodice. She wore an extra long jersey knit hijab that was rolled around the top of her head and draped around her neck and chest regally. Fariba topped the outfit off with several brass necklaces around her neck and similar bracelets on her wrist.

"Girl, I wish I could play some dang hooky. I got too many bills," Fariba huffed.

"Don't start, Reeba," Ya'coob warned her as he switched the Miswak to the other side of his mouth.

"Oh, hush up, Yah!" Reeba grumbled as she swatted her brother's arm and laughed. "Anyway, I was working from home today. You really good, though?" Fariba turned around and questioned me. "I know this must be crazy stressful for you. But you need to really know that we are all in this with you, honey!"

"Thanks! I'm still trying to wrap my head around everything. It really helps to be open and honest and to know that ya'll got my back. I was living pretty foul and that's why I am in this mess now. But Insha'Allah, I am hoping this is the final door that I have to close. Enough is enough. I am really ready to move on. This time is different... I am different, you know?"

"You are, alhamduleelah! We all are. And I am really proud of you! Don't overthink it. Put your trust in Allah and fight forward. I done went up against some crazies myself in my days. They sure will make you reflect that's for sure. Anyway, Yasmeen and Mas'ud bring that baby home yet? I am so excited for them. I can't wait to go shopping for her."

"Oh my, yes! I almost forgot. Today is baby girl's day. They should be on their way home in a bit. Ya'll gotta come by,"

"Yep, you know I will, Insha'Allah. Yaz is probably so happy to finally get out of that hospital. Moody too!"

"Yeah, poor baby! He was looking beat down this morning from all the late nights with Yaz, baby girl, and running back and forth from work and home."

"Stop that. Don't be poor babying him, Imani. He's a grown man. He'll get through it, Insha'Allah," Ya'coob noted. "That's his responsibility to take care of his family. And he has help, too, so he gotta roll with it. Everybody don't have the support we have here."

"Ain't that the truth. It's why I had to carry my tail on back home. It's hard to be responsible without a village to help you carry the load."

"Man, bump the village. You needs a husband ASAP, Reeba!"

"Bruh! How many times I gotta remind you to M.Y.O.B?" Fariba snapped. We all laughed.

Minutes later Ya'coob pulled into the Islamic Center's parking lot. The lot was already semi full. He drove down to the middle section and found an open spot to park in right next to his brother's SUV. When I got out I saw Mas'ud sitting in the passenger side. Jibril and Mas'ud exited and walked over to us. Ya'coob offered salams and handshakes to my brother and Jibril. Fariba and I left them be and started walking together back down to the Islamic Center.

After I entered the building, I took off my shoes, placed them on the large wooden shoe rack and went to go make ablution in the women's bathroom. A group of young Muslim girls who attended the Islamic Center's Day School were huddled around the wudu stations and bathroom's mirrors. The girls giggled and chatted as they reworked and styled their hijabs with their friends' assistance. Some of the other girls applied eyeliner and lip gloss to their mouths. Oblivious to my presence, I listened to the girls chatter about their classes, Islamophobia in the news, their parent's fears, and their plans for the weekend as I washed my face, hands, arms, head, and feet.

The conversation made me smile. After they exited, I finally made my way to the mirror and fixed my own hijab before heading into the prayer area.

The Islamic Center of Pittsburgh was one of the largest centers in the city for Muslims to congregate at and worship Allah. Besides the full-time Islamic school, they also operated an evening technical training program and free English classes for refugees and immigrants. It had blossomed and grown into a much more diverse center than when my parents and other elder Muslims had helped to start it. The Islamic Center of Pittsburgh was both home and host to Muslims from all over the world including Syria, Nigeria, Somalia, Egypt, Saudi Arabia, and Pakistan while also remaining the flag post in the city for dawah efforts to indigenous Latino, White, and Black American Muslims.

Muslim women of every color, size, fashion style, and ethnicity sat folded leg on the carpeted floor side by side in the women's section of the praying area. I scanned the room from side to side with my eyes until I spotted my mother sitting up front in the first row right next to Sister Adilah. I excused myself and found a narrow path to tiptoe through until I got to the second row. I patted my mother on the shoulder lightly. Ummi turned around and beamed proudly at me. She extended her hand. I placed her hand in mine, brought it up to my mouth and gently kissed it before I shook it. I lowered myself down to bended knee and we kissed cheeks thrice as the Imam started his khutbah.

I stood up in my little space to offer two units of prayer. By the time I finished praying, there were over 100 women, children, and babies jam packed into the hall listening to the Imam talk about the importance of charity. Some of the children were playing, crying, and talking on the sides or stuck on their mothers' laps. When I turned my head to the left, I spotted Fariba all the way to the end of the row I was in. She was sitting right next to sister Tahirah, her ex-husband's wife and they were holding hands.

I tried hard to tune in to the Imam's words and get my mind to shut-off the other chatter that had been swirling around it since Mateo had called me, but for some reason I suddenly felt nervous. I felt like something bad was going to happen. It was louder than ever before. I raised my hands high and began to supplicate silently for protection, peace, and strength. Mas'ud had already told me that he would protect me. But what he didn't really understand was that Mateo was my fight to win. Even if he physically hurt me, I would heal, by the permission of Allah.

As the *Muadthin* called the iqama for salat, the sisters all began to stand up. I followed. As I stepped up a bit to toss my handbag up to the front of the room, my mother reached for my hand and pulled me up into her row. We squared our shoulders and lined up our feet, heel to heel, to remove any spaces between us. Other sisters shuffled around as well. By time the Imam started the prayer, standing in the same line as Ummi and me was sister Adilah, sister Tahirah, and Fariba.

The Imam recited in a fluid and sweet melodic Arabic:

(The Prophet) frowned and turned away because there came to him the blind man. But what could tell you that per chance he might become pure (from sins)? Or that he might receive admonition, and that the admonition might profit him? As for him who thinks himself self-sufficient, To him you attend; What does it matter to you if he will not become pure. But as to him who came to you running. And is afraid (of Allah and His Punishment), Of him you are neglectful and divert your attention to another, Nay, (do not do like this), indeed it (these Verses of this Qur'an) are an admonition, So whoever wills, let him pay attention to it. (It is) in Records held (greatly) in honor. Exalted (in dignity), purified, In the hands of scribes. Honorable and obedient. Be cursed man! How ungrateful he is! From what thing did He create him? From male and female semen drops He created him, and then set him in due proportion; Then He makes the Path easy for him. (Surah Abasa, 1-20)

"Allahu Akbar!" As sisters, we bowed our heads, supplicated, and bent our bodies to the grown. Each time I followed along, supplicating and praising His name, I feel refreshed and renewed. I had to only place my trust in His might to find the light I needed to guide me out of the darkness I'd been trapped in. The end was near.

"As salamu alykum wa rahmatullah," - "As salaamu alykum wa rahmatullahi wa barakatuh."

The prayer finished and one of the elder brothers immediately got up on the mic on the brother's side.

"Uh Uhm Uh, As salamu alykum, brothers and sisters. This is brother Amir Mirza, your newest board member. As you all know, we are on the cusp of Ramadhan. Today is the 29th of the month of Sha'ban so we have our group of moonsighters ready for tonight. Insha'Allah, the volunteers will gather to look for the moon and also work the phone lines to record any credible moon sightings anywhere in the world. As is this Islamic Center's long standing opinion, we will accept any credible moon sighting locally or internationally. Bukhari and Muslim recorded that the Prophet of Allah (sallallahu alayhi wa sallam) stated: Do not fast until you see the new moon, and do not break fast til you see it. That is a collective duty or fard kifaya. Whoever sees the moon first, has the obligation to share it and spread it. So, Insha'Allah, please don't clog the phone lines up or gather unnecessarily here tonight looking for answers prematurely. But do add your number to our database before you go, if you haven't already. As soon as we receive credible information, a local or international sighting, we will contact all of you automatically, Insha'Allah! May Allah bless us all and allow us all to meet the month of Ramadhan with Eman and health.

"Another thing I wanted to mention is we have been dealing with a growing number of parking issues lately and with Ramadhan coming we know that even more people will start to come out to worship. This is what we want, of course. However, brothers and sisters, remain mindful that this is the house of Allah and we are all guests. Be careful of where you park and how! Don't take up more than one space, don't block each other in, don't park in the prohibited areas or areas designated for our brothers and sisters with disabilities. Also, don't park in front of our neighbors' driveways! But please, do use the extended parking lot, if you cannot find a proper spot to park in the main front lot. Please be respectful of the brothers on security. We would hate to have to have cars towed, but if you don't follow the rules, we will have to maintain order.

"Lastly, the sisters' committee has cooked up some delicious halal meals today: curry chicken and jasmine rice or fried fish and macaroni and cheese - my favorite. It's all downstairs in the multipurpose room. This is the last lunch meal until after Ramadhan, so do support their efforts and help support the Islamic Center. As salamu alykum wa rahmatullah."

Chatter, grunts, hisses, and every other noise you can imagine stirred up in the hall after the announcements. Sister Adilah stood up and clapped her hands twice quickly to gain attention,

"Sisters, please stop this fussing right now! Make your sunnah and go head down to the basement or over to the Imam's office, if you have questions. We not going to have no arguing on the musallah!"

Respectfully, sisters quieted their voices and went back to their prayers. Sister Adilah shook her head before sitting back down in her spot on the carpeted floor to dhikr her remembrance of Allah with her hands.

Ummi and I stood up and changed spaces before we continued on to our prayers. I didn't have much time to get back to work so I finished praying, kissed my mother, Sister Adilah, Tahirah, and several other elders before I made my way out of the praying area and back into the shoe rack room to fish my shoes out of the massive pile. I tossed and brushed shoes out of my way until I spotted my own flowered nursing clogs.

By the time I got outside and started on my way to Ya'coob's car, the once tightly packed parking lot was already clearing up. I obviously wasn't the only one headed back to work. My cell-phone beeped as I reached my brother standing there waiting for me.

"You talk to Ummi?" Mas'ud asked.

"Yeah. She went down to eat lunch with sister Adilah," I told him.

"Is she riding home with her too?"

"I think so, but make sure you confirm that before you leave. Or let Meera know she needs to swing by to get her. You going up to the hospital to pick Yaz and baby girl up now?"

"Yeah Insha'Allah! I'll have her give you a ring when they get settled in 'cause I actually gotta get back to the shop and finish up some work. Jibril and Fariba will scoop you up from work so that Meera and Umar can stay with Yaz and the kids."

"No problem! I am so excited to see her and so excited for you and Yaz, baby boy!"

"Pray for us, she's a tough little bit."

"Tough is good. May Allah make her strong, healthy, and forever guided," I prayed as I leaned in kissed my brother's forehead.

"Ameen, ameen! See you later tonight. Text or call if you need anything." I smiled as I watched my brother walk further down to the lot, get into his car, and drive away. Leaning on Ya'coob's car as the sun beamed down on to my already sweating body, I reached into my handbag and pulled out my sunglasses and slide them onto my eyes. I reached back in the handbag, dug a little further searching for my cell phone and wet wipes. As soon as I grabbed my phone, pressed a button to call Fariba, a car blasting old-school reggae came roaring down the street in front of the Islamic Center. Walking away back towards the musallah, I put the receiver to my ear and my hand over my ear so that I could hear the call.

"As salamu alykum, Reeba, where ya'll at?

"Wa alykum as salam. So sorry, Imani. Ya'coob and Jibril are with me. I had to have them holla at Mahir real quick. We coming right now!"

We offered and returned salams and I clicked the end button on my phone before sliding it back into my handbag. I took out one of the wipes from the package and wiped the perspiration off and cooled my face off. I started walking back to the Ya'coob's car when a car's alarm went off across the street. It ended as quick as it started. Then the reggae started blasting again. The booming trunk speakers blasted, forcing the ground to bounce with the rhythmic island drum and whistle beat. I turned my head to face the street and there was group of men and a lady standing around a black Mustang with tinted windows laughing and talking. All of the guys' backs were to me, but the lady was staring right at me. I looked away for a second to see if Reeba and her brothers were anywhere, but the coast was clear. By the time I turned my head back to the party across the street, the woman had already crossed the street and was walking towards me. I knew exactly who she was. I walked towards her. I met her at the Islamic Center's gate as the Mustang's radio began to crank out a familiar reggae tune:

"*Yu waan test the rocket launcher?*
Well let mi tell yu sum'ting
Mi are di original butcher
Mi hav fi chop up
Lord, hav mercy, hear dis
Yu'll hear dis?
Wake di man
A who dat a come?
Wake di man
Who no tink me the don?"

Cutty Ranks' voice, deep, heavy, and full Patois accent was an ironic reminder of who I was dealing with. She smiled as she approached me. Those stilettos clicked and clacked to the beat of the music. Then she swung the matching hand bag around her shoulder. I stopped walking. This woman was wearing my leftovers.

"*Que lo que, Mami?*"

"*Yo no se, prima. ¿Como tu ta?*"

"*No te preocupe, to'ta frio.* Evelyn, mi prima, sent me to find you. Sorry it took so long. *Oyeme,* they're here," she explained as she glanced over her shoulder back at the Mustang across the street. "Diego popped up at my spot late last night so I was worried. I didn't know how to get you quickly so I brought Danny to see you at the clinic. Here," she said handing me a small piece of paper. "Mateo wants you to meet us at the library tonight,"

"*De verdad?*"

"*Si.* Don't worry, I'll be around. I promised Evelyn that I'll not leave your side. Manny knows they're here, too so hopefully they'll act right. Gotta go so Diego won't get mad. But, I'll see you at seven. Come alone, okay?" she warned before turning to power walk back across the street towards the Mustang. As soon as she reached the car, Diego, taller and buffer, than I remembered him, dressed in black slacks and a checkered black and white buttoned down dress shirt, turned and finally faced me. A quaint smile stretched across his clean-shaven face before he turned around and opened the driver's side door to let the woman in. Evelyn's cousin. Danny's mother. I didn't know her name. Diego sped off as Reeba and her brothers approached. I was deep in my feelings.

"*Si Dios quiere!*" I whispered as I looked down at the paper the woman gave me.

"You all right?" Jibril asked me breaking into my private thoughts.

"Yeah, yeah. I'm good. I have to get back to work now," I told him as I tapped on my wrist watch.

"What's that?" he said pointing at the paper in my hands as Ya'coob chirped the alarm on his car and unlocked the doors.

"This?" I said looking down at my hands. "Oh, nothing. Just a number someone gave me." I told him as I stuffed the paper into my hand bag.

"Okay so Ya'coob will bring you back to work and I'll be over there shortly. I need to run back to work real quick. Anything funny, strange texts or calls, call me, call everybody. Got it?"

"Of course, will do...Insha'Allah. All right, as salamu alykum, Jibril. Go to work!"

"Man, slow down, sis," he said laughing before extending his hand and offering me a small Styrofoam container. "I bought you lunch,"

"Why thank you, brother! I hope you didn't get me the fried fish,"

"I wouldn't dare. Nothing but salad in there, a side of curried veggies, and a bottle of water,"

"Sounds good."

"See you later, Insha'Allah," he told me as he turned and walked away to his car.

I was silent all the way back to the clinic.

With two minutes to spare, Ya'coob got me back to work on time. I changed my clothes, grabbed my roster, and headed in to see my next patient. Even though I had been cornered once again by Mateo, I wasn't going to break down in front of my co-workers. I had a choice to make: I could tell Mas'ud and Jibril and let them square out a plan. Or I could meet up with Mateo, Diego and Evie's cousin or go buy a bottle of Frio and find somewhere to hide. Those were my choices.

As I worked I kept going through all the choices in my mind. The outcome was bad for all of them. I didn't want to slip up and make the wrong decision. I forced myself to smile at each patient. I tried to think about Yaz and baby M.A.J at home with Ummi, Meera, and all the other kids. My family. Those were the people that I loved and that loved me. Those were the people I had to stay loyal to no matter what.

As soon as I got a minute alone in the staff room around four in the afternoon, I locked the door and offered the afternoon prayer. When I finished, I sat down at one of the tables and grabbed the lunch out of the fridge that Jibril had bought me to eat. The Fattoush salad was sprinkled with pomegranate seeds, pita chips, olive oil, and a light but tangy salad dressing. It paired well with the spicy curried potatoes, peas, and carrots. As I munched on my food, I toyed with my cell phone and read a couple of emails online. When I stumbled across an old note from Miss Labibah, I knew I needed to call her. Pulling up her office number at the Clover Recovery Center, I hit the send button and waited until I heard the dialing sound.

"Labibah Bey speaking,"

"As salamu alykum, Miss Labibah. This is Iman. Do you have a minute to talk?"

"Wa alykum as salam, Iman. Of course, I have a minute. Is everything okay?"

"Everything is rotten. I... I was thinking about drinking today. I am stressed, angry, overwhelmed, I guess. I am so very tired of feeling all of these emotions all of the time."

"All right, so you expressed your feelings and got it out of you. You know what comes next?"

"Yes, the triggers."

"Good. That's right. You are not an alcoholic, Iman. You have PTSD and drinking was your coping mechanism. You don't need it to cope. You have already learned some management skills. You know that because you've been doing it. So what's triggering your stress and fear? And what coping methods can you use to reduce your anxiety right now?"

"That's it, I don't know. Mateo is here, Miss Labibah! His brother was bold enough to roll up to the masjid. He sent a woman to deliver a note to me. He wants to see me tonight. I really don't know what to do. Do I go alone? Do I send my brothers? Do I run away again? Why won't this man leave me alone for good?"

"You know why he won't leave you alone, Iman. He has a major control problem and you not being there to do what he wants diminishes his power and control. Now I understand you are feeling conflicted, but there really is only one choice here. It would not be safe for you to go meet Mateo alone. He might play nice, calm, or sweet for a little while but you know he can't maintain it. He is an abuser, a bully, and a victim too. He can't change until he gets real help. So don't even think about putting yourself at risk like that with that man. You have the restraining order. You have family and friends that want to help you. You have me. And you have 9-1-1."

"But if something was to happen to my family - they're all I have, Miss Labibah. I couldn't live with myself if I put them in danger,"

"You will always have Allah, Iman. Put your trust in Him. He's here and He will protect all of us. Trust is key! And you know how you build your trust in anyone up, it's by trusting them! You know that you can't trust Mateo! He has proven to you that he is untrustworthy! I really think you should call the police and let them deal with him."

"What will they do? Lock him up for 30 days, 60 days? And then what? He'll get out angrier than now seeking revenge, right? I want to be done with him for good! I need him to divorce me so this can all end."

"Okay, call brother Jibril and your brother. Let them handle it. Trust your trustworthy people to go to battle for you. Let them get the divorce lawyers involved and have them settle this for you."

"Miss Labibah, I really wish it was that easy. Mateo wants me to come see him so that I can beg and cry to him for my freedom. He wants to hear how sorry my life is without him and that I made a stupid mistake by leaving him. He's not going to help me if I don't grovel, beg, and do whatever else he's planning in his sick, twisted mind."

"But it will not go down like that! Listen, Iman, I don't care what that man wants. He doesn't deserve anything from you, certainly not an apology. Mateo is your trigger, Iman. Stay far away from him. He doesn't mean you any good and he can't be trusted. So I want you to hang up with me right now and call your family. If you want this to end the right way, let them handle it. Can you promise me that?"

Sighing deeply with my chest and exhaling through tears, I nodded before I responded, "Yeah, Insha'Allah. I guess it's the right thing to do."

"It *is* the right thing to do. And it's the brave thing to do, Iman. Ask for help from the people who love you. And I love you, sister. I am proud of you for calling me. I am proud of you for acknowledging your anxiety and expressing your feelings. I am proud of you for crying and listening and hearing me when I tell you that Allah is there for you. Take one step."

"And Allah will take two."

"Ameen, sis! I'll check on you later. Okay?"
"Okay. Thanks, for listening, Miss Labibah."
"None needed, beloved. As salamu alykum."

I clicked the end button on my cell phone as I dried the tears from my face with the palm of my hand. I had a couple of more patients to see before it was time to go home. I needed to go clean myself up so that I could do what I had to do. I figured I would tell Jibril and Mas'ud about the meeting in person. No need to get them antsy right now.

Forcing a smile, I left the staff room and I headed back out into the clinic. I had work to do and patients that needed my help. Those children and their parents didn't care that I had been an abused wife for over ten years or that I had abandoned my family and then lost my father in the midst of it. They just cared that I helped them feel better and got them the right medicine. There wasn't any time to keep feeling sorry for me. I had a job to do.

"Hey, Iman," Michel'le called as I exited an exam room.

"Yes, Ma'am? What's up?" I asked her.

"How was your service? I hope you made it there on time. I was listening to WAMO and the DJ mentioned that traffic had been terrible during the midday."

"Oh, it was bad. But I made it there and back on time. I enjoyed the service."

"That's good to hear. Listen, I wanted to drop this bug in your ear 'fore I forget. I know you remember when I mentioned to you about the women's support group here at the clinic?"

"Yeah, I do,"

"Well, we have a program coming up the last Saturday of the month and we need one more speaker. I think it would be great to have a Muslim woman health professional present because we have a growing Muslim community that we serve. And," she said, emphasizing the conjunction, "you speak that *Espanol* and you have a powerful testimony to share. Now, I don't wanna push you if you're not ready, but this could be a great platform for you," Michel'le explained.

"How about I think about it?"

"That's perfect! Give it some thought. Meanwhile, I'll email you the program, the sponsors' information, and some photos from prior events so that you can see some of the participants. It's an all women workshop, very intimate and healing."

"Miss Michel'le I appreciate you always looking out for me. I'll get back to you soon."

"Don't even mention it. You take your time. And thanks for not shooting it down right away. It's about time for you to sign out. See you Monday, Iman. Have a good night!"

"You too. See you next week."

I honestly didn't even have time to think about the women's health summit. I had to think about my life right now and the healing and spiritual journey I was on. Telling the truth. Trusting my family. Having faith that He would see me through. I had to do the right thing in order for the right things to come my way. I had to talk to Mas'ud and Jibril and tell them about the meeting with Mateo.

Chapter 11

I went back to the staff room and grabbed my handbag out of my locker. I decided to change out of my scrubs and back into my jilbab. After I pulled it over my head I noticed that the wrinkles had stayed at bay. It still looked freshly ironed. I packed up my clothing, my medical equipment and headed out of the staff room. I texted Jibril to let him know I was done and coming out as I walked towards the exit. He replied back immediately:

I am already here. You can come out.

Right out front waiting.

I saw Jibril and Fariba sitting in his car as I soon as I walked out of the doors. He popped the locks as I reached for the car's handle. I climbed in the backseat as I greeted them both. Fariba had changed her clothes. She wore an eye catching pink and black Ankara dress. The royal blue headwrap she wore was twisted and looped around her head, neck, and bosom. It draped regally around her body.

"When I get my next check, we gotta go shopping, Reeba," I remarked.

"Bet, Imani. You know I am a shopaholic. Let me know what you're looking for. A lot this stuff I make myself, though, or I find it at the second-hand stores and then repurpose it myself," she revealed. "I been gave up on straight retail."

Jibril laughed. "We can tell," he quipped at his sister. "Don't let Reeba style you, Iman. Most days she be lookin' like Queen Latifa meets Mariam Makeba circa 1989 with a hijab. Pittsburgh can only handle one of her."

"You got jokes, Jibril?"

"Why you think they call me Fresh? I can help you, little sis," Jibril explained as he pulled out of the clinic's parking lot and into traffic.

"I'll have you know, boy, that my sewing services are requested all over Pennsylvania, trust me. But anyway Iman, I received a little good news today," Fariba started as she turned her body around in the front seat to face me.

"Well do tell, sweets. What's up?" I asked her.

"Jibril probably already knows this, but Shareef wrote me and Alhamduleelah – he's getting out next week!" she shrieked.

"No, really? What? My brother is coming home?" I asked through tears.

"Yes, Insha'Allah, and right in time for Ramadhan! His case went up for review last month. He was being tight lipped 'cause he didn't want to get his hopes up. But the review board let him know he's good to go. Insha'Allah, he's coming home. Right, Jibril?"

"Yeah, Insha'Allah, he's coming. But you two keep this under wraps for now. Don't go spreading this around the community and don't tell Aunty Muneerah yet."

"Why not?" I asked.

"Surprise element," Fariba pondered. "Probably. Shareef is silly like that."

"Ya'll know my Ummi don't like no surprises and her heart ain't in the best shape. I don't know if him popping up like that would be a good thing for her. I wouldn't want to overwhelm her, even with good news."

"Good point," Jibril agreed. "Maybe we can let her know she will have a visitor on the day I go get him. She'll have a little time to prepare and won't be caught off guard, Insha'Allah."

"That sounds better," I agreed. "We should host an iftar or something."

"Ooh, good idea, of course. Maybe we can get the brothers to slaughter too," Fariba suggested.

"Whatever ya'll want to do is fine with me. Just plan it and I'll pay for it. I'll pass the information over to Shareef, too," he told us.

"Jibril, did you tell Mas'ud yet?" Fariba asked him excitedly.

"No, but I'll let him know tonight though, Insha'Allah,"

We pulled up to my house and Jibril parked in the driveway behind Umar's car. Everyone was home. Ameera, Mas'ud, and Yasmeen's cars were all parked on the street. Baby M.A.J was home with her family. For a minute, I felt excited. It was 6:15. I still had time to get in the house, be with my family and pray. By 6:45, I'd have to leave to go back to Mateo.

Hasan opened the door with the biggest smile on his face. After salaming Jibril and Fariba, he grabbed my hand and yanked me into the house then steered me and Fariba into the living room. Jibril headed upstairs to Mas'ud's apartment where my brothers were.

"Aunty Iman, look we got us a baby living with us now," Hasan quipped as he pointed over to Baby M.A.J lying sound asleep in her bassinet.

"Yes, we do. Allah has really blessed us, hasn't He?" I asked Hasan before he stole away with Imran and Munir to go upstairs and play. Yasmeen, now looking much slimmer, laughed before picking up her baby and bringing her over to me. Fariba offered Ummi and Yasmeen salams while I smelled, hugged, kissed, and gazed in the baby's pretty face. I didn't want to, but I passed the baby girl over to Fariba. I didn't have much time.

I headed into the kitchen to grab some drinks for the guests. Ameera was in the kitchen cooking in what looked like her date night clothes. She wore a pair of white skinny jeans paired with a short-sleeved strappy black t-shirt. Her shoulder length brown hair was curled tightly and hanging down. She looked cute.

"You're looking good, girl!" I told her as I grabbed glasses, a tray, and bottles of water from the refrigerator.

"I'm trying. Down another two pounds this week, Alhamduleelah," she admitted.

"*It's going down!*" I sang teasing her. "Seriously, it's really noticeable. You already look like you're 18, in a minute you'll be back at 16," I laughed.

"You ought to talk, Iman. You have not aged, period. I am trying to follow your footsteps," Ameera told me.

"Don't do that. Don't ever do that, Meera. Be you. Healthy habits, Insha'Allah," I warned her as I picked up the full tray. "Got some news to share with you, but I gotta go pray and make a run. Tell you 'bout it later, kay?"

"Kay, but how much later? Umar is gonna take me to the movies around eight. You'll be back before then?"

"Meera, you're not gonna leave Ummi here with all these kids tonight, again? You know she gonna have to help Yaz and Mas'ud with the baby."

"I will put my kids to bed before I go. I told Imran he gonna have to watch Saba already. Besides, Yaz should stay down here with the baby. It'll be easier for her,"

"Um, not really with Umar sleeping down here too. If ya'll can catch a later show, that would be better. Please. I should be back around eight thirty or so. May be nine, Insha'Allah. I'll take Saba and Munir when I get back. Deal?"

"Not trippin' today, Iman. I'll run it by Umar and let you know," Ameera said. Nodding, I excused myself, carrying the tray. I passed by the living room and dropped off drinks for Fariba, Ummi, and Yasmeen before heading upstairs. I climbed all the way up to the attic. Imran came running to the door so I handed him the tray.

"Can you ask Uncle Mas'ud and Uncle Jibril to come here for minute?" I asked him. The smell of Nag Champa incense wafted through the air and made its way to my nostrils.

"You got it, Aunt Iman," he agreed before turning around and strong-arming the tray with a two-step stroll. Knowing Imran would never ask me for help, I giggled and shook my head as he slowly made his way to his father and dropped the tray into his lap. Umar wailed out in pain, "Boy, what's wrong with you? You 'bout to get me all wet!"

"Aunty Iman wanna talk to Uncle Mas'ud and Uncle Jibril. She out there by the door," he told them.

Leaning against the doorway, I could see my brother's face. He looked calm as he got up off the floor to walk towards me. Jibril trailed behind him.

"Salams, what's up?" Mas'ud asked. He'd changed into his house thobe, a short sleeved striped Islamic gown for men. It sure was hot enough for it. Jibril seemed quiet.

"Mateo," I revealed as I handed my brother the note the woman had given me after jumu'ah. "He wants me to meet him at the library at seven."

Mas'ud turned around shaking his head and smiled at Jibril. "You were right, akh - again, man! I'm down two."

"What can I say, bro? I'm a winner. Patience is a virtue… it takes time. You and Shareef can kick rocks," Jibril explained through a laugh.

"Wait. What are you two talking about? What you mean he was right? About what?"

"It don't matter right now," Jibril told me. Mas'ud handed him the note. He glanced at the words quickly and rolled his eyes upward as he folded it back into a square. "Anyway, you can go get ready. We gonna go offer the salah at the masjid. Be back in like fifteen,"

"Yeah, okay, but what's the plan? Am I meeting with Mateo alone?" I asked.

Mas'ud and Jibril exchanged silly looks before my brother shook his head. "Not happening. We'll talk about it on the way, though, Insha'Allah. Go pray and get ready to go," my little brother instructed me before walking away. Jibril stood there looking down at the floor pensively. It felt like he wanted to say something, so I waited for him to speak. He said nothing until Umar off in the distance called out to him.

"Go make salat. And um, make istikharah, too, please," Jibril advised me before he walked away.

Istikharah prayer was a special prayer used when someone needed guidance from Allah about a serious issue. Moving from one place to another place, job hunting, medical procedures, and marriage choices all fell under the category of things that salatul istikharah could be used for. But there was a requirement for the prayer. The one caveat was one needed to be clear on the direction you wanted to go. With everything going on today, this year, these last 12 years, I wasn't sure if I was coming or going. Or running. I walked back down the stairs and headed to the bathroom to make ablution for prayer. By the time I got back in my room, I heard all the men's heavy feet galloping down the stairs followed by the lighter and quicker steps of Hasan, Imran, and Munir trailing behind.

I yanked my prayer garment out of the tightly packed closet full of mine, Ameera, and baby Saba's clothing before pushing and then slamming the door closed. I slipped the loose garment over my head, laid my prayer rug out, and then made takbir:

"Allahu Akbar!"

It was getting harder and harder to find focus while praying. The urge to give in to the whisperings of defeat and failure were all around me. Was it because I was weak? I *was* weak, I knew that. It was my weakness for Mateo initially that had pushed us both into something that neither of us was ready for. I'd blamed him for my troubles, but maybe I created some of his troubles too. He hadn't been ready to be a husband. Like so many other Black and Latino young men, he was born into a world where there were too many hardships and far too much pain waiting to harden him up and spit him out. He didn't have much of a chance. We never had a chance.

"Sami'a Allahu liman hamidah - Allahu Akbar,"

Allah hears those who praise Him. Praise Him, Iman. Whatever you did in the past, leave it there. Stop worrying. Praise Him. Focus. Trust. Seek refuge from all that doubt. You know help is near. You know he cares for you and is trying hard to show that you can count on him. Loyalty. What do you call this? He knows your truth and he didn't run away? That's something real.

Prostrating to the floor, I made sure my forehead, nose, palms, knees, and toes all touched the ground. *Well, get down on your knees and call on your Lord,* Abu had always reminded us whenever we had any problem. This position was the closest I could get to my Lord in this world to demonstrate to Him my weakness while simultaneously demonstrating my need for His guidance, pardon, and everlasting love.

"*Subhana Rabbiyal A'la,*" I recited three times.

The second, and finally the third units of prayer came much easier, sweeter, even. By the time I got to the last sujood, I rested my face on the floor and let the tears flow. The washing was such a needed relief from the depths of my soul. It felt good to pour out my needs and wants and fears and shame with the One who had created me. The Only One whose love for me was limitless and full of mercy. This was a connection that had carried me through the darkness and illuminated my steps back to the family He had chosen for me in the beginning. This was what I always needed to learn. This had always been the test.

I rose from that evening prayer refreshed, strengthened, and with certainty. I had made my decision. But, I didn't have time to offer the prayer for guidance. I rushed out of the bedroom, ran into the bathroom, and jumped into the shower. I quickly rinsed my body clean and sprayed the water from the showerhead over my head. A few minutes later, I was back in my room drying off. I decided to change my clothing too. I busted open the closet and scanned until I found a jade green umbrella abaya made out of Koshibo. It was light, loose, and feminine. I wore a simple slip underneath it and matched it up with black gladiator high heel sandals and a black on black Swarovski studded shayla. I wrapped the long material around my head, pinned it in the back, and brought the flowy chiffon material back around my chest area to cover up the front with a silver star pin.

I grabbed my large leather bucket handbag stuffed the divorce papers in it, threw my cell phone, keys, and mace in it. I didn't know what I needed to take really, but I needed to cover my bases.

"You look nice. Where *you* going?" Meera asked as she carried Saba in her arms and placed her down on the bed. Hands on her hips, she sucked her teeth before I had a chance to even answer her. "Umar said we can't go to the movies now. He said he gotta go somewhere with you and Mas'ud," she told me.

"Really? Umar's going?"

"That's what he said. I wish you would have invited me too. I know you worried about Yaz and Ummi being here with all the kids, but them two can manage. Whatever ya'll got going on, I should be there too."

"Meera, you sound silly. This isn't some outing to Kennywood. You're not going to miss anything, believe me. Fariba's here with ya'll, too," I tried to explain to her.

"And? I am saying why can't I go? Umar is leaving Sunday. You're stealing my time. At the very least I should know where ya'll going!"

"No, you shouldn't, Ameera. But you know what, I almost forgot I had some good news for you," I told her as I walked over to door to close it. "So alhamduleelah, Jibril and Fariba got word that Shareef is coming home next week, Insha'Allah," I told her smiling from ear to ear.

"You're kidding? You better not be playing with me?" she demanded with a big smile of her own.

"Wouldn't dare. Keep this to yourself, meaning do not tell Ummi yet. Those are Shareef's orders Fariba said."

"I cannot wait to see that man! Guess we'll be going from having the aqiqah for the baby girl to planning a wedding," Ameera noted.

"A wedding? For who?" I snapped.

"Iman, ain't nobody tripping over you no more, girl. I'm talking about a wedding for Fariba and my big brother Shareef, Insha'Allah"

"Oh, okay. Yeah, yeah, Insha'Allah! Now that will be fun. Everybody will come."

"True, you know all the old heads will come. Ummi and Aunty Adilah will officially be family. They been waiting and praying for this to happen some kind of way for decades. That good ol' dua from mothers. Can't mess with it."

"Hmmm, that is something."

"Ain't it."

The door busted open and Imran came running in. "Aunty, Uncle Mas'ud said for you come down and hurry it up," my nephew told me. Ameera popped him on top of his head.

"He did not add all the freshness, boy! I know my brother better than you do. Watch yo' mouth around me for I tell your Abu,"

Imran mouthed sorry to me before racing right back out of the room. I hugged my sister and got up off the bed.

"As salamu alykum, Ameera. Insha'Allah, I'll be back a little later. We'll talk more then."

After kissing my Umm, my sisters, and baby M.A. J. I headed out the door. Outside I saw Mas'ud in his van with Umar sitting upfront. Behind his vehicle was Jibril in his Infiniti with Hamad, Ya'coob and two other big boned, security guard looking Muslim brothers that I recognized from my childhood. They were friends of Shareef's. They'd brought the squad. What were they planning?

I walked over to the other side of the van, opened the door, and sat behind my brother. Umar and him were talking loud and intensely. It seemed like they didn't even register my presence. Mas'ud tossed some papers over to Umar. Umar seemed annoyed. He gathered up the papers and carefully folded them in half before putting them in his little file folder.

"That still doesn't change what you did!" Mas'ud informed him.

"Akh, how's that? You really won't believe nothing? What I do? Huh? What did *I* do? This," Umar said holding up his file, "This right here proves I was truthful, concerned, and protecting myself and my family. That's what this is. You know so, when you come around to it, an apology would be fair. But it is what it is and you know what akh, we family. I ain't holding nothing against you. Take your time," Umar offered solemnly.

"I intend to." Mas'ud noted as he pulled out of the driveway. Now was my time to interject my concerns.

"Why so many people, Mas'ud? Don't you think this might be a little intimidating for Mateo?"

My brother turned around to look over his shoulder at me and his gaze said it all. The furrowed eyebrows and tight lips were the judgment he didn't have to speak. He didn't like the way I phrased it. I sounded too much like a wife, too concerned for the safety of my monster. I was concerned for everyone's safety but admittedly, I had included Mateo's safety as well. This was hard. Feeling anything for him was now *haraam* for me. I knew it and I knew that I had to stop. I didn't know how to scrub my heart and mind clean quick enough.

"Ain't enough brothers, if you ask me. He lucky, though," Umar started. "Boy oh boy, I wish he'd showed up in North Philly like this. We could've really showed out. Now, you promised me Mas'ud, if he bucks, I get first crack at him."

Mas'ud shook his head and laughed. "Bro, I ain't tell you no such thing. We got this all worked out and we gonna follow the plans. No bucking, no cracking heads - none of that. We gonna treat this man decent and give him some simple options. He gonna have an opportunity to do the right thing. He take it, Alhamduleelah. He buck or show out, then it's whatever it's gonna be."

"And that's when I get first crack at him?" Umar asked excitedly.

"No," I barked knowing full well what I was saying. Umar turned around and looked at me this time. "No violence. Really you guys, no violence. That's all Mateo knows. It's why he's messed up now. And it's... it's not right! Look, you're here, Umar, and I am glad you want to help. But I think we gotta show him a better way. We're Muslims. Right?"

"Ah, man, I'm sorry, Iman. I like to joke around a lot. I don't mean nothing by it. I know this can't be easy," Umar noted apologetically. "My Mom's had this slim crazy dude that she would go back and forth with. He was so greasy he'd pop her in the eye for breathing too loud. She'd kick him out for a spell. He be right back a week or two later sleeping on our couch. One day, Mom couldn't take it anymore. She had a heart attack and died at 35. Me and my sister got sent to DCYF, the school of hard knocks. It ain't easy for nobody dealing with that crap. But Iman, you gotta make a choice right now. You want us to roll up and give this bull his shahadah and marry ya'll for real? Or you ready to end this by any means necessary? How you want this to go down?" my brother-in-law asked.

I fell back into the seat and sighed. They didn't get it. Or me. I was the one who had risked my life to get away from Mateo. I had already made my choice. How many times and ways did I have to tell these people I wanted out? Did they have a right to know that I was trying to find some forgiveness in my heart for him and me? We had both done a lot of wrong. If I was going to forgive myself, I had to forgive him too? Right?

"No violence," I warned. "That's all I am going to say about it," I insisted as I folded my arms across my body and looked out of the window.

"Aye," Mas'ud called. "Isn't the library closed on Fridays? Why you think he picked this spot to meet at?" he asked me as he pulled up in front of the newly remodeled branch. All the lights were turned off. But still, it looked nothing like it had years ago, when I'd worked there. It was now sleek with high glass windows, bright, shiny paint and colorful murals decorating the outside and inside and a nicely manicured lawn. Back in the days, Mateo and I had spent many evenings there reading books, scanning through travel magazines, looking at pictures of Santo Domingo and dreaming about visiting Calle Las Damas and Casas Reales - together.

"We met here. I used to work here after school. Abu used to pick me up right over there on the corner," I said pointing out of the window. "You probably don't remember. You were really young then, Moody."

"Wow!" he gasped dragging the sound out too long. "So this fool is reminiscing 'bout ya'll past or something? Now that's some crazy and sick stuff," Mas'ud quipped.

Rolling my eyes upward harder than I needed to, I turned my whole body to the other side. This was all starting to suck the air out of my lungs. I was suffocating. In a split second, I saw *him* walking up to the car. He had this walk that was such a calm and focused bop and he always looked clean. Not until that moment did I realize how much his presence had the ability to spread calmness and balance to my world. He stopped right in front of the passenger's side and tapped on the window. Umar popped the locks.

"Salamu alykum," Jibril greeted us as he climbed into the back of the van smelling like Cool Water cologne. He sat in the row behind me. "Everything is ready to go," he informed us. "Iman, you doing alright?" Jibril inquired.

"Yeah." I told him without making any eye contact. My eyes were fixed on the shiny black Lexus that had passed us twice and was now parking across the street. I was waiting for the text to come to confirm who I thought was in the car. It didn't come. Instead my cellphone started ringing. I held my hand up to my brothers before I answered the call to get their attention. Everyone turned towards me and stopped talking

"*Si! Tato. Donde esta?*" I asked him as I watched him get out of the driver's side of his car. He never responded. I hit the end button.

"Is that Mateo? Is that your ex husband?" Mas'ud questioned me as he looked at him walking over to the van as if he was confused. Mateo didn't look like a big bad wolf. He always knew how to present himself.

"Uh huh, that's him." Time slowed all the way down during the seconds it took for him to walk those few steps across the street towards us. I wasn't afraid. I wasn't angry. I wasn't hurting. I was facing him. All of him. The soft, funny, and handsome *tigre* with the pronounced and rich accent who loved his mama and his brothers. The angry little boy whose father was aggressively killed on the streets of New York before he got a chance to father his sons. The bibliophile who introduced me to the works of Jose "Cha-Cha" Jimenez, Julia Alvarez, Frank Baez, Fred Hampton, and Stokely Carmichael. And then there was the man who was my husband who had been so mean, so possessive, and so abusive all at the same time.

"Stay in the car," I heard Jibril instruct me before he and my brothers got out of the van leaving me behind with the Qur'an playing in the CD changer.

Mateo looked healthy and sober. He'd lost a bit a weight and was looking much slender. His eyes were clear and dark. His skin was tanned a rich toffee complexion and his moustache and goatee were freshly lined up. He'd let his curly hair grow out some too. It was now bouncing right above his shoulders. He was dressed casually in a pair of khaki fitted Chinos, and a pale green button down shirt that he paired with black leather sandals. Maybe he really did go get therapy.

Mas'ud was the first to speak up to him. Mateo responded by extending his hand out to Mas'ud and then shaking his head with a smirk. Mas'ud refused to shake his hand and started to say something back to Mateo when Jibril interrupted, stepping right in front of my window blocking my view. I pressed my ears on to the glass. Praying silently that they would all stay calm and reminded of Allah. But that wasn't the case. They were all talking and I heard Umar throw out an expletive and boom I turned my head just in time to watch Diego and this big black guy get out of the Lexus from across the street. Demented Diego was what Evelyn had always called him. I jumped up and pulled the keys out of the engine and slid across the seat to pop the locks. Yanking open the door, I ran out the van as fast I could in my heels. The fear finally found me. It slapped me so hard, I felt a dull throbbing right in the middle of my chest. In the blink of my eyes, I was standing there facing my monster.

Mateo sighed deeply and hard as if he was comforted by my sight. A real smile full of milky white teeth spread softly across his face as he beamed at me. He tenderly spoke the name he created for me when I used to be his. "*Imania!*" he sang out. "*Mi primer amor. Tienes los ojos mas bonitos del mundo.*" He used to always say that to me when he was in a good mood. He was in a good mood today. Mateo was infectious. I had to force myself not to reciprocate. I had so much hate and love for him still festering inside of me. I felt ashamed and cast my eyes downward.

"*Basta ya, Mateo! Que lo que?*" I questioned him before turning to my brothers, "What's going on?" I said repeating myself.

"We're good here," Jibril told me stiffly. I immediately sensed his attitude. "You wanna go back in the van?" he questioned me but really it was an order of protection. I was hesitant to follow suit.

"What? Why? She ain't in no danger. Mi vida, stay," Mateo ordered walking closer to me than he should have. Mas'ud immediately stepped in front of me and sized him up and down. Mateo stepped back with one foot, but became noticeably agitated. "I was about to suggest we go sit down somewhere. I'd like get to know your brothers more. And you and me can talk too. I'd like to finish our business. Pallantia is right in Shadyside. Nice cocktails, some of the freshest seafood. Let me treat your family," he suggested, glancing back to Diego. Diego seemed anxious, though, as he glanced around the streets.

"Actually, we don't do bars," Mas'ud told him. "But there's a spot in the Strip, Saleem's Market. We could go there if you talking about getting the papers signed tonight. If not, we not trying to waste no time with you eating."

Mateo smiled politely before looking back and eying Diego again and the black man that was with them. Diego checked his cell phone before nodding his head. "Of course, I'm here to talk about the papers. Long as your sister is ready to talk about some marital things too. I'd like to discuss some business issues with Colon Nacional Dominicana. Right, Nia?" he informed us. Mateo knew good and well he was pissing off my brothers, but I tried to show I wasn't fazed by it. I shook my head no. I had nothing to do with his company any more.

"I already done told you to only address us," Jibril advised him. "We're here to talk to you, not Iman." Jibril's voice was stern and cold. Mateo eyebrows furrowed and his lips tightened. He was definitely angered now.

"Look, my man, all that loud talkin' ain't necessary. I heard what you said the first time. Ya'll wanna represent her and discuss the situation, cool. But let me now be very clear with you: Imania is *my* wife. I ain't here to take no orders from you or nobody else about *my* wife. Ya'll posted and wanna stunt, it's all good. I'm trying to be easy and handle this like a good guy 'cause I got nothing against you people. Never have. But I ain't new to the game. I can roll my sleeves up and bring it, my man."

"Oh, it can be whatever and however you want it!" Jibril replied sternly. "But if you trying to lead this, it ain't happening. Iman," he turned around and called my name before he pleaded with me, "Go get back in the van. Please." My eyes scanned the circle of men and my heart dropped as I sensed the thick tension encircling us. Mateo and Jibril's bravado was blinding them. I glanced across the street and I could see Danny's mother's eyes peering right at me. I raised my hand and waved at her. She quickly opened the back-passenger door of the Lexus and jogged across the street. She clicked and clacked her hand me down heels right up to Mateo and took his hand into hers and rubbed it. I wondered who she really was there with.

"*Gracias, prima,*" I whispered before I started to walk away.

"*Me llamo Lissette, prima!*" she said revealing her first name finally. "*Hey, Manito, tenga uno problema!*" I heard her say. "Di que, I got a call about Danny…"

I hadn't taken more than two or threes steps before Mateo sighed loudly ripping his hand away from the woman then pushed her away from him all at once. He raised his fist into the air then punched it his other hand, "Imania!" he barked, stepping away from Lissette. "Mami, I asked you nicely to stay put. I wanna talk to you! Look at me! This is about us – you know I love you! You know I am not here to hurt you." Mateo's angered tone was one I knew all too well, but him begging was new to me. My feet froze mid stride as my heartbeats became louder. I didn't know how I could defuse him without giving him what he desperately sought from me. Turning back around slowly, I tried to walk back towards him, I extended my hand towards him and he began to reach for me but Mas'ud wouldn't allow it.

"Don't do it, Imani! Get out of here!" my brother commanded shoving me harshly back the other direction.

"*Stupido!* What is this? Nah, that's your wife right there," Diego growled at Mateo prompting him to suddenly drive his full body weight right into Mas'ud knocking him backwards off his heels as he reached out, grabbing my arm tightly. "Don't let them change you, baby. Come with me, Nia!" he yelled voraciously. Before I could find the words to explain to him that it was him who had changed me for the worst, there was a pile up of men all around me. They were boxing, tussling, punching, and kicking as I was knocked to the ground as well. Shareef's other two friends came galloping down the street like jaguars and wasted no time jumping into the struggle. I fought to get up but was dragged away from the altercation by Mas'ud kicking and screaming. He picked me up and threw me in the van before locking me in.

Screaming as loud and as hard as I could until my throat felt raw while bullets of tears streamed from my eyes I caught a glimpse of both Mateo and Fresh entangled together. Mateo was being out weighed, out hit, and outsmarted. He was losing. Umar and the others were holding off Diego and his boy, but they were giving it everything they had to get through to Mateo.

Then blood sprayed out from Mateo's mouth as his head violently knocked from one side to the next. I screamed louder, kicked faster, and banged with all my might on the inside of the door calling on Allah through sobs for it all to stop. That's when I saw her run over to Diego. She was screaming and crying too. She was screaming for Diego to help *Mateo*! She threw something to him. Umar ran up on her to try to disrupt the flight of the chrome gliding through the air. He was too late. It landed right in Diego hands – in what seemed like slow motion. My ears went deaf, my voice went flat, my thinking paused and then my breathing slowed all the way down.

"No! No! No! Allah! No! No!"

Diego fired his gun several times into the crowd of men.

I couldn't watch anymore. My heart burst. Darkness engulfed me.

Chapter 12

ↄ

"When you have taken a decision, put your trust in Allah" (Quran 3: 159).

"Abi, I gotta lot of work to do tonight at the library. Can you please, please, please pick me up at 7? Please!"

"Iman and I got alotta sleeping to do. I get one day off you know that? Why can't I ever use it how I want to? Don't seem right to me," the father chuckled as he sat reclined in his La-Z-Boy chair with his Noble Qur'an folder on his chest. "Now how I remember it going was you telling your Umm and me that you needed this job and it's so close to the house and it's safe 'round that way and it's the greatest job for a Muslima to have and it's gonna look good on your college applications. All you said you needed was that bus pass that I went ahead and paid for. You got the bus pass, right?" he questioned her as he tipped his head down and his glasses slid down the bridge of his nose.

"Abi! Can you please pick me up? Pretty please! I hate taking that bus at night. It's so smelly and slow. If you pick me up, I can watch Moody tomorrow night while you and Ummi go to your karate class."

"And? What else?"

"Abi, really! C'mon, that's bribery."

"You started it. Now sweeten the deal,"

She laughed hard. "Man, oh man! Okay, Abi. I'll watch Moody and Meera for the rest of the month, every Saturday. And I'll wash your car, too."

"Allahu Akbar. Now you talkin' that talk I like to hear, Imani. But you know what?

"What's that, Abi?"

"I would've done it for a hug too. You didn't offer me that, though. Guess you're too big now to give your father a hug these days."

"Abi, I will never be too big to hug you," she told him as she walked over to him and wrapped both her arms around his neck and lightly kissed his bushy bearded face. "I love you to the moon and back. You're the best. See you at seven, Insha'Allah."

"Make sure you make salat before you go to work. And be safe on the bus too. Don't talk to any strangers, kiddo."

"Abi, I'll be fine. Salaams!"

***

"Shhh! Young man, please lower your voice. And Miss Johnson, please talk to your friend after hours," the reference department's supervisor warned her before turning on her heels and walking out of the room.

She rolled her eyes upward. He stuck up his middle finger and blew raspberries at the woman's back. The girl muffled her laughter as she shook her head. He was something else. He always knew how to get a smile out of her when she needed it.

"Mi amor, mi vida, mi mujer! See you later." the young Afro-Latino man promised. He stood about six feet tall, walked with a confident bop, had pretty dark brown eyes, super curly hair, and smooth skin. He came to the library every day and always took out one or two books. He was older than her by a few years.

"Six fifteen out front," she reminded him. She was covered modestly in a long jean skirt, a pink button down collared shirt, and a white flowy Georgette hijab pinned around the front of the shirt.

A smirk spread across his face as he nodded his head and bopped out of the library's swinging doors. Inside his car, he sat reading Soul On Ice by Eldridge Cleaver while Brand Nubian played softly in background. As he licked the tip of his finger to turn the page, his beeper went off. He yanked the clip off the side of his belt that was under his Karl Kani shirt. Glancing at the number, he grimaced and cursed out loud, threw his book down into the passenger seat, reached into the glove compartment and *pulled out the small shiny Smith and Wesson revolver. He quickly stuffed the handgun in his pants before turning the engine on. He sped off right before she walked out of the library.*

She waited and waited. He wasn't anywhere to be found. Her heart sank as she slowly walked back into the library to finish working. At seven on the dot, she packed up her things into her bags, waved good bye to her co-workers, and went outside to wait for her father. He wasn't there yet, but she knew her Abu was on his way. His word was his bond.

It was the guy she wanted to be her guy who pulled up first. He looked fly to her in his old black '85 Toyota Corolla with those fancy retractable headlights. She beamed brightly as he parked up on the curb. Her heart sped up and her hands got all soft and clammy. She was excited that she was going to get a chance to talk to him for a few minutes before the night ended. He jumped out of his car wearing those heavy Lugz' boots on his feet. Concern was painted all over his face. Her smile faded. Her eyes were fixated on him as he looked over his shoulder like he expected someone to jump out at him. She didn't want to get worked up. She remained calm as he met her. He didn't speak. He grabbed her hand forcibly and pulled her over to his car, opened the door, and then said, "Get in!"

"Well hello to you too, Mr. Colon" she said through a jittery smile. "You're a little too late, though. My father is coming now, Mateo."

"Yea, I know. But I need you to come make a run with me. Get in," he ordered again. Dropping his head in shame at his harshness, he loosened up. "Por favor, mi amor!" he asked her nicely. Iman sighed and he smirked. "You know I wouldn't ask you to help me if I didn't really need your help, your intelligence, and all that beauty. I'll get you home soon. You know you can always trust me, right?"

She did trust him. He'd only shown her kindness, respect, and sugary sweetness. She knew exactly when she started to trust him too. It was three months ago, when he took her to the movies and snuck her into see House Party on its opening night when everyone from her high school was there. Mateo had been nothing but a gentleman. He'd bought her an extra large buttered popcorn, a box of Swedish Fish, and a large cherry slushy all for herself. He didn't try anything either. He kept his hands to himself the whole time even though his brother Manuel's girlfriend Evelyn was sitting across from them being fresh. Mateo told her that night he was happy and proud she was different and covered. He loved that she was a good girl.

From the back window of his car, Iman saw her father driving up the street. Mateo dropped his foot on the gas and sped off.

That was the last time she saw her father alive.

She sat at the table watching him eating his food. She cooked him Guisado and white rice the way his Abuela Aida showed her how to. He liked it a lot. In between mouthfuls, he'd smile and thank her for his food so graciously as if she was some star chef at a five-star hotel. It was time to speak up. She had nothing to lose. Everyday since she arrived in Santo Domingo with his family she'd dreamed about this moment. She'd tried to bring up going back home to her own family so many times. But every time she'd strike up the conversation, he'd get agitated so she would decide to change the subject. He was drinking, smoking, and hanging out with his brothers and cousins all the time now. She'd seen the guns, the stolen cars, the jewelry, and she knew now that she was in the wrong world. She couldn't live like this much longer. Ramadhan was coming too. Surely Allah would make a way out for her.

"I - don't - want - to ...... do - this - any - more!" Iman pushed each word out of her throat one at a time in a clear and loud voice. "It's been over a year and I haven't seen my parents," she tried reasoning with him in a much softer tone. "Can you please take me home, Manito?"

"Oh, okay. Really? So, you going to go and leave your man like that?" he questioned her as he threw down his fork, pushed the plate of remaining food away from him, and stood up. He grabbed the shot glass from off the dining room table and downed the remaining brown liquor in one gulp before slamming it back onto the table. Her shoulders flinched. "I take care of you. I provide for you. I love you. Now you got the nerve to be ungrateful?" he scolded Iman while taking a couple of steps closer to her. She sat calmly, avoiding eye contact with him as he stood over her

breathing wildly flexing his muscles. She was hoping he would cool down. She had no reason to fear him. She trusted him. It didn't work that time, though. Mateo grabbed her ponytail with his hand and snatched back her head forcing her eyes to focus on his face.

"Basta ya, Mateo! You're hurting me," she wailed as tears rolled down her brown cheeks. "Por favor!"

"Why should I stop, huh?" he yelled at her yanking her head with each word. "You don't know how to appreciate nothing. You don't got nothing to worry about, but you. I saved you, you know that? I protected you. Could've let them wet up your whole family. But I didn't. I thought about what you needed. I'm always taking care of you, giving you everything I got and now look at you? Look at you, Imania! Stupida! Should've left a hoodrat in the hood," he concluded before slamming her head into the wooden table and storming away.

The warm blood from her nose dripped down her lips mixing with her salty tears and stained her arm and then the table. The sobs rocked through her body. Iman knew good and well she wouldn't ever be able to bring up her leaving ever again. She also knew she no longer had any trust in Mateo.

"Haven't you realized by now that it's not going to change whatever happened to you all those years you were out there alone? You were hurt. You made bad choices. You got issues. I am sorry that it happened to you and that I couldn't have been there to help you and protect you. Allah put me here right now. I am offering you help right now. Take it. Don't let Shaytan win this round. Take the help," he barked at her.

She wanted to be able to. She wanted to be able to know that he would be there for her. But she was afraid. She'd lost so much life, honor, and peace in those 12 years. How could she really trust again? Would he really be able to be trusted with all that pained her and that made her strong? She wanted to finally get a chance to stand in her truth and be the woman that Allah created her to be. She wanted to know that he would help her heal and be a better woman, a better Muslimah, a better daughter and

*sister. She knew she couldn't do it alone. She'd have to take the help. Iman
reached out her hand...*

"Iman, wake up, baby! Bismillah, you can do it! Open your eyes up
right now! You hear me? Iman, wake up right now, girl," Ummi begged
me. As my eyes fluttered open and I tried to regain control over my
sight, I caught focus of the room. The bright lights. The tiled walls. The
white shades. Turning my head right and then left to take in the whole
room I shot up quickly to sit up straight. I was frightened by what I
saw. None of it was familiar.

"Where am I? Mas'ud? Where's Jibril? Oh, Allah?" I screamed. My
mother was sitting right next to me in the bed. She grabbed my body
and hugged me tightly before kissing my forehead. Sitting across from
her was Ameera. She got up out of the chair she was sitting in and came
over to us. She sat on the edge of the bed and grabbed my hand. She
looked so sad.

I cried harder. "Where are they?" I yelled again shaking in my
mother's warm arms.

"Would you quiet up all that loud yapping, Iman! Calm down,"
Mas'ud's voice cut through the air sharply as he entered the room
carrying a pitcher of ice water. "This is a hospital. There are real sick
people in here trying to get some rest," he informed me. He walked
around to me, leaned his tall frame down and gave me a big hug.
"Alhamduleelah," he said kissing my cheek, "glad to see you awake,
sis."

"What am I doing here?" I asked everyone. Ummi poured me a cup
of ice water.

"You fainted," Ameera said rubbing my arm now. "How you feeling
now, sis?"

"The doctor said it's was a minor concussion," Ummi told me
cutting off Ameera. "How do you feel, Iman? Does anything hurt?"

"I feel okay," I admitted as I rubbed my hand through my loose
hair. "Where's my hijab?" My mother got up and grabbed my black

jersey knit scarf off the window ledge and brought it back over to the bed and handed it to me. I quickly wrapped the hijab around my head and chest so I felt covered. Ummi handed me the cup of water. Sipping the liquid slowly, it dawned on me again that I hadn't accounted for everyone. I placed the cup of water on the tray next to my bed.

"Where is everyone else?" I demanded.

"Umar is at the house with the kids. Yaz too," Ameera offered first.

"Ya'coob, Hamad, Musa, and Kareem went to the masjid," Mas'ud went on. "They'll be back later."

I nodded my head up and down. They knew I was waiting on more information. I didn't feel the need to say it out loud again.

"Oh, and Jibril is here too," my sister finally announced happily. "I saw him talking to the police a little while ago."

I inhaled slowly but hard as I could and thanked Allah silently before releasing it. "So, that's everybody. Everybody is okay. Right?" I questioned my brother.

"It got crazy, but Alhamduleelah we made it out. You're safe and that's what matters now. Guess I will go get the officer so that you can give your statement and then we can work on getting you discharged. I'll be right back." Mas'ud got up off the bed and walked out of the hospital room leaving me behind with Ummi and Ameera.

"Ya'll know ya'll all need a butt whoopin'. Nobody told none of you to go do something so dangerous and foolish. Putting everyone in danger unnecessarily when that's what the police department is for. Their job is to serve and protect. I almost had another heart attack when Jibril called me. Like to 'scare me to death."

"I am so sorry, Ummi. I didn't mean for any of this to happen. It got out of hand so fast and it didn't even accomplish anything. He didn't sign the divorce papers. I am still married to a monster!"

"You mean these papers right here?" Ameera said as she grabbed a stack of white 8 x 12's. "He sure did sign them. My husband made sure of that before he left the hospital. Umar said to tell you that you made the right decision," before she handed them to me.

I sat up straight in the hospital bed in disbelief. I flipped through all the pages slowly until I reached the last page. There in black ink was Mateo's signature. I started laughing lightly out of sheer disbelief. The monster set me free. He really did it. I was finally free of him after almost 13 years. Alhamduleelah. Allahu Akbar. He finally had made a way out for me too.

There was a light tap on the door. Mas'ud appeared again. "You ready? I have the officer who needs to speak with you," he told me.

"Yeah, let him in," I instructed my brother. A short stout Latino officer with a receding hairline walked in wearing all the on duty gear he could find. It looked like it was weighing him down the way he was shuffling across the floor over to me. The equipment was either too heavy or he was too overweight to bear it. It really wasn't my business, but it was noticeable.

"Good evening, everyone. I'll only take a few minutes of you folks' time here," he assured us all as he scanned the room looking at each one of us individually and pulled out a note pad and pen. "Mrs. Colon, I know you were out for a good amount of time and maybe you are still experiencing some amnesia surrounding the deadly altercation with your estranged husband. But any information will help to move this investigation forward for the victims' families so that they can have some closure."

"Wait! What? What victims? What was deadly?" I asked getting riled up again. My heart thumped. I had accounted for everyone. Mateo signed the papers. "Who died?" I yelled at the officer.

"Ma'am, I am very sorry. I thought you knew already," the officer alleged. He looked over to my brother. Mas'ud shook his head at the officer granting him permission to discuss the details with me. "Mr. Diego Thomas Colon was DOA. One self-inflicted gun wound to the head."

"Diego! ¡La hawla wala quwata ila billah! Oh, Diego." My eyes immediately started to release tears for the crazy and wild younger brother of Mateo that I had lived with for many years.

"And also, Miss Lisette Karina Reyes. Two gunshot wounds to the chest. She passed away in the ambulance enroute to the hospital."

"What? ¡Mi prima! ¿Mi prima? No," I kept asking in Spanish how that could have happened. It didn't make sense. I saw her throw the gun to Diego! "Y ven aca! I saw Diego catch the gun. I saw him shooting. Lisette, mi prima, she was trying to help, right?"

The officer was shaking his head as he wrote words down on onto his note pad. None of this was making sense.

"From all accounts thus far, Miss Reyes was shot by Mr. Diego Thomas Colon," the officer informed me. "Lo siento mucho, Mrs. Colon."

"Diego shot up into the air a couple of times and then pointed the gun right at Mateo," Mas'ud explained. "Diego was trying to kill Mateo. Mateo yelled at the other guy to get at Diego, but it was too late. His brother shot at him and the woman came out of nowhere and jumped in front of him. We all stopped. Mateo grabbed her and Jibril and I tried to help stop the bleeding while Ya'coob called for an ambulance. Kareem and Hamad went to my van to grab some bandages but that's when they found you knocked out. It was crazy. I ran around to go check on you and the gun went off again. Diego had shot himself."

I froze.

"Mrs. Colon, we have a lot of old charges on the Colon brothers. With your active restraining order against Mr. Mateo Victor Colon and a testimony from you against him detailing some of his illegal operations, we potentially have a really strong case against him. With your help, you can help us put him away for a very long time. Can you give me any information about his import business, Colon Nacional Dominicana headquartered in Atlanta, Georgia? Mrs. Colon? Mrs. Colon, can you hear me?"

"Call the doctor! Now," Ummi yelled.

The darkness found me again.

Chapter 13

The sun was setting. She sat on the deck at the patio table with a steaming cup of black coffee, a bowl of walnuts and dried cranberries, flipping through an Essence magazine as she chewed her snack leisurely. The weather was warmer. The aromatic spring air mixed with the early blooming daffodils and forsythia adding a splash of color to her garden she gazed out on every once and awhile. She was settled. She knew exactly what was going to happen, when, and where. It had to go down like this. She took a sip of the coffee.

"Dimelo, Mami!" he crooned as he pulled open the sliding door and walked out onto the patio wearing his workout clothes and sneakers. He had just come back from the gym and hadn't showered yet. His scent offended her space. Then again, everything he did or said or didn't say offended her too. He pulled out a chair and sat down. He smirked at her boyishly before he reached over touching her hand to take the cup of coffee out of it. His fingers glided over her hand ever so lightly.

"Que?" she asked annoyed. "What's the matter with you?"

"Mi primer amor. Tienes los ojos mas bonitos del mundo," he reaffirmed to her before sipping several gulps of the hot liquid then placing the cup back down on the glass table.

She sucked her teeth boldly before hissing: "Were my eyes the most beautiful in the world when you hit me upside my head last night?" She asked it knowing it could spark a flame she wouldn't be able to put out. It was too late to take it back, though. He flexed the muscles in his jaw. She'd made him uncomfortable. He didn't like to talk about the abuse. He never acknowledged the hurt or pain she felt publicly. He'd leave the house just so he didn't have to hear or see her cry. He'd convinced himself she always asked for it by pressing his buttons. He'd convinced himself that his love, his provisions, and his care for her were always greater, more important than the abuse he inflicted. They were still together. She was still his muse. That was all the proof he needed.

"You know they were. Of course they were. They always are," he revealed hesitantly. He surveyed her body from head to toe slowly, enjoying the view. She was wearing a silky, flowy black and cream long caftan with batwings embellished with little white balls of fringe. Just the edges of her shoulder length curly brown hair peeped out from underneath the cream colored pashmina scarf she wore loosely wrapped around her head and neck. Her youthful smooth butter pecan face was scrubbed clean of any make-up, but her dark almond shaped eyes were still mesmerizing. Her hands were soft and delicately manicured. And her feet were bare and soft. This was the girl he had fallen in love with. She had always been such a good girl. "You're still the most beautiful woman I've ever seen, Imania. I don't know what I'd do without you. Life is just... hard, though,"

"Life has been hard," Iman agreed. "Too hard."

"I know and I'm ssso..." he struggled to bring himself to formally apologize to her, but just couldn't pull it out. He recognized her suffering and all the losses she'd borne over the years while carrying his seeds. She didn't deserve that. That hurt him. But it was those beautiful babies he never got to hold that would come to him in his deepest sleep and chastise him whenever he'd go too far with their mother that he was ashamed of the most. He was failing them, just like his Papa had failed him. He'd give anything to just touch his children and feel their love just one time in his life. He prayed faithfully that the Almighty would forgive him and finally give them a chance to be parents. "Things can change, you know. I can change. I want to, for you. I am trying, Imania. It's just... it ain't easy for me to control it," he confided to her in a low voice. Admitting he had a problem finally after all those years of being confused and angered by his own anger felt freeing. He hoped she still could be sympathetic.

"I know, I know." Iman had sympathy. She even still had love for him. It was complex simplicity. She saw all of the good and evil evenly. Most days, though, the evil inside him overpowered him. This was a rare

moment when they were both mourning what could have been.

"Last time I went to go see Manny he told me about this counselor he was seeing."

"Manny is in therapy? Really?" she asked quizzically with a raised eyebrow.

"Yeah, he is. He said it's the best thing he did, too. It's helping him a lot to work through the past. And this shrink he sees has an office out in Decatur. I think I might go check him out. Let him run a full battery of tests on me. Gotta start somewhere," Mateo admitted to his wife.

"Velda? You are going to go see a shrink? Mateo since when have you been open to the White man's psychology?" she asked incredulously with a smirk on her face. She thought back to their early days back in Pittsburgh when he would talk her ear off about how Afrocentric politics, health, and psychology were missing from their communities. Back then, Mateo had been for the people, an idealist prone to socialism and in full support of black and brown power movements.

"Who said the shrink practiced Eurocentric psychology? You know me better than that, Nia. I wouldn't sit with those nut cases for nothing. Dr. Femi Kwesi is a master herbalist, ordained Yoruba priest, and has two degrees in psychology from Morehouse." he rattled off proudly.

"Interesting," Iman scoffed. She grabbed the cup from the table and took a sip.

Mateo smiled at his wife playfully. "I know you ain't into those ancestral beliefs and whatnot, but it's deeper than that for me. I need help, Nia. I'm getting way too old to be living like this. Not being able to control nothing, I don't like it," Mateo admitted.

"May be if you stopped drinking so much, Mateo. Maybe that might help some," Iman offered.

"True. Maybe that would help the both of us," he replied with a wink at her before leaning back into the chair and putting one of his hands behind his back. He pondered and then offered, "I ain't mean nothing by that, really. I know most of our issues start with me. I gotta find the willpower to make some big changes or this crap I got inside of me is *gonna kill me. Imma go to see the doc and if he can help me get myself together, that would be good. So you know, I hope you will come with me and support me through this too." Mateo leaned forward to get closer to Iman. He picked up and placed her small slender hands inside of his larger ones and lightly kissed them. "I still need you!"*

Iman was quiet as he massaged her hands. She could offer him no response appropriate for that moment. She just prayed to Allah he was sincere. Not for her sake. But for his own. She had her plans. By the will of Allah, she had every intention to follow through.

"What time's your flight tomorrow?" she asked him in an attempt to change the topic of conversation.

"Oh, um, early. Too early. You just reminded me to get Jorge for that too. That boy's useless, you know? Who schedules a flight for four am? If Mama goes back to D.R. this summer she's gonna have to take her nephew with her. That boy doesn't have a brain and my hands are already full watching over Diego like a hawk. Diego having kids all over the place he don't even wanna have anything to do with and child support payments I gotta pay for him. I don't like him doing family wrong like that. Then that fool still messing up simple orders. I really wish I could get rid of Diego too. They're both costing me thousands every month. It's just too much all the time. I really need Manny back. Hey, you sure you don't wanna come with me to London? I could use your intelligence and all that beauty."

"Hmph, I wish! It would be a nice break. But my stomach is still queasy and my head is still light from that flu. I wouldn't have the energy to be much of a companion," she lied so easily as she flipped another page of the magazine.

"Yeah, yeah, I forgot. Well, I'll bring you something back real special, Mami, okay? And uh, maybe when I get back we might be able to get you in to see Dr. Amanda again. Just to talk. You've been feeling this way for awhile. Maybe the flu isn't the flu. Maybe it's..."

"Ya!" Iman cut him off quickly! She felt like throwing up right there on the table and she never even had the flu. How could that man even think about a pregnancy? He was so far gone she knew there was no

saving him. She would never provide Mateo with a child if it was up to her. "Mateo, it's too soon. I don't have the energy or the strength or the heart right now to go through that again. We have to focus on one thing at a time. I think counseling is the right thing for us. It's what we should have done years ago."

Mateo raised his hands in defeat. He knew she was right. She'd been through too much. The day would soon come where she could look at him and would feel happy and in love with him again, he prayed. Right now, he had to focus on himself. If Iman wouldn't give him a baby, there were plenty of women who would line up all around the corner to. He'd hoped it didn't have to come to that, but he knew it was the one thing he couldn't force her into. She had a right to mourn his babies as long as she needed.

"Si!" he confirmed as he stood up out of his chair and stretched his arms. "I'm going to shower. Don't stay out here too long. It's getting chilly and I wanna see you before I go."

"Taa Bien!"

Ramadhan Mubarak sister Priscilla! Shukran for coming out!" I remarked as I saw one of my mother's friends leaving.

Ameera and I were running around like chickens with our heads cut off. If I was running left, Ameera was running to the right. Yaz was sitting pretty on the sister's side, hosting and cradling the baby girl. Mas'u d was with the brother's on the other side of the building. With Ummi and Sister Adilah running the aqiqah like two old sergeants, everybody, including Hasan and Imran, were working. The Islamic Center was filled beyond capacity. It was the last weekend in Ramadhan and my family had finally started to rebound. On this night, we had pulled together so we could welcome Mas'ud and Yasmeen's baby girl.

"As salamu alykum wa rahmatullah wa barakatuh, everyone," Mas'ud started as he stood at the podium inside the dining hall. "Alhamduleelah, my wife Yasmeen and I and our families wanted to thank you all for joining us tonight in the last days of this blessed month to welcome our newest addition." Yasmeen walked up to the front of the room and handed her baby to her husband. Mas'ud cradled the sleeping baby in his arms and lightly kissed her cheek. "May Allah bless, protect, and instill goodness into my first born, ameen. My daughter; Madeenah Aya Johnson, may Allah love you for all of your days and bless you with the best home in the hereafter, ameen."

The crowd repeated "ameen" after Mas'ud and several of his friends shouted "Takbir" and we all responded, "Allahu Akbar".

"I know it's almost time for Ishaa so *Jazak'Allahu Khayran* for coming out. We'd appreciate it if you make sure you place your empty plates, cups, and napkins in the trash or recycle bins. Any leftover food can be given to our volunteers. And speaking of volunteers, the messenger of Allah, *sallallahu alayhi wa sallam*, is reported to have said: You haven't thanked Allah, until you have thanked the people so I really want to take a few seconds to thank my dear mother, sister Muneerah, my mother-in-law Khadijah, my sisters Iman, Ameera, and Fariba, my Aunt Adilah, my big brothers Shareef, Jibril, Ya'coob, and Hamad and everyone else who assisted Yasmeen and I. May Allah accept your fasts and reward you all abundantly." Mas'ud handed Madeenah back to Yasmeen as they walked away from the podium.

With everything that had happened, we didn't really get to give Shareef the welcome home we'd wanted. Tonight was his night too.

"You want some of these oxtails, Shareef?" Ameera asked him through her face veil. "There's too much food left. We won't have enough room to bring it all home."

"Meera, I done ate three plates already. I came out the joint with a six pack, ya'll trying to undo all my hard. That's not fair," Shareef teased. "Plus, it's almost time to stand for tarawih. I ain't gonna make it through the first three raka'at let alone eleven before the sleep creep up on me."

"Fariba made these oxtails," I chimed in.

Shareef laughed. "Ya'll crazy. Go 'head and make me a to-go plate. But that's it. Whatever the people here don't finish, we can bring over to the homeless shelter and the halfway house downtown tomorrow," he suggested.

I watched *him* walk right past my sister and me without any acknowledgement. He shook my brother's hand and they embraced. He was sporting a beige kurta with white stitching across the bodice over pressed khaki colored pressed slacks with a white kufi on top of his head. He looked clean and fresh as always. Half of a miswak tooth stick dangled out the side of his bearded mouth. He talked but it never fell from his mouth. I couldn't make out what he was saying. He was probably doing that on purpose too. He hadn't spoken to me or even dropped by the house to check on me since I'd gotten out of the hospital. Was he still mad at me? Or maybe everything that had transpired had been too much for him to handle. Maybe I was too much to deal with. Hasan and his son Saud ran up to them and he limped off with them. He'd been hurt that night. That night we had all lost so much. Jibril's foot was encased in a brace.

"Imani!" Ameera called. "Ummi said to go bring up the rest of the veggies from the kitchen. She said they're ready to start packing up."

"All right, I'll go and get them. If you see Fariba, tell her to come help me, please."

"Will do," she told me. Saba was strapped to her back in one of those babywearing wrapping thingies. I loved the style, but Saba was getting entirely too big for any of us to be carrying her around all night. Ameera was gonna be sore tomorrow for sure, but it sure was helping her get her exercise in. She had already dropped a couple more pounds and you could see it in her face. She looked completely different than when she had first came back to Pittsburgh.

Walking briskly trying to work off all the food I'd eaten, I took the stairs three at a time to go down to the kitchen. I removed two large foil pans full of seasoned green beans and cabbage from under the warmer. As I picked them up, I heard my name called:

"Here, let me help you with those," Fariba offered.

"Shukran, Reeba. How's it going upstairs on the sisters' side?"

"Good! We've fed everyone at least twice and the lines are done. These pans just need to be sealed with aluminum foil and packed up. As soon as brother Wahid calls the iqamah for Ishaa we can start cleaning and stacking the tables."

"Sounds like a plan. So you happy now?"

"What you mean? You mean him?"

"Yeah. That's exactly what I mean," I exclaimed.

"I am. I am really relieved too, Alhamduleelah. This is exactly where he belongs." she beamed. "Still cautious, though. Trying to take things slow."

"Good." I offered.

"What about you?" she questioned me.

"What you mean?" I repeated. Fariba laughed.

"Iman, my brother has wanted to marry you since we were kids. Uncle Musa used to pop him upside his head for staring at you those with googly eyes when we use to play double dutch outside. 'Member that?" she laughed.

"Yeah, I do. He and Shareef would be in the street playing football and we be out there double dutching as our hijabs flew in the wind. We'd be doing double duty watching all the little kids while Ummi and Aunty grilled burgers and hotdogs. Yep, those were the days, sis!"

"Sure was. Jibril ain't changed none."

"He's hasn't ever officially asked to marry me. I was expecting Shareef to mention it when he came home, but nope, nada!"

"Is your divorce finalized yet?" Fariba asked me.

"No, not yet."

"He's waiting," she informed me with a smile. "Maybe we can have a double wedding!"

"I thought you weren't in a rush?" I pointed out.

"I'm not. I mean when we're all ready! It would be nice to do it together – and cheaper!"

We both laughed. Jibril had been right. Fariba was frugal with everything.

"Maybe you're right."

We carried the food back upstairs and set them up on the buffet table. She was right, the room full of sisters had almost cleared out.

Yasmeen was packing up Madeenah's things. Ameera and Aunty Adilah were busy wiping off the tables.

"As salamu alykum, Iman!" a woman said as she embraced me tightly. "I didn't want to leave without seeing your face," Miss Labibah told me.

"Wa alykum as salam wa rahmatullah. Miss Labibah, shukran for coming. I feel so bad I didn't get a chance to sit and chat with you. I was just too busy with everything tonight. But Insha'Allah, don't you worry, I promise to get over to see you for my session this Tuesday."

"Very good then. How's fasting going? Are you sleeping any better?"

"Alhamduleelah, so far so good with the fasting. I really needed this, I can tell you that. And you know even with everybody in the house, I am sleeping better than I have in years. It's getting better - I am getting there."

Miss Labibah squeezed my hand tightly. "Allahu Akbar. You will get there! There is nothing like being surrounded by loving and praying family. And that new niece of yours is just too cute!"

"Did you get a chance to hold her?"

"I did! The lusciousness of a new baby... my ovaries, ouch!"

"Yeah, tell me about it! I am just glad she is in the house with us. I get all hugs and holds I need. And I need them for sure!"

"Well, I'll tell you this: you, Iman, are a strong, strong woman and Allah has something so special for you, Insha'Allah. Believe and trust that, beloved. Any time He puts difficulty and hardship in our path and you fight through it and come out of it increased, subhan'Allah, whoo! That's His blessing. It's a cleansing. You just keep doing the right thing. Keep pushing onward."

"I don't know any other way to live, Miss Labibah. It's what I learned growing up around all these elders!"

"I know that's right! Ain't nothing like old school 'Merican Muslims," she teased and we shared a laugh.

Ummi walked up behind me carrying some of her cooking utensils and pots. "Salamu 'alykum," she greeted Miss Labibah with her best smile to cover up the fatigue. "Don't mean to intrude, but Iman I need you to go give these things to one my sons and have them take it out to the van," she told me.

"Okay, no problem. I'll go find them in just a sec, Insha'Allah. Ummi, I want to introduce you to Miss Labibah. This is my counselor and... my sponsor," I declared looking her directly in her eyes.

Ummi looked at me and then back at Miss Labibah a couple times before she spoke. "Is that right?"

"Yes, As salamu alykum, sister," Miss Labibah started as she extended her hand out to Ummi to shake. "Alhamduleelah, you got a really wonderful daughter. She's overcome a lot."

Ummi shook her hand and then turned right back towards me. "Is that right?" she reiterated.

"It sure is!" Miss Labibah continued. "Insha'Allah, I only see her getting stronger and more confident each day. She will overcome her struggles and Allah is all of our best Helpers,"

"He certainly is," Ummi noted with increased curiosity. I still had never told her my whole story.

"Well, sisters, I have to get going. I wish I could stay for tarawih, but it's my husband's night to pray in congregation. I gotta get home to my children. Insha'Allah, I'll see you later, Iman. May Allah bless your granddaughter, sis. Muneerah!" Miss Labibah explained to us before walking out of the room.

Ummi and I stood there. She stared at me. I dropped my eyes before I spoke, "You want me to take the pots out now?"

"That took a lot of courage to tell me, right?"

"Yes," I mumbled on the verge of tears.

"Iman, don't you be acting scared to be real with me. How many times I got to tell you now? I prayed for you before you were even you. I birthed and nursed you. There is nothing that you and I can't get through! I don't know how long Allah gonna keep me on this earth, but I am not going to run away from you. You hear me?

"Yes, Ummi!

"Go 'head and give Shareef these things. Tell 'em I said send Hasan and the rest of the boys to come help clean up. I ain't gonna be able to stand up and pray with ya'll tonight. I got to sit down and rest these bones."

"Okay."

Turning on my heels, I wiped the tears from the corners of my eyes with my sleeves of my abayah and walked out of the sister's dining hall. My arms were starting to feel weak. I'd been working like an old mule all evening. Resting sounded good. But I had to stay.

Chapter 14

I scanned all the main halls, but I saw no one I knew. My brothers were nowhere to be found. They had all gone up to the *musallah* to get ready for prayer. I headed upstairs carrying the pots only to be met by a steady stream of Muslims, adults and children, coming in and out of the prayer area. I decided I would just bring the things out to the car myself. I slipped my feet into my flip flops and I headed outside.

With the copy of Ameera's keys in my pocket, I power walked through the parking lot looking for her car. The security lights illuminated the darkness some, but it was still dark enough that I needed to squint my eyes as I scanned the cars I passed. I approached her car, put the pots and utensils on the hood, and grabbed the keys out of my pocket. I don't know why I felt the need to turn around before I put the pots in the wagon, but something deep inside me prompted me to check my surroundings. As I slowly twisted my body around and looked over my shoulder, I didn't see anything. I turned back around, opened the trunk and started packing Ummi's things inside. I locked the doors and was headed back when I saw lights flashing across the street. I stopped in my tracks.

The car was parked in the exact same spot as Diego's had been weeks ago. It was where I had met Lisette. But this car wasn't the Mustang Diego had been driving. This car looked like a Lexus. The car's headlights flashed again. I started walking. At first I walked briskly, then I started jogging in those cheap flip flops so hard, I could feel the dust hitting the heels of my feet. Panting out of breath due to the sheer fear that had flushed into my lungs, I rushed into the Islamic Center and tripped over a pair of shoes and landed right on my butt.

Why are you still running? Get it together, Iman! You are now safe!
You are free!

As the adhan for salatul Isha was being called, I got up and followed the crowd of sisters into the washroom. After cleaning my body for prayer, I took a minute to fix my hijab by repinning it. My hands were so shaky; it took me several tries to get it right. That wasn't him. It couldn't have been. He would have gone back to Atlanta for Diego's funeral. He wouldn't have stayed in Pittsburgh. It wasn't him. No fear, not today!

I squeezed into one of the lines in the back near the wall and waited for the Imam to start the prayer. Those flashing lights had nothing to do with me.

"Allahu Akbar!"

At the Islamic Center, the Qur'an reciter that was visiting the community for the whole month of Ramadhan prayed 23 units. But after the first 11 he would take a break. Most nights, the congregation would decrease by half after the first break. I always tried to push through all 23. But this time, I left with the first group of worshippers. I had to go to work in the morning coupled with the early Morning prayer and all the servitude I'd just put in, my body was begging for some rest.

Ameera's car was full with her children, the pots, dishes, table cloths, and utensils. Mas'ud had his van full with the leftover food. Plus, of course, Yasmeen and Madeenah were stuffed in there too.

That just left Ummi and I since Shareef and Hasan had drove with Jibril. We got into Fariba's tan Hyundai Santa Fe with her three daughters. They were all family anyway.

"Aunty Muneerah, how'd you think everything turned out?"

"Oh, Alhamduleelah, we had a good night. And ya'll did good! We fed the people and we prayed to Allah. Mas'ud and Yasmeen introduced Madeenah to the community and Shareef is home. That was what we came to do, right?"

"Yeah, that was it!" Fariba agreed. "I just hope we have this type of turn out for my nikah!"

"Of course you will, Fariba! Just don't rush nothing. You deserve a nice night too. I don't care if Shareef my son or not. He got to take care of his business and Hasan. He got to prove to you that he is ready to be a husband. His Abu wouldn't have it any other way," Ummi lectured her.

"Aunty, now you know me better than that. And you know your son, too. He ain't gonna let me get ahead of myself. He got a job and he'll make it do what it do," Fariba insisted. "Besides Shareef and Hasan need time to get adjusted and settled."

"That's what I know. Shareef got to get on his feet, Fariba, and do what a man's supposed to do for his family. We got more trouble lurking around than a little. Not until this child of mine," Ummi told her and pointed at me, "is safe from all that trouble she got 'round her, will I rest. Shareef got a whole lot of work to take care of before we gon' celebrate anything."

Fariba nodded her head and shot me a look. We both knew Ummi was right. Things had to be settled. There were two court cases I had to take care of. And Mateo wasn't in jail. He was free. I closed my eyes and nodded off.

The weekend was too short. Monday morning ran right into me. Ameera woke me up for suhoor around three thirty in the morning. By time I got down to the kitchen she had already finished cooking the morning meal for everyone. Ummi and the little boys were sitting at the table chomping down on eggs, cheese grits, and turkey bacon. Shareef was chopping fruit and boiling eggs. Mas'ud was eating toast as he rocked baby Madeenah. Yasmeen wasn't able to fast, so she was sleeping.

"I made you a protein smoothie, Imani," Shareef said he handing me a glass.

"Oh, nice, bro," I responded as I sat down at the table. I said "*Bismillah*" and started sipping the thick liquid down.

"Don't worry about it. You going to work in the morning?"

"Of course," I said with a nod of my head.

"I was talking with Mas'ud and we both agree that, for now, it's best to keep the brothers posted around your job. Just until the case is settled. How does that sound to you?"

"That's fine."

"Good. Hamad, Ya'coob, and I will take turns throughout the day. And Ameera and Fariba will drop you off and pick you up. And on Tuesday, Mas'ud will take you to see Hussayn, the lawyer. Insha'Allah, he'll help wrap the case up so you can get some closure for yourself."

I just kept nodding.

"That man should be in jail. He oughta stay there for the rest of his life!" Ummi interjected. "He kidnapped my child and hurt her and he gets to walk the earth free? What was the protective order for? Shareef, there ought to be something we can do 'bout this now. Next thing you know it he be done fled this country."

"He has a lawyer, Ummi. A pretty good one too. Lot of evidence building up against him but if Imani doesn't want to testify against him, he isn't going to jail." I could feel their eyes burning a hole into my neck. I kept drinking.

"Iman Shahidah Johnson, you got to do the right thing, baby. Your Abu," she paused and shook her head. "Your Abu, he would want that man to pay for his crime. He tore apart this family and broke your father's heart," Ummi revealed through pained eyes. I could see her holding the tears back.

I didn't respond. She sighed loudly before stomping out of the kitchen. Ameera shook her head and sucked her teeth loudly before announcing, "C'mon boys! Hurry up and clear up your dishes. It's time for ya'll to get washed up for Fajr."

"Hurry up, ya'll. Get ready to go the masjid. Hasan, make sure you help them make wudu properly," Shareef added before getting up from the table to put his dishes in the dishwasher. "So, I had a quick meeting last night that I think you need to know about," Shareef started.

"Really? With who?"

"Ah, Me-tio, is that how you pronounce it?"

"Mateo. What in the world is he still doing in Pittsburgh?"

"I guess he didn't want to go to his brother's funeral. He's here helping with the arrangements for the funeral for the young lady who was murdered. Guess they were close?"

"Is that so?"

"Close enough, I gathered," Shareef told me. "Look, I know you might have been considering attending that funeral just to pay your respects, but I don't think it's a good idea. The families are beefing and you already done got caught up in the middle of their family shootouts. And Mateo will be there so that's another reason to avoid it too."

"What did he say?" I asked.

"He said a lot stuff that you don't you have to concern yourself with anymore. You're done with him. Insha'Allah, we'll continue to work on this til it's all finished legally, but don't look back. All right, it's 'bout time to stop eating. This is the last week of Ramadhan, so finish strong."

"Shareef?"

"Yeah?"

"Do you think I would be sinful if I decided not to testify against Mateo?"

"I don't know, Imani. It's a good question, though. I don't think it's an easy decision for you to make. I mean you could go talk to the Imam or call one of the scholars overseas, if you wanted to hear their opinion about what's going on in your life and how they think it should be handled according to Qur'an and Sunnah. But at the end of the day, you're going to be the one who has to live with the consequences. You need to feel at peace with whatever decision you make and be able to go on with your life. Make salatul istikhara and stick to whatever Allah leads you too. I do know that you don't owe anyone anything - not even Ummi."

"Yeah, I guess."

"Nothing to guess about. This is your life and you gotta live it and make the best choices for you, Imani! Ain't nobody perfect 'round here.

Ummi and Abu made their mistakes too and they got through it. We'll get through ours too, Insha'Allah."

"Ummi thinks testifying against Mateo is the right thing to do for Abu! Don't you think he would want me to?"

"That's what Ummi wants. And maybe Abu would have wanted it to. But what do you want to do? If you choose to forgive him and let Allah handle him - how is that wrong Islamically? You were married to the man legally. You had to have some good feelings and love for him at one time or another. Ya'll went through whatever ya'll did together - the good and the bad. Allah is the best to judge us. But now, that's all in your past. You're here now and you gotta forgive yourself and everyone else too.

"Look at me," Shareef said motioning his hands up and down. "I am the oldest, was supposed to be the most responsible, but I messed up big time. My ex-wife screwed me over. She didn't put me in that jail, though. I did that. And now I just got out of the joint and she done went in. I didn't wish that for her. If I could have helped her avoid it by doing more time, I would've took that bid for her. Real talk. See, even though she did me dirty, it wasn't like that always. There were some good days too. I'd give her a second chance if I could. You might not get it…"

"I get it. I do. Second chances are blessings. Allah gave me one."

"He gave me one too. The best advice I can give you is to just focus on you and Allah, Iman. I'll see you later, Insha'Allah," my brother said before mushing me in my head.

After my talk with Shareef, I felt a big weight lifted off my shoulders. I had already made my mind up but to be given support was comforting. Mas'ud left Madeenah with me so that he could go pray at the masjid with the rest of the menfolk. She was sleeping already so I placed her in the baby swing while I prayed alone. Ameera and Ummi prayed together upstairs without me. It wasn't the first time I had felt ostracized by them and I knew this wouldn't be the last.

After Ameera dropped me off at work, my day started rolling. Fasting and working was tough. I hadn't fasted the whole month in years. No one to blame for that but myself. Some years the miscarriages prevented me. Others years the PTSD was too deep and dark. Despite the hunger pains some days, it really felt good to be fasting. With a billion Muslims around the world fasting and praying during Ramadhan with me, I knew I could make it through the days and long nights. I could feel the cleansing happening in my body. My skin was glowing and I felt stronger than ever by forgoing food and drink for over 17 hours a day. Now that it was almost over, I had finally found the right pace for success.

I made sure I drunk at least a gallon of water each night, ate a protein and oatmeal most nights for iftar, and had green smoothies, protein, almonds, and dates for breakfast. On the weekends, Ameera, Ummi, Yasmeen, and I would go walking at night. Sometimes Fariba and Aunty Adilah would come too. We would laugh and talk about everything we needed to. Sometimes, we would even hold hands.

Like with everything else, I just keep pushing myself through each day of fasting. It was a month full of blessings and now that the drama was behind me, I had every intention to reach my happy ending.

After I returned from the exam room checking in on a patient, I headed back to the nurses' station to input her updates into the computer when one of my co-workers called out to me.

"Really, chica! Really? Why you been holding out on us, Iman?"

"What you talking about Tasha?"

"I know ya'll Muslim womens be getting ya'll husbands and marriages in all quick! But I didn't think you would hold out us like this though, yo!

"What are you talking 'bout, Tasha? I don't have a husband!"

"Well, looks like you got an admirer sending flowers and what not! For alls we know you already married the man – oh, the brother, my bad! Why we don't know nothing about him, huh?" she fussed at me before handing me the package of red and orange roses and pink carnations. Surprise and worry draped my face. I honestly had no idea who had sent them. "Just read the card already," Tasha ordered. I slowly pulled the card out from under the box and prayed for the best as I opened it.

"What it say?" my nosey co-worker requested. I just smiled. It was good and fresh.

"It says," I started, "After difficulty, comes ease."

Tasha screwed up her face and wrinkled her nose. "Is that it?"

"Yeah, that's it. It's sweet," I smiled with relief. Jibril reaching out to me was unexpected, but welcomed.

"Well, shoot, if you like it, I love it," Tasha quipped before grabbing a patient's file and heading out to the waiting room.

I scooped up the flowers and my card then carried them into the staff room. After smelling them one more time, I locked them in my locker. It was time to offer the Asr prayer. Even though everything wasn't perfect, I felt fine. My prayer was light and I was focused. I sat on the floor on top of the prayer rug my mother had gifted me. It was dark green and gold colored with a faded black mosque on the center. The rug was old and ragged around the edges, but it had belonged to my Abu. He prayed on it often when I was growing up. Now I had the chance to use it daily for my own prayers.

As I sat on the rug making supplications, I pulled the pocket Qur'an out of my bag and read a couple pages. Reading in English was much easier than fighting through the Arabic. But every once and awhile I would glance over to the foreign letters and slowly sound out some of the words just to challenge myself. My pronunciation was horrible. Abu always said if we didn't use what we learned, Allah would remove it from us. He hadn't snatched all of the Arabic from me, but the little that I had left embarrassed me.

Shareef, Ameera, and Mas'ud all could read and recite Qur'an in Arabic beautifully. They all had also memorized large portions as well. Much of the 15 or so chapters that I had once memorized as a child, I was relearning in the classes at the Islamic Center Ummi I still went to. My progress was slow. With working, counseling, being in the hospital, and baby Madeenah and Shareef coming home, I didn't have a lot of time to study. It was frustrating some days. I hated making excuses, but my memory wasn't anything like it used to be. Ramadhan was the driving force pushing me to pick up the Qur'an more and read it page for page. With or without the Arabic, I wanted to reacquaint myself with the themes, the messages, and the faith it contained for me.

Miss Labibah often read passages from the Qur'an during our counseling sessions. "It's a healing! If you want to find Allah, read His book, and see if you don't find some peace. He's always there," she told me right after I got out of the hospital. I'd been trying to read a couple of pages each day ever since.

Once I finished reading the Qur'an, I went back out to nurses' station hoping to grab a computer and enter data until my shift finished. That wasn't the case, though. Phone calls, calls for assisting the medical assistants, and doctors kept disrupting me. By the time I got back to the computer, it was time to go home. I gathered my bags, the flowers and card, and locked up the files before heading out into the waiting room to wait on Fariba.

"Imania?" I heard my old name being called just as I stepped into the hallway. The female voice was familiar so I walked towards her confidently.

"Imania?" Our eyes locked then we both sized each other up and down. As I scanned the middle aged, tawny-beige face of the woman standing in front of me as I took in her wide, dark eyes, and full lips covered in blood red lipstick on a face that was framed by wild, curly cropped hair dyed a striking platinum blond. I smiled. She smiled back.

"Oh, my God! It's been so long," she squealed as she stepped forward and embraced me tightly.

"Evie! My God! How did you find me?" I asked as I squeezed her and rubbed her back. "How are you holding up? I am so sorry you had to come back like this."

"Shoot, this funeral is the only thing that would have ever dragged my butt back to this city," she admitted as a couple of tears escaped her eyes and rolled down her cheeks.

"You doing all right? Have you talked to anyone yet?"

"Nia, I am alive, but this life don't make no kind of sense right now. It's all crazy. You know, I spoke to Lee that morning. I was yelling at her, 'make sure you take care of Imania. Don't let her out of your sight! And she listened all right! She was in too deep. Deeper than she let me know. God! I am okay, though. I tried to warn her, but everybody can't be saved. Que lo que?"

"I know it. But I am standing and breathing. I am alive, too. Thank you so much, Evie. I am just so grateful for all of your help. You really came through for me and you are here now. I thought you were going to leave me high and dry!"

"What? Like really? You know I am loyal. We been through so much! Life and death stuff - we are closer than sisters. You looked out for Corazon and me when no one - I mean no one in the world would give us anything. That money you let me have… and how you kept your word and never told on me - you saved our lives," she explained as we started walking towards the sliding doors and exited the clinic. Fariba was parked right out front. I waved at her to let her know to wait a minute.

"Listen though, I need to get back to my aunt's house 'cause Corazon is there. But we really gotta talk, Imania. I am not staying here too long with all the crazies. But there some real red hot info you need to know. I know something that Mateo doesn't want you to know," she whispered in a hush tone. "Straight from Manny."

"Okay, let's meet up a little later. I gotta go check in with my family and pray."

"What time you going to be free?"

"Let's meet up around eight. Aladdin's on Forbes. You know where that is?" I asked her.

Evie shrugged her shoulders. "The GPS will find it. See you," she told me before walking away and climbing into a silver Nissan Murano.

Chapter 15

I walked across the parking lot and got into the car with Fariba.

"Hey, salams, sis. You good?"

"Wa alykum as salam wa rahmatullah," I replied as I secured the flowers and my bags in the back seat. "I am good. Sorry to keep you waiting."

"Who was that lady? She work with you in clinic looking like that?"

"No, she doesn't work in the clinic. She's an old friend from before."

"Uh oh! That's probably not good. Is she mixed up with the ex-husband and the murder victim?" Fariba inquired.

"You know it. Evie is Mateo's oldest brother's ex-wife and Lissette's, the woman who was murdered's cousin. She came up for the funeral and to help her aunt out."

"That's awful! That guy, the other brother, must have been really crazy killing that woman and himself like that. I wonder what in the world made him hate his own brother enough to try to kill him?"

"Honestly, Fariba, I don't even want to know. Diego always was wild and reckless and just a mean-spirited guy. But when I was there, those brothers loved each other. Whatever went down, had to be a really raw deal. I don't want to be involved."

"I know that's right. Leave good enough alone. So what's with those flowers? What you do to get them?"

"More like what did you say to make someone give them to me? I was surprised at work with this delivery from some little pricey flower shop downtown. Your kind brother sent them."

"Really? Jibril sent you flowers? That's new. I ain't never seen him do that before. Do you like flowers or something?"

"I love them. I had a really small but beautiful garden in Atlanta. Yaz and me just started gardening in the backyard, too. So what did you tell that brother of yours?"

"Nothing major. I just told him the truth about his ways. He saw it my way," she giggled before starting up the car and pulling out of the parking lot.

"Alhamduleelah, thank you anyway. Hey, what you doing later 'round eight?"

"Nothing much. Why?" Fariba asked.

"You wanna go to Aladdin's and grab a bite to eat for iftar?"

"Sure. I haven't been there in ages. I'll drop the girls off at their Abu's house a little early and come back by to get you around seven thirty."

"All right, Insha'Allah, I'll see you then." I got out of the car and grabbed my things from the backseat.

As I entered the house, I called out the salams and headed straight up to my room. I could hear Ameera in the room using her around-the-way girl voice. She sounded like she was really mad. Needing to put my stuff down and use the bathroom, I knocked on the door and then pushed it open?

"Who you talking to like that? I swear you got more problems than a little—! Why you ain't never happy? What you want me to do, Umar? Why? Now you're just being childish? So what? I said so what? You can talk to Shareef, Mas'ud, Ummi, Jibril - any damn body you want! I said so what!"

This was clearly the off week for Ameera and her husband. For every week that they did well, they had to follow it up by doing bad. I guess I couldn't expect them to solve all their issues over night, but their lows were always dangerously low. I wasn't sure what had caused this flare up, but I didn't want it to get any worse. I waved at Ameera and blew her a kiss. While I gathered up a change of clothes, my sister let out a few more curse words. Bothered by her tone and lack of control, I walked over to her and shoved her. With furrowed brows, I mouthed to her,

"You're fasting! Let - it - go!"

Ameera shouted back to me, "I am not fasting right now. Mind your business."

I shot her another concerned look and then walked out closing the door behind me. Sometimes you gotta leave people be. Ameera was just so thick headed. Umar had proven to me that he wasn't a real monster like then one I had got hooked up with. He was a decent guy trying his best to be a decent husband. Problem was he just wasn't evenly yoked with Ameera. They were like oil and water.

I washed up, prayed, and then headed upstairs to the attic.

"As salamu alykum," I called out as I knocked lightly on the door that was slightly ajar.

"Wa alykum as salam. Iman?" Yaz came to door holding Madeenah in her arms. I smiled and reached out my arms to hug my sister-in-law. She didn't look too good, though.

"Hey, sweets! How you feeling?"

"Good. Tired. Overworked. Sleepy. Oh, *Astaghfirullah*," Yaz admitted. "Come on in," she sighed with a wave of her hand. We walked back into her small sitting room and I immediately noticed that the usually neat space was unkempt. Sprawled across the cream and black carpeted floor were old gift bags, wrapping paper, blankets, packages, soiled baby clothing, and several instruction booklets for different baby equipment. The bassinet that Ameera, Ummi, and I bought her was in the middle of the floor and so were her breakfast, lunch dishes, and a couple of cups.

Yasmeen was wearing a ripped pair of black leggings and one of Mas'ud's old high school football jerseys. Her long curly hair was flying every which way with several strands framing her face. She lowered her body to the floor and balanced the fussy baby at the same time before pulling a heavy blanket over her body and cradling the baby on her chest. I didn't like what I was seeing. Without a word to Yasmeen, I started to pick up the mess on the floor before I grabbed the broom from the kitchenette to sweep up.

"You get to take a shower today, Yaz?"

"Nope. I just wait for Mas'ud to come in to do all that. It's just easier when he is here."

"Ummi and Ameera are here, you know? They can help you during the day. We all are here to help you guys out."

"Yeah," Yasmeen sighed deeply as Madeenah's cries began to get louder. Yasmeen shot back up and rocked her baby from side to side roughly. Madeenah's wails wouldn't let up. Yasmeen began to cry. "I've been nursing her all day it seems. I am so sore. I am just so tired of the crying," my sister-in-law admitted.

I put the broom down on the floor, walked over to Yaz and slowly took my niece out of her hands. "It could be gas or she needs to be burped or maybe she needs to be rocked slowly," I offered as I cradled Madeenah upward and placed her on my shoulder and patted her back gently. "She's a baby, but she's a human too. Just like you, she has so many feelings going through her mind in this new world that she can only express through those cries. She's not trying to anger you. She's just communicating. You haven't done anything wrong, Yaz. Has Mas'ud finished putting together the other the swing yet?" I asked her as I walked up and down her short hallway, but she didn't answer.

When I turned around, I saw Yasmeen had fallen asleep that quickly.

"Okay, baby girl. It's just you and Aunty! We are going to have some fun until your father gets home. But first we have got to clean up this mess in here and then we get some food on that stove so that your parents can eat and have some more energy to take care of you. Is that alright, baby girl?"

Madeenah stopped crying and quickly flashed a smile at me. "We gonna be alright, Insha'Allah. Yep, we will!"

I grabbed the baby sling Ameera had bought for Yasmeen and secured my niece in the padded carrier and got to work. Madeenah fell asleep without any problems as I washed the dishes, bagged up the trash and tidied the kitchen up. Before I knew it, it was about seven. I finished cooking a pot of creamy pasta with spinach and sun dried tomatoes.

"Salamu alykum?" Mas'ud called out. I trotted out to the sitting room and whispered, "Shhhhhh," Mas'ud was leaning over his sleeping wife and pulled the blanket up over her some more.

"She's been really tired," he noted.

"She should be. Her body went through a lot and is still working hard. It takes a lot of time to adjust to motherhood and for babies to adjust too,"

"We're learning," my brother admitted with a smile. "How was Madeenah for you?" he asked as I took her out of the baby sling and handed her to him.

"She was good and tired too. Have the boys help you finish fixing up that swing. She likes a lot of movement. I made you guys' dinner. It's on table. It'll be time to break soon. Make sure Yaz eats something," I told him as I headed towards the door.

"Thanks, Iman."

"None needed. Bring her downstairs later if you want to take a nap too. Ameera can watch her," I told him as I walked back down the stairs and headed towards the bathroom. I jumped in the shower quickly and then dried off. Wrapped in my towel, I rushed into my bedroom to find it empty. After I dried off, I pulled on a pair of mint green wide-leg crepe pants, a cream kurta top with a pale green and gold stitching around the bodice, paired with a silver necklace and bangles. I covered my hair with a cream jersey knit hijab and slipped into black leather mules.

It was almost seven thirty in the evening. I knew Fariba was either already here or on her way. I grabbed my handbag and went downstairs.

"Aunt Iman, you look nice!" Hasan commented when he saw me. "You going out with Aunt Fariba? She's dressed up too," he told me.

"Yea, we're going out to break fast tonight," I said as I walked into the living room.

"You're running late. This is just like old times," Fariba pointed out as I shook her hand and kissed her cheek.

"Well, I was going to wait to Maghrib came in first. We can pray here and then go. So no rushing."

"Okay. It's your date anyway. Where is everybody?"

"I don't know. I was up in Mas'ud's spot with Yaz and Madeenah until he came home. "Hasan," I yelled back in the front room. "Where's your dad, Jeddah, Aunty Ameera, and the littles?"

Hasan paused his game then came into the sitting room. "Jeddah and my dad went to the grocery store with Aunt Ameera. The kids went too."

"Thanks for that update, Hasan," Fariba responded. "They might be out for a while. Should we cook something for iftar so they have something to eat when they get here?"

"That's a good idea. But I don't really feel like cooking in these clothes," I lamented. "I can order a couple of pizzas."

"That'll work, too" Fariba agreed. "Call Samir's Spot. They deliver over this way and have halal pepperoni and sausage too."

I nodded before walking into the kitchen to make the call. Ameera had cleaned the kitchen. Everything was shining and in its proper place. I fumbled around for a few minutes looking through the cabinets for the menu to the Turkish Muslim owned pizza place until I found it. I pulled out my cell phone and dialed the number as I walked back into the living room.

"Wa alykum as salam. Can I get two party-sized pizzas with pepperoni and sausages? How long? Hmm. Yeah, it's for *iftar*. Okay, 40 minutes is fine. Wa alykum as salam."

Fariba and Hasan were in the front room playing video games. I sat down on the couch and started scrolling through the messages on my phone. I only had a chance to delete ten messages before the door opened and the children came running into the house.

"We're back!" Imran and Munir squealed. Saba wobbled behind them with a face full of smiles. She was holding her little baby doll and a banana. I got up off of the couch and scooped her up into my arms as I walked over to the door. I spotted Shareef directing Ummi into the house so she couldn't pick up the bags.

"Ya'll gonna stop treating me like I can't do nothing in my own house," my mother told us as she dragged her tired feet across the threshold. She immediately kicked off her shoes and headed straight for her comfy La-Z-Boy chair and plopped down.

"You know we are just trying to help you, Ummi. Besides, you're fasting - and you really shouldn't be out!" I told her.

"Iman, I'll have you know that I've been fasting longer than any of you have been living. I know how to fast. It's just once a year and—"

"But you have medications that you need to take, Ma!" Shareef reminded her as he carried in the bags. "You can't just make-up your own way with this kind of stuff. You gotta follow the rules when you have an illness. It's serious."

"Don't you be worrying about me, Shareef! Worry 'bout yourself and Hasan. That's what ya'll all need to do - worry 'bout yourselves. And I ain't gon' take you to the store with me no more either. Next time, I'll just wait on Mas'ud. He know how to sit in the car and leave me be."

"Ma, you know Moody is busy. He got the baby, Yaz, work, and school. Besides, he's too afraid to speak up to you and help you make good decisions. I ain't afraid to tell you can't have cookies and chocolate. What you gonna do? Whup my butt? I know how to dodge with the best of them." Shareef teased. Ummi started laughing.

"Boy, you silly."

I sat Saba down on the couch right as the *adhan* for *Maghrib* sounded off the computer in the back room.

"Hasan!" Shareef called out to his son. "Go get Imran and Munir. Tell them to come pray."

Fariba brought out from the kitchen at tray of dates, grapes, and sliced honeydew melons and a pitcher of lemonade for everyone to break their fast before sitting on the floor. As the kids ran into the living room one by one she offered them something to eat.

"Imran, do you wanna call the *adhan* for *salat*?" Shareef asked him as he walked back into the living room from making wudu in the bathroom.

"But Abu, I'm the oldest!" Hasan blurted out. "Jeddah always lets me call the *adhan*. It's my job."

"It's good to share responsibilities sometimes, Hasan," Shareef reasoned. "Leaders always help others to be great too. Plus, Imran is getting older. He needs the practice."

Imran beamed proudly as he stepped forward to make the call to prayer. As soon as he finished, we all lined up, except for Hasan. He sat pouting.

"Come on now, Hasani!" Ummi called. "Get up in that line, boy, and stand tall and shoulder to shoulder with your cousins," she advised him with a smile. "Go on!"

Hasan slowly stood up and walked to the prayer line and stood next to Imran and Munir. After we finished the Evening prayer, Shareef sat down with Ummi and read Qur'an to her. I sat back down on the couch and put my shoes on.

"Fariba, you ready?" I called into the kitchen. She was in there helping Ameera finish putting the groceries away. "Oh, Ummi, before I forget. I ordered pizzas for you guys. Here," I said pulling out two twenty dollar bills from my bag and handing them to her.

"Where ya'll going this time of night? It'll be time for Isha soon," Shareef questioned me.

"I can see that. We're going to grab something to eat over at Aladdin's. A little treat."

"It's gonna be crowded over there," Ummi commented.

"It's late," Shareef stated again. I sighed then rolled my eyes. Shareef laughed before offering, "Be safe."

"We will, Insha'Allah," Fariba promised as she entered the living room and headed towards the door.

"Okay so ya'll just gonna go out to eat and didn't even invite me?" Ameera griped right as we were about to step out.

"Sorry, Meera! We didn't mean to overlook you, mama" Fariba insisted.

"What? Ameera you know we all can't leave out at once with all the kids here. Yaz and Mas'ud could really use some help with Madeenah tonight, too. Could you please go up there and take her for a while?" I pleaded with her.

"Yeah, whatever. I guess I am just a babysitter, cook, and wife to you too. Don't nobody really value me or think about what I want ever!" Ameera blurted out before stomping up the stairs. Like a little duck, Saba followed right behind her mother.

"I don't know what Ameera's problem is," I admitted to Fariba as she drove down the highway. She has the worse mood swings these days and it is really getting on my last good nerves. In the mornings, she seems fine. But then it's like she just flips the script at night. She can really be immature too."

"You know how your sister can be," Fariba offered.

"Really, I don't. I knew Ameera as a little girl. This grown up Ameera is new to me."

"Well, all I will say is this, she has been through a lot. Just like the rest of us. She's got a lot of baggage to work through and it's heavy. She's trying, though. Her and Umar both are trying. That's all any of us can do."

Chapter 16

When we reached Aladdin's, the restaurant's parking lot was full. We were running late but couldn't find a parking spot.

"Why don't I just let you out, Iman? I'll keep looking for a spot to park and meet you inside in a bit," Fariba suggested.

"Stop playing, Reeba. You know if anything happens to either us, they'll kill us twice," I joked and Fariba joined in laughing. "Let's just keep looking. If Evie leaves, that just means I wasn't meant to talk with her,"

"Yeah, but it could be really important. You don't have her cell phone number?"

"No, I don't – oh, look over there on the right. Someone is pulling out of that parking spot!" I shrieked.

Inside, Aladdin's was cozy. Crimson red plush carpets lined the dining area that was filled with cappuccino stained wooden tables and chairs. White monorail track lighting hung from the high ceilings that were paired with bronzed antique lanterns. Throughout the restaurant were miniature camel figurines and date palm trees. The strong scent of Oud incense wafted through the air and mixed with the smells of cardamom, cumin, and turmeric spices that the chef used in the dishes.

"Party of two?" the White female waitress wearing black tuxedo slacks and a white short sleeve button down shirt enquired.

"We are joining a party already here. Miss Evelyn Colon?"

"Oh okay. Right this way," she instructed us. Fariba and I locked arms together as we followed behind the young woman through rows of diners already seated. Most of the tables were filled with young professional looking White people. Some of the them looked up at Fariba and I as we walked by. Fariba, as always, was dressed brightly and unapologetically African. Her jade green maxi skirt was decorated with black geometric shapes. She paired it with a long a mint peplum shirt, wooden bangles, silver necklaces, black peep-toe flats, and a black jersey knit hijab.

The waitress led us to a booth table at the back of the restaurant. Evelyn was sitting there sipping on a cup of water holding a menu. She had changed her clothes too. She had a grey scoop neck tank dress on. Her uncovered arms revealed several intricate designed tattoos that covered scars from the abuse she had endured for too many years.

"Hey lady!" I greeted her. "Que lo que. ¿Dime ave?"

"Aye! ¡Que lo Que, Mami! I am good. Thought you weren't gonna make it! Come, sit," Evie instructed us.

"Thanks! Evie this is my brother's finance Fariba," I told her. "And Fariba this is Evie Colon, Mateo's brother's ex-wife and my sister-in-law."

"Nice to meet you!" Fariba extended her hand out to Evie.

"Same here, Mami. Nice to meet you too!"

The waiter cleared her throat before interjecting her script. "Can I start you all off on any drinks and appetizers?"

"Sure, I am starving." Fariba admitted. She grabbed the menu and scanned it quickly. "I'll take the lime Perrier, a small falafel bowl with hummus."

"Sound good, Reeba" I agreed. "I have the lime Perrier and a small Fattoush."

"Okay. I got that. And you, Miss?" the waiter asked Evelyn as she finished writing down the orders.

"I don't what know this stuff is!" Evie admitted. "What should I try, Nia?"

"You want some meat?" I asked.

"Yup?"

"The chicken sambosek is pretty tasty! A lot of our first-time customers start there," the waitress suggested.

"Okay, I'll try that and the fresh squeezed orange juice on ice too."

"Got it. Coming right up, ladies."

"All right, I know you are probably wondering what I got you out here for. I know I heard a lot of stuff coming out here and like, man, I'm just really proud of you. Seeing you put together, free, and just doing your thang, we prayed for this," Evie reminded me before taking a few sips of her water.

"I have you to thank, Evie. You started all of it. I would have never even had it in me to leave, if you never left me. When you and Cora left, I just knew I couldn't stay caged up there forever. You really forced me to wake up and do something for me," I revealed.

"Yeah, I don't know. It's been real up and down ever since I left, you know. Some days I think I didn't do what was best... for Corazon, you know. She loves that creep Manny and he might die before he gets out! I did that. Now Lisette's gone and Cora loved her too. I did that too. I put Lissette in the mix. Diego gone. Cora's uncle is dead! You know how much she loved Mateo and Diego. She hasn't stopped crying since we got here. Mama Paola wants Cora to go to Atlanta and spend some time with her since Mateo wouldn't take her to the funeral. And I am stuck, man. I don't know how I'm gonna explain all this to her. I feel like I let my baby down, way down. If her father was free, ain't none of this would've happened." Tears rolled down her eyes and huddled in between her lips before splashing onto her hands that were decorated with acrylic wrapped nails.

"Evie, you can't carry that! That's too much!" Fariba noted. "You have to let the other people involved carry their own weight."

"Fariba is right, Evie! You didn't kill Lissette. Diego did! And yeah, you asked her to help me, but you didn't know Diego would try to shoot at Mateo. You were trying to help keep us all safe. Whatever was going through Diego's mind had nothing to do with any of us. It never did. You know that, Evelyn! Don't beat yourself up."

"I got to! I should have known that Diego and Mateo were beefing! I should have told you that Diego and Lissette had a child together.

I should have known that Mateo was taking care of Lissette. I have should have known better than to trust Lissette around any of the Colon brothers. I should have listened to Manuel! He told me not to trust Lissette anymore because she wasn't being true to herself any more. The cars, the money, the house - these girls be trippin' thinkin' they gon' get upgraded. All that fancy mess come with a real steep price," Evie confessed.

"All right, ladies," the young waiter carried two trays of food with her. She placed our appetizers in front of us before sauntering away to grab our drinks. "Can I get you ladies anything else?"

"No, we're good. Thank you very much," Fariba told her. I had suddenly lost my appetite. We all sat quietly for a few minutes while Evie continued to cry.

"Lee... she... Lee was pregnant. She died and the baby too. I did that," Evelyn revealed through sobs.

"Allah! No! No, Evie! What? How did that happened? Why would she do what she did if she knew she was pregnant?" I questioned her.

"It's wasn't Diego's baby! It was Mateo's baby, Nia. That's why they were beefing. When Lissette told me she wasn't dealing with Diego anymore I just thought it was over. But I didn't think it through. Manny kept writing me and asking me about her. Why was she in Atlanta staying with them if she wasn't going to marry Diego? I thought she was there to help Abuela and for Danny to be with Diego. I am so sorry, Nia. I just didn't think any of this through."

I didn't know what to feel. Lissette had been in my closet. My garden. My kitchen. My bed. She had taken my life. Whatever she thought it was worth couldn't have been worth her life. Or the life of another Colon baby.

"Mateo knew she was pregnant?" I asked her. But I already knew that answer.

"Si. Tu lo ave. He told Manuel they took a paternity test and everything. It was his baby. Plus, he's here and not there with Mama Paola burying his brother."

"*Laa ilaha illalah!* How is he doing with knowing that his own brother killed his unborn baby and the mother?" Fariba wondered.

"Not good. I don't think that I have seen Mateo like this ever. He has never ever disobeyed Mama Paola. None of them have ever. But when she told Mateo to go back to Atlanta and help her with Diego's funeral arrangements, he refused. He is here with Corazon and Danny making sure they are okay. It's just so much. It'll never be the same. I think I destroyed their family," Evelyn cried.

"You didn't! The brothers did that to themselves," I explained. "So what did Manny tell you to tell me?" I finally asked Evie. I was ready to go. So much information had been unloaded on me. I didn't know what to make of it. I needed space.

"He said that Mateo needs you to get his head straight. He trusts you, and with Diego gone, me - I am divorced from the family, you are the only family he has."

"Mama Paola is alive. That's his mother! I can't help, Mateo. I can't."

"Mama Paola has dementia. She's been sick for years, you know that! It's not gonna get better, Nia."

"I can't help, Mateo! What are you even saying this for? You know I can't go back, Evie!"

"Imania, you own shares in Colon Nacional Dominicana! They used your name because it was clean. With Diego dead and Mama Paola sick, you now own ⅓ of the shares. But if you go through with that divorce—"

"She'll forfeit the ownership!" Fariba gasped.

"Exactly!" Evie added. "Manny said Mateo came here to tell you about the money and get you to sign a new contract so that you could have control of the money, but I guess Diego didn't like that. It just all probably pissed him off. Mateo was winning. He came here to try to reconcile with you and he had a baby on the way with Lissette."

"And he had lost again to Mateo. Sick! That's just sick. I don't want any of the Colon's money. I would have given it to Diego, if he'd just asked. This is crazy. I need…"

"Presidente or Bohemian Especial?" Evie reported in front of Fariba. A flash of shame engulfed me. I shook my head back and forth.

"Not anymore. I need to go pray!" I assured her.

"Good for you. I need shots daily. It takes the edge off of all this pain. I got a long way to go to be free. That's why I can't take Danny. It's hard enough keeping my head above water and raising Corazon. I can't take Danny."

"Lissette's son?"

"Yea. Her mother, my Aunt Lourdes, is old. She not too healthy either and she ain't got the money to really take care of Danny. Danny is Diego's son, though. So, if I can't take him, then... then he'll have to go with Mateo. Really, Mateo is the only one left to take him, right?"

"Right what? You think Mateo can raise a child safely?"

"I don't know. I mean, so far from what I've seen, he's been great with Danny. He loves his nephew just like he loves his niece. He wouldn't hurt Corazon. You said so yourself. So of course he wouldn't hurt Danny. Right?"

"Evelyn, I don't know. Mateo has never taken care of a child for more than a few hours. Just when Corazon was little. I don't know what to say."

"You gotta decide this now. You don't want to stay married to Mateo to get that check, okay. Your call. But Danny is my cousin's son. He needs a legal guardian in good health to take care of him or the state will send him to some strangers."

"What are you saying?"

"You can take a pay out. Mateo will pay you your fair share of Colon Nacional Dominicana,"

"What does Manny want from me?"

"Mateo, you mean. If you don't testify against Mateo, he can legally adopt Danny."

"And avoid jail."

"Yeah, that too."

I should've known some things too. I should've know that Evelyn would eventually find her way back under Manuel Colon's thumb. I should've known that Mateo had ulterior motives for coming all the way up to Pittsburgh. I should've known that this life just ain't easy.

"Here's my number Evelyn," I said as I pulled out one of my business cards. "Stay in touch. Whatever you decide to do, pray about it. Be safe, okay?" I told Evie as I got up to hug her.

"The funeral for Lissette is this Thursday. I hope you'll be able to make it. Cora would like to see her aunt," she mumbled in my ear as she embraced me warmly. "Don't be a stranger. Nice to meet you Fariba!" Evelyn threw a hundred dollar bill onto the table before walking away.

"Same here! Take care of you," Fariba advised.

After Evelyn left, we waved down the waiter to pay for the food.

"You good, Iman?" Fariba asked me as soon as we got into her car.

"I think so."

"That was a lot to take in and try to digest. But you know you don't have to carry all of the information by yourself. Talk to Shareef and Mas'ud and see what advice they have to offer. Okay?"

"Yeah, you're absolutely right. I'll probably sit down with them tomorrow after Fajr and see what they have to say."

"Good! My Umm is having her annual iftar tomorrow night. Make sure you remind Ameera she is invited and wanted. And make sure Aunty Muneerah and Yaz and the baby come out too. We'll probably discuss Eid activities and have a small halaqah."

"Oh nice. You need us to bring anything?"

"We pretty much have everything covered. If you wanna bring some juice or water, that'll be cool. Can't never have too much to drink."

"Got it. All right, Insha'Allah, I need to get in this house and pray and pray some more before I go to bed." I opened the door and stepped out.

"I hear you. I gotta go into to work early tomorrow so that I can be out early enough to help Ummi with the food preparations. We'll talk tomorrow, Insha'Allah. As salamu alykum."

"Wa alykum as salam wa rahmatullah."

I turned around and saw the porch light on. Both of my brothers and some of their companions were hanging out front talking. I walked up to the porch carrying my takeaway bag and greeted them all. *He* responded to me last as he stood up wearing a short-sleeved beige and black thoub, a black and cream kufi, black ankle socks, and Adidas slides. Reaching in front of me, he opened the screen door so I could enter.

"Thank you, Jibril," I offered him.

"You are very welcome," he returned with a small smile and full on eye contact. And just like that he had broke his self-imposed silence. That was enough for now.

"As salamu alykum, Ummi!" I greeted my mother as I came through the door. She was holding Madeenah as she walked back and forth.

"Shhhhhh, Iman! Almost got this girl back to sleep."

"Sorry!"

I brought my untouched food into the kitchen and stuffed it into one of the drawers in the fridge.

"Hey!" Ameera's voice cut into the room. "As salamu alykum,"

"Wa alykum as salam. What's up? You feeling better?"

"No. But it'll pass, sooner or later, Insha'Allah."

"You eat anything? I just put some Fattoush in the refrigerator."

"No appetite."

"Same here."

"You and Fariba have fun at Aladdin's?" she threw out at me while she poured a glass of water and plopped some ice into her mouth.

"Ameera, we didn't leave you intentionally. It's just that I've been worried about Yaz. She needs our help. We can't all leave her alone."

"I know."

"You know?"

"I know, Imani. Yaz needs our help with the baby. I know. I've had babies before," she spat at me.

"I know that."

"In case you forgot. And I didn't have a house full of people babying me. I just did it on my own. Me and Umar, we pushed through."

"I don't think I am asking you to baby her. But regardless, people are different. We all need help. Different issues, different strengths - we all need help with something. Besides, she's our sister. And little sis, you were babied too. I remember that."

"It stopped right after you disappeared. After you ran away and left us. Abu stop babying me. All he could ever think about was his baby that got taken away. But you weren't taken away. You left us. You left him heartbroken and ruined. He never babied me ever again. He was too busy praying for you."

Ameera picked up her cup and brought it to her mouth slowly. She stared me down before she drank all the water in one swallow. She shuffled her feet in her slippers and placed her cup in the sink and walked out of the kitchen without another word to me.

I was getting really tired of her passive aggressive antics. Ever since I'd came out of the hospital and Yasmeen brought home Madeenah, Ameera had been undone. If she wasn't picking fights with Umar, blowing up at her boys over silly stuff, she was finding something to fuss at me about. The only ones she didn't argue with were Shareef and Ummi, of course. I honestly didn't have the time or energy to strap her issues on my back. I was busy trying to unload and drop off my own.

I got up off the chair and walked back into the living room. Mas'ud, Shareef, and Ummi were sitting quietly watching Madeenah sway back and forth in her swing. She was asleep. Another small victory.

"Shhhhhhh!" they all warned me.

I smiled as I waved my hand at them. I didn't have to be told twice. I had to let my night simmer and my thoughts dim down. I had to make ablution and let that water refresh me. I had to pray. I didn't have to talk anymore tonight.

Chapter 17

The next morning, I woke up on my own. I headed downstairs early. Shareef and Hasan were the first downstairs. My older brother and his son were making oatmeal, eggs, and smoothies. Shareef was a good cook too. When we were younger, he would often help Ummi cook meals for the whole house. Shareef would watch us, play with us, and walk us to school. I don't remember him ever complaining or being disrespectful to our parents either. Hasan was really fortunate to have him as a father.

"Salamu alykum, sis. How goes the morning?" my brother asked me while he poured some of the smoothie from the blender into a cup for me. "Here you go."

"Salam, you guys. It's going," I said with a light chuckle. "I think I need something a little stronger than this. Any coffee made?"

Hasan jumped off of the stool he was standing on at the stove and jogged over to the other side of the kitchen. He grabbed the coffee pot full of dark liquid and brought it over to me.

"Here you go, Aunty Imani. You want sugar and cream, right?" he predicted.

"Just a little," I told him as he poured the coffee into a different cup for me. "Be careful, Hasan."

Shareef plated the eggs and brought them over to the table. He grabbed the pot of coffee from his son and poured himself a cup. He drank his coffee black.

"Ummi said you were working. Where you at?"

"Back at the old barber shop on Penn Ave and working nights at the Birch Inn."

"It's a little crazy down there at night. Gotta be careful," I advised him thinking back to my time staying there.

"Yeah, man! It's a zoo some nights. But Jibril, Hamad, and I run a tight block. The pay is decent, though, so it's working right now. I gotta pay off all the legal financial obligations or they'll send me right back."

"Court fees?"

"Yeah and anything else they can tie on me. They get back jury fees, attorney fees, filing clerk fees, and my incarceration costs. I owe them about $2500 and they taking about $150 out of my check every payday."

"Gee, going to jail is expensive."

"You better believe it. Its big business is more like it. In more ways than a little. But Insha'Allah, I'll pay it off by the end of the year and then be able to do something better with the money. I'm thinking 'bout getting a food truck next year. Maybe sell some vegetarian soul & Caribbean burritos? Fariba thinks it could work downtown."

"I like that. If you gonna put Fariba on the burner, I would definitely be a regular customer. She can really cook."

"Yeah, you know she get it from her momma. But I ain't too shabby myself. I'm gonna make some jerk collard greens tonight for Aunty's iftar. Be sure to tell me how the sisters' like it."

"Oh! Okay. Sounds like a good combo. Hey? Wait a minute. How come I was asked to bring drinks and they asked you to cook?" I complained. Shareef laughed.

"I'm trying to tell you, I am Michael Jackson bad when it comes to this cooking stuff."

"Yeah, well, I'll have you all told, I know my way around the kitchen pretty good too. I learned from some of the coldest Dominican cooks in Santo Domingo. *La bandera*, *Moro de habichuelas*, *quipe*, *tostones*, and I can even bake a serious *tres leche*, too!" I bragged.

"Alright, competition is healthy! Next time we'll have to put you to the test," Shareef promised.

"As salamu alykum," Ummi greeted us.

"Wa alykum as salam," we all replied in unison. I got up from my seat at the table and offered it to her. Ummi sat down and poured herself a cup of coffee.

"Ummi, do you want eggs or some oatmeal? There's some fresh fruit too."

"I'll take a peanut butter sandwich and fruit," she insisted.

"Ma, you need a little bit more than that since you gotta take all those meds now. How 'bout some oatmeal or toast and eggs with the peanut butter and fruit," Shareef reminded her.

"Toast with the peanut butter and eggs. I've changed my mind about the fruit. It might make my sugars go too high."

"Do you want an apple? It's higher in fiber and not so sweet," I suggested.

"No, just the toast and eggs will do. I'll be alright, ya'll," Ummi told us.

"Okay. Ummi, you know Aunty Adilah is having the *iftar* tonight. What time you wanna get dropped off?" Shareef asked.

"Yeah, she done reminded me fifty-eleven times. I'll be there, Insha'Allah. Whenever one of ya'll can drop me off will do," Ummi picked up her cup of coffee and drank the last of the liquid. "Oh, and Shareef some paperwork came the other day from the school department 'bout Hasan. Said his math test scores were really high and he might be able to go to that new school out at Squirrel Hill North. They say it is a really good school."

"Is that so?"

"Yeah, he'll do good there I think."

"Insha'Allah, I'll check it out. It just all depends where I end up. If I get that house over by Shadyside that brother Mubarak showed to me last week, he probably won't be eligible for that program. But Hasan will be all right whichever school he ends up at. He's a smart boy."

"Why you looking at places so soon, Shareef? You just got here. And Hasan needs time to adjust to all of this. I thought ya'll was gonna stay here in the house with us at least for this next school year."

"That was contingent on me finding work and the marriage, Ma. I got my old job back and I am working nights. Hasan is all right. I am not a stranger to my son. I've always had him back and forth. You know that. He'll bounce back better after the marriage and we all get settled as a family, Insha'Allah," Shareef assured us.

"I don't know why Fariba is pushing you to marry her so quick. You need time yourself to get on your feet solidly and help out here in this house with Iman and you know good and well Ameera and the kids need your help too. You don't need to rush into another marriage. Fariba ain't going nowhere."

"Reeba is not pushing me, Ma. I want to marry her. Like yesterday if I could have. I mean there really isn't a reason to wait a year or even six months. I've known her my entire life and you practically raised her. And it ain't like we're 18 or even 25. We're both grown. But I can't move Fariba and the girls into this house. There isn't enough room. It's not like I'm leaving you hanging either. I'll be in the city and by here every day. Mas'ud will still be here in the house with you. Umar is trying to get over here sometime soon so he can move in til they get settled. Being married isn't going to take me away from you, lady!"

"Yeah, you said that the last time, when you married Renay. I told you not to do it and you did it anyway. You see where that one led you? I don't see nothing wrong with you and Fariba waiting til next summer. It'll give ya'll both time to save and plan and let the kids adjust. But what I know? I was married 40 years, though."

"Ma, c'mon don't be like that!" Shareef snapped. He stood up from the table then leaned over Ummi and kissed her cheek. "It will be okay, Insha'Allah. We'll have your constant guidance and rebuttals every step of the way - how we gonna fail?" he joked. "Hasan, go wake up the boys and Uncle Mas'ud. Tell them to hurry it up too."

"Well, if I may interject," I announced but Ummi quickly shut me down.

"Worry about yourself, Imani!"

"Ummi! I was just going to say that I think Hasan and Reeba will do well. They already love each other. And Reeba's girls love Shareef.

They're already family. Them moving in together will only strengthen their bond," I argued.

"I don't have a problem with Reeba! I love her. I want good for her and Shareef too. I am just saying that they need to plan things a little better. Patience ain't never hurt no one either. Hasan been here with me all this time. And they just gonna snatch him up from me. He needs time. That baby been through a lot."

"Kids are resilient, Ma. And you will still have a house full of grands to fuss over. In just a little bit Madeenah will be running 'round here with Saba. And Hasan will be here on the weekends. You will be okay, lady," Shareef assured her again.

Ummi bit into her toast and shoved some eggs in her mouth then swallowed without chewing it up first. Change was always hard. It never got easier to digest.

After we all prayed together, I went back upstairs to shower so that I could get ready for work. Ameera never got up. When I asked her to drop me off at work, she shook her head vigorously for side to side.

"Take the keys. Bring the car back when you're done."

I made it to Hilltop Clinic at the same time as my supervisor. She smiled as she unlocked the door then held it open for me to enter.

"Early bird catches the worm, or in my case, catches up on a stack of paperwork," she giggled softly.

"Ah, yes! We're in the same predicament, Miss Michel'le! Some days it just seems impossible to get it all in on time."

"That's the joke. It is impossible. But we're nurses. The mules and superwomen and supermen who are supposed to do it with a smile. Don't worry 'bout it, Iman. Do your best and give the rest to God. And if that doesn't work, blame it on the tech department. Something is always not working properly."

"So that's the plan?" I laughed. "I couldn't hurt those guys in IT. They work too hard."

"We all do!"

Michel'le and I sat in our station then got busy on our laptops going through files that needed updating. By the time the rest of the staff showed up, I was ready to roll through my roster of morning patients. The time flew by. The first week of August had brought in another steady stream of children needing their physicals and vaccine paperwork updated. The other wave of children were the sick children. Those children never ceased to come see us.

When Asr prayer rolled in I was grateful. My afternoon prayer wasn't just my time to read Qur'an, but it was also my countdown time. It was almost time to go home. Throughout the day, I had collected even more paperwork but there were just a couple more patients to see.

"Tasha, love, que pasa, Mamita?" I asked her playfully as I entered the medical representatives' station.

"Aqui." She handed me a new file. "Mija, esta que estilla!" She warned me about the looks of someone in the waiting room.

"Who you talking about? The child?" I demanded to know.

"No, silly! The dad! Just go get them!"

Shaking my head with a laugh, I walked out towards the waiting room. I opened the file and saw a familiar name. It stopped me in my tracks. Pacing my breath and reassuring myself that I was safe at work and that there could be a really good reason why I was reading Danny's name. I was okay. I started to walk again until we all stood face to face.

"Tia! That's my Tia! Tia Nia!" Corazon ran at full speed with her waist length pigtails whipping back and forth behind her. She jumped into up into my arms. I bended down and embraced the little girl that I had rocked and kissed many moons ago as I pretended she was mine on so many nights.

"Mija Cora! Oh, sweet Cora!"

Danny walked over to me wearing plaid shorts, flip flops, and a white short sleeve shirt. He stood with his hands stuffed into his pockets looking down at the carpeted floor for a minute before he too fell into my arms. I hugged him close to me and kissed his forehead.

"Dannito! ¿Que lo wha, pana?" I asked him before hugging him again. I was so deeply touched by seeing the children; I didn't notice him standing there quietly. He was staring at me with his hands stuffed in a pair of white-washed jeans with a couple of rips in the knee area paired with a beige polka dotted oversized button down shirt, caramel color suede loafers on his feet and a brown round fedora over his curly shoulder length hair. His tanned face was adorned in new facial hair.

"How can I help you, Mateo?" I finally managed to say.

"Hello, Iman," he recited my name with a rhythm I had spent the last couple of months trying to forget.

"Hello," I responded coolly.

"Evie said you could help me get Danny's medical records. I'll need them to enroll him in school in Atlanta."

I glanced at Danny and then at Corazon who had both now retreated back to their uncle's side. I scanned their faces looking for any signs of fear, anger, or abuse. It wasn't for me, it was my job's requirements. I was a mandated reporter of child abuse. I couldn't find anything. Corazon's smile was endearing: full and genuine. She held Mateo's hand tightly and stood almost in front of him as if she needed to protect him from me.

"Yes, I can have his records prepared for you. It'll take 24 hours for the department to pull it and get them printed then over to me, though."

"A'ight. I'll stop back tomorrow around same time."

"I'll need a release form signed first. But I am not sure you can sign it right now. Can you have Abuela Lourdes sign it and bring it back tomorrow?"

"Whatever needs to be done," he responded with a shuffle of his feet. He looked withdrawn and quiet. It was the quiet that people in pain displayed when they didn't have enough fight left in them to cry or run.

"Okay, have a seat and I'll go fetch the form for you."

I turned around one foot at a time and walked back through the double doors that separated the waiting room from the nurses' station and the examination rooms.

"Did you see him? Ma-ma-mia, he's butter pecan fine, right? Girl, el es guapo!" Tasha quipped.

"Can you get me a medical release form?"

"Iman? Did you see him or what? That dad out there is so freaking…"

"Tasha, get the release form!" I ordered. I walked away from her to take Danny's file back to cabinet.

"Here you go, Mizz Iman," Tasha whimpered as she dropped the paper on the counter. She rolled her eyes and sucked her teeth on the way back to her cubicle. I didn't let it bother me. I was sure she didn't understand my lack of enthusiasm over Mateo's appearance. It had been years ago when I had to bury away all my affectionate feelings for Mateo. I couldn't call his beauty beauty. He was just Mateo. He was my pain, my heartache, my regrets, my fears, and my past. I didn't owe her that information.

"All right, here you go," I extended my arm out from a considerable distance. I was so far away from him, he couldn't reach the paper. He stood up and stepped towards me. I stepped back two steps and he sighed deeply as if I offended him.

"Have Abuela Lourdes sign it. If you can attach a copy of the death certificate or any other legal documents that she may have and bring it with you, it'll help the record department get the request filled faster."

"Understood." Mateo turned around and looked at his niece and nephew. "All right, let's go guys. Give Tia Nia a hug and thank her for her help." Corazon and Danny walked back over to me and I hugged them again. I grabbed Corazon's face first and kissed her cheeks again. "I love you, Cora, okay? You're such an amazing, sweet girl. And Dannito, we haven't known each other long, but you, my friend, are an intelligent young man and loved. You are both loved so much. Don't forget, okay?" I reminded them as a couple of tears escaped my eyes. I quickly wiped them away.

"I love you too, Tia!" Corazon said. Danny began to cry. I hugged him tighter. Mateo reached out for him and started to wipe his eyes.

"Big man, no more tears. You're good. I got you, okay!" Danny hugged Mateo and the little boy leaned against him for support. "My man! Hey, Nia, thanks and ah, I really hope that we can talk. Mediate some of the loose ends... with the lawyers."

"Speak to my brothers."

Mateo nodded his head then guided the kids out of the waiting room. Corazon waved good bye. I didn't know who that man was, but I breathed a sigh of relief. I hadn't been harmed. I had pushed through my anxiety. This was a win for me. I was moving on and conquering my fears. Just take one step towards Allah...

"Iman, I am going to be out on leave for about a week starting tomorrow," Michel'le started. "My husband is having surgery finally on his knee. I'm going to stay home and nurse my man back to health," she gushed.

"Wonderful. Don't worry about peds, we'll be okay!"

"I know it because you are here with us! But there's a meeting tomorrow that I was supposed to attend with management about funding for some of our programs. Our women's support group might be on the chopping block. I think you could present a strong defense. Would you step in for me, pretty please with a cherry on top, Miss Iman?" Michel'le clasped her hands together and prayed in to them.

"My Lord! If it means that much to you, Miss Michel'le, I will stand in for you at the budget meeting. Send me the details and I will try to put something together. Is there anything else that I need to do for your while you're away?" I asked.

"Yes, in fact there is something else. I need you to relax, smile, and know that you're doing a great job!"

I laughed and beamed at her brightly. "I appreciate that, boss lady. Have a good time at your staycation and tell Dequan I hope he feels better."

"Thanks, will do, hun."

Chapter 18

When it was time to go home, I couldn't leave fast enough. I was too happy to have Ameera's wagon. Fariba was busy with the iftar preparations, Shareef was home cooking for the iftar, and Ameera was still stuck in her funk. Mas'ud was still at work, and Yasmeen had Madeenah. It was time to wean off the security anyway. I was ready. Moving forward was what I was doing. It felt like I had cracked the ceiling ever so lightly. I could smell a little fresh air. It was light, but full of sweetness waiting for me to claim it.

I walked out of the clinic towards the staff parking lot tugging my bags along the way. The keys were in my mouth dangling back and forth as I struggled.

"Looks like you need some help there," Jibril suggested with a hearty chuckled that I hadn't heard in a while. I handed him the bags without any hesitation. "What you got in here rocks? You training for a Golden Gloves boxing match or something?"

"You got jokes," I jested with him as I unlocked the doors. Jibril carried the bags to the passenger side and placed them inside without any strains. His foot had healed nicely and he was walking smoothly again.

"Of course, always!"

"You know, you didn't have to come out of here. I am okay."

"Alhamduleelah, glad to hear that, kid. But I got my orders."

"I see. So you were just following instructions?"

"Yeah. Following instructions is important. Especially when it involves protecting people that you are invested in and care about. That's wajib on me," he disclosed. "I'm following you home too."

I got into the wagon, threw my handbag in, sat down, pulled the seat belt around me, then started the engine. I watched Jibril walk back to his SUV and get in. He backed out of the parking space he was parked in across the street and pulled up to the curb outside of the staff parking lot. I put the car in reverse, backed out of my parking spot, and drove out of the parking lot. Jibril pulled into the traffic and followed behind me the whole way home. Just like he said he would.

The short ride home allowed me to clear my mind a bit. I kept thinking back to the way Mateo's face looked. The way he acted was drastically different than my last year with him. He was hurting for sure. Diego was a big loss for their family. But I just felt like it was more than that. He finally looked defeated. All the years of anger, dishonesty, and abuse of me and himself had caught up to him. I hope he was finally ready to let go of his monster and just be a man and find healing.

I parked Ameera's car on the street because the driveway was full. Umar's car was parked in the driveway behind Yaz's. The boys were out front playing football.

"As salamu alykum, Aunty!" Imran, Hasan, and Munir yelled at me in unison. Imran ran over to me and gave me a big hug.

"Wa alykum as salam, guys. Hasan and Imran, can you help me with my bags. Each one of you take one, please and thank you," I added.

"I can take both bags, Aunt Iman," Hasan told me as he snatched the other bag away from his cousin.

"No, that's not what I asked you to do, Hasan. I want you to take just one bag. Please, give the other bag to Imran to carry. They're heavy and even though you might not think so, it's safer to share the task. Okay?"

Hasan sighed and dropped the bag on the ground before walking away. I didn't chastise him further. Hasan was going through his changes too. With his dad back home in the house, he wasn't able to be babied by us as much as he was used to. Shareef was also giving some of his attention to Fariba and her girls. Hasan had to adapt. I was confident that he would. Fariba and Hasan had a good relationship and she would make a great step-mother, Insha'Allah.

I noticed Yasmeen as soon as I entered the kitchen. She was sitting at the table cutting cheese into cubes with Ameera wearing an old looking white long sleeve t-shirt and full jean skirt with a black Georgette hijab. Shareef was at the stove stirring his pot of greens.

"Hey, salamu alykum, good people! How goes the day?" I asked them.

"Wa alykum as salam," my family replied. Ameera was dressed up looking pretty. She wore a maxi dress with a peach body t-shirt undeath, big gold hoop earrings, and her hair was curled into bouncy ringlets that framed her golden-brown face.

"Is that what you're wearing to the *iftar* tonight, Ameera?" I asked my sister.

"This is it."

"It's cute. I don't know what I am wearing yet," I said as opened the refrigerator's door and scanned all the drawers and shelves. Then it hit me, I still had an hour of fasting time to go. I slammed the door shut.

"Yaz, you're coming with us over to Aunty's house tonight too, right?"

"I don't know if I feel up to it yet. I'll have to pack two or three outfits, diapers, water, creams, snacks for me, the car seat, her rocker - it's just too much," she complained. "She'll just end up crying the whole time."

"It's good to get out," Ameera declared. "Like I was telling you earlier, you can't let that little girl rule you. She is a baby and you are the Mama, Yaz. If you want her to nap, then you have to teach her. The nursing is a different story, though, but you can get it on a routine too. Insha'Allah," she continued.

"True, Yaz. This phase will pass. It will. Come out with us. You're friend Hasanah and her baby boy will be there and so many other sisters will be there to help you," I pointed out.

"Fariba can watch Madeenah for you too, if you need her to, Yaz," Shareef chimed in. "Way too many family members around for you and Mas'ud to do it alone. Just say the word, we can all help you more."

Yasmeen shook her head in agreement. Tears dashed from her eyes then she sobbed loudly. Ameera looked at me. I looked at Shareef. He screwed his face up and then shrugged his shoulders as if to say he didn't know what was happening either. I sat down at the table next to her and rubbed her back.

"How are you feeling, Yaz? What's making you cry, honey? Does something hurt?"

Yasmeen shook her head her up and down before wiping the tears with the sleeve of her dress. "Everything hurts. I don't know why? I don't know why this is all so hard. I don't know why I am failing at this. I just wish my Umm would've stayed a little longer with us," Yasmeen confessed.

"You are doing exactly what all new mothers be doing," Ameera started. "Oh my goodness, you should have seen me with Imran. It was bad. I didn't know how to nurse, couldn't change his diapers fast enough. He must have peed on me and Umar a gazillion times before we figured out that we had to cover him up while we changed his diaper. I gave him formula for the first three months because I just couldn't get the nursing down. I cried all day and he would cry all night. Abu was sick around that time so Ummi couldn't stay with me in Philadelphia too long either. But you know what she told me?"

"What?" Yasmeen asked.

"She told me to call on Allah," Ameera revealed with a giggle.

"That's classic Ma!" Shareef added as he grabbed the pan of macaroni and cheese off the table.

"I thought she was being cold then. I mean, I probably still do feel like that a little today. But the point is, I followed her advice. I learned that it gets a little easier, but welcome to motherhood, Yaz. Having babies is tough. Raising kids is tough. Guiding adults is hard. You just gotta roll with the punches and do your best."

"Even though I don't really know much about motherhood, I do know that at my clinic we have some great mother and baby support groups offered in the morning. We also have several female family counselors. I think it might be good for you come to work with me tomorrow and see if any of the programs might be a fit. What do you think, Yaz?"

"I think I'd like that, Iman. Shukran. I'll have to talk to Mas'ud first, though."

"Okay, good. So anyway, let's all go get ready for *iftar* at Aunty's. I am hungry and you sitting here nibbling on all the food ain't helping," I joked

"Perks of childbirth," she reminded me.

"Right! Why don't you go wash up first, Yaz? Ameera and I will get Madeenah packed and ready."

"Are you sure?"

"Yes!" Ameera and I said in unison.

Yasmeen got up and smiled at us before walking away towards the stairs.

"Hey sisters," Shareef whispered.

"What Shareef?" Ameera responded.

"You're both are two cups of awesomeness."

"You're so corny," I shot back.

"Seriously though, Nurse Iman, you think Yaz has the baby blues?" my brother asked me through furrowed brows.

"She'll need anti-depressants for that and they make you even crazier," Ameera cautioned us.

"Maybe not. I think the first step is just to get her to see some professionals at the clinic, keep helping her with Madeenah, and make sure she gets up and gets out so doesn't feel so overwhelmed."

"Yeah, seems like she needs help getting back to her old self," Ameera admitted.

"I'll talk to Mas'ud about the clinic so that she doesn't have a reason to back out," Shareef promised.

"That would be best," Ameera agreed. "I'm going to go finish getting me and Saba ready. You good, Shareef?"

"Uh huh. I got it from here."

Shareef waved us out of the kitchen so that he could finish up cooking his dishes for the *iftar*. I grabbed my things and headed back to the living room to get my niece. Madeenah was swinging quietly in her swing sucking on her pacifier watching the carousel spin toys above her head. She looked like she was almost about to fall asleep. I left her be so that she could rest while I got myself ready.

An hour later, I had finished showering, tamed my hair, and had found an outfit to wear. I put on a silky magenta hi-lo shirt mid-length dress with a black stretch knit maxi skirt and pink and gold leather high heeled sandals. I paired a couple of brass and silver bracelets with it to complete the outfit. I switched my black jersey hijab out for the cream pashmina. I wrapped it loosely around my head and chest area and pinned a gold brooch onto my shirt to keep the ends of the hijab in place.

I went back down the stairs and found a fully dressed Yasmeen and Ummi, and the boys lining up for the evening prayer.

"Where's Madeenah? Is she dressed?"

"Mas'ud took her. He's upstairs getting her ready now," she told me.

I kicked my shoes off and brought them out to the shoe rack and bumped into Shareef. He was carrying his trays of food out the door.

"'Scuse me!"

"You're excused," my brother noted. "Watch out now," he warned me.

"Ya'll ready to pray? Where's Ameera and Saba?" I asked everyone.

"She's in the backroom talking with Umar," Yasmeen told me.

"Okay, we'll let's go ahead and pray without her," I suggested. Ummi shot me a look that let me know she wasn't sure about my suggestion. I moved into the middle of the line, raised my hands above my head, and professed, "Allahu Akbar."

Ten minutes later, we had completed our prayer. Mas'ud brought Madeenah and her car seat downstairs. He'd done an excellent job cleaning and dressing his daughter. She was playfully dressed in a pink tutu and a white t-shirt that read: "Got Milk", and pink crochet slippers with pink and white ribbons decorating them. Mas'ud had even slipped a pink and white flowered headband on her head.

"She looks perfect, sweetheart!" Yasmeen gushed.

"You sure? You don't think I over did the pink?" he asked his wife.

" Can't overdo pink!" Yasmeen reached into the car seat and picked up her daughter and swooned before kissing her cheeks.

"Ummi, ya'll ready to go?" Mas'ud turned and asked our mother. I was sitting on the couch ready to go. I hadn't even broke my fast yet. I was reserving my appetite for the good meal that we had waiting on us.

"I guess so. Just waiting on Meera and Saba. Go and check to see if she riding with us or if Umar gonna take her," she instructed my brother. He pursed his lips together and looked over his shoulder towards the backroom and sucked his teeth as he walked away. I had the same feeling that Mas'ud had. The saying goes, leave good enough alone. In Ameera and Umar's case, it meant that if they weren't arguing or fighting, they were good. Asking if they were okay could potentially start a problem.

"No. What? Nah, I ain't checking nothing. I didn't say I was on anyone's side. I ain't playing, Meera -- Meera! What is wrong with you? Shareef!" Mas'ud yelled.

I jumped to my feet and ran to the door to go get my older brother from outside.

"What in the world is going on now with them?" Ummi snapped as she struggled to get up out of her chair.

"Jeddah, do you need help?" Hasan asked her.

"Yes! Come pull me up, boy!" Ummi ordered him.

"Ummi, stay out here. Ya'll go 'head to the car. Hasan, take the kids to the porch!" Shareef instructed his son as he ran passed me in the direction of the backroom.

"I don't care! NO! Get off of me, Mas'ud. Tell him to tell me the truth! I wanna hear you say it! I swear I'mma hurt you, bust you right upside your head! Yeah, okay. So who sending you these text messages? Who is she?"

Ummi shook her head and clasped her hands over her face and fell back into her chair. "Something ain't right with that child of mine," she whispered through a few tears. "She just ain't right."

"GET OFF OF ME! Shareef, no! STOP!" We all stood frozen in place as we listened to Ameera yell and scream at the top of her lungs. There were a few bumps in the wall and then the door opened and shut several times before there was one last loud slam. I knew it was time to go.

"Let's go, ya'll. Let's go. Mas'ud and Shareef will take care of her," I told them as a hope and prayer both. I held my mother's hand and grabbed Madeenah's baby bag as we walked out of the door.

After we all packed in Mas'ud's van with the Meera's boys, I realized that my niece Saba was still in the house with her parents. I had to send Hasan to go get her. She'd already seen enough, she didn't need to see any more fights between her parents tonight.

A couple of minutes later, Mas'ud came out of the house holding Saba with Hasan walking by his side. Yasmeen opened the side door and grabbed Saba.

"Everything okay?" Yasmeen asked her husband. Mas'ud face looked grim. He shook his head then wiped his face.

"Ya'll go on. We'll talk about it later."

After Hasan got in the car, we strapped Saba into the child seat built into the van and I pulled out into the street. It was a good thing that Aunty Adilah lived close to us. The silence that filled that van was so loud it hurt my ears, stomach, and mostly my heart. We were all worried about Ameera and Umar, but her sons were crushed. Munir sniffled and sucked up his tears the whole way there.

"You know that your Umm is all right. Your father is there with Uncle Mas'ud and Uncle Shareef. They gonna take good care of her. She is probably just tired," Ummi lectured them. "Call on Allah and ask Him to keep her safe. Yup, that's what you do," she told him as she patted his head.

Aunty Adilah's street was packed full of cars that belonged to all the sisters she'd known after over 40 years in the community. There was a small group of brothers, mostly her sons and some of their friends standing around her front yard. I let the kids, Ummi, and Yasmeen out so that I could find a parking spot further down the street. I texted Shareef and told him to call me whenever he had a chance and update me about what was going on with Ameera. We were going to have a family meeting about her behavior sooner rather than later. We all needed to know what the problem was and how we could help her.

Full of thoughts in my mind that wouldn't stop dancing, I had forgot all about Shareef's food in the back of the car. I walked backed down to Aunty's house and approached the group of brothers.

"Hamad, have you seen Jibril?" I questioned his brother.

"Yeah. He's in the backyard on the grill with the boys. You need him?" he asked me.

"I do. I got a couple of platters of food in the back of Yasmeen's van that Shareef sent."

"Uh oh, Reeba got big Reef back cooking!" he joked. "I'll go get it," he quickly assured me. I reached in my wristlet, pulled out the keys, and handed them to him. "And uh, I'll tell Jibril you looking for him too."

I nodded as I walked to the porch. The screen door was locked, but the door was open. I heard groups of women laughing and talking jovially. "As salamu alykum? Can someone come unlock the door?"

Habibah and Hadiyya, Fariba's identical twin daughters who were about eight years old came running to the door carrying a basket to let me in. The girls were dressed the same in pretty bright yellow lace print shift dresses with white lace leggings. Their hair was pulled into one big puff that let their curly hair fall out and bounce around.

"Ramadhan Mubarak! Please come in," they stated in unison. "Here you go," the twin with the missing tooth said as she handed me a small Samosa filled with meat.

"Shukran! Now, you two are going to have to remind me if I mess this up - are you Hadiyya?" I said pointing to the little girl who handed me *iftar* snack. The girls began laughing. I knew that my guess was a miss.

"Nooo," she said shaking her head with a big smile that exposed her dimples. "I'm Habibah, the oldest," she told me and then pointed to her sister, "And that's Hadiyya, my younger sister!"

"Alright, I am going to do my very best to get it right the next time."

I followed the girls into Aunty's dining room where some of the sisters were eating.

"You can also go downstairs to the basement. My uncles and my mom set up tables and we have some games to play later tonight."

"Okay. Thank you...um, Hadiyya? Did I get it right that time?"

The sisters smiled. "You got it right this time."

"Alhamduleelah."

I sat down at one of the chairs and nibbled on my samosa. Fariba spotted me sitting. She walked over carrying a full pitcher.

"As salamu alykum. I was wondering where you were?"

"Wa alykum as salam. I was trailing behind like always. What's in there?" I asked her.

"This is lemonade. Freshly made with a little mint, honey, and pineapples."

With my mouth full of food, I grabbed a plastic cup and held it up for her to pour me a cup of the juice.

"You know Jibril was looking for you a minute ago," she told me.

"Can you just ask him to go round back by my house, please."

"Is everything okay?"

"Ameera and Umar," I confided in her in a hushed voiced.

"Oh boy. If it ain't one thing, it's another. I'll go tell him to go over there now 'fore the cops show up."

"Thanks, hun."

Buffet serving trays sat upon sparkly white and silver table cloths that covered several folding tables around the perimeter of the room. White and silver balloons were tied together and looped around all the bay windows in the dining room and inside the hallways that lead to the staircase and around the kitchen doors. Small white lights were twisted around the staircases leading up stairs and down to the basement. Paper lanterns colored in silver and gold were hanging on the wall over the fireplace along with a big gold crescent moon and smaller stars. There had to be over 20 sisters plus little children and babies moving through the rooms. Another 25 were probably downstairs in the basement. I smiled at and politely salamed everyone who passed by me or sat down at the tables.

Smaller trays filled with several different types of hor d'oeuvres kept me occupied. Different types of cheeses, grapes, cucumber sandwiches, shrimp, and sausages, watermelon slices, veggies, and dips were some of the offerings. The tray that kept the sisters coming back was mini waffles and fried chicken bites that were drizzled with honey and powdered sugar. I tried my best to avoid it. I followed my rules to put the healthy in first. I had nibbled on the veggies, a couple of olives, and had even chomped down some watermelon slices. My tummy was still talking to me, though. My tummy wanted some of the waffles and fried chicken.

I got up and grabbed a napkin then picked up one of the little decadent and savory bites. I placed the whole thing in my mouth and chewed it up quickly. It was delicious and dangerous. They were so good, I needed to leave the buffet. After I threw my trash away, I headed downstairs to find my family.

"As salamu alykum! Iman?" a new revert sister from the halaqah group that Ummi and I attended reached out her hands to embrace me.

"Wa alykum as salam wa rahmatullah, Carla! You look stunning, sis," I told her.

"Oh, this right here is old. But I guess I do clean up pretty good," she agreed with a light giggle. "You always look well put together and beautiful. Love that shirt. If I was a couple of pounds smaller." Carla had a habit of putting herself down. It made me feel uncomfortable because I didn't want her to feel like I agreed with her doubts. At the same time, I hated trying to find reassuring words for strangers.

"You look fine, Carla. Absolutely fine, sis."

"Ah, thanks. So do you know how long the Eid break will be for our class? I missed the last two classes. Didn't have childcare," she admitted.

"Just a week. And you know Ustadha Maysa doesn't mind the kids. You should bring them. They can play in the classroom right next to ours or sit with you in the class," I suggested.

"I know but my two boys are too big for the playrooms but not big enough to stay home. They would get bored and bug me the whole time and I wouldn't get any learning in. I am behind already."

"I understand. I still think you should bring them, though. If they are over ten, there are some classes for them too. Speak to Ustadha Maysa and see what she has to say."

"Alhamduleelah. I'll do that. Good seeing you, sis."

"You too, Carla."

The basement was full of the other half of the sisters talking, playing board games, eating their hors d'oeuvres, and fussing after their children. Soft nasheeds played in the background from the surround sound system that Aunty Adilah had hooked on the back wall close to her washer and dryer. It was nice a turnout and the perfect opportunity for my sister-in-law to relax and get out the house. I just hoped she wasn't worrying herself about Ameera like I was. I still hadn't heard from Shareef, Mas'ud, or Jibril.

Chapter 19

⟨⟩

Saba waddled up to me as I was in stride towards Yasmeen and Ummi sitting with Aunty Adilah. I picked up my niece and grabbed a chair, dragging it towards the group. "You look good, Iman. How you feeling?" Aunty Adilah asked. She was holding Fariba's youngest daughter, Hafsa.

"I feel all right. Pushing through these last days, Alhamduleelah. Ya'll did a good job with everything. Did you know there's a crowd of sisters swooning over those snacks upstairs?"

"That was all Fariba and Shareef's doing. I ain't had to cook nothing, really. I made the lemon and limeades, though."

"Those juices were delicious. You might want to brand it and package it up!" I complimented her.

"You kids all sound the same. Shareef told me the same thing. Said he is really thinking about getting a food truck and he is gonna need that juice!" She chuckled. "We'll see, Insha'Allah. Any way, Jibril and Hamad should be finishing up with the chicken on the grill so we'll start serving dinner soon, Insha'Allah."

"Hey, Muneerah," Aunty Adilah turned around to her other side and started talking to my mother.

"What's that?" Ummi answered her.

"Do you remember the first time we put together this sisters' *iftar*? It was just me and you and the husbands?"

"That's right. We cooked and cleaned for days. Aqil worked so hard building those benches for the sisters to sit on out in the backyard," Ummi laughed.

"Sure did. Back then, if I even whispered an idea he just run with it. And how 'bout Musa running around Pittsburgh with all the kids riding in his station wagon looking for a farm that would let him bring the lamb back to the city so he could slaughter it at the masjid? You didn't think he could do it, did you?"

"Nah, not a bit. I thought he was crazy myself," Ummi eyes were lit up and she was smiling ear to ear as memories of my father flooded her mind. "He and Aqil together were something else. Weren't they something?"

"Sure 'nuff, they were a team. But you know what, we ain't topped that first iftar yet."

"Can't top it. It was the whole city. We told them just sisters, but every brother came out to do security. I thought they were going to call the cops on us that night with all them black and brown men out on your front lawn making salat. That was something, wasn't it Adilah?"

"Sure was! Those were the days. We fed every Muslim in the city and we didn't know them all, either. All they had to say was that they were Muslims and Musa gave them the salams and told to come on in. Eat, pray, and enjoy yourself," Aunty Adilah pointed out to us.

"What happened to those days and those Muslims?" Yasmeen asked.

"Life, Yaz. You know hardships, struggles, jealousy, and enmity. All that crap gets in the way of Muslims coming together and working together. It just sucks the love right out of us. Now everybody got they own clique. They own look, passwords, masajid, and Imams too. We done got away from the basics. I was downtown at the bank yesterday sitting in the line. I see a little young Muslim girl come in the door. She covered up and looked nice. I waved and offered her the greeting. She gonna turn all the way around. So I raised my voice and greeted her again. She gonna look at me and then point at herself like, 'who you talking to?' I said forget it and went on with my business. I don't got time for the foolishness. It's so sad how we are, it's funny!"

"Since I've moved to Pittsburgh, I've found the sisters to be really warm. Especially at the Islamic Center. I've made some really good friends, Alhamduleelah," Yasmeen declared to us about her own experiences. "Granted, it still doesn't feel exactly like home to me here. But it's been good."

"Glad you feel that way, Yaz. It's always tough moving to new Muslim communities as a young person," Ummi told her. "Ain't really enough of us anywhere nowhere. Even in the city with large numbers of Muslims split up by race or culture."

"Don't forget the haves and have nots," Hasanah, Yasmeen's friend added as she rocked Madeenah in her arm. "Sometimes wealth is a greater divider among the Muslims than anything else, even race. I think we do a good at the Islamic Center because we have the school and the community works hard supporting it to keep the fees affordable. But there are still a lot of Muslim families who can't afford the school. So those children and their families miss out on some of the opportunities to develop their Islamic identity."

"Well now hold up," Aunty Adilah interjected. "We didn't have that school when ya'll were children. We homeschooled during the week, we had Islamic weekend school, and in the summer time we had the camp right at the Islamic Center. We didn't charge nothing but three or four dollars per child to cover lunch and some activities. And if the family couldn't afford it, we didn't turn them away. It was a lot of sacrifice. The goal was always greater than the struggles.

"Nowadays, you young Muslims more concerned with stuff looking nice and pretty. Activities got to be at the biggest and best places. Schools got to be in high rise buildings with the latest computers for anyone to wanna go. Problem is you don't reach all the people like that. In fact, you exclude the poor completely and that ain't from Islam. And I know Hasanah, you's a good teacher over at the school. Eventually, we got to get back to the basics. We gotta get back to hearts of people. That's where change can happen."

I listened as the sisters continued to talk about issues in our community. I didn't have much to add at that point. Overall, I felt like I still had a lot of heart work to do on myself. I also had my family to support. I was needed both financially and emotionally. Worrying about the next sister giving salams, budgets at the Islamic Center, summer camps and trips just weren't on my bullet list yet.

My phone vibrated inside my wristlet to let me know that I had a message. I pulled the phone out and swiped it to see the landing page. Two messages awaited me.

Reef: Taking Ameera to the ER. Riding with Umar.

Reef: Don't tell Ummi. Mas'ud is at the house. Jibril will keep the boys tonight.

My heart dropped. I inhaled slowly and pushed out the breath I couldn't hold in anymore. I hated how vague my brother was being. How did he expect me not to tell my mother that her daughter was on her way to the emergency room? This wasn't what we needed tonight. I grabbed Saba and walked away from my mother and sister-in-law and headed back up the stairs. As soon as I got to the kitchen, I saw Fariba and her brothers preparing plates for the sisters to eat. I sat down in one of the chairs with my niece and clicked on my brother's number.

"Salamu alykum," he answered the phone.

"Wa alaykum as salam. Shareef what's going on? Why are you guys taking Ameera to the ER?"

Fariba looked over to me and then at the kitchen door before she walked over and closed it. She waved her hand at me to let me know that I could keep talking.

"She wasn't feeling well, Iman. Umar felt it was best to take her in to be seen than to try to wait it out."

"Wait out what? What is wrong with my sister, Shareef?"

"Iman, the doctor is coming back for her now. I think she is probably going to have stay overnight to be checked out. If they keep her, we'll get you and Ummi over here. All right? Saba good?"

"She's fine. She's sitting with me now."

"Okay, cool. See ya'll later, Insha'Allah. Salamu 'alykum."

He ended the call. I had no answers. I looked over to Fariba. I knew she knew more than me. She always did.

"Reeba! What is going on?" I yelled. "Why Shareef not telling me nothing?"

Fariba was standing over the sink. She washed her hands then dried them off before turning towards me. Her lips were pursed together. She cut her eyes at me before walking over to the table.

"Iman, some things are not our place to speak. Some things sometimes need to be explained directly from person that it is about. Insha'Allah, Meera will get some much-needed rest tonight. Try to talk to her tomorrow when she is feeling better, okay?"

I rolled her explanation around in my mind for a moment. I quickly thought about all of the things I had been through during my marriage and since I returned home. I knew my story, so my narrative could only be spoken through my mouth. Anything else wouldn't make sense nor carry the vowels, adjectives, or the pitch correctly. Ameera's story was her own tale to speak. That made sense to me. My heart slowed down. My breathing began to normalize. I knew Ameera hadn't been physically hurt. Shareef would have told me. Whatever she needed to rest from was emotional. Sometimes our feelings hurt more and were heavier than any physical pain. I would have to wait til tomorrow to talk to my sister. My task now was how to explain it to my mother.

"What do I tell Ummi?" I asked her.

"Just tell her that Shareef and Umar will talk to her later," Fariba offered.

I stayed in the kitchen helping Fariba to finish plating food for the sisters downstairs in the basement. The rest of the food we brought into dining room and added to the warm serving trays. Fariba and I also served the ten or so brothers out in the backyard before I got a chance to sit down again.

I fixed a double plate for Saba and I then sat down with some little girls to eat on the floor. A large white cotton table spread was laid out for the children in Aunty's prayer room. Fariba and her three daughters came to eat with us. We both ended up cutting up food for the children, pouring and wiping up spills and singing songs the whole time. I enjoyed spending time with all of the little girls. It reminded me of all of pregnancies that I'd had and lost. Some of my babies would have been close in age to Reeba's daughters. I still felt that they were better off. I just prayed and hoped I would get to a place in this life where I would be fit to care for a child of my own.

After prayer, I gathered all of my family members and got them in the car. Jibril came up to give us salams just as I was about to drive off.

"As salamu Alykum, Aunty Muneerah and company. Ya'll enjoy yourselves?"

"Alhamduleelah," Ummi pondered before telling him, "It was good. Always nice to see the sisters. Your Umm had to remind me that this is our tradition. Started with your Abu and Umm. It's good it's still going. May Allah accept it for him on his good deeds."

"Ameen. Ameen. *Alhamduleelah*, this whole city meant a lot to him before… before everything else got to him. So just wanted to let ya'll know I got Hasan, Imran, and Munir. They coming over to my place hang out with Saud and me."

"You ain't got to work tonight?" Ummi enquired.

"Nah. Shareef and Ya'coob on it tonight. It's my night off."

"All right, well if you want to take them all," Ummi quipped. "Just make sure Munir go to the bathroom before he sleeps. Don't give him nothing to drink 'cause he'll spray the room down," my mother warned with a light laugh.

"Yeah, I know how it goes with that boy. Insha'Allah, we good," Jibril reassured her. He tapped his fist onto of the van before offering the salams and walking away.

I drove the van home and parked it in the driveway behind Ameera's wagon. Umar's car wasn't there. They hadn't returned yet. I knew I needed to tell my mother about the situation before she got in the house looking for Ameera.

"Ah, Ummi, Shareef and Umar decided to um, take Meera to the ER," I slid out. I turned the lights on and unlocked the doors. In the mirror, I could see Yasmeen's surprised face. "Mas'ud is here, Yaz. Can you text him and tell him to come help take these kids and plates in?"

"Yeah sure," my sister-in-law pulled out her phone and called her husband.

"What they take Meera to the ER for?" Ummi asked me too quiet for my liking.

"She wasn't feeling well. Umar wanted her to get checked out."

"Did he hit her?"

"No. He didn't hit her. Shareef said she wasn't feeling well. She gonna have to stay the night."

"Allah! Yasmeen, bring Saba up to your place with you and Mas'ud. Keep her til I get back, please."

"Okay, Ummi," Yasmeen replied just as Mas'ud came up to the van. He offered the salams.

"Ummi, where you going?" he asked our mother.

"I am going to the hospital to check on my child. Ya'll not gonna talk to me like I don't know what is going on. Meera is my child. I carried and birthed her, you understand me?"

"Yeah, we know that, Ummi," I noted.

"Then ya'll better act like it. I am going to go to that hospital right now to see about my child."

"Ummi, she is resting. That's it. Umar said they gonna discharge her first thing in the morning with a follow-up appointment. Shareef and Umar are on there way back here right now. So if you wanna go up there, just wait on Umar. He'll take you. Meera is safe and resting," Mas'ud pleaded with our mother.

"They on their way now?" Ummi questioned him again.

"They comin' right now, Insha'Allah. Come on in the house and wait for them," he urged her.

"All right, I'll come in and wait on 'em to get here. Got my baby out in some ER and gonna tell me to go to sleep. I don't know who ya'll think ya'll are?!" Ummi mumbled as Mas'ud helped her get out of the van.

He shook his head and I shook mine in return. Muneerah Johnson wasn't the one to get on her bad side. I guess that's where Ameera and me got our ways from.

I took my niece with me upstairs to our room. Mas'ud and Yasmeen had their hands full with Madeenah.

She was wide awake too so they weren't going to sleep any time soon. Saba and I were ready to call it a night. I changed her diaper, put her pajamas on, then laid her down. Before I could change into my bathrobe, she was asleep. After I washed up and made my night prayers, I snuggled up next to Saba with my Qur'an. I recited the words from surah An Naba over and over again until I finally dozed off.

I woke up the next morning and slid out of the bed without waking Saba. I pulled the blanket up on her little body then placed a couple of pillows next to her so that she wouldn't know I had left the bed. Wrapped in my bathrobe and slippers, I headed down stairs to start cooking breakfast. Since Shareef was working overnight and Ameera was in the hospital, the duty fell on me.

Turning on the lights as I walked through the house, I realized that a couple of them were already lit. There were sounds coming out of the kitchen too. Someone had beat me down there.

"As Salamu alykum," I said as I opened the door. My mother was standing at the stove in some sweats and a T-shirt. Her short curly hair was shining underneath the soft light. She looked like rest had done her well too.

"Wa lykum as salam, baby. I got some grits and eggs cooking. "Bout to make the toast and cut up some fruit. You want some yoghurt or something?"

"Yeah, I get it, though. I was coming down here to cook for ya'll. You done stole my blessings, Ummi!" I joked as I sat at the table and poured myself a cup of coffee.

"I been up, Iman. You gonna cook, you can't rely on that alarm clock. You got to use your own internal clock."

"I guess so. What time Umar bring you back?"

"He dropped me off 'round three. I just stayed up. Prayed then read a little."

"And how was Ameera? Did you get to speak to her or was she just sleeping?" I questioned.

"She was mostly sleeping 'cause they had to give her something to calm her down. She came in and out. I let her know I was there. Umar let her know he was there. I spoke with a doctor and therapist about her and then I came on home," Ummi nodded her head then went back to stirring the grits. "Let me turn these off before they burn on me. You want a little cheese in yours?"

"No, that's okay. So what were the doctors saying about her?"

"He said something about Meera having some type of mood disorder. That she ain't been taking the meds properly and that can lead to periods of crazy thinking. I don't understand everything he was trying to say. But Umar said they had both known about her condition all this time. I don't understand why they ain't tell me nothing," Ummi shook her head then brought over the pots of grits and eggs and a couple of plates. "Go up to the attic and get Mas'ud so he don't miss suhoor."

I got up with my cup of coffee in my hand and left the kitchen to go wake up Mas'ud. I was pretty certain I knew the name of the disorder my mother was describing that the doctors had discussed with her. Just thinking back on some of the things Ameera had shared with me. The anger, the fighting, the mood swings, the overeating, the exaggerated worries that seemed to be episodic. Mas'ud had told me a while ago her changes seemed to start right after I left which was around the time she would had been just starting puberty. He thought it was because of me when it was really a chemical imbalance.

"Morning, salamu 'alykum, sleepy head," I greeted my brother at the top of the stairs of the attic. He was already up.

"Morning," his groggy, low, deep voice didn't seem steady.

"You didn't get much sleep, did you?"

"Madeenah was up all night. She just dozed off," he revealed. "I let Yaz sleep."

"Moody, did Shareef talk to you about the support groups at the hospital? I can bring Yaz with me this morning."

"I don't really think that's necessary," he told me as we walked back into the kitchen. "Good Morning, Ummi! You lookin' pretty!" Mas'ud greeted our mother and then kissed her cheek. Ummi smiled.

"Thanks, baby. Go 'head and eat 'fore you miss the salat," she instructed him.

I poured my brother a cup of coffee then grabbed up my own plate and dug in. We all sat there quietly eating and thinking. I wasn't done with Mas'ud and the support groups. Yaz needed to go talk with a professional about her challenges with Madeenah. They both needed to learn some techniques to deal with her or they were both gonna crash and burn out.

"Aye, Iman, before I forget, Shareef said you got a meeting with the lawyer this afternoon around 4. I know its short notice, but do you think you can make it?"

"No, there's no way I can cut out early. My boss just went out on leave. I have to stay til closing and make sure some of her work gets done as well. Do I have to attend? I didn't come the other times ya'll met with him."

"I know, but you need to sign some more documents so they can get filed with the courts. Also, I think Mateo requested mediation. I guess he just gotta get some stuff off his chest. So, it has to be after 6, right?"

"Six thirty. That's the earliest I can do it."

"All right, I'll let them know. Jibril might be able to get them to give you an evening slot. But if not, you might have to take off a few hours in the morning. This is important. The quicker you finish the paperwork, the sooner you get it filed so that you can be legally divorced."

"That's right," Ummi added. "That's something you need to make a priority. You need to go on and do it today. I am sure if you asked somebody over at that clinic can close up for you. This is an emergency. You don't need to have nothing to do with that evil man ever again. Go on and get this done 'cause he gonna be thinking you stalling cause you got something left for him."

"That's certainly not the case, Ummi. I think Mateo knows now after everything that has happened, everyone we both have lost, our marriage is dead," I charged.

"Well then get it done legally. Don't leave no loose ends hanging around for him to grab onto."

I sighed. But my mother was right. I needed our marriage to be over. I would have to find someone to cover for me.

"Okay, okay. Point taken. Once I get to work, I'll ask around to see who can help me out. I'll give Shareef a call later on today once I know what's up. Meeting is at four?"

"Yeah," Mas'ud responded.

"I'll get there."

"Good."

Chapter 20

As soon as I got to work, I texted Michel'le to let her know what I had to do. I also needed a little more details about the financial board meeting that I had to present at this morning. I set up my rooms, unlocked the doors, then settled in the nurses' station at my computer desk to work on some files. By time the rest of the staff started rolling in I was already finished with Michel'le's work for the day.

"Top of the day, Iman," Kyle Burgess, one of the I.T. department's technicians called out to me. Kyle was a young Caucasian guy who had transferred to Hilltop Clinic from UPMC Mercy. It's a much larger facility. As a graduate student, he'd told me he needed a slower paced position so he could concentrate on his studies too.

"Morning, Kyle. Did you get my messages yesterday?" I questioned him.

"I did. I was trying get over here, but got backed up. Here now, though. Which one was giving you some trouble?"

"This one," I told him as I pointed to the laptop I was sitting in front of. "It shut off on me twice yesterday. And it's been acting really slow so far this morning."

Kyle nodded his head as he listened to me. "Not sure if you checked out that memo I sent out last week, but today starts the upgrade. We got to rewire the wires, add some new equipment to the server too. Some of the other clients will be affected which could be the source of the slowness. But the computers shouldn't be shutting off on you," he explained as he examined the laptop. "Can I take this with me for a while? I'll have Jason or Romello bring you down a loner for the day."

I rolled my eyes. Kyle laughed. He knew what was coming. "As long as nothing changes. No data lost, no different passwords, no janky crap. I gotta lot of work in there, Kyle."

Got it! I promise you she's safe and I will have her fixed by the end of the day. Have a great day, Iman."

"You too, Kyle."

Around eleven thirty, my cell phone rang as I was coming out of the examination room. I glanced at the number and recognized it.

"Hey, boss lady!"

"Hi, Iman. I got your message but I caught up with Dequan during the surgery."

"No problem. How's he feeling? Was the surgery successful?" I asked her.

"Glory be to God! He's doing well. Talking and complaining," she laughed. "But the surgery went really good. I don't think Dequan got a chance to run with them Steelers, but he'll be able to play a couple flag football games with his boys this fall. Anywho, go on to your meeting. I spoke to Alyssa in HR. She said you have more than enough time banked this cycle to leave early."

"Thanks, Michel'le. I didn't mean to interrupt your day. But it's nice to hear from you. I am glad Dequan is going to make a full recovery," I told her.

"Not a problem. I am glad to help. Shanice or Miss Roberta can close up. Don't forget about the meeting today. I am counting on you, Iman."

"Oh, Lord. Don't remind me. I didn't get much time to write anything. I don't want to be up there stuttering and messing up."

"Just be calm and speak from the heart. You know this community and you know the people we serve. You serve them everyday with love and compassion. Just speak the truth. You can't mess that up."

"I guess not. I'll do my best, Boss!"

"That's what I'm talking about. You'll be fine. I'll talk with you tomorrow. Bye, Iman."

"Bye, Miss Michel'le."

I walked back to the nurses' station to put away my file then sat at my desk to text Shareef. When I looked down at the screensaver on another laptop it dawned on me that I had just missed Lissette's funeral. It saddened me that I hadn't been able to get over there to pay my respect to her mother, Danny, and Evie. I prayed they found peace out of all the violence and family problems the Colons brought with them every where they went. I was actually glad I was gonna have an opportunity to speak to Mateo.

A year ago, I wouldn't have been able to do it. I would've cowered or drunk myself into a stupor out of fear of even fumbling into to a confrontation with him. The tables have turned. I didn't want to release any more tears over that. I wanted to look him in the face and make him reconcile with what he did to me. I wanted him to hear my emotions; the shame, the anger, and the love that he ruined. I needed to throw all of it from my stomach like the bug he had been to me. That's what I wanted from him. I wanted to be heard.

I tucked my phone into my jacket's pocket then strolled to the back of the nurses' station to pick up the next patient's file. I had more work to do here at the clinic. I was needed here. The crazy thing that had just dawned on me was that it had been Mateo who had begrudgingly paid my way through nursing school. He had made it difficult every step of the way for me to get that degree. Every fear that lived in his head, he brought into our lives and let it torment me. I wasn't grateful. I got what was due to me. As far as I was concerned, he still owed me.

I knocked on the door to one of the examination room then entered. "Kayla Houston?" I called.

"This is Kayla. I'm her mother, Rowena Houston," said a young girl who looked no more that fifteen or sixteen years old. She had shoulder length cornrows in her head that were adorned with small clear beads at the ends of them. Rowena wore blue jeans that were worn at the knees, a pink Old Navy t-shirt, and white slip-on Converse. She held a sleeping baby girl in her arms.

"Nice to meet you, Miss Rowena!" I said, sitting down next to her in one of the chairs. "What brings you and Kayla in today?" I asked. I had already checked the file. I knew what she was here for, but I wanted to see if she could explain it to me.

"Kayla fell this morning," she whispered. Tears welled in her eyelids then burst into streams that rolled down her rosy brown skin. "I didn't mean for it to happen," she coughed out through sobs that rocked her body and her daughter. "I didn't mean for it to happen, I swear. I just want my baby to be okay!"

I gently rubbed Rowena's back up and down then around in circles before slowly reaching out my hands for Kayla. Rowena glided her baby into my arms. "It's gonna be alright, Miss Rowena. You are certainly not the first Mama to drop her baby accidently. Sometimes it can be hard to hold on to babies that are Kayla's age. They like to wiggle and toss and turn a lot so they don't miss out on any action. Kayla just turned six months, yes?" I held Kayla upright to check for any bruising on her face or head. There was a small scratch on her forehead. I opened up her onesie and checked her stomach and legs.

"Last week."

"Good and now, Miss Rowena, can you remember what you were doing when Kayla fell?"

"I was arguing with Chaucey. That's Kayla's dad. He kept on trying to pull her out of my hands and stuff. He said he was gonna take her over to his girl's house with him. I wouldn't let him, though, cause Moriah be smokin' and lettin' anybody up in her place. She ain't even Chaucey's girl. He just callin' her that 'cause she lettin' him stay over there," Rowena explained.

"So you and Chaucey were tussling back and forth and arguing. He tried to grab Kayla but you wouldn't let him?" I repeated back to her as I weighed Kayla on the scale.

"Nope. I didn't let him hold my baby. So he got real mad. He started talking junk then he just grabbed me and jacked me up by my shirt while I was holding my baby! I started yelling for my cousin Tynisha to come and get him off of me. Tynisha came running at him with the broom in her hand. Chaucey shoved me and my baby into the kitchen door then he ran out the backdoor. That was when she slipped out my hands. I picked her right up, though, I didn't mean to let her fall."

"No, I am sure you didn't. Was this the first time Chauncey has grabbed ahold of you?"

She paused. More tears flowed from her eyes. She took a deep breath and then blew it out.

"I don't want to get into no mess with Chauncey. I don't be with him no more. I left messing with him before I had Kayla. I don't really want his help, but sometimes I need it. I take classes at the Literacy Council and I'mma take my HiSet certificate test and finish school up this December. I watch my cousins' kids most nights while she work at Walmart. Tynisha pay me a few dollars when she can. Chauncey brings me diapers twice a month, that's it. I gets her milk with my W.I.C. checks," she added.

"I understand, Miss Rowena," I told her with a smile. "Well, the good news is that I don't see anything alarming on this tough cookie. But the doctor will still come in and give her a thorough check-up. Okay?"

"All right," Rowena sniffled through her nose. I grabbed a tissue from off the counter and handed it to her.

"Here you go," I said as I handed Kayla back to her mother. "What I would like for you to do is," I started as I reached in my pocket and pulled at one of the clinic's cards, "call here tomorrow morning and ask for me. My name is nurse Iman Johnson. We have some really good programs for young moms like yourself where you can meet some helpful community organizers who have resources available to help keep you and Kayla stay safe. You don't have to talk about Chauncey or anything you don't want to. You can just come in with Kayla and say 'Hey, I need help with getting diapers or I want to know about some job training opportunities or hey, I'd like to meet some other young moms'. Does that sound good?"

"Yeah, it does. I'll call you tomorrow."

"Great. I'm gonna be expecting to hear from you now. All right, you and Kayla have a good day."

I shut the door behind me and headed towards the elevators. It was time for the budget meeting and I knew exactly what I was going to tell them about the support programs. I was going to tell them my own story.

It was also almost three thirty when I finally had a moment to call my brother Shareef. He answered on the first ring.

"Wa alykum as salam. You still coming?"

"Yeah, of course. I am packing up and will be on my way in a few. What's the address?" I asked.

"1220 Shady Ave, Suite number 2. We'll wait out front for you."

"We who?"

"I'm riding with Jibril," he told me.

"Okay. See you in a few, Insha'Allah."

"Alright, as salamu alykum."

I grabbed my bags out of my locker in the staff room then closed the door. I headed out the door toward the nurses' station. Tasha was at her computer typing away.

"Aye, mija! Have you seen Miss Roberta?" I asked her with a big smile to break the ice. Tasha slowly looked up at my face before rolling her eyes.

"Hmph!" she murmured. "Now you got words for me? Por que?"

"Tasha, really? You can't still be upset about the other day?"

"Really, I'm not. It's the principle," she reasoned. "I don't really care too much for funny acting people. I don't have to be around them and could care less. But when my friends act funny, that's concerning," Tasha explained.

"You're right, Tasha. A personal issue came up but that didn't give me the right to snap on you. I am sorry if I offended or hurt your feelings."

"It's not that deep, Iman. We're good!" she smiled coyly.

"Good! Now, can you page Miss Roberta? I gotta get'ta steppin'," I informed her.

"One sec," Tasha swung her chair around then dialed a number on the phone. She put the receiver to her ear as I listened to her enquire Miss Roberta. "She's still in a meeting with Kyle. What you want me to tell her?"

"Tell her I am leaving for the day and she'll need to clock out last."

"Got it. See ya' tomorrow, Iman."

"Later, mija!"

The traffic in Pittsburgh during the afternoons was the worst. Well, not as bad as the traffic in Atlanta was. Still, it was difficult. I had been forced for many years to be a passenger even though I had a license and a car. Mateo strongly preferred I didn't drive. He didn't even like me driving around with his brothers. Mama Paola and I usually sat in the backseat and Mateo would take us to run errands and shop twice a week. The car he'd said was mine was really just an alternative car for him to drive around in. When it came to me, it was strictly for emergencies. It had given me such great pleasure when I sold it right from under his nose. It was in my name. It was paid for. The dealer had no idea I hadn't paid for it.

When I pulled onto Shady Avenue, I spotted Jibril's black SUV parked outside of small office building. I parked behind him.

"As salamu alykum," I greeted my brothers.

"Wa alykum as salam," they responded. Shareef was dressed in gray slacks, a white button down shirt, and black mules. His locs were braided back into a French braid that hung on his back. Jibril wore a French blue Polo, khaki pants, and brown leather sandals. I still had my scrubs, a plain magenta top and skirt with a thin beige buttoned down sweater to cover my arms and keep me warm inside the air-conditioned clinic.

"Did he come yet?" I asked.

"Yeah, he's here. He came with his lawyer." Shareef affirmed. "Let's go inside 'cause we a little late."

We all walked into the building together. The building looked even smaller on the inside. There was a small reception area in the front and elevators to the left. The lady sitting in the reception was fully engulfed in her cell phone. She was laughing and smiling but never looked up at us to help direct us. We took the elevator up to the second floor. As soon as we got off, the door to the lawyer's office was right there. Jibril opened the door and held it for Shareef and I to enter.

"Hello, Mr. Ibrahim and Mr. Johnson," an Arab woman sitting at the front desk spoke. She was a slender woman with olive skin, round brown eyes, and short black hair. She wore a black pencil mid length skirt and a white silky top with black pumps. "You're all here for mediation?"

"Yes, is Hussayn here?"

"He's here. He just went to the meeting room."

"Oh, all right, that's good. I didn't see his car out there."

"Good eye. I got it into a little fender bender. It's in the shop."

"Awe, man. You all should've called me. You good?" Jibril inquired.

"Alhamduleelah, it wasn't too bad. We're using a car service this week. And did you get the papers I sent to you last week?"

"Got it. Just taking some time reading through. I'll get it to you tomorrow, Insha'Allah."

"Okay, I just want to make sure we meet the deadline. Why don't you all go back now," the woman instructed us.

"Thanks, Rahaf."

Jibril turned around and looked at Shareef before he stepped to the side and waved his hand forward so that we could walk ahead of him. The meeting room was a short distance from the front desk. Outside of the door, Shareef stopped.

"Okay, so Insha'Allah, we go in and the objective is to get this all solved today. You sign all the papers, and then Hussayn files it. We are not going in there to argue or fight or to dig into who did what. Mateo is probably gonna try to attack you and get you riled up. Don't get into that. Stay cool. We don't want the lawyer to try to take this to court. Ya'll don't have any kids so this is just about taking care of any property and signing the papers. You cool, Iman?"

"I'm ready." I announced. Jibril nodded at me then told me,

"I'll be out here in the waiting room."

"You're not coming in?" I questioned him.

"It's better if I don't," he advised me.

My brother opened the door and we entered together, holding hands. The lawyers stood up but Mateo remained seated at the table. I didn't even know which lawyer was representing me because I hadn't had the chance to meet him. The first time Jibril took Mas'ud to meet up with him I had just gotten out of the hospital. After hearing about the murder of Lissette, I slept for days straight. I only got out the bed because I had to go to work. Helping the patients at the clinic and fasting had helped to keep me sane. It had helped me to focus on those who needed more help than me. It had helped me to see with my eyes how Merciful Allah was. Now I was about to cross the finish line.

Chapter 21

"Welcome, Mrs. Colon, I am Hussayn Al Ajmi, lawyer and lead mediator for Al Ajmi Family Counseling and Law," a short middle aged Arab man greeted us. Mr. Al Ajmi was dressed in a white dress shirt, a green tie, and black dress pants. His reference to me as one of the Colons turned my stomach. I cringed so hard I felt the disgust all the way to the bottom of my feet. I tried to suck it in. He then extended his hand towards Shareef. "And Mr. Johnson, good to see you. Please, let's all be seated."

"Miss Johnson, I prefer." I expressed to him as I sat down in a chair across the table from Mateo and older black woman with short cropped hair cut, thick glasses, and a mole on the bottom of her chin. She looked mean too. Shareef sat right next to me and then Mr. Al Ajmi sat at the top of table.

"My apologies. Miss Johnson."

"First, good afternoon and welcome to you all again. I am glad you all could make it to this mediation. I want everyone to feel comfortable. There's water, coffee, and tea available for those who are able to drink and there are restrooms right outside to your left. I know some of you are fasting so I don't want to take up too much of your time here. This mediation is confidential. Nothing said today can be used in court, nor can I be subpoenaed. Are all parties in agreement with this meeting being confidential?"

"Yes," I answered. Mateo nodded his head.

"Is that a yes or no," Mr. Ajmi questioned Mateo.

"Yes to the confidentiality."

"Good. The next thing is a request. Mutual respect is important and one of the main reasons why mediations are a great alternative to litigation, not to mention it is less expensive than dealing with the courts. So at all times, I would like for us to maintain mutual respect for each other. Also, if possible, let's all address ourselves by first names.

"I am Hussayn. And Miss Johnson, what first name would you like for us to address you by?"

"Iman is fine."

"Good to have you here, Iman."

"And Shareef, I know that we can go by that. Mr. Colon, how can we address you?" Mr. Al Ajmi asked.

"Mateo," he answered quickly.

"Great. Thank you for being here, Mateo. And Leshanda is your attorney and I know her. Thanks for being here, Leshanda. I am going to pass around the agreement to mediate. Please just sign your name on the line next your printed name," he instructed us.

"While you all do that, I'll tell you the good news. I usually go through four different areas with clients during divorce mediation. However, there are no children between the two of you. Correct?" the mediator asked us. I responded alone in the affirmative.

"There were several miscarriages and one stillborn," Mateo offered solemnly. "But none living."

I sighed loudly. I knew at that moment that it was going to be extremely hard to maintain mutual respect.

"Okay. And I am very sorry for your losses. However, without any living children between the two of you, we don't have to deal with child custody or child support. That leaves us with just the division of net worth and alimony. But, before we get to that, I would like to give each of you the opportunity to state what is important to you with this divorce. I would also like to request that you speak only for yourself and your own perspective. Please don't try to go into what the other person is up to or what they think or what they do… just speak for yourself. Mateo, can you speak to us first?"

Mateo nodded his head again then sat up in his chair. His hands were clasped together. He kept twisting them around and flexing his fingers. He sat directly across from me. I thought about dropping my head or turning away as his mouth opened. But I had agreed to give him respect. He didn't deserve much respect from me at all. Still, I tried to do better. I looked at him as soon as the words flew out of his mouth.

"I am here because I recently experienced more losses. They were life changing losses within my family. It shook me in a way that that I've never felt before and it's forced me to really take inventory of my life - my struggles within my marriage to Imania and my own personal life with the people around me. It hasn't been easy to look in the mirror these past few weeks. I know, though, that I need to make some changes and get my life back on track. I also know that I need to make amends to Imania, I mean ah, Iman and to her family. I am here to do that," Mateo announced.

"Okay, that's understandable. Iman, are you willing to accept an apology from Mateo?" Mr. Al Ajmi asked me. I heard him but I hadn't decided what to do yet. Why would Mateo apologize now? Because he was hurting? Because Lissette lost his baby? Because he lost his brother? What did this apology have to do with me?

"Iman," Mr. Al Ajmi called out to me again. Shareef rubbed my back gently. I knew he was trying to encourage me to speak up, however, I was focused on maintaining mutual respect. That's what I had agreed to do. Be respectful, Iman.

"Yes," I responded finally.

"Is it all right for Mateo to offer you an apology?"

"Yes," I heard myself say. I inhaled deeply then exhaled.

"Mateo," the mediator began, "Please go ahead."

"Nia, mi primer amor. Mi esposa. Tienes los ojos mas bonitos del mundo," he started with his same old sorry lines. I sighed heavily. His attorney Leshanda tapped him on the arm and whispered something in his ear. Mateo shook his head, then cleared his throat before he started speaking again.

"Iman, even though I never wanted to be here with you...with lawyers ending this marriage, I know that I gotta let go of you. I need to do so much to get right. I know that I really have to do this on my own. From the time I met you, I just knew you were perfect for me. You were beautiful and smart and I just...I felt like you understood me and no one else did. I wanted you to be perfect for me and was just stuck on that. I did things that I shouldn't have done to you thinking I could change you and make you better. All of that was my immaturity and it ended up hurting you and pushing you so far away. I did a lot of dumb stuff thinking it was manly because I saw older guys and family members doing it. I followed them in everything and it just ruined my life.

"I want you to know that even though I didn't always show it, I loved you. And I appreciated everything you taught me - the good and the bad. I appreciated how kind and patient you were with Mama and Abuela. I appreciated that even when we fought, you still took time to listen to my problems and advise me. I appreciated all the work you did to help with Colon Nacional Dominicana with Manny and me. I loved that you made Tres Leches for my birthday every year even when you were tired, angry, or just plain sick of me. I was so excited every single time you got pregnant and broken every single time you lost one of our children; it felt like the world was closing in on me. I am sorry I never could love you good enough. I am sorry, Imania. And I know this don't mean much to you right now. But I want you to know that it means everything to me. I've lost so much in my life. I lost my brothers, my father, I lost my babies, and now I am losing my first love. I just wish I had been strong enough to be a better man to all of you. Now, I need to be able to take care of Danny. For Diego," Mateo cleared his throat then he wiped his eyes. His eyes were watery, but he did a good job holding back the tears.

"Thank you for that heartfelt offering, Mateo," Mr. Al Ajmi told Mateo. He turned to me and said, "Iman, is there anything you would like to state or request at this time?"

"Of course," I said.

"Alright, please go ahead."

"I'm sorry as well. But I am not sorry for you, Mateo. I am sorry I made a drastic decision to marry someone I didn't really know well enough at such a young age without my parents or siblings being involved. I am sorry that I allowed my fear of hurting someone who was hurting me to imprison me for such a long time. I am sorry that I wasted so much time holding on to someone I was never meant to be with. Someone I couldn't ever fully love because I really didn't understand how to properly love my Creator or myself," I confessed.

"I have moved on and I'm taking small steps every day to shed the fear, the hurt, the embarrassment, and the anger that I lived with for so long that I considered them to be my only friends. I haven't totally forgiven you, Mateo. But I am working on it because I know that I have to eventually forgive myself as well. I don't want anything from you anymore Mateo, not even your name. Any monies or legalities, I just want to void it. I want to start anew. I want safety. I want complete freedom. I want to be me again, Iman Shahidah Johnson."

"Those issues we were going to address next, Iman," Mr. Al Ajmi noted.

"There's nothing to address. I don't want anything except for this divorce to be completed and my name to be removed from all of his business dealings." Mateo leaned over and whispered something in his attorney's ear. At the same time Shareef tapped my shoulder then held up his notepad for me to read. He had wrote:

Let him pay for the court filings and mediation!!!

Mateo raised his hand and Mr. Ajmi nodded his head at him. "Yes, Mateo, please speak."

"Right now, I am trying to secure guardianship of my nephew and I need to make sure that the path to do that remains clear. If Nia, uh, I mean Iman would be willing to sign a non-disclosure agreement in regards to our marriage and Colon Nacional Dominicana that has been prepared by my attorney handling my legal proceedings, I am willing to dissolve legal business partnership immediately. In addition, I am prepared to offer her a sum of $50,000. It's from the Rahma account, our daughter's money, clean money. It's belongs to her."

"Iman, are those acceptable terms for you?" the mediator asked me. I turned to my side. Shareef shook his head at me before he mouthed, "take it".

"Those are acceptable terms for me," I agreed. Mateo's attorney reached down under the table and reached into her briefcase. She pulled a stack of papers that had small tabs of colored tape stuck to them.

"Iman," Mateo's attorney spoke to me for the first time. "This first set of paper work is the non-confidential disclosure. Once you sign these papers and you accept the payment, it will bar you from testifying, giving any statements publicly in a court of law, online, or any written form to any legal organizations in regards to Mateo about your marriage or any of the businesses operated by Mateo and the Colon brothers. The second paper is the statement of dissolution to dissolve your partnership in Colon Nacional Dominicana. Would you like to take them home to read them over for a day and then submit them to me tomorrow?" she asked me.

"No, Ma'am. I'd like to sign now," I told her. She grabbed a black pen off of the table and handed it to me. I took the pen from her and picked up the first stack of papers. I flipped through pages that had a stickies on them where I was to put my signature. I inhaled then exhaled before I placed the stack of papers back on the table. I signed each page quickly then handed the first stack back to her. The last sheet was left. I sped read it. Nothing jumped out at me as alarming. It really didn't matter, though. I was going to sign it. I was getting out of the marriage by any means necessary.

"Here you go," I said as I extended my hand for her to take the paper that I had just signed. "Are we finished?"

"Um, well I did want to recap," Mr. Al Ajmi pleaded. "We've reached an agreement that no alimony will be sought by Iman. We also have reached agreement that assets will not be divided. Iman has signed the nondisclosure agreement and the statement of dissolution. Those documents guarantee Mateo confidentiality and Mateo has agreed to reimburse Iman $50,000. Mateo, please make that payment by the end of next week at the latest. Are all parties in agreement?"

"Yes," we all said in unison.

"Then this concludes our mediation. If either of you have any further questions, please don't hesitate to contact the office," Mr. Al Ajmi turned around in his chair and extended his hand out to Mateo and Leshanda. Each one shook his hand then he turned around and extended his hand to Shareef.

"Ramadhan Mubarak!"

Shareef pulled out my chair and helped me to stand up. He grabbed my hand in his and we walked out of the meeting back into the front of the office. Jibril was sitting in a chair reading a magazine.

"Finished?" he asked.

"It's done," Shareef told him. "Papers get filed and stamped tomorrow."

Mr. Al Ajmi came out into the front office guiding Mateo and his attorney. While he was thanking them, I could feel Mateo's eyes on me as I stood with my brothers. Feeling guilty for everything that had just went down, I started to walk out of the office. I stood at the elevator, waiting for it to reach me. I saw the door open, then it closed hard. I turned around and started to walk back to the office but the door opened again. Shareef stormed out followed by Jibril. Mateo opened the door. His attorney Leshanda was holding his arm, but she let go. All three men were in the hallway with me. The air felt stale.

"What's going on?" I asked. Mateo stepped closer to us.

"Nia, can I talk to you? Please?" Mateo begged. "I know I don't deserve it, but just let me…"

"No! You don't deserve nothing from my sister, man!" Shareef told him. He stepped up in front of me and into Mateo's face. "You"—he pointed into Mateo's face—"got what you wanted in there. We got what we needed. That's it. Ain't nothing left between Iman and you.

You don't get to speak to my sister any more. You don't get to follow her or harass her or scare her or even whisper nothing at her. Not even by mistake," Shareef told him.

"I got you," Mateo shook his head as he raised his hands up in the air. "I mean no disrespect, my brother."

"I ain't ya brother, Mateo. But I am Iman's brother."

"Look, my man, I still ain't got no beef with your family. I am asking your permission, respectfully, can I speak to Iman?"

"And I done already told you no. There's nothing else you need to say to her."

"There is," Mateo yelled. "Nia, please. Nia!"

The elevator door opened. Jibril stepped into it. Shareef grabbed my hand and pulled me into the elevator with him. I looked at Mateo standing there with tears filling up in his eyes. In all the years that we had been together, he'd never shed tears in front of me. I hated that I thought about his feelings, but I did. It was deeper than loyalty. It was instinctual. I let go of Shareef's hand, slapped the hold button on the elevator, then I walked out.

"What else can you say?" I asked. "You're gettin' off. You get to go back to your family. You get Danny! You get the business. You get the house, the cars, and the money. I get to pick up the pieces you broke within me and try to put them together. I was 16, Mateo! I put all my trust in you…."

"Not for nothing, Nia. You trusted me, even when you shouldn't have because you know you saw something in me nobody else saw all those years ago. You had hope in me and you had your prayers for me. That wasn't for nothing. All those years, I admit were the worst, but I am here to tell you, I know I can change. I didn't come here to divorce you. I came here and I stayed here because I ain't never loved nobody or nothing more than I loved you. I know I don't deserve no second chances from you or you family. I know we both need to heal. Change. Pray a lot more and grow. But Nia, me and Danny need you. I am gonna do everything I can to do better, to be worthy of you… some day. La familia over everything," Mateo expressed to me as those tears finally rolled down his face.

I shook my head from side to side. I wasn't sorry for him. I was no longer afraid of him. I had nothing left for Mateo but our memories. Those were the horrors.

"I can't help you, Mateo. I've been sick and tired of you from years and years of neglect and abuse. I don't have anything left to give to you. And I know you ain't even worth the trouble. You did a real dirty number on me. If it hadn't been that even on my darkest days, Allah was there keeping me, I would've died from the sorrow. Everything was necessary. Even being down and without has actually been good for me. I love someone. And I know now that what I felt for you all those years ago, wasn't never ever anything close to what love really is. Some school girl's infatuation. A lot of fear. Abuse. PTSD. None of it ever equaled love, though. I pray for your forgiveness and I pray Allah helps you and Danny heal and grow together for the better, Mateo." I turned around and stepped back on the elevator. Jibril let go of the hold button. The elevator doors closed.

"I guess you told him," Shareef busted out laughing.

"She sure did. Real brutal. A real heart breaker," Jibril added. A satisfied smirk tugged onto his mouth.

"Jokes, guys? I really don't think this is the right time," I insisted.

"I felt a little bad for him," Jibril added.

"Me too. That was ice cold. What she say, Fresh?"

"She said, 'I don't got no love for you 'cause I am in love with another man, but I'll pray Allah helps you,'" Jibril gushed before he broke out into full blown belly laugh.

"Oh my! I didn't say it like that guys," I insisted again. "You two are so immature," I had to join in their laughter.

The elevator opened. We all exited and walked through the reception area where the young woman was still chatting away on her phone. It was going on six in the evening. As we left the building, I noticed that the sun was turning the sky all sorts of warm colors as it got closer to setting. The air was just right. Not too hot and not too cold. It was the perfect afternoon.

Shareef and I got into our sister's wagon. Jibril got into his SUV and drove off ahead of us. We weren't too far from home. I turned off the air conditioner and pressed the buttons that controlled the windows and sunroof so that they could all open. The breeze, the sun, and the freedom filled me up even though it had been almost 16 hours since I had eaten or drank anything but I didn't need it. I had finally found a piece of contentment.

Chapter 22

❧

"When you love someone," Shareef began as I pulled onto Webster Ave and drove down the street towards Ummi's house, "you should marry them. That's the sunnah. It also can make life a little easier."

"Yeah, well, I think I just made my intentions clear. Full honesty," I admitted. I parked, turned the car off, and unlocked the door. "The ball is in his court. If he loves me too, he should ask to marry me. That's the sunnah, too."

Shareef smiled at me as he got out of the wagon. Hasan and the boys ran up to us as they did everyday. Shareef picked up all three of them and dragged them to the front porch.

"As salamu alykum!" Yasmeen greeted us. She was sitting on the porch in a light grey jilbab and white Georgette hijab playing with Saba. Baby Madeenah was asleep in her swing. I kneeled down and softly kissed her hands.

"Wa alykum as salam, Yaz. How you feeling today?"

"Good. Out here getting Madeenah some sun. She's still so pale. She needs some color," she smiled before she picked up a can of grape soda pop and sipped it through a straw.

"I don't know if she is tanning but this good ol' summer sun done got her sleepy. That's for sure."

"I know! It was Ummi's idea to bring her out. So I guess she knew what it would do," Yasmeen thought.

I followed Shareef into the house. The house smelled like good food cooking. I sniffed my way to the kitchen. My brother-in-law and my sister were standing over the stove talking and giggling like they hadn't been just fighting the night before.

"As salamu alykum, family,"

"Salams, Iman," Ameera smiled.

"Wa alykum as salam," Umar responded.

"What ya'll cooking?" I asked.

"Creamed spinach, fried catfish, stir-fried cabbage, and we got some hot water cornbread and banana pudding," Umar rattled off.

I turned my nose up and squinted my eyes. "Why?"

"Why what?" Ameera asked.

"Why catfish when you know it is my weakness. I just ate mac and cheese and barbecue chicken yesterday at Aunty's house. I can't eat fried catfish today!" I revealed.

"Too bad, so sad," Ameera teased. "I didn't get to eat at Aunty's yesterday. So I made my own feast. Ya'll didn't even bring me a plate back," she huffed. Her husband rolled his eyes, then waved his hand at her.

"It's Ramadhan," Umar offered. "Leave that diet stuff for after the Eid, Iman. Ya know Ramadhan is for eating good. Don't knock your blessings."

"I suppose," I walked over to the oven and pulled it open. The catfish, golden brown and crispy, was piled high in an aluminum pan. "It looks so good."

"You know it is. I used Abu's recipe!" Ameera bragged.

"You have Abu's catfish recipe? How'd you get that?" I questioned as I remembered him locking us all out of the kitchen, including my mother, when he made his famous catfish.

"He taught me right before I married Umar. He said I needed a trick up my sleeves to keep my husband happy," she laughed.

"It worked. May Allah bless him," Umar prayed. "You got the best catfish around, Meera."

"I do!"

"When you get home?" I asked.

"Early this afternoon. I got a couple of follow-up appointments next week, though."

"Sound good. What you think?"

"I don't know. I know what they want," Ameera revealed.

"And what would that be?"

"They gonna add more meds. I hate the stuff. It really doesn't work anyway," she complained.

"That's why you gotta keep meeting with them doctors, Meera," Umar interjected. "If one of them or all of them are not working then they need to know so they help you find something that will help you better. Not taking your medicine or reducing the dosage on your own don't work either. *That* we do know," he explained.

"You talking like it's so easy. All those meds have one side effect or another. I tried my fair share already. Plus, there's the weight gain, the bloating, the acne. I don't want to deal with it."

"Well you have to do something. Not taking any medication isn't an option for you right now, babe! You're Bipolar. Without the medication, you not only are at risk, you put others at risk," Umar reminded her. Ameera turned to me and said:

"Iman, do you have any doctor friends that work with my kind of disorders? Holistic doctors?"

"No, not that I know of. But I can ask around, though. Insha'Allah, we'll find something, Ameera. Just do what you need to do to stay on track now."

"I am going to try," Ameera nodded.

"Nah, I am going to make sure you do. Now that I done got this job closer to ya'll I'mma go back to Philly and close up. I'll be around daily, Insha'Allah. I should have known you wasn't on your meds, though. Every since you left, I had a feeling something wasn't adding up."

"Whatever!" Ameera blurted out. "You think you know me so well."

"I do, woman. I do."

"Don't eat all the catfish," I interjected. "Going to go take a quick nap. I can't keep my eyes open."

"Yeah, I'll put a plate away for you. You know, the way you was supposed to do for me yesterday," Ameera nagged.

"Girl! If you don't stop!" I warned her before dragging my body off the chair and out of the kitchen.

After I performed wudu to clean myself for the afternoon prayer, I prayed in my room alone. I laid on my bed, still in my work clothes and immediately felt relief to be off my feet and inside my parent's home with my family. Reflecting on the day's event as I laid there staring up at the ceiling, I felt for the first time in my adult life like I had accomplished something meaningful. Then again, I still knew that I wasn't where I wanted to be. I had significant amount of progress that I needed to make and a laundry list of goals to work on. I wasn't going to get overwhelmed, though. What mattered was that I was on my way. I was heading in the right direction.

It didn't take long to fall asleep. It just didn't last long enough.

"Aunty! Aunt Iman," Hasan yelled into the room. "It's time to break fast and make salat. Aunty Meera said you better come get the plate she made for you 'fore uncle eat it!"

I shot up in the bed and ran my hands through hair to smooth the flyaways from my face. "Nobody better touch my catfish. Hasan, go tell them I'm coming down now. Don't let them pray without me."

I pushed my body out of the bed and slipped my bare feet into my slippers before shuffling out of the room and into the bathroom. After relieving myself, I turned on the faucet and quickly washed my hands, mouth and nose, face, arms, wiped over my hair, my ears, and last I washed my feet.

"Iman, hurry up now! We are ready to pray," my mother's voice echoed throughout the hallway as she yelled up the stairs. "Make sure you're dressed. We got company."

Whenever someone told a Muslim woman to make sure she was dressed, they weren't referring to any type of clothing. It was a reference to hijab. They were alerting you that your hair and other body parts needed to fully covered because a man who was not biologically related to you was present.

I ran back into my room, pulled a black jilbab out of the closet and yanked it over my body before finally wrapping my black hijab around my head.

"I'm coming," I yelled as I jogged down the stairs in a hurry. Mas'ud, Umar, and Shareef were in the front room with all of the kids. Some other brothers were standing up in rows waiting to pray as well. In the living room, Fariba, her three daughters, and Aunty Adilah were all lined up with Ameera and Saba. As soon as I got in a line, Shareef said, "Allahu Akabr!"

"As salamu alykum wa rahmatullah! As salamu alykum wa rahmatullah!"

Shareef finished praying salatul Maghrib and I got up and went into the kitchen to break my fast. Ameera and Fariba followed me.

"As salamu alykum!" Fariba offered me the greetings.

"Wa alykum as salam," I responded after I took a sip of water from a bottle from of the fridge. "What all ya'll doing over here?" I asked her.

Fariba looked over to Ameera and they both gave each other some silly look. I don't think either one of them knew what to tell me. "We came to eat!" Fariba finally told me. "And check up on Meera, too! I brought some sweet potato pie and Ummi's pound cake."

"Really, Fariba? More sweets?"

"It's Ramadhan," Ameera and Fariba said at the same time.

"I know but stop tempting a sister! Aunty's pound cake and your sweet potato pie. I am going to have a slice of both!"

"You wanna go walking tomorrow night? Or maybe let's all go out bowling and take the kids, Legacy Lanes has games for the kids and really good pizza."

"Bowling?" I grumbled. "Bowling? Where is my catfish?"

"We like to bowl," Ameera whined as she reached into the oven and pulled out my plate. She had put way too much food on it. Fariba had started to make plates for the children so I grabbed one of theirs and added the extra food from my plate.

"That's fine. I'll go wherever. Any word on Eid yet?" I questioned.

"The brothers are going to go tonight for the night prayers. They'll wait on any announcements," Ameera confirmed.

"We should all go pray tonight too." Fariba suggested. "It's an odd night."

"Yep, we should go. You think Ummi will watch Saba for me?" Ameera asked us as she worked on the plates for the men.

"You know she will. Saba's easy to care for. She'll be asleep before it's time to go."

"Iman, come help me take these plates out for the children." Fariba ordered me. I grabbed a tray and a tablecloth from out of the pantry and then brought them out to living room. Ameera followed behind us with cups, juice, and a jug of water. I laid the flowery tablecloth on to the floor and Fariba started placing the plates and utensils down for the kids. I sat Saba down with Hafsa, Habibah, and Hadiyyah.

Hasan came running into the living room with Saud, Jibril's son. Ummi fussed at them for running in her house like she always did.

"Sorry, Jeddah. My Abu wants to know if we can be served," Hasan asked.

"Cause we hungry too," Saud added.

"It's coming now," Ameera yelled. "Sheesh! Ya'll be doing too much complaining. They know good and well we gotta get the kids and elders fed first. Here, come bring this juice and cups over to them. Then ya'll come back over here and get some of the plates," Ameera instructed the boys.

Fariba, Ameera, and I served everyone in the house double times before we got a chance to sit down and eat ourselves. We didn't feel abused, mistreated, or bothered. Well, we did feel a little bothered that the older people couldn't make up their minds quick enough. Overall though, all three of us believed there were blessings in serving people. This was, after all, Ramadhan and everyone in the house was related to us by blood or faith and we cared for them. Serving them wasn't a chore. Serving them was an honor.

"So, we bowling tomorrow night?" Ameera asked through bites of her food.

"Yeah, let's do it," Fariba agreed. "We haven't all gone out in years. Plus, we can give the grandmothers a break and let them have the night to themselves. I know my Mama needs some rest. The girls are talking her head off."

"Yeah, I'm in. I don't know how to bowl, but I'll give it a try," I told them.

"Abu used to take us bowling a lot. You don't remember, Imani?" Ameera questioned me.

"Yeah, but I couldn't bowl then either."

"You ain't never go bowling with your ex?" she furthered dug.

"No. That's wasn't his thing," I explained.

"So you only got to do things he liked?" Ameera nagged for more information.

I sighed deeply then nodded to affirm her question before getting up to go clean my plate of food. It still hurt to remember how not so long ago, I didn't have a life many women could exist in. I was alive and breathing, but I wasn't living. Mateo shopped for me often and gifted me regularly. We never went hungry. And I always had comfortable housing. Mateo considered himself a hard worker and a family man.

"It don't even matter no more," Fariba interjected. "That man is old news. He is finally history. Gone with the wind and played out like jelly shoes and… and…"

"And crackerbox rings," Ameera laughed.

"You took it back. Good one," I smiled. "He's played out like Jherri curls and hairspray!"

"Yes," Fariba hit the table as she grabbed her stomach and giggled. "Remember my Jherri curl used to leave those big ole greasy wet spots in my hijab? Ugh. It was bad. He's so played out like perms and chemicals and those ugly Starter football jackets all the guys wore with the Steerlers' logo on it in the '90's."

Ameera sucked her teeth. "You always gotta go overboard, Fariba! Leave my perm and my Steelers alone. My hair is laid to the side and dyed and I am black and gold, every day!"

We all laughed. The kids started bringing the food and plates back into the kitchen. I brought a pot of coffee into the living room. Ameera brought in plates of sweet potato pie for Ummi, Aunty Adilah, and the girls.

"Whew! I am full. I don't think I got room for your pie, Adilah."

"Don't stuff yourself, Muneerah. You don't want to make your sugar shoot up. I'mma save mines for tomorrow 'cause I ain't take my medicine yet."

"You should've took that blood sugar medicine before you ate," Ummi advised her friend.

"I know the doctors say that but I think it works better for me to push the sugar out of me quicker if I take it after I eat."

"Adilah, you making that up?"

"Nah, I ain't either. That medicine slow moving cause I only take it twice a day. By dinner it done wore off. That's why I give myself another shot right after I eat 'stead of before. It work better."

My mother and her friends went back and forth debating how they best should take their medicine. I took everything in me not to comment on their musings. I left them be because this just wasn't the time to chastise them about their behaviors. Especially not my mother.

"Iman, Shareef wants you," Yasmeen called me as she carried in Madeenah.

"You need help?" I asked her. I was worried that she hadn't gotten enough sleep again.

"No, it's okay. She's been asleep for like three hours. Mas'ud and I just came back from Applebee's. Our first outing with her," she gushed.

"Wow, that's great, Yaz. Alhamduleelah, I'm glad you guys enjoyed yourselves. Next time let me know ya'll are going out. You know I don't mind watching her," I suggested as I walked out into the hallway. Shareef was waiting for me by the stairs.

"You busy?" he asked me.

"No, not really. We cleaning up. Did the boys bring the coffee and slices of pound cake over?"

"Yeah, yeah, we got it. Stay in the living room with Ummi, I am going to open the door to the front room. All right?"

"Okay," I promised my brother. I walked back into the living room with my mother and Aunty Adilah. Yasmeen, Fariba, and Ameera had all gathered in the room as well. We were all sitting on the floor waiting for something. Shareef opened the door and peaked into the room.

"Salamu alykum. Are y'all ready?" he questioned us. Looking around the room at everyone, I didn't have a clue what Shareef wanted us to get ready for. I shrugged my shoulders.

"Tell him go 'head now. We're all ready, dog! I am sleepy and ready to go home to get in my bed. We ain't got all night to messing around with y'all," Aunty Adilah blurted out.

"Insha'Allah," Shareef noted. "Bismillah, wa salatu wa salaamu ala Rasoolilah. We all bear witness that none has the right to be worshipped except Allah alone and we send the salams on the last prophet and messenger of Allah, Muhammad ibn Abdullah, *sallallahu alayhi wa sallam*. We wanted to gather everyone here tonight as a family because that's what we have all been to one another for most of our lives. Alhamduleelah, we know it is none but Allah who puts love and mercy into the hearts of the believers and we've all benefitted from them both. From our fathers' friendship - may Allah have mercy on them both and illuminate their graves and grant them the best of rewards in the hereafter, ameen – and from our mothers' friendship that has endured and lasted for over 30 years.

"Allah has continued to bless us to be together despite our trials and tests. As you all know I've placed intentions on sister Fariba and, Alhamduleelah, she has agreed to marry me. Is that right sister Fariba?" Shareef asked.

"YES!" Fariba and her daughters cheered. Fariba raised both of her hands up and waved them in the air. We all laughed at her enthusiasm. Aunty Adilah grunted before she snatched a magazine off the end table and swatted at her daughter playfully.

"If you don't act right!" Aunty Adilah threatened her. "And when is the date is what I want to know?"

"Soon is the date, Insha'Allah." Fariba noted. "Still ironing some details with my wakeel. Making sure my contract is right."

Shareef cleared his voice and then said, "May Allah make it is easy on you, sis! We'll talk about the contract later. Right now, though, I want to go back to the concept of love and mercy. It's from the love and mercy of Allah that our families were brought together and that He continues to increase us in love and mercy for each other. And so, when my brother from my other mother, soon to be my mother-in-law, came to me and started to talk me about his intentions and desire to join my family through marriage, Allah knows my heart was overjoyed. Not only do I consider him my brother already, but I trusted him with you all and by Allah he did his absolute best in my absence to be here to help and to support everyone," Shareef's voice cracked a bit and he had to clear his throat again. My brother was getting choked up and we all felt his sincerity. This had been the best Ramadhan I have had in a long time, but it wasn't without its hardships. Shareef went on and said quickly, "So I love this man for the sake of Allah and for myself. So, come on up bro and tell our family what you wanna say."

"As salamu alykum wa rahmatullah wa barakatuh. This is Jibril," he told us. I knew then exactly what was going on. My sisters, my mother, Aunty Adilah, and even the children were all looking at me. My eyes dilated. My heart began to pump faster. My hands started get a little wet. I clasped my hands and inhaled. Was I ready for this moment? Was he only speaking up now because of what I had said earlier? I wasn't sure.

"Can ya'll hear me or do I need to speak louder?" Jibril asked.

"Louder!" his mother replied.

"This - is - Jibril," he stated his name again really slow and then did that low belly laugh he always had to share with others, especially when he was nervous. "Son of Aqil and Adilah Ibrahim. The prophet of Allah said there isn't anything better for those who love one another than marriage. So tonight Aunty Muneerah and Shareef, I am here with my son Saud, to request the hand of your daughter and sister, Iman Shahidah Johnson - if she would have me as her husband, Insha'Allah."

Chapter 23

As soon as Jibril finished speaking it seems like the whole house filled up with squeals and shouts of "Allahu Akbar!" Aunty Adilah got up and hugged me and kissed my cheeks. Ameera was rubbing my back as she cried real tears. Fariba and Yasmeen and all the kids were still shouting Takbir so that everyone could continue to say "Allahu Akbar".

I didn't know what to do or say. This was the first time in my life that I had been asked for my hand properly, Islamically, and in front of my whole family. It did feel like an honor, like I was some important woman and he was this important man who was ready to announce to the world that he cared about me and that he wanted to make me his wife. I did love him.

"As salamu alykum, Imani," Mas'ud called over to me from the other room he sat in with the brothers. "You gotta give him an answer."

I heard one of the other brothers in the room ask if my silence was my consent? "Nah, she has to answer. She's previously married. She has the obligation to clarify if she wants to be married again or not. Maybe she don't want him no more. After all, Fresh got a big head and eat a lot. My sister may not want to deal with that," my little brother argued. The brothers all busted out laughing.

"You coming for me, Mas'ud like that, akh?" Jibril teased back.

"I'm just saying what it is. Aye, Imani? You still over there?" Mas'ud called out to me again.

"I am here," I finally croaked out. The whole house became silent again. Eyes and bodies spun around and refocused on me. I felt like I was under a spotlight. My chest tightened, my breathing quickened, and a lump settled at the top of my throat.

"I'm still here too," Jibril spoke again. "I get it. You don't have to answer in front of everyone if you don't feel up to it. You can tell Shareef and Mas'ud your decision later. It's all good," Jibril added. Some of the brothers booed and he shushed them up. "I'm good," he told someone.

Ameera leaned over closer to me, wrapped her hand around my shoulders and whispered in my ear, "Don't embarrass him, Iman. Say something!"

I knew Ameera was right. It took courage for Jibril to do this and he earned my support. I did want to marry him. I just didn't know if he would want to still marry me if he knew all of my truth. I didn't know and that scared me. I had been afraid so many times in my life, now was the time to rise above the fear. The worst thing he could do was not marry me. I would still be Iman. Allah would still raise the sun up in the sky, hold the birds in the air, and take care of me.

I stood up and walked closer to the door in the front room. "As salamu alykum, brother Jibril?"

"Wa alykum as salam, sister Iman," Jibril laughed his hearty laugh again. "We back to that again? This might not be looking too good for me after all."

"Well, wait a minute. Be easy. I have a question."

"Yes, Ma'am, what's your question?"

"Why do you want to marry me?" I asked him. I heard him sigh loudly before he blew air out of his mouth. "Do you even know? Is it because you liked me as a child? Is this some childhood crush being played out?"

"Little sis, I'm a grown man and uh, wait, are all the sisters covered? Ameera, do you have your niqab on?"

"One sec," Ameera jumped up and scurried into the kitchen to get her face veil. Jibril and Umar started talking but I couldn't hear what they were saying. Ameera dashed back into the room fully covered from head to toe.

"What's happening? What going on?" My mother asked. I shrugged my shoulders.

"I don't know, but I don't wanna miss it. It's 'bout to get real. I can feel it," Ameera insisted.

"Ya'll covered?" Jibril asked again.

"Yes," we all replied. Jibril pulled opened the double doors fully and stood in the middle of the divider. He stood a couple of feet away from me wearing a navy blue collared kurta top that had buttons down the bodice, some dark wash blue jeans, topped off with a blue and white knitted kufi.

"Now, to answer your question, sis," he started as he looked me directly in my face. "I'm a grown Muslim man. I've made a million mistakes. But Allah has continued to save me from me. I consider myself a hard worker and a decent Muslim, but honestly, I am not the best at anything in this life. My intention is to be with the best in the next life, though, and to see my Lord's face. I want to marry you Iman, because I need help now in this life staying the course: believing, praying, and worshipping Allah. I want to marry you, little sis, because I see paradise in you and Allah knows best, but I wanna get there with you. I want to marry you, Iman, because I have always loved you and I am a selfish man," Jibril explained. "Can you help a brother out?" he grinned.

I nodded my head. My heart was beating a thousand miles a minute. A smiled tugged at my mouth and few tears escaped my eyes. No one had ever shared with me words that were that were so heavy, so honest. I covered my face and stepped back away from the door. Fariba stood up, walked over to me, and wrapped her arms around me tightly. "Yes. Yea. I mean really, of course, Jibril," I managed to get to out as I gazed into his face with labored breath.

"This brother done started writing Hallmark cards and everythang. He up here speaking in couplets, giving a soliloquy," I heard Umar joke.

Hamad joined in. "Nah, he the smooth operator tonight. Trying to stunt on us with that Sade' '85." The brothers were laughing and joking among themselves. Jibril didn't return their banter this time. He stood there in front of us women quiet. Pensive and fixated as he watched his sister, Ameera and me hug. I wiped my eyes clear, refocused and saw Saud, his son standing in front of me. Saud was dressed identical to his father. He extended his hand towards me. At the end of his hand in the clenches of his little fingers he held a medium sized silver gift box. Fariba reached out and took the box from her nephew then handed it to me. Jibril turned around and closed the double doors.

It wasn't until the night was over and the kitchen, both front room and the living room had been cleaned and lights had been turned off and the Attar incense wafted through the air that I sat alone in my room breathing one breath at a time. In my mind, I retraced every moment of the night over again as I held that silver box in the palm of my hand. I was intended and betrothed. I was wanted exactly as I was.

Ummi came to me right after everyone had cleared out with tears in my eyes, "Your Abu always wanted Jibril for you," she revealed to me. "Every since you two were children, he prayed for you to grow up and be husband and wife. His dua to Allah all those years ago *finally* reached you." She hugged me tightly and said, "Be happy, Iman."

I was happy. I was full, I was satisfied. I was thankful. But I was still concerned. I would eventually have to talk to him about some hard subjects. He would have to decide if I was really able to help him and Saud. I gripped the box tighter in my hand then put it on the side table next to the bed. I decided I didn't want to open it until I knew what Jibril's real decision would be. Right now, the box didn't really belong to me yet. That gift might be meant for someone else.

The night had been restless but I still woke up to a new day. My nephews were tapping on the door and giggling out in the hallway. I threw back my covers, hit the light switch on the lamp, and swung my body to the side of the bed. I fumbled around the room like I always did until I found my slippers and overgarment. After I pulled it over my head, I grabbed my hijab and loosely wrapped it around my head before I left the room.

It was finally Friday, the best day of the week. My brother-in-law Umar was staying over for the weekend so that meant I had to creep around the house. I had to make sure my hijab was nearby or already on me just in case our paths crossed. It wasn't as horrible as it sounded. Ameera and Umar mostly hung out with their kids outside the house when he visited. They both had plenty friends in Pittsburgh and were often invited out to one event or another over at Masjid Al Awwal. Now that he had found a job in Pittsburgh, I was hoping Ameera would really get serious about her health.

"Salamu alykum, ya'll. Morning," I greeted everyone in the kitchen as I headed to the counter to look for the coffee pot.

"Wa alaykum as salam," Ummi, Shareef, the boys, Ameera responded.

"Coffee over here," Shareef told me as he held up the pot. He grabbed a mug off the old cup carousel my father had purchased as a gift for my mother years ago. "Cream and three sugars?"

"Ah, let's try two," I instructed him. Shareef smiled.

Ummi was standing at the stove cooking eggs, pancakes, sausages, beef bacon, and hashbrowns. The stove was full of pans and pots. The kitchen smelled better than IHOP. I shook my head and sucked my teeth as I looked over my mother's shoulder. I knew I was going to eat everything she cooked. I was tired of telling them to eat better while they teased me with butter, grease, and fried chicken. It *was* Ramadhan.

"We got some leftover sweet potato pie," Ameera announced as she scanned the fridge. She pulled out the pies and brought them over to the table. Mas'ud walked into the kitchen and picked up one the pies and grabbed a fork.

"Really, Moody? Really? You taking the whole thing?" Ameera griped.

"I ain't even get none last night. This half is mines." The both of them sounded like little kids going back and forth over a dessert.

"Your wife had some," Ameera threw back at him.

"That ain't got nothing to do with my stomach," he declared before he sat down and dug his fork into the pie.

"Where's Madeenah, Mas'ud?" Ummi asked.

"She's asleep with Yaz," he smiled. "She only woke up twice. Yaz nursed her and I changed her diaper and she went back to sleep after like ten minutes," he gushed. Everyone congratulated him.

"Alhamduleelah. That's good. Madeenah just needed some time to bond with you and Yaz. Babies got to get comfortable with their surroundings. Just keep her on the schedule," Ummi insisted as she brought over a plate full of the food she had cook. "Hasan, Imran, and Munir, ya'll come on get some food."

"What time we meeting up at the bowling alley?" Ameera asked as she made the kids their plates. I could tell she was excited to hang out.

"We're going right after Maghrib," Shareef announced between bites of his pancakes and beef bacon. "Just have the kids ready so we can get there on time."

"Mas'ud, are you and Yaz coming?" Ameera asked.

"Yeah, we coming. Madeenah did pretty good last night at the restaurant. So we'll try it again tonight. Yaz like to bowl anyway."

"Good! She needs to get back to doing all that she used to do. And you gotta help her find her way. Don't let Yaz sit upstairs holding Madeenah all day like that's all her life is going be. Mothers gotta have balance. And if she need to go talk to somebody about that, Mas'ud, don't you stop her. Everybody got different needs. Your job as her husband is to support her in doing the right thing for herself. Don't be getting in her way thinking 'bout yourself, you hear me?" Ummi scolded my little brother. Mas'ud tightened his jaw, but kept his mouth shut. We all just continued to eat. Ummi had spoken and her word was law in her house.

"All right, boys, go get washed up. Almost time to get to the masjid."

"Shareef, are you working this morning?"

"Yep, Ma. I gotta be up to the barbershop for an eight o'clock client. Insha'Allah, I'll get to Jumu'ah on time, though. Hamad is gonna pick me up."

"You working an awful lot, Shareef. You need to slow done some. You ain't 21 no more. You do need to rest. I ain't seen you sleep none since you came home. That's not healthy."

"Bills, bills, and more bills. Imani and Mas'ud not supposed to be taking care of you. That's the responsibility Abu left to me, Ma. I was doing it before without them and I'mma do it again. I'll be alright, Insha'Allah," Shareef explained as he got up from the table. He picked up his plates and the boys' plates and brought them over to the sink and started washing them.

"I am doing okay, Shareef. I don't need you getting yourself hurt or sick out there in those streets tryin' to take care of me. We getting by. Just slow down some."

"Insha'Allah," Shareef promised. But it wasn't really a promise. It was more like an acknowledgement that he had heard her concerns. I knew my brother had no intention of slowing down one bit. He was going to push ahead until he got what he wanted: to be the head of our household again.

I headed back upstairs to prepare to offer the Morning Prayer. Ameera was coming out of my room.

"I put my car keys on the dresser. I don't need them this weekend. Just put a little gas in there for me," she instructed.

"Okay, will do. Did you take your meds, Meera?" I questioned her as we passed each other. She sized me up and down, then huffed. "Just trying to help," I added.

"Not like that, Iman. I am a not a child. I know what I am supposed to do," she insisted.

I raised my eyebrows, then nodded at her comment. But my mouth stayed closed. She knew good and well what she was supposed to do and doing what she was supposed to do were two different things. She hadn't been doing what she was supposed to do.

"Golly," she finally huffed at me again. "I took my meds. So nosy."

I nodded my head and walked away. We were all fragile. That I knew. I also knew some things had to be confronted and battled with teeth and nails.

I pulled up into the clinic's parking lot at my regular time. I loved the early morning. The quiet, the summer clouds, the birds chirping mixed with the sounds of the inner-city. It was a marriage unlike any other. It was sweet, melodic, and dramatic. It was home.

"Top of the morning to you," Kyle greeted me as I walked into clinic. I jumped backed out of fear and shock.

"Kyle! You seriously scared the crap out of me!" I shouted at him. "What are you doing here this early?" He looked down at the laptop he was holding and smirked.

"Got caught up yesterday. Wanted to get in here early and fix you up. She's ready for the day," Kyle told me as he held out the laptop. I walked over to him and took the laptop from him.

"Thanks, Kyle."

"Nah, don't worry about it. Sorry I scared the crap out of you!" he laughed. "Have a great day, Iman."

I prepped the examination rooms, refilled the printer, and updated my files while I had the clinic to myself. As the other staff came through the doors. I spoke with each one. When Tasha finally arrived, it was time for me to go see a patient.

"You're late, Tee!" I alerted her.

"Car trouble, man trouble, house trouble, sleep trouble, life trouble," Tasha unleashed on me before she threw down her bag, keys, and sweater on to the counter. She raked her hand through her short brown hair then fell into her chair and sighed.

"I pray it all gets better for you, mija!" I wished her sincerely before leaving her with her thoughts.

With Miss Michel'le out of the clinic, the energy had changed. It seemed like the whole staff was dragging their feet, over worked, and needy. Michel'le gave each of us the best pep talks each morning. It was almost like she was a best friend to all of us. I missed her and needed her too. She wasn't there, though, so I had to fill her shoes. Right after lunch break was over, I gathered with all the nurses and nursing assistants in the staff room.

"Family, the day is almost over. You have all been great today. You're great every day, but this has been a bumpy, long week. With network issues, scheduling issues, and Miss Michel'le out of the building, your professionalism, teamwork, and efforts been duly noted. This is the best nursing staff in the system and we know that Hilltop Clinic is one of the best clinics in Pittsburgh and it's because of each one of you. Your presence is what makes peds a great place to work and to treat our clients. Let's finish the day strong so we can get to that weekend and get some much-needed rest," Tasha was the first to clap but suddenly a roll of applause erupted. One by one, my co-workers thanked me with hugs and hi-fives as they exited the staff room.

"Great job, Iman! Miss Michel'le would be proud of you," Sandy Parks from the HR department told me. I had no idea that she had been down in the clinic today. "Let's talk Monday?"

"Sure, no problem, Miss Parks," I replied. I didn't know what she wanted to talk about. She smiled, though. Would she smile if she had a pink slip to give me?

It was jumu'ah, but I wasn't gonna be able to make it. We had too many appointments, two doctors out of the clinic, and our nursing supervisor on leave. It always bothered me when I couldn't go pray in congregation at the end of the week. Every week came with its struggles, the small and the big. Standing shoulder to shoulder with other Muslims who were all dealing with their own problems, calling on Allah, and seeking His purification and patience gave me relief. It gave me a community to be a part of. It gave me balance, too. This week though, the staff room was what I had.

After I performed wudu, I laid out my prayer rug in a small corner next to the windows and stood by myself to pray. When I finished my prayer, I sat on top of the rug and read a chapter Qur'an for a few minutes. Right as I finished, my phone vibrated in my pocket. I pulled the phone out and scanned several short messages that had come through:

Mrs. Bey: As salamu alykum, Iman! You missed your session this week. We need to meet soon. Insha'Allah, have a good Jumu'ah.

Brother Jibril: No comment on the gift? Did we do that bad? Saud made the final choice. Blame him if you don't like it, j/k!

Ummi: Going to the market after Jumu'ah. You need anything?

I called Labibah back first. With everything that had happened this week, I'd completely forgot to check in with my sponsor. I listened to her number ring several times before it went to voicemail. She was probably at Jumu'ah. When the automated voice prompted me with a quick beep, I left her a message:

"As salamu alykum, Miss Labibah. Thanks for reaching out. Another crazy and stressful week has come to an end. I am not sure I'll be able to get to you this weekend. But Insha'Allah, I will be in right after Eid is over and things settle down a bit. I think I finally have some good news for you, too. The dust is settling and I can see clear skies are coming my way. Jazaki'Allahu Khayra for all of your help, prayers, hugs, and for listening to my story."

I hit the end button, swiped the screen several times to I go back to the messages. I read Jibril's message again. I still hadn't looked in the box. I decided to just tell him the truth. I hadn't lied to him yet and I didn't want to start. I wrote him back.

Still waiting to open it. Insha'Allah, I'm sure you both did a great job. It was a thoughtful gesture. Shukran.

I took a deep breath and then hit send. I swiped the screen and entered the next message sent from my mother.

Can you get me a case of bottled water and two bags of grapes? I'll pay you when I get home, Insha'Allah.

Before I could hit send, the phone beeped. I knew it was Jibril's reply. I decided not to read it. I had to get my next patient. I'd see him later at the bowling alley for iftar. I stuffed the phone back into my jacket, and then put away my prayer rug and Qur'an before heading out of the staff room.

"Iman!" Tasha called out to me. I walked around the back of the nurses' station and sat down next to her in one of the swivel chairs.

"What's up? You feeling better, mija?" I asked her as I smoothed back a flyaway hair from her face.

"Ostros 20 pesos, but you won't believe who just rolled up in here?" she told me excitedly.

"Que fue?" I asked her.

"You remember that fine, fine, fine dude that rolled up in here with the two kids? You ordered his kid's record, 'member that?" Tasha got up, walked to the printer, and took out the papers. She handed a new folder and the papers to me.

"Mmm hmm," I nodded. "Y que?"

"He just left!" She smiled before handing me an envelope. "He came in looking for you, *Mistin*! I can't believe you knew him all this time, Iman! He's so beautiful. Please, girl, give him my number? I need an upgrade. He even smell like success!"

"Tasha, you're married!" I swatted at her playfully.

"Yeah, but I ain't happily married!" she informed me. "Today, these dudes only good for one season."

"Baby girl, if you ain't happy on your own, no man will be able to help you find it. In fact, that man probably would have you buried under dark clouds and storms. Don't knock your blessings," I reasoned.

"How you figure?" she asked.

"Some women haven't ever experienced even one good season with their husbands. Just coldness, darkness, abuse, and pain. If Armando is trying to be a good man – and you know he goes hard for you, Tasha – don't give up on him. Support him, encourage him, and keep praying for him. You got a good guy! There's nothing better than that," I advised her.

Tasha was quiet for a minute before she said: "Ay bendito! Mija, that's him, wasn't it? Dude was your ex, huh? Diablo!"

"It's okay, Tasha. You didn't know."

"Why didn't you tell me? Iman, I would've spit in a cup of water and gave it to him or something!"

"Tasha, you are crazy girl!" I laughed.

"Why didn't you tell me before? That's not cool. I wouldn't kept bringing up all that stuff about him being cute. I take everything back, all right! He's a Gremlin when it gets wet, okay!" We both laughed.

"He's old news, Tee! Nothing more needs to be done to him. He's done enough to himself. I am good. But I love you. Gotta go," I told her. I took the file with me and went into the waiting room and called up my next patient.

An Arab-looking Muslim woman dressed in a black abaya and white hijab stood up. She grabbed the hand of a little girl with light brown curly hair and a little boy with the same curly hair and milky white skin and big dark brown eyes.

"As salamu alykum," I greeted.

"Wa alykum as salam wa rahmatullah," the mother responded with a heavy Arabic accent.

"Aliah and Ali Yahya?" I asked. The mother shook her head. "Twins?" I gushed as I glanced back down at my file. The mother shook her head again. I got the impression that her English was limited. I waved my hands and indicated for her to follow me through the doors into the corridor where the examination rooms were located. As we passed by the nurses' station, I called out to Tasha:

"Page an Arabic translator for me and see if Dr. Mohsen is on the available list," I instructed her.

Once we were inside examination room four, I glanced into the file again. They were Syrian refugees. The mother and the two children were still standing up. I smiled at them and then pulled out the chairs for them to sit in. She looked at me and I waved my hands towards the seating. She smiled back at me as they sat down. *"Hal tatakalameena al Inglizeyya?"* I asked slowly pronouncing all of the letters exactly how my teacher in the Arabic classes I had been taking for the last six months did. She shook her head then sucked her teeth.

"Laa!" she responded to let me know she wasn't fluent in the English language. She pointed to her son Ali and pushed him forward. My file said that the twins were eight.

"Okay. Ali, my friend, do you speak English, buddy?" I asked him. Ali and Aliah laughed but they both nodded. Relieved, I knew I would have help doing my job with them and getting home on time.

Chapter 24

The end of the day snuck up on me once again before I had time to finish up all my reports but I still breathed a sigh of relief. I had completed the week without any major problems, completed the mediation and signed the divorce papers, someone that I respected and had grown to care for had asked my entire family to marry me and Mateo had delivered a check to me. Alhamduleelah, for Islam because without it I would've probably felt like things were too good to be real for me. Without Allah, I would've been afraid to face the weekend. The old me would think all that good that came my way would have to be balanced out with something bad, upsetting, or just ugly and stressful. I grabbed my bags, locked up my laptop and locker, and headed out of the clinic feeling happy for everything that I was able to accomplish.

I got into my sister's wagon, tossed my bags in the back seat, strapped my seatbelt on, and hit the CD changer. The melodic recitation of Saad Al Ghamdi flowed through the speakers into every crevice of the car. The sun was setting and the air was moist. I pressed the button to roll the windows down. I put the car in drive, backed out of my parking spot, and steered the car towards the exit. My cell phone began vibrating in the center console. I drove the car out into the street and parked next to the curb. I don't know why, but I figured it had to be family. I picked the phone and swiped the screen to open the text messages.

Brother Jibril: Woman, open your gift up! Please! See you later, Insha'Allah

I started laughing at Jibril's message. He was getting desperate. I still felt that it would be better to wait until after our talk to find out if that gift was really intended for me. It wasn't that I thought he would lose respect for me based on what I wanted to share with him. I just wanted him to know the whole truth. My truth. I wanted him to have all the facts to make an informed decision. Maybe he wanted something I couldn't give him.

I put the car back into drive and drove off down the street. When I arrived in front of my mother's house about fifteen minutes later, I was surprised by the scene. None of the kids were outside playing. The front lawn was empty. No one was on the porch either. I didn't see Umar's car or Yasmeen's. I grabbed my bags from the back seat and got out my sister's car. I knocked on the door a couple of times but no one answered. I had to put one bag down on the porch and look through my handbag for my keys.

"As salamu alykum!" I called out as I entered. Still no answer. "Ummi? Ameera? Hasan?" I yelled through out the house as I walked through the front room, then the living room. I peeked into the kitchen and then knocked on the back-room's door where Umar and Ameera were sleeping in. "Salamu Alaykum!"

The house was empty. I pulled out my cell phone and started texting my family members one by one.

Salams. Ummi are you still out shopping? Text me back, please.

Ameera, where you at? You got all the kids? Text me back, please. I am at the house.

Salams Yaz. Where you at? Are you okay? Text me back, please.

As salamu alykum, Shareef. You still at work? Where the kids at? Hit me back.

I locked the door then headed up the stairs to pray and prepare for the iftar at the bowling alley. After I finished praying, I took my bathrobe, towel, and bath soap out of the closet and went to take a shower. I washed my hair, blew it dry, and even put some of that instant henna from those disposable tubes on my finger nails and toes. I must have been in the bathroom for over thirty minutes when I heard someone bang on the door. I tightened the straps on my bathrobe, walked over to the door and stuck my head out.

"Who is that?" I called out.

"It's me!" a little voice responded.

"Who?"

"Me, Munir," the voice said then my nephew walked closer to the door so that I could see him, He was shuffling from foot to foot. "I gotta go to the potty, Aunty!"

I opened the door to let Munir in as I gathered my things to leave. "Make sure you use the instinja bottle to clean yourself with the water first, Munir," I instructed him,

I walked back into my room and closed the door behind me. Ameera was in the room changing Saba's diaper on the bed.

"As salamu alykum,"

"Wa alykum as salam," Ameera responded as she put Saba's clothing back on.

"Where ya'll coming from?" I asked her as I stood in front of closet looking for something to wear.

"I had a doctor's appointment after Jumu'ah, then we stopped by the park and let the boys play for a bit," she told me as she picked Saba up then sat down on the bed. I turned around and faced her. Ameera was staring up at the ceiling.

"You feel all right, honey?" I walked over to my sister and sat next to her. I rubbed my hands over her face then grabbed her arm and felt for her pulse. Nothing registered as abnormal.

"A little,"

"A little what, Meera?" I begged her.

"Pregnant!" she pouted. "Can you believe that I am six weeks pregnant?"

I sucked my teeth and pushed her shoulder before pointing in her face, "Keep playing with me, Meera, if you want to. Imma get you!" I promised her. I walked back over to the closet and pulled out a teal and navy striped maxi dress with dolman sleeves.

"What?" Ameera fell back on the bed and belly laughed.

"You know what you did. And I don't think it's funny, Meera" I warned her.

"I was joking," she insisted. "Anyway. That's a cute dress. You should wear something like that to your wedding. Maybe in a creamy beige with satin and lace. You know sister Suhaiylah can make it," Ameera suggested. She laid her daughter on the bed then reached over and picked the gift box off the night stand. "What Jibril and Saudi give you?" she asked as she lifted the top off of the box. Ameera gasped then covered her mouth.

"Meera, didn't nobody tell you touch that box. I haven't even looked at it yet. Why don't you go downstairs and get the boys ready, please," I shouted at her as I tried to snatch the box out of her hands. She wouldn't release it to me, though. She turned the box around and showcased it for me to see.

"Where did he get this? This is so beautiful!" I covered my eyes with my hand.

"I will not look at it. Put it down now, Meera. Close the box and put it back where you found it," I ordered her.

"Oh my goodness, you are so nutty! I can't believe you haven't looked at it yet. It's really unique and it's..."

"Ameera bint Musa Johnson! *Astaghfirullah*! Get up on out of here, girl!" I grabbed my handbag and swatted at her with it.

"Fine! It's your gift. Don't look at it then." She rose up from the bed, readjusted her shayla and wrapped it around her neatly again. "We leaving in like ten minutes. Try not to wake Saba. She's staying here with Ummi."

"I hope you asked her first,"

"She offered, for your information," Ameera explained. "You act like I be leaving my kids with her all the time."

"I said no such thing," I told her as I pulled the dress over my head and smoothed it down. "I'll be ready."

"It's a beautiful gift. You should look at it!" she suggested before she left the room. I walked over to the nightstand, fixed the top of the box then centered it back to where I had it. Now I was really curious to find out what was in the box. It would have to wait until after tonight, though.

I found a navy-blue georgette hijab and wrapped in around my head. I pushed in a couple of straight pins and a golden flower brooch onto my shoulder to secure the ends of my hijab. I glanced back at the box on the nightstand and I started walking towards it. I stopped in front of it and took a deep breath. *Don't rush this, Iman!*

"Oh, Allah, make this box for me," I whispered a prayer before leaving the room. I left door cracked a bit and the light on in the room so that when Saba woke up she wouldn't be frightened. Downstairs Yaz, Mas'ud, baby Madeenah and Ameera were sitting in the living room with Ummi.

"Where's the boys?" I asked as I looked in the closet for my navy-blue sandals that were embellished with clear rhinestones. "Ameera, did you borrow my sandals with the sparkles and not give them back to me?"

"It wasn't me." She sucked her teeth. "And the boys are all outside with Umar. Shareef is on his way back now. I think we should just go and he can make his way out there with Hamad and Ya'coob. I wanna get a good lane and table. Ummi," Ameera called out to my mother. My mother came out of the kitchen wearing her apron.

"Yeah, what you calling me for Ameera? I got chicken on the stove."

"Saba is asleep upstairs. She'll probably sleep another hour. But don't let her sleep longer than that 'cause she'll be up all night."

"Meera, I know. You told me already. I'm gonna get the baby just as soon as I put this chicken in the oven. I ain't gonna leave her. Ya'll go ahead on to the bowling alley," Ummi suggested. Ameera flipped her niqab down over her face as she mumbled under her breath and walked out of the house.

"I found them!" I announced as I dug my shoes out. I stuck my feet into the sandals, picked up my handbag, and walked towards the door. Mas'ud shut off the television, fastened Madeenah in her car seat, then took her out to the car.

"You ready, Yaz?" I asked my sister-in-law. She was sitting on the couch wearing a fuschia linen abaya with pleats and buttons down the bodice and scrunchy sleeves. She paired the outer garment with a plain beige Georgette hijab.

"I am ready. Tired, but I am ready," she told me as she tried to push herself off the couch. I walked back into the living room, grabbed her hands, and pulled her up off the couch. We both laughed. Yasmeen wrapped her arm around my waist as we strolled to the door.

"How you feeling, Miss Engaged?" she opened the screen door for me.

"I am feeling it, you know. Lots of mixed emotions, I guess. Salaamu alykum, Ummi," I yelled out before locking the door behind me.

"Good emotions?"

"Yeah, I am feeling some good emotions. I am also feeling cautious too. I just don't want to get too far ahead of the situation and end up disappointed," I explained. Mas'ud unlocked the doors and we both got into his van.

"Nothing wrong with that. I didn't expect you to even to accept the proposal. You shocked me. I guess you are different than me."

"How so?"

"You all grew up together. Ummi and Abu Shareef and Aunty Adilah were best friends. Ya'll have been family all along. You know them."

"That's true. But I haven't been around them in years. I feel like I am being reintroduced to Jibril."

"Maybe so, but you have memories to build on. I didn't know Mas'ud. I was tripping hard," Yasmeen turned around from the front passenger seat and told me.

"She was Inspector Gadget. And she turned me down twice. The third time I asked her to marry me, I'd told myself on the way to Jersey, I wasn't going back."

"But I said yes!" she gushed. "You should have seen him, Imani. He was the saddest, cutest guy I'd even seen. I had to say yes that time," they both laughed.

"Dag! So you said yes to me out of pity?" Mas'ud joked. "I am offended."

"No! I said yes because I believed you and I felt like I could trust you, sweetheart!" Mas'ud rolled his eyes playfully at his wife. "You're backpedaling, Yaz. It don't really matter, really. I got you. Forever and for always," my brother promised his wife as he drove onto the highway.

"Forever and for always, Moody."

"Yeah well," I had to interrupt their honeymoon. "Trust is important. I think I can trust Jibril, Insha'Allah."

"You can!" my brother and sister-in-law said at the same time. "We trust Jibril. If we didn't trust him, respect him, and love him, Iman, we wouldn't have accepted his proposal for you. It takes time to trust someone, but he is trustworthy so that is half the battle. If you have questions or you're worried about something, ask him. Start communicating with him now. Don't wait until the wedding day to talk about the hard stuff. Get that out of the way now," Mas'ud advised me.

"Communication is important in marriage. It builds trust," Yasmeen added. I agreed with them both. I needed to have my talk with Jibril sooner rather later. Mas'ud exited the highway, drove down a couple of blocks, then pulled into the bowling alley's parking lot. He parked in a spot right next to Umar's car.

We got inside the bowling alley just as the servers were bringing out the food Fariba had ordered. Inside the bowling alley was dimly lit with flashing lights in red, green, and blue. Ameera had chosen a seating area towards the back. There were three long tables connected to each other, white and green balloons scattered around the table, black carpeted floors, a small food and salad bar in the back, and the game room over on the other side. The bowling lanes were upfront. They were lit up in different colors as well.

Ameera, Fariba, and Umar were helping the servers with food. Ameera had brought extra deserts and she had placed one on each table. "Umar, you think that's enough for everybody?" she asked her husband.

"It looks good, doll. We here to bowl anyways. They gonna eat good tomorrow, Insha'Allah."

"What's tomorrow?" I asked as I looked at my watch. "Three minutes left til iftar," I announced as I surveyed all the food sitting on the table.

"Got word from the masjid that the moon was sighted in Saudi Arabia and some other countries."

"Really? Alhamduleelah, so this is it? This is the last night of Ramadhan."

"This is it," Fariba chimed in as she brought over another jug of juice. "Alhamduleelah, we made it. May Allah accept it from us and bless us to meet it again next year."

"Ameen!" Ameera, Umar, and I responded.

"It's 'bout time to pray. I'mma go get the kids from the game room. We gonna have to pray outside in the parking lot," Mas'ud told us.

"Yup, that's fine," Fariba told him. "Jibril said he is five minutes away. And I think Hamad, Ya'coob, and Shareef are probably already outside in the parking lot."

"Who else are we waiting on?" Ameera asked.

"Mahir and Tahirah and my girls are on their way too," Fariba told me.

"Okay, good."

Fariba, Ameera, and I went to the bathroom to wash up for the prayer. Yaz stayed behind with the baby.

"I hate praying outside in these areas," Fariba started telling me as she stood watch by the door while Ameera and me made wudu. There was nothing worse than trying to quickly make ablution in a public restroom, than having a couple of non-Muslim women walk in on you washing up in a sink. The mean looks and sighs boiled the blood in my veins. People tried so hard to look down on Muslims for every little thing, even cleanliness. "You know there's a lot of crazies in Pennsylvania."

"For real. Ever since 9/11, I don't really pray out in public like that, except if I am at an event with other Muslims. I ain't trying to catch a case 'cause you know I can act a fool, if need be."

"Don't we know it!" Fariba laughed. "I guess it's different for the men. They always wanna try sisters, especially our immigrant sisters.

But ain't nobody gonna go knock the brothers upside their head while they're praying. At least not our men," she smirked.

"They'll have to bury mines under the jail if they tried him while he was praying," Ameera suggested.

"They'll have to bury all of them under the jail together if they tried them - period," Fariba explained.

Chapter 25

When we got outside the bowling alley, Mas'ud and Umar had gathered everybody over to the side of the parking lot on a grassy patch. Mahir, Tahira, Shareef, Ya'coob and his wife Ishaa, Hamad and his wife Wahida, Jibril, and all the kids were together. Yasmeen was helping the little ones' get in a straight line for the prayer.

Ameera and I laid down sheets to pray on before going to the back of the group where Fariba, Tahira, Wahida, and Ishaa were lined up at. The boys were lined up in front of us and the men were in front of the boys. Shareef led the prayer. Each time my brother recited "Allah Akbar" I scanned around us with my eyes before I bent down. My sisters were right, it just wasn't safe to pray in places we didn't know.

Years ago, when I was a child, my father and Jibril's father would always take us to the park in the summers. We would eat and pray and it was fun. We shout "Allah Akbar" and sing songs about Allah at the top of our lungs as we played on the monkey bars and took turns on the swings. We didn't think anything of it. Now praying publicly and shouting Allahu Akbar in the wrong neighborhoods could get the police called on us. Now we had to be careful of where we prayed at and who was around us when we did it.

"As salamu alykum wa rahmatullah," Shareef called out as turned his head to the right and then the left to end the prayer. We followed his motions. When I looked to the right and then the left, I was relieved. No one was in the parking lot but us. We were safe.

After we got everyone inside the bowling alley, I handed out dates, cups of milk, and the mini beef patties Tahira had made. The brothers were at one table. The boys sat in the middle and all of the sisters and Fariba and Tahira daughters sat at another table. We'd ordered pizza, salad, and juice from the bowling alley. Tahira and Mahir brought fried chicken and peas and rice, and Ishaa had made banana pudding.

"Congratulations, Iman," Tahira offered me in between bites of her food. "Alhamduleelah, Jibril is good brother. At least that's all I know of him."

"Thank you," I told her as I reached for another one of her beef patties. I hadn't even visited the salad bar once. "I only know good about him too. Insha'Allah, he's a good match for me."

"Insha'Allah, he will be. No brother is perfect. Mines sure ain't. We have our up and downs and we been through a lot, but I always try to be mindful of the same forgiveness that I want Allah to have with me, I got to give it to others. Especially with my husband. As long as a brother is making his salat and giving you your rights Islamically, what else is there? This ain't jannah," Tahira reasoned with me.

"Compatibility matters. A brother making his salat is for his own soul. And every woman isn't in need of financial support. Some of us can pay our own way, if need be. But we all need compatibility. I gotta like the dude I am married to. If I can't laugh with you, hang out with you, let my hair down, and just be me with you and know that you are really cool and in my corner, I don't want 'em."

"Haqq," Ameera chimed in. "I couldn't be with a lot of brothers. They're good brothers' out there, but not many of them would have patience with sisters with medical issues…"

"That's different, Meera," Tahira told her. "If you have a medical condition and your husband won't help you or support you, then he ain't no good brother. He's selfish. I am talking about how a lot of sisters try to act like brothers got to be exactly how they want them to be in order to respect them. Let a man be a man. You didn't create him. Allah did. Find the love somewhere in him. Stop trying to make men over in your own ideas. Like a common issue sisters complain about is that their zawj is not romantic. Okay, *you* be romantic. Teach a brother a thing or two. Be forgiving and be easy. Don't throw a good man away just because he's not everything you want."

I shook my head and said, "I agree with that." Fariba rolled her eyes.

"If Allah said to call on Him for what you want and that He will respond, then that's what I'll do. I don't think its right to ask sisters to settle. If a sister wants a romantic man, she should pray for that type of a man and wait on him to come. Don't settle 'cause you know what the elders say, whatever you do to *get* the man, you gonna have to keep *doing*. Most men are not going learn to be romantic, they'll just sit back and enjoy the work his wife is putting in the marriage. He'll thank Allah for blessing him with a romantic wife from time to time, but if you're waiting on a backrub, roses, candles, and sparkling cider from him at the end of the night, the Trumpet will be blown and the day of Judgement will be here first," Fariba insisted.

We all laughed. "Reeba, you on the money with that one," Ishaa agreed. "But I think you both have made good points. As long as you like enough of what your husband is doing, meaning his good outweighs the bad, then a wife should be able to find patience, forgiveness, and love for him. If you need romance, laughter, close friendship or even a brother that is studious and up praying all night, go get it. Whatever it takes to make the hard parts easier to get through, try to find that. Nobody is perfect, but we don't have to be miserable in this life either."

"Exactly," Wahida noted. "Go get him, Iman," she joked.

"I got him, Insha'Allah," I told her with a wink.

"It's good that you both come from a big family. That's helpful. Especially since Jibril got that new baby and you'll have to help with him," Tahirah told me. I thought I heard her clearly state that Jibril had a new baby. I looked around the table and it seemed like everyone had froze or was gasping for air. Fariba's grumbled face said it all. I had heard right.

"Now why in the world would you say that, Tahira? You stay starting some mess and carrying tales that ain't got a darn thing to do with you," Fariba yelled at her ex-husband's wife.

"Astaghfirullah, Fariba! What are you talking about? I didn't..." Tahira started.

"Wayment, wait, hold up!" Ameera yelled. "Who got a new baby? Jibril got a new baby? Jibril, come here!" Ameera stood up and yelled as she yanked up her face veil.

It was time for me to go. I pushed my chair out from the table, picked up my handbag, stood up and started walking towards the door. I didn't know how I was gonna get home, but I was going to get out of there.

"Imani! Iman, wait a minute. Where you going?" Yasmeen yelled after me. I didn't slow down or turn around. I knew my sisters would explain everything to my brothers. That was their job. Mas'ud and Shareef would probably come after me too. All of that didn't matter. Right now, I needed air, I needed space, and I needed to talk to Allah in public. I hadn't lied, I hadn't drank a drop of liquor in months, I had faced Mateo, I had prayed. I'd been praying so much, some night the heels of my feet hurt by the time I gotten into bed. I fasted all of Ramadhan for His sake - gave up my food and drink so that I could get closer to Him.

I was trying.

I just wanted one thing.

I know I asked to be led to the right way. But like this? Did I have to be humiliated? Hurt? Hurt again? Crushed? Why I am still being tested? "Iman!" he called me. I heard him, but I kept walking.

"You about to walk right into the highway if you keep going this way. Imani!"

I stopped walking and opened my tightly closed eyes. A few tear drops released and blinded me. I roughly wiped my face before my eyes adjusted. I saw that the street was going to end. The sun had set and there were cars driving up and down the road too fast. He got of his car, and locked it before he crossed the street.

"Iman, can we talk?"

"They said they trusted you. My brothers. Umar. Mahir. Tahira. Ummi, Yaz, Meera and Reeba too. They trusted you because they already knew, right?"

He lowered his head and stuffed his hands into his pockets. "Some of them knew. Not all of them. I was going to tell you. I swear by Allah it was my intention to tell you months ago. Just never really thought it was the right time. A lot of stuff happened. A lot of stuff was going on. Didn't think we'd be here right now."

"And where is that? Where are we, Jibril?"

"With love the Allah gave us. Waiting to marry. I didn't see this coming. I been prayed for it. But my mind was all over the place. A month ago, you were ready to defend your ex. You were sticking up for him and it confused me. Why would I tell you about the trouble in my private life if you still in your feelings for another man? Not just another man – your *legal* husband at that?"

"Really? You gonna take it there, Jibril? Because I was concerned about my family - my brother, *you* getting hurt by getting involved with my criminal *ex*-husband, means I was in my feelings about *him*? You were confused about me loving him? The man I *ran* away from? The man *who beat me up*? The man who took me away from my family? You thought I had romantic feelings for *that man* still?" I whispered through tears. "You *can't* be serious!"

"Iman, these days, stranger things happen all the time. Plenty of women loving up on men right now who smacked them this morning. Look, I don't expect you to fully understand what I was feeling, but know that I have feelings, though. Stuff happened and I was looking for some signs from you just to know which direction this was gonna go. When you signed the papers and told Mateo to get lost, I took the opportunity to propose. There's a lot about me you don't know. I know I ain't been a good guy. I made some mistakes. I was honest about that, right?"

"You didn't say anything about how you was out making babies in the streets!" I yelled at him.

"Why you *assuming* the worst? Who said I did that? Do you want to hear the truth or you done already made up your mind about my situation?"

I folded my arms across my chest and exhaled. Did I want to hear the truth? Would truth help me? Would the truth save us? I had to choose something right now. There was nowhere else to run.

"Iman!" Jibril yelled my name.

"Yes." I answered him,

"Did you hear me? Do you want to hear the truth?"

"Yes. I do." I chose the truth.

"Okay, I had a quickie marriage last year. I didn't really tell anybody about it 'cause it wasn't the best situation. A lady I was working with was hollering at me for a while. She wasn't Muslim and she was kinda wild. But you know, I'd been single and taking care of my son after his mother died. Shareef told me not to marry her just 'cause of how bad his situation had played out. I honestly didn't want to marry her. But I was lonely, though, and just working with her everyday Shaytan was playing with me. I didn't want to sin like that. So, you know I married her."

"Was she pregnant before or after you married her."

"I'm telling my story! Can I finish?" Jibril asked me.

"Go ahead."

"Thank you. Listen, please."

"Just talk, Fresh! 'Cause this is some *dirty* stuff," I rolled my eyes upward and sighed.

"Mahir performed the marriage for me and Tahira was there 'cause it was at her house. My brothers and Mas'ud were witnesses. I gave her a little cash and that was it. She was working for me at the Birch Inn but things didn't work out. I was married to her for like four months. She never moved in with me, she never met Saud. She never met my mother or my sister."

"Why not? That doesn't seem very Islamic."

"I caught her stealing from the cash register. Twice. I caught her smoking... I couldn't deal with that again. Drugs and marriage don't mix well. I divorced her. She said she was pregnant. I helped her go to rehab. That's how I met sister Labibah," he informed me.

"So this woman was working at the Birch Inn when I was staying there?" I asked him.

Jibril shook his head. "She still works there sometimes now."

"Short, big-boned, olive skin, long black Janet Jackson from Poetic Justice hair extensions dyed pink and red, and the bad attitude," I rattled off as an image of the woman who always banged on my door while I stayed at the motel formed in front of my eyes. "You married *her*?"

Jibril lowered his head then laughed. "That's some sharp memory you got there. Remind me never to cross you, little sis!"

"When did she have the baby?"

"Almost two months ago. Amari Zaire," he revealed. "I just got physical custody of him yesterday. My mother has him now. Hussayn Al Ajmi was helping me. He went to school with Shareef and me. We used to ball together."

"So what's your intentions with your son's mother? Do you plan to keep helping her get her life together and revert her to Islam, then remarry her?"

Jibril laughed lightly again then shook his head. "Slow down with the conspiracy theories and hidden agendas."

"I just want to know what you want in your future. How are you trying to set this up, so I am clear?"

"I just want to marry you, sis and build a good life with you and my sons. I want to spend the rest of my life with you. No, hidden agendas."

"I may not be able to give you children," I heard myself admit to him finally. "I've had several miscarriages. I birthed and buried a stillborn. With Mateo. I may not ever have any children."

"I am sorry to hear that. For your losses, your pain, your heartaches, I am sorry. May Allah heal you completely and give you what you want and need. May Allah make my children yours too. I don't mind sharing them with you. In fact, I think they would be blessed to have you as a step-mother. We all would be. That is, if you still want us?"

Jibril waited for me to respond. But I couldn't find the words at that moment. I shook my head up and down and mouthed "yes".

"Alhamduleelah. You should know, though, Iman that I can't promise you an easy life, sis. That'll be up to Allah alone to grant it to us. But I can promise to give you whatever I have, to protect you, to love you, and be honest with you. No more secrets?"

"No more secrets!"

Jibril put up his hands in the air and exhaled. "Alhamduleelah!" he sighed. "C'mon, let's go bowl."

I followed him across the street back to his SUV. He opened the back-passenger door and held it open it for me to get in. He walked around the front and got in on driver side.

"Did you ever open your gift?"

"No," responded as I fastened the seatbelt around my body. "Not yet."

"Can I tell you what it is?" he asked me. He put the car in drive, backed up then turned the car around.

"No, thank you. I'll open it and find out on my own," I insisted as he drove back down to the bowling alley.

"Open your gift tomorrow before salatul Eid," Jibril begged as he held the door open for me to enter.

"I will."

Everybody was over in the front bowling in the lanes. Fariba, Yaz, Ameera, and Tahira all came over to me. Ameera hugged me and kissed my forehead. "You good, boo?"

"I am good. I am all right," I told her.

"You still engaged to my big-headed brother?" Fariba put her palms up in the air and made a dua silently. I pushed her and smiled.

"Yeah, I am. Insha'Allah, I am gonna marry that big-headed brother of yours." Yasmeen hugged me.

"I just want to say I am sorry, Iman. I really didn't know any better. I hope you will both forgive me for this mess I caused. Fariba called it right, too. Sometimes my mouth needs to be checked. I don't mean no harm to no one, but I gotta do better. I love ya'll sisters," Tahira explained.

"We're good, Tahira. I just need those little beef patties you made tonight for the wedding," I asked her.

"I have beat you to it. You know I have already ordered 200 of them thangs for our weddings! You still gonna do the double wedding with me and Shareef?"

"I am still in, Insha'Allah."

" I just wish our fathers could've lived to see this. Uncle Musa would've hooked up the food so good. And my Daddy would've built us the dopest reception ever. I miss them both so much."

"Insha'Allah, we will see them again!"

"Yup, Insha'Allah, we will."

Chapter 26

◈

We got home from the bowling alley and my mother was in Eid mode. She had Qari Abdul Bassit playing on the computer, she had washed and dried clothing for the kids, ironed her clothing and thoubs for Mas'ud and Shareef. She was sitting in the living room with Saba bagging up candy to give out at the prayers.

"No! Don't you think about eating one piece, Imran. Ameera and Umar, get those boys washed up and in the bed so that they can get up on time."

"We on it," Umar told my mother. "Imran and Munir, upstairs."

"Abu, we just got here. Can't we play first?" Munir whined.

"Not tonight, son. Insha'Allah, tomorrow you can wild out. Now we have to get ready for Eid prayers in the morning. C'mon, right now!"

Umar marched the boys upstairs. Ameera, Yaz, and me were laying in the living room.

"Meera, I already washed up Saba. I washed out a couple dresses and pretty socks for her too. I didn't know what you wanted her to wear."

"Shukran, Ummi. But Umar bought her a new dress so she'll wear that. I'mma do her hair tonight."

"Oh, alright. Yasmeen, you good? You need me to iron anything for you and Madeenah?"

"Madeenah and me are good, Ummi," Yasmeen acknowledged. She was lying down holding her baby on her chest.

"Iman, tell Hasan when he get here to finish bagging up this candy. I'm going to pray and go to sleep."

"Okay." Shareef and Hasan was over at Aunty Adilah's house packing up the supplies for the Eid breakfast in the morning.

Next thing I knew, it was eleven at night when I woke up to the sounds of my brother's voice.

"Yeah?"

"Go to bed, Imani!" Shareef called out to me. I pulled myself up and waded through the rooms until I found the staircase. I held tightly to the banister, put one foot in front of the other until I got to the top of the stairs and found my room.

I yanked my hijab off, threw my shoes in the closet, and fell into the bed and pulled the covers over my face. I rolled over and looked at the clock and it hit me heavy. I jumped right up and got out of the bed. I hadn't prayed ishaa yet. I headed to the bathroom, made wudu, and came back to my room. It was clear the night had been long and full. I grabbed the one piece prayer garment out of the closet and pulled it over my clothing and head.

"Allahu Akbar," I stated to begin my prayer. Each motion I made, I willed myself to I focus on what I was saying and who I saying it to. When I bowed, I cried. I knew Allah had sent me an answer and I knew it was the right answer.

"As salamu alykum wa rahmatullah," I offered the greeting of peace to the angels I couldn't see, but was sure was all around me recording my actions.

I sat in place on top of the prayer rug offering dhikr. The room was dark and quiet and I felt safe. I stood up and walked over to the lamp. I turned the light on then sat on the bed next to the night stand. The silver box was still there where I left it. I picked it up and held it my hand. It wasn't heavy at all. I turned it around and then flipped it over to see if anything was written underneath it. My fingers danced on top of the box before I finally eased the top of the box off.

Inside the box was a silver key engraved with Arabic from top to bottom that was connected to a silver diamond cut necklace. I picked up the key and turned it around. The Arabic was on the other side as well. There was a small note attached to the top of the box. I peeled it off, unfolded the paper, and spread it out. It neat print it read:

This key was given to me to by your father a couple of months before he passed away. This is the first key to the Islamic Center that my father and your father had made. Once the board took over and renovations were completed, they had the locks changed. Your father had it engraved with Surah Fatihah by one of the teachers at the school. I believe this key is rightfully yours and will help remind you of the strength, patience, and love your father showed us all. Saud picked out the necklace. I hope you like that too. Fatihah, the beginning or the opening. Let's begin the rest of our lives together with everything we have for everything we want for the sake of the One who holds the keys to paradise. - Jibril ibn Aqil Ibrahim

I enclosed the key in my palm tightly as the chain dangled through my fingers and brought it up to my heart. "Abu!" I wailed. Jibril had given me a gift that was priceless. He'd gifted me something that my father loved so much in this life, that he used it every single day. I smelled the key hoping to pick up a trace of the first man to love me so deeply and so complete. It was because of Abu that I trusted so easily. I loved easily too. I never thought of it as weakness until Mateo came into my life and spoiled the goodness I'd been fed. But now, in my hand, on my heart, I could love and trust again.

"Thank you, Allah."

I turned off the light and laid down. I held the key in my hand until I fell back to sleep. When I heard the loud banging and footsteps in my room, I knew it wasn't my nephews.

"Get up, Iman. We got a system in this house for Eid prayers and you gonna have to get with it. You only got five minutes to get in and out of the shower. Dry off and get dressed here in the room. We gotta get all the kids, you, and Ameera washed up and out so the men can get in. You hear me talking to you? Iman?"

"Yes, Ummi," I mumbled with covers still over my face. "I heard you. I am up."

"All right then. Let's go!"

"Shouldn't you wash up first?" I asked her.

"I did already. I am getting ready to get dressed. Then I am going downstairs to make some oatmeal for the kids. That should tide them over til Eid breakfast, Insha'Allah."

My mother left the room and left my door open. I knew she meant business about me not messing up her system. I swung my feet out of the bed, grabbed my prayer garment and threw it over my head. As soon as I stepped into the hall, I felt the pandemonium. Shareef was yelling downstairs at Hasan to turn off the video games. Ameera was running up the stairs holding Saba and calling for my mother. Then Mas'ud opened the door from the attic.

"You going in the shower?"

"Yeah, I'm next."

"A'ight, well hurry up. You got five."

"Ummi told me."

I reached into the cabinet and pulled out my toothbrush from the shelf. I turned on the shower and spread toothpaste onto the toothbrush. After I took off my clothes, I got into the shower with the toothbrush in my mouth. I showered and brushed my teeth at the same time.

"Hurry it up, Imani. I gotta wash up the boys," Ameera yelled from outside of the door.

"Really, Meera?" I yelled back. I turned off the water, wrapped myself in my towel, then yanked the prayer garment over my head and body. I unlocked the door and Meera was standing there with all of her kids rolling her eyes. I rolled my eyes back and mumbled: "I gotta get my own place."

"You will soon, Insha'Allah. But don't think you won't be back here in Ummi's house. Sooner or later - or at least for Eid, you'll be here just like the rest of us and it'll be crazy! It's our *Sunnah*."

I didn't reply to her. I just headed into my room. I was glad that for the time being I could dress in peace. My eid outfit was waiting for me to pull it out from the back of the closet. It was a jade green satin abaya with a full swing skirt and a lace overlay on the sleeves. I had purchased a new gold shayla with matching crystals studded on the hemline and gold BCBG sandals with a small heel. I had also bought a golden statement necklace and a thin gold belt. I had a change of mind though. I decided to leave the dress as it was and to wear my engagement gift instead. Even though it was silver, it worked.

"Let's go, ya'll. It's time to get in the cars!" Ummi yelled up the stairs.

I started down the stairs but had to go back up to take some money with me to pay my *Zakat*. The charity was a religious obligation due on Muslims who had enough savings. I had learned in my Islamic studies class that *Zakat* literally meant that which purified. Under the pillars of Islam, it came right after praying five times a day in its importance. It made me feel good to know that I had earned enough money by myself to pay it and share my earnings with other Muslims who needed help. I'd been in their shoes. I'd been without even when I had.

"As salamu alykum, ya'll!" Ameera shouted as she rushed her kids out the door. She looked beautiful in the same jade green full swing abaya that I wore. Her long black shayla and princess niqab complimented the green perfectly. "See ya there, Imani. Don't forget to have Mas'ud bring those extra prayer rugs and the chairs for us to sit in."

My whole family was making Eid prayers together at the Islamic Center. In past years, Ummi said Ameera and Umar would go off to a different masjid in Pittsburgh or offer salatul Eid in Philly. But this year was different. This year she had all of her children, grandchildren, and soon to be in-laws coming together as one.

"Okay, sweetie, we'll be on the way right behind you."

I drove Ameera's car with Shareef and Hasan. Ummi, Yasmeen, and Madeenah drove in the van with Mas'ud. With Ummi's system we all left out of the house by six thirty in the morning. It was a sunny and warm early morning. Hasan had his windows rolled down letting the fresh air blow in his face. As we got closer to the Islamic Center the traffic started getting tighter. There was a line a cars waiting to turn into the masjid that my father and Jibril's father started years ago. Now it had grown into a big community of Muslims from so many backgrounds, countries, and languages. Balloons were flying in the air and the police were out helping to direct the traffic.

"How many Muslims do you think will come?" I asked my brother Shareef, astonished at the hundreds and hundreds of people we were caught in middle of.

"No less than two," he shrugged his shoulders as he carried chairs for us.

"Only two hundred?"

"Two thousand!"

Aunty Adilah, Fariba, her three daughters, Ameera and Saba were all sitting together. "As salamu alykum! Eid Mubarak," Fariba greeted us. She got out of her chair and kissed my mother on the cheek before offering her a chair. Shareef handed her a couple more chairs to set up.

"Eid Mubarak, Aunty Adilah. Eid Mubarak girls!" Shareef handed each one of his step daughters to be a gift and bag of candy. He winked at Fariba before handing her a gift.

"You know I don't need nothing but the wedding."

"Insha'Allah, it's coming, darling. You know I am working morning, noon, and night for it. See ya'll later."

Fariba laughed. She looked regal as always in dark emerald and gold African two-piece dress. The peplum top had an elegant train while the mermaid skirt fanned out behind her. Her gold shayla was long and wrapped around her body loosely. She accented her hijab with a gold rope chain that was layered and matched her gold bangles and gold pumps.

Fariba stuck her nose down into the bag then laughed again. "He's so corny!" she giggled. "He gets me though and that makes me happy," she explained to me as she pulled out a jar of Manuka honey and a jar of coconut oil. "And I sure was completely out of honey and coconut oil. He's such a good listener!"

"Allahu Akbar, Allahu Akbar, Allahu Akbar. Laa ilaha ilallah! Allahu Akbar, Allahu Akbar, wa lilahi hamd! Allahu Akbar Kabira!" the Muslims were chanting the takbirat loudly. Shareef had been right; there were thousands of Muslims out on the field. There were so many sisters I could no longer see my brothers anymore. It was just a sea of Muslims. I rubbed my fingers on the key that was hanging onto my neck. My Abu would've been so proud to see what he had helped to create with me standing in the middle of it.

"Allah Akbar! Allahu Akbar!"

We all stood up to pray shoulder to shoulder and foot to foot. I cried the whole time. A rush of emotions filled my heart and I knew that it was partly because I had made it. I had achieved what I set out to do a year ago.

It wasn't until I was out in the parking lot serving the Muslims the breakfast buffet with my Aunty Adilah that I looked up and saw Fresh coming towards me with his sons. He held his baby boy so gently, and then extended him to me.

"Imani meet Amari - your son," he told me. I just gazed at that sweet baby and I knew my life was about to change again. I knew that so much love and some more pain was waiting on me too. But it was okay. Insha'Allah, this time I would have help.

I rocked, hugged, and loved on Amari for half of the day. The other half I played with Saud, Hasan, Imran, and Munir out on the basketball court, on the playground, and in the parking lot. We had waterball fights, tug-a-war fights, and Shareef even set up an archery spot. There was so much food left over Mas'ud and Umar was standing in the parking lot forcing people to take it home with them.

"Akhi, take some of this food, Insha'Allah. Share it with your community. Give it to your neighbors or bring it to the homeless," Umar begged a brother he seen leaving the Islamic Center with his family. "Eid Mubarak!"

"We gotta start cleaning all this up?" Shareef did a 360 and scanned the center.

"Yup! We all gotta clean this up. The women's committee is helping out too. It was a good turnout, wasn't it?" Fariba asked us.

"It was beautiful. So different and bigger than anything I can ever remember. Truly Allah makes the Muslims and it's only Him that can bring us together," I pondered.

"After we done fought, pushed, turned away, cried, and suffered the whole year. Ramadhan comes and washes it all away. We fast for a whole month getting by on dates, water, and half the sleep most adults need, but our hearts…," Ameera explained. "There's nothing like Allah or Islam in this world, but Allah and Islam."

"Shareef, I almost forgot to give you your Eid gift. Here you go," I extended my hand out to him and handed him an envelope.

"Here's yours Meera and this is for Yaz and you, Moody." I gave each one of my brothers and my sister envelopes as we all sat outside the musallah in front of the food hall. They all looked at me and each other quizzically.

"What's this?" Ameera asked as she ripped into the envelope first.

"A little sprinkle for your life you said you needed for me to give you when you first came, right?"

"Imani, big sis, you didn't?" she screamed. Umar tapped her shoulder and she showed him the check.

"Whoa, *Subhan'Allah!* You ain't rob no banks, armored trucks or nothing now did you?" Umar jested.

"No, but I did get a settlement that I didn't want so…Eid Mubarak."

"Iman, is this the money you got from …" Shareef started.

" It's yours, Reef. Pay off your bills, get married, get the house and let's buy that food truck!" I told him. Shareef walked over to me and hugged me tightly.

"Imani, you don't have to do this," Mas'ud told me as he looked over his check. "You don't owe us nothing."

"I do, Moody. This really isn't enough. I wish I could give you all more."

"Well," Umar started. "Meera and I will take it. God bless you," he joked. "Jazak'Allahu Khayr, Imani."

"Looks like we're getting married sooner rather than later, right?" Fariba gushed.

"Let's get married right now, darling!" Shareef insisted.

My mother walked up pushing Saba in her stroller. Jibril following behind her with all of the boys.

"Somebody need to bring me and Saba home. I am tired. This has been a blessed day, but it's been a long! Ya'll have a good time?" she asked her children.

"It was a beautiful day," I told her as I picked up Amari out of the car seat Jibril had him in.

"Can you hold on a little longer, Ma?" Shareef requested as he hugged his son to him.

"For what? It's almost Maghrib. There's nothing else planned for us to do but clean up. I'm too old and my knees ain't going to make it much longer."

"You can go rest in the musallah right after I get married to Fariba and Jibril marries your daughter!"

"Word?" Jibril choked out. "Come again? We getting married tonight?"

"Fariba said yes to me. You better ask Imani."

Jibril turned to me as I held his son in my arms and then looked over at his sister.

"Do it, Jibril!" Fariba urged her brother.

"Miss Johnson, will you be my companion for the rest of your life?

My mother walked over and took my hand. Her smile told me everything would be okay. Her smile let me know that it wouldn't be easy. But that smile, that strength that she and my father had passed down to me let me know that I was okay. I was safe. I had endured so much pain. I'd been stubborn. I'd been lost. I'd been angry. I had even abused my own body. Yet, when I called out and sought help, my Lord opened the doors, the windows, and even the front door. I ran right out the front door and made it home to the love He written for me before I was even born.

"Is your silence your acceptance?" Mas'ud joked.

I've been tried and tested, but I was created to be tried and tested by the One who holds the key to this world and the hereafter. And He, Allah, the Most High, He gave me this story to share with you.

With confidence, I said, " I would love nothing more than to marry you, Mr Ibrahim. Somebody better go find the Imam 'cause he has two marriages to perform before he leaves, Insha'Allah," I announced. I hugged my mother and she hugged me back.

ABOUT THE AUTHOR

Umm Juwayriyah, also known as Veiled Writer, is an American born and raised Muslim in her late twenties. She has an A.S. in Communications and is currently completing her B.A. in English at BayPath College in Massachusetts. Umm Juwayriyah has been writing and performing Islamic inspired poetry and fiction for a number of years. She is the former assistant director and website creator for the Islamic Writers Alliance and currently the editor for the New England Muslim Sisters' Association.

AUTHOR'S NOTE TO READERS

Bismillah

Alhamduleelah! You've just finished reading an Urban Islamic Fiction Book and I sincerely thank you! You know, I've dreamt of writing this book since I was in the eighth grade. I won't tell you what year that was, but what's important to know is that at that time I had already developed into an avid reader. I read all sorts of books and would often wake up early Saturday mornings to rush to the library in hopes of finding just one book that told the stories of people like me, in my neighborhoods and with my background: as an indigenous American Muslimah, born and raised. It never happened, mashallah, but it fueled a desire in me to do what I just did: tell the stories of Jameelahs, Nurahs and Aaliyyahs and even Bilals living in inner-cities across this country.

Of course, I know some people may still question the relevance of this sort of genre. Does it call for separation or glorification of "hood life"? The answer to that would be a resounding no! For sure, we are one Ummah and there is a uniting factor that crosses every race, socio-economic line and country border and that is Tawheed, the Oneness of Allah, which we all share and cherish. As such, in Islam we also have guidelines of morals and boundaries for most things and writing is not excluded from that. Which is why I write with the intention for Urban Islamic Fiction to be a way to identify and share the stories of millions of Muslims in this world, the young and the old, striving to practice Al Islam with all of their might and hold on to the rope of Allah, in spite of their surroundings.

However, know that my characters will continue to have struggles, drama, and major set backs every now and again. They are not perfect and I would never want them to be. Why? Because my stories are written for you, my beloved readers; the little covered pearl in Roxbury, MA who never has any friends from her public school to be with on the weekends but she wishes she did, the sister in Brooklyn, NY working nine to five and has a long ride on the train and wishes she wasn't there, and that brother in Detroit, MI vending on the streets. I know it's a test and I know it's difficult out there in this dunya for us. I also know that Allah is so good and He has given success to many of us as well. For you all, no matter who you are in this life; I am honored to be your sister and I am honored and proud to share your stories.

Wa billahi At Tawfeeq – With Allah Lies All Success

Umm Juwayriyah

CPSIA information can be obtained
at www.ICGtesting.com
Printed in the USA
BVHW01s1532100118
504923BV00001B/77/P